SERIAL DEALER

Book One of The

SEVEN, YOU'RE OUT

Series

A Novel by Richard Barton

SERIAL DEALER is a work of fiction. Names, characters, places, and incidents either are products of the author's imagination or are used fictitiously. Any resemblance to actual events or locales or persons, living or dead, is entirely coincidental.

Cover design by Isabel Espinoza

Cover photo by Keith Price of Tahoe Photographic Tours

I would like to thank my wife, Marisol, and my children, Carlo and Niza, for bearing with me during the long, arduous process of the creation of this story. Big thanks to Cinnamon Vann for your editing expertise, your constant support, and for sharing your literary acumen. This would not have happened without you Cuz. I also want to thank Stephanie Bartholomew for your proofreading help and all your enthusiasm. Last, but not least, I want to thank my numerous beta readers; co-workers, friends, and clients (you know who you are) across the nation for your interest and input.

This story is dedicated to everyone who has ever worked in the service industry.

Table of Contents

PROLOGUE

Paradise. Hell. Paradise or Hell? Perhaps it was Paradise and Hell, two parts of a perverse yin and yang, each unable to exist without the other. Billy wondered if this was truly how it had to be. As he walked across the parking lot of his workplace, the autumn sun warmed him, casting ephemeral rays in a dusty shade of orange that cut like laser beams through the pine trees. The western sky was a deeper shade of fiery orange. The clouds to the east glowed with soft shades of purple and pink. The crisp, pine-scented October air was a pleasure to breathe, to smell. When God created the Earth, he paid special attention to Lake Tahoe. Paradise....

A glance to Billy's left revealed the dichotomy of his existence, perhaps that of the Jewel of the Sierra as well. The glass tower of Harry's Casino rose nineteen stories into the mountain sky, blocking his view of Heavenly mountain, but providing guests with a dramatic view from their hotel room of the lake and its pristine blue waters full of sexy vintage speedboats that only millionaires could afford. Which was more important? Billy surely couldn't tell, but he knew the perspective of the men controlling the casino was that the greatest importance lay in what the customers could experience when they came to Lake Tahoe. Yeah right. These were the same idiots who spent most of their time in Tahoe wasted in the casino, gambling away their money, hard-earned or not, drinking far too many watered-down "free" cocktails, and losing touch with themselves and the beauty that surrounded them. Billy knew that most of them wouldn't make it outside to see the sun. Many would not even use their room that afforded such a fantastic view of the lake. The worst part about it from Billy's standpoint was that he had to go in and be nice to these people. He had to play referee in a free-for-all for drunken adults. Billy had been a casino dealer for ten years now. Hell....

"Paradise and Hell, one cannot exist without the other" Billy thought to himself as he entered through the rear employee entrance and walked down the familiar hallway lined on both sides by hundreds of six-inch wide sheet metal lockers stacked two high from floor to ceiling. The carpet, low-grade and worn, reeked of cigarette smoke. This view was the other end of the spectrum compared to what Billy had been enjoying outside. Polar opposites.

Billy headed up the prefabricated metal stairwell that led to the casino floor along with all the other six-o'-clockers and prayed for a slow night. He wasn't in the mood to deal with a bunch of obnoxious drunken gamblers. Maybe he would sign the early out list for dealers who didn't feel like working a whole shift.

Three things always hit Billy upon entering the casino floor: the bright lights, the myriad of noises, and the stale but acrid stench of cigarette smoke. All three were an inherent part of casino existence, constant and unavoidable.

Billy was numb to the lights that covered virtually everything from floor to ceiling. Their underlying purpose was to add to the confusion that people felt when faced with the prospect of risk for great reward. They had subliminal messages for everyone that walked by: "Try this slot machine. It will be lucky for you", or "Play keno and you will win."

The noise came from everywhere: Classic Rock playing on the overhead, live bands on various stage bars, bells, whistles and ditties from the slot machines, and most importantly, the human element; the sound of winners. While walking though the casino toward the main pit, Billy heard snippets of people's stories of victory fade in and out as he passed by.

A six-spot winner of ten thousand dollars in Keno: "I always pick my birthday, my Mom's birthday, and my Daughter's age and it finally paid off."

A slot machine jackpot winner: "I've been playing this machine every week for the last four years, and I just knew it would hit for me one day!"

A ten-pick football parlay card winner of forty-five hundred dollars from a five-dollar bet: "College football is easy; there are always ten favorites that cover the spread. You just have to pick the right ones."

Everyone loves to hear a winner's tale. Unfortunately, these folks weren't revealing the brutal truth; that their "big" jackpot didn't get them close to even from what they lost since they arrived in Tahoe, nor did it come remotely close to covering what they lost in their gambling lifetime. Regardless, the stories flowed and the people listened.

Billy reached the table games area and noticed that the smaller pits outside of the main pit weren't open yet. There was chance for a slow and short night. Once he turned the corner and saw the main pit, his hopes were dashed. Every game was full, with patrons watching from behind, waiting for a seat to open. Billy figured it would be a waste of time to sign the early out list. He might not even get out on time...Hell.

From that far end of the main pit, Billy could hear the craps pit. The main game was blowing up, and it was the only craps game open. People were screaming and yelling while others were waiting two-deep to get a spot. Billy walked into the main pit with his fellow dealers, put on his apron, and stopped at the podium in the middle of the pit where the dealer coordinator known as "The Pencil" was waiting.

The Pencil was Peter, an old friend of Billy's roommate, well, his ex-roommate. Peter glanced up at the group and started barking orders. "Stone, go to craps 301 and push out J.R. Try to clean up that mess a little since I can't open another game until eight o'clock."

Billy looked over at craps 301, surrounded by a sea of people, and figured that someone in scheduling had dropped the ball for this day. Maybe they forgot that a junket of 200 Texans was arriving, and that it was Blackjack tournament night which brought in a hundred more players. Regardless, Billy was walking into a mess with no reprieve for at least two hours. Imminent Hell...Paradise may as well have been a thousand miles away instead of just out the side door. He walked into the craps pit to notify his box man that he would be on the game and was thankful that it was Brian Seran. Brian had over thirty years of experience in the business and was a boss that backed up his dealers one hundred percent. At least with Brian here, Billy knew things wouldn't get entirely out of hand.

"Good morning Brian. I'm here for J.R. He gets to go home."

Brian looked up, a pained expression on his face. "Thank God you're here. Take the stick and get that kid the hell out of there.

Billy looked up at J.R. standing in the croupier's spot and realized that he was in the middle of a craps meltdown. A hard eight had just rolled. Everyone who bet that a pair of fours would roll before some other form of eight was going to get paid nine times their bet. Poor J.R. appeared to have forgotten his multiplication tables of nine. His face was blank. There were at least fifteen bets that needed to be calculated, and everyone on the game was screaming, yelling, and cheering. No one would get paid though until he snapped out of his funk. The player immediately to J.R.'s left was hollering "Hey man, I have a twenty-nine dollar hard eight. Gimme my three hundred and fourteen dollars!" Billy did a quick calculation in his mind and realized that guy was asking for way too much money. A couple of Texans on the outside hook of the game were complaining so everyone could hear. "Y'all got a bunch o' terrahble dealahs in this heah casino. Golly, I ain't nevah evah seen a craps game move so damn slow! Them dealahs in Vegas are so much bettah!" Their accent irritated Billy to no end. Ten years of dealing craps had instilled in Billy a hatred of all things Texas. J.R. still stood there, head still in his ass, still confused.

The words "controlled chaos" popped into Billy's head. The whole scene was laughable. He looked up at J.R. and said "Hey buddy, break that first bet down into two parts that you can handle. Twenty dollars pays a buck-eighty and nine dollars pays eighty-one. Now add those two together and pay your most impatient customer two-hundred sixty-one dollars, not the three fourteen he's asking for. When you're done paying everyone else, you'll be off". Relief washed over J.R.'s face, and he started authorizing the payouts.

Billy walked around the game and tapped J.R. on the shoulder to let him know he was there and ready to push in. He made a quick assessment of the crowd while J.R. was finishing his payouts. The two complaining Texans were typical high-rollers. They were betting one-hundred dollar units on most of the numbers and currently had about ten thousand dollars in chips in their tray. Their wives stood right next to them like bookends, mirroring their play with twenty-five dollar chips. Both women were young, well maintained, and bored: the kind of gals that stick around just long enough to get some alimony from their old, overweight, loud-mouthed, cigar-smoking, tobacco-chewing, swearing, complaining, ten-gallon hat-wearing Sugar Daddies.

There were three Hawaiian guys on the other end of the table also playing big money. Hawaiians for the most part were known to be good players and great tippers, but Billy had dealt to these three numerous times over the years and knew they were "stiff", the casino term for not generous. They also had some whacked system of play that they learned on an internet site that was labor-intensive and irritating for the dealers. All three were a worthless pain in the ass from Billy's perspective.

Next to the three Hawaiians were four middle-aged women in cheesy, matching velour sweat suits, screaming at the top of their lungs "woot, woot." Their fat asses told Billy the story: Housewives in dire need of attention getting away from their husbands for a "girls only" weekend, most likely from Sacramento.

There were a couple of locals on the game who were regular grinders referred to in casino talk as "fleas". They were still betting the table minimum on the six and eight, grinding away in hopes of earning enough comps for a free buffet. They were also worthless from Billy's perspective, as they didn't tip at all, and they took up space on the table that could be filled by someone who might tip.

Right next to the base dealer on the Texans' side were two dudes covered in tattoos betting large stacks of five dollar chips, or "chunking" in the field. "What a motley crew" Billy thought to himself. He steeled himself to step into the chaos.

Billy leaned in to J.R.'s right to get the verbal rundown before pushing in and choked on a cloud of cigar smoke that spewed out from the first player to his right. Damn cigar smokers; they always ended up standing right next to a dealer. Billy wondered if they positioned themselves there on purpose. Through the acrid haze, poor J.R. finally turned and said "The shooter is three to the left". Billy had no problem identifying the current shooter since he was pounding his palm on the table and screaming "Give me the damn dice! You guys are trying to cool me off!" The Texans began complaining about the stick change and their high-maintenance trophy-wives took up the cause as well. "Why y'all always switchin' the stick like that? Y'all's always tryin' to break ouah luck!"

As J.R. escaped, Billy thought about telling the Texans to shut the hell up and realize that the stickperson changed every twenty minutes in craps like clockwork. He also wanted to tell the shooter that he wouldn't move the dice an inch until he stopped pounding his damn fist on the table. The fat-ass housewives had taken up the cause, chanting "Dice! Dice! Dice! Dice!" He wanted to shove both the dice and his fist into their shrill fucking pie-holes. In the thirty seconds it had taken Billy to push in to this game from hell, things moved that much closer to hell. He thought to himself. "Controlled chaos? Hardly."

The shooter was still pounding on the table, so Billy intentionally waited another five seconds to send the dice. The chanting and complaining reached a crescendo. The cigar smoke was thickening. One of the tattooed guys was screaming "Where's my hard eight?" Billy ignored him and finally sent the dice out to the shooter. As the shooter began his delivery, Billy applied some of his own personal voodoo, opening his left hand to reflect the number five while his right hand was holding the stick and flashing the peace sign underneath his left hand to reflect the number two. His eyes were on the dice constantly from the second they left the shooter's hand. At this point, everything went into slow motion.

Billy saw the intense look of concentration on the shooter's face as he released the dice. He saw the housewives, all in mid-scream with angry, rabid looks on their faces. He followed the dice as they arced in midair to the other side of the table and caught a glimpse of the Texan Sugar-Daddies with their bright-red alcoholic gin-blossomed faces looking like they were at a cockfight instead of in a respectable establishment. A tattooed arm was out over the game, still trying to wave someone down for a hard eight that didn't get paid. The first die hit one of the large stacks of nickels in the field and stopped dead in its tracks on the number two. At this point, time slowed even more for Billy as the second die bounced against the wall, came back, and hit the tattooed hand which was still pointing at the hard eight bet. One of the Hawaiians screamed out “No roll”, but unfortunately for him and everyone else on the game, the stickperson makes the final call, and everything counts, even some idiot’s hand that is in the way. The second die fell right next to the first one and slowly, painfully, settled on the number five.

Billy made the call without hesitation. “SEVEN, YOU’RE OUT! That’s the end of that”. Everyone loses, and for a brief moment, the mess is cleaned up. Paradise.

CHAPTER 1

MR. BIG PURPLE TEX

"What the hell am I doing?" Billy thought to himself for at least the third time in the last twelve hours. From a small wooden bench at the top of the Powder Glades chair, he watched the multitudes debarking from the chairlift three or four at a time, chair after chair. Falling snow had accumulated inches on parts of his body. He hadn't moved in over an hour. It was Saturday in December. Billy had never been on the mountain on a Saturday; he didn't need to join the tourists on the most crowded day of the week. He only went up on the weekdays. Yet here he sat, watching them go by in droves. Watching. Waiting. Wondering.

The Dark Thoughts had spoken. Those voices in his head that had been silent for over a decade, locked away in the furthest recesses of his mind during a life-changing psychoactive experience, had emerged last night with strength, compulsion, and conviction; and here he was, waiting patiently for a man who most likely wouldn't show, a man he had aptly named Mr. Big Purple Tex.

Memories of the previous night with Big Purple Tex flashed through Billy's mind like dysfunctional frames of an old black and white movie. He recalled the moment when the man landed on his craps game about an hour into his shift. Billy had been standing on a dead ten-dollar game, watching basketball on the flat-screen television that hung conveniently on the wall in front of him, when a booming voice laced with a surly, irritating accent that could only come from Texas called out "Ten dollah craps game? Well let's fire this muthah fuckah up! Gimme ten thousand, now!"

There stood a man in a garish purple one-piece ski suit and a goofy multi-colored fleece court jester's hat, complete with little round balls at the end of each tassel. His face appeared to be sun burnt from a day on the mountain, but closer inspection revealed a field of gin blossoms. Billy could smell alcohol on the man from three feet away. He threw in his player's card, which hit Billy in the chest, and started giving orders. "Gimme that ten G's all in hunnert dollah chips, and when y'all pay me, pay me in hunnerts too. I want a waitress to bring me some good fuckin' scotch, not that rotgut shit y'all serve to the common folks, and get someone down here to get rid of mah Goddamn skis. Gimme five hunnert on the pass line, a hunnert on the yo eleven, and gimme them damn dahss!" In a matter of thirty seconds, Billy's night had gone straight to hell, and he was sure it would stay there until this shitty human being left.

Billy looked at the name on the player's card. It said Chas Wellington, but Billy had already named the man in his mind: Big Purple Tex. He called out to his pit boss. "Hey boss, I need a ten thousand-dollar marker please! Platinum player." Platinum players were the elite tier of Harry's gamblers. To achieve that status, one had to gamble millions of dollars annually at Harry's. Everyone was on top of their game when a Platinum player landed. Billy knew this man would be a challenge. He was already pounding his hand on the layout, screaming "Gimme my damn dahss! We gon' fire this game up!"

Billy did his best to maintain some professionalism with Mr. Big Purple Tex. He began cutting out the ten thousand dollars, all in hundred dollar chips; a ridiculous task since the man was betting in five hundred dollar units. It wasn't his place to question though. "I'll get your money to you as soon as the boss gives the okay sir. How was your day on the mountain?"

Big Purple Tex ignored Billy's question. "What is the mother fuckin' hold up here? When ah go to Vegas, they have me set up immediately. Ah wanna shoot some damn dice." Coming out of his mouth, it sounded more like "dahss". "Y'all are some of the slowest dealers ah've ever come across in mah forty years of gamblin'." He looked up at three young, attractive, voluptuous women who had stopped to watch. Billy could tell that these girls were looking for a money situation. When they saw no money on the layout or in the rail, they kept walking. Big Purple Tex, determined to start his show immediately, pulled a wad of hundred dollar bills from one of the pockets of his purple one-piece and threw them at Billy.

"Dealah, hook this lovely young lady up with a hunnert dollah line bet. She goin' be mah lucky chahm. Come here, sweetie, you wanna make a hunnert dollahs the easy way? Just be mah lucky chahm and shoot some dahss for me". He then fixed his viper-like gaze on Billy. "Now get me my fuckin' money before I go across the street to your competition! Ah bet they could get me a ten thousand dollah marker in less than fifteen minutes. Y'all are pathetic."

The Big Purple Tex show continued into the evening while he solicited every attractive or sleazily dressed woman that came up to the game to 'Be mah lucky chahm and shoot some dahss for me.' The insults to the dealers continued, as did the comments about how they were so much better in Vegas. He propositioned the cocktail waitresses with twenty-five dollar chips but gave nothing to the dealers. At one point, he actually told Billy "Y'all dealers are a bunch of beggars and thieves. Y'all ain't gettin' nothin' from me."

That was when The Dark Thoughts spoke in Billy's mind for the first time since the Gulf War. *"There are those in society who by their very actions corrupt it; those who abuse their place and power to belittle or take advantage of those who have none; those who haven't a care in the world for someone in need, but instead care only about having their own needs satisfied. Engage. Find the enemies' weakness and prey upon it. Work this jackass. Something will eventually come."*

Billy was shaken. He thought he had banished The Dark Thoughts after the war. The life he had created for himself in Tahoe was his salvation from their hungry desire to kill, yet here they were again, strong and compelling as ever, as if they had never left. He had to obey.

Engage. "So, Mr. Wellington, how was the skiing today?"

Big Purple Tex was taken aback by Billy's sudden change of demeanor, but his need to talk about himself prevailed. "Ahm a purty good skier and ah ski at Vail or Aspen most of the tahm. Y'all don't have no good tree skiin' out here in the west. Ah spent mah whole day at Heavenly looking for untracked powdah and ah couldn't find me none."

Find the enemies' weakness. Billy leaned in close to Big Purple Tex. "So you like tree skiing huh? I'll let you in on a little "locals secret" if you will. The Powder Glades chair on the Cali side serves only intermediate runs, so most of the people that ski there are afraid of going into the trees. The trees there are pretty tight and challenging but they also stay fairly pristine since no one really goes in there." *Prey upon it.* "It's supposed to dump tonight and then snow steadily for most of the day tomorrow. Those trees should be epic for most of the day. There are also some wide open areas in there that appear out of nowhere if you like to throw up giant waves of snow. You should have the place to yourself for most of your runs."

Big Purple Tex seemed pleased with Billy's change of attitude. He tossed him a hundred-dollar chip. "Billy Boy, I never tip 'cause y'all dealers are a bunch of hustlers and beggars, but here's a black chip for sharing some good information. If y'all want to join me tomorrow and show me around there's another hunnert in it for you." Billy chuckled to himself. The going rate for a personal mountain guide was at least two hundred fifty bucks for half a day. "Sorry sir. I don't go up on weekends. I snowboard, and most skiers don't like to hang out with boarders. I haven't been on the mountain on a Saturday or Sunday in ten years. You have yourself a good time though. There should be some good powder there tomorrow." *Something will eventually come.*

Billy wondered what the hell he was doing.

Around midnight Big Purple Tex was beyond wasted and had either insulted or pissed off enough of the other customers that John Hughes the shift manager finally had to get involved and send him to bed. Of course, there was a huge scene when Big Purple Tex was finally escorted away by security that involved him telling John, Billy, and anyone else in the vicinity "Y'all can go fuck yourselves. Ah'll go back to Vegas where they know how to kiss a rich man's ass!" The

Dark Thoughts had whispered then in the back of Billy's mind. *"Those that need to disappear."*

•••

As Billy sat alone on the cheap wooden bench at the top of Powder Glades chair wondering why he still hadn't moved in over an hour, he heard a booming voice with that oh so recognizable accent come from the debarking area of the lift. "Yeehaw! We got ouahselves some mothah fuckin' powdahh!" There he was, still wearing the gaudy purple jumpsuit and the idiotic court jester's hat. Billy wondered if the guy had even taken the time to change his underwear from the previous night. He stood up as Big Purple Tex shot down the run that went directly under the chairlift. Still covered in snow that had frozen to his body due to lack of motion, he followed Big Purple Tex as he went down the run about a hundred yards and cut a hard right into the trees. The man was a good skier but Billy had no problem shadowing him from afar. He had ten years of snowboarding experience combined with tracking skills he had learned in The Marines. He could keep his distance and a close eye on his prey at the same time.

Big Purple Tex picked his lines well. He moved with relative ease around boulders and fallen trees. He stayed high on his traverses until he saw a good line of untracked powder then attacked that line aggressively, weaving through the trees like they were part of a preordained course. He carved a huge swooping turn, sent up a wave of snow in an untouched wide open area, and immediately shot back into the deeper trees through a three-foot wide gap between two giant cedars. Billy could tell the man was a veteran skier.

At the bottom of the run, Billy entertained the idea of packing it in and heading back home or maybe to the beach for some cross-country skiing. He still had no idea why he was on the mountain on a Saturday, following Big Purple Tex through the Powder Glades trees. The lift line was probably horrendous. He headed toward the lodge and watched Big Purple Tex veer to the left toward the Powder Glades lift. The Dark Thoughts echoed in his mind with compulsion.
"Engage."

Billy cut a hard left and almost took out a skier. He had just broken a cardinal rule of mountain etiquette; no sharp turns. That was how most accidents occurred on the mountain. The compulsion of The Dark Thoughts was impossible to resist though, and he found himself merging into the crowded lift line that accessed the Powder Glades chair. Big Purple Tex had gone into the regular lines where three or four people loaded at a time. Billy got into the singles line and kept an eye on Big Purple Tex as he advanced in his own line. Luckily, the singles line was moving faster than the regular lines and he could pace himself perfectly to get on the chair in front of his target. Once at the top, all he had to do was sit on his old friend the bench, tighten up his bindings, and wait for the court jester's hat to appear.

Big Purple Tex took the exact same route as he had the previous run, heading straight into the trees over the tracks he had made before. As Billy followed, he wondered once again what he was doing tracking this disgusting man up and down the Powder Glades. The Dark Thoughts provided an answer. *"This jackass isn't wearing a helmet."* They were now speaking quite frankly to Billy, just as they had back in Baghdad. *"Engage your enemy and take him out."*

"Yes, and go to jail and lose the only life I've ever liked?"

"You won't go to jail if you don't get caught."

"But this guy hasn't done anything."

"Just another bane to society. Think about the way he treated you and everyone else last night."

"And what am I supposed to do up here, slam his head into a tree?"

Silence. Then the faintest whisper. *"This jackass isn't wearing a helmet."*

Billy was stricken with a bout of shuddering as he shot out of the trees and onto the cat track that brought him down to the lift line. He had to stop and tried hard to vomit, but only came up with a single dry heave. He almost lost sight of Big Purple Tex, but at the last moment saw him entering the regular line for the Powder Glades chair again. At least the man was predictable. This time though, Billy had to be aggressive in the singles line. He got to the front of the line at the same time as Big Purple Tex. This meant that he would have to sit with and possibly talk to the man for at least eight minutes, the duration of the chair ride. Once again, Billy wondered what the hell he was doing.

Worst of luck; an open spot appeared next to Big Purple Tex. The lift operator waved Billy in. He chose to take it because circumstances could have otherwise kept him too far behind.

Billy didn't say a word as the lift propelled them into the air. He was sitting next to the man who had belittled him, worked him to death with petty demands, called his place of work "the biggest piece ah shit ah've evah seen", insulted everyone that came near him, threw his money around to attract a crowd, used the influence of his money to get people to do things that they normally wouldn't do, and ultimately told Billy, his managers, and his work associates to go fuck themselves. He kept quiet and waited to see what would come out of that rotten pie-hole today. It didn't take long. He looked at Billy first, and seeing that he was a snowboarder, turned instead to the couple to his right who were both wearing skis.

"Y'all been getting' some powdah runs today?"

The husband responded. "Nahh, this is only our third time skiing, so we're sticking to the groomed runs."

Big Purple Tex chuckled. "Well if y'all want to try some of the best powdah on this run, ah can guide y'all into the trees just to the right there when you get off the lift. Ahh was given some privileged information by mah dealah last night on the craps game. I probably tipped that monkey over a thousand dollars and he sang like a canary and gave away one of the best kept secrets on the mountain. Y'all wanna come?"

Billy gritted his teeth at Big Purple Tex's blatant lying, but he kept his mouth shut. He could tell that the couple were getting creeped out by the disgusting, rude, arrogant man.

The young man answered back. "I think we're just going to stick to the runs. The way it's snowing right now, we're getting a couple of inches of powder after each chair ride which is fine for us." He looked ahead, saw that the top of the chairlift was approaching and started in with the niceties. "Enjoy your powder sir, and have a great rest of your day.

Maybe we'll see you in the casino tonight. We're going to the right."

Big Purple Tex was getting himself ready to debark from the chair. He crowded Billy in close to the edge of the chair and said "Ah'm going left so let me pass first." That was the worst thing to try to do from one spot in on the left. That person was supposed to debark straight out so that the person on the far left could move to the left and clear out. This guy was a complete idiot. Regardless, Billy still said nothing.

As they reached the offloading ramp, Billy stayed on the chair a few seconds longer than he should have to allow Big Purple Tex to get off and clear out. Then he jumped off at the last minute before the chair began its 180 degree turn to head back down the mountain. It took him a moment to sit down and tighten up his bindings. Big purple Tex was already headed down the mountain. Billy was sure where he was going. He quickly cut to the right into the trees and began scanning the open area for his target.

There was the court jester's hat, moving toward the open area where he would carve up a few waves of snow before heading toward the two giant cedar trees. Billy dropped into the bowl, making a beeline straight toward Big Purple Tex. He could see the frills on the court jester hat flapping in the wind. He closed the distance between them by bombing down the open area where Big Purple Tex was carving around and throwing up his big waves of snow and came in right behind the guy as he headed for the two cedar trees. The Dark Thoughts began to give orders: *"Target is not wearing a helmet. Engage."*

Billy followed orders, still unsure of what he was doing. He spoke to The Dark Thoughts as he closed the distance between them to less than ten yards. "What now?"

"Attack the weakness."

Billy locked his gaze upon Big Purple Tex's fleece court jester's hat. He could see the two large cedar trees getting closer and closer. He wasn't sure who or what he was talking to as he muttered "I can't do this."

"You MUST do this. You must remove this bane from society."

"But I'll go to jail. They'll lock me away forever once they figure out my past."

"Look around. It's only you and him. You know you want this. Engage!"

Big Purple Tex was rapidly approaching the two big cedars while at the same time Billy was rapidly approaching Big Purple Tex. The Dark Thoughts spoke with conviction. *"You can do this without breaking a sweat. All you have to do is get up close to him just before he cuts through those two cedar trees. Anyone that wears a fleece court jester's hat instead of a helmet while tree skiing is a fool."*

"I Can't." Billy was distraught.

"You will." The Dark Thoughts spoke with conviction.

In a dream-like state, Billy closed the distance between himself and Big Purple Tex until he could reach out and touch the man. They were rapidly approaching the two giant cedars and sure enough, Big Purple Tex was going to lunge between them. This would be a difficult maneuver for Billy to perform without running himself into one of those cedars as well. When Big Purple Tex was about ten feet from the trees, he suddenly looked back over his shoulder and into the orange-tinted lenses of his death. Billy's outstretched glove made contact with Big Purple Tex's chubby neck. He shifted his momentum downhill and both he and Big Purple Tex were headed straight for the cedar tree on the right. Big Purple Tex started to yell something, but it was cut short when his head went straight into the tree. It made the same noise that a crab leg made when crushed with a pair of those special pliers. Billy's arm was ejected away from the impact with enough force to swing him around and cause him to fall head first into some deep powder about ten feet from where Big Purple Tex's body had landed. He was in a troublesome position, especially since a man with a crushed skull was only ten feet away from him.

Billy swung his snowboard downhill, which popped his buried upper body out of the snow. Once his head was free and he could calm his breathing, it only took him a minute or two to get back to standing. Big Purple Tex's dead body lay amidst a pool of blood that grew larger by the minute. His head had truly been crushed like a crab leg.

Billy looked around, both up and down the hill. Not a person in sight. He stood there for a moment, staring at Big Purple Tex's corpse, then muttered to himself, "Seven, you're out. That's the end of that"

•••

It was dusk. Billy sat in a foot of powder in the trees a hundred yards up the mountain from Big Purple Tex's corpse. The pool of blood had disappeared once the snow began falling hard enough to bury it. The Dark Thoughts congratulated him from the furthest recesses of his mind.

"Well done, soldier. You have removed a bane to society, another degenerate who used his wealth, place, and power to demean and belittle those he deemed below him. You weren't meant to have a regular life. You are a killer. You weren't meant have a fiancée. That gold digger left you for a rich guy anyway. You weren't meant to have a best friend and life mentor. He was a liar and a thief who stole tips from the same people he called friend. You were meant to evolve. You are a protector of those who can't protect themselves, a purveyor of vigilante justice."

The snow let up and the western horizon came ablaze in shades of purple and pink. The rays of the setting sun reflected off the clouds in the east, bathing the mountain in Alpenglow. Billy sat, unmoving, and absorbed the glorious spectacle until it diminished to twilight. He stood up and shook off the pile of snow that had consumed him during his sit. He felt like he was shedding a cocoon of rebirth, for he had truly detached himself from humanity today and entered a higher existence, no longer subject to the regular rules of "justice". Billy was a killer once again. With a sense of empowerment and just a small bit of trepidation, he bombed down the Powder Glades run in the twilight, all the while thinking about how blessed he was to have the opportunity to do something that most people only dreamed about. Whether it was the Powder Glades run in twilight or the killing of Big Purple Tex he wasn't sure, but he felt blessed nonetheless. As he passed the mound of snow that he knew was Big Purple Tex's dead body, he muttered to himself again, "Seven, you're out."

CHAPTER 2

THE TALE OF MIMI MERRIDALE

In the fading twilight, Billy approached the bottom of the mountain near The California lodge. He had a vision of police officers waiting for him. He knew that his concerns were a product of nervousness and an overactive imagination, but he was worried nonetheless. He had just killed Big Purple Tex, Chas Wellington, oil man from Houston Texas. He would go straight to jail for a long time if he was caught.

A more realistic concern was that someone from ski patrol might have seen him poaching the mountain after hours. Once all the lifts were done running for the day, the ski patrol team did a final sweep of the mountain to get all stragglers to head on down to the bottom. This usually entailed rousting young snowboarders from hiding places in the trees where they stopped to get stoned or lovers trying to get in a quickie in a secluded spot with a view of the lake while the sun set. Many people liked to try to get in that final twilight run in at the end of the day. There were workers who scanned the runs from the bottom with binoculars after the final sweep to catch anyone who might be poaching. Perpetrators were charged with trespassing, and either had their pass taken away or were eighty-sixed from the resort for the rest of the season.

Billy didn't want to lose his pass, but more damning was that his name would be on record for having been on the

Powder Glades run around the time of Big Purple Tex's demise. His concerns were unfounded though. He stayed in deep pockets of trees on the way down, as far from the open runs as possible. No one was waiting for him as he shot out of some thick pines onto Roundabout, the cat track that accessed the California side of the mountain. Instead of heading toward the parking lot by going down either the Gunbarrel or World Cup run where he would surely be seen by anyone who might be watching, he followed Roundabout to its' end at a dead-end street in the neighborhood, Sherman Way. He was a half- mile from his cabin on Needle Peak. A quick glance at his watch showed it was almost five o' clock. He had to be to work at six so he started jogging.

•••

Billy pulled into the employee parking garage with ten minutes to spare. The reality of what he had done today, what he had become, was slowly setting in. He felt that at any moment some Douglas County Sheriffs or perhaps some FBI agents would stop him and ask him to come with them for questioning. He tried to tell himself that he was overreacting since he was the last person on the planet to see Big Purple Tex's body before it was completely covered in snow. The odds were slim that the body would be discovered any time before the resort opened tomorrow morning. The storm that was currently dumping inches, perhaps feet of snow over Big Purple Tex's corpse also served to decrease the chances that it would be found anytime soon. When the body was finally found, the cause of death would appear to be nothing but a normal skiing accident; a skier without a helmet ran into a tree and crushed his skull, like Sonny Bono back in January of '98. If no witnesses surfaced, his crime was perfect. He walked on to the casino floor at five minutes before six with a sense of empowerment and a feeling of rebirth.

Later in the evening, the main boss of the craps pit, Johnny A, came up to Billy's game and whispered in his ear. "Hey Billy, do you remember that drunken idiot from Texas that you were dealing to last night?"

Billy's heart skipped a few beats, then began to pound in his chest. He tried to remain calm as he answered. "How could I forget that obnoxious bastard in that outlandish purple jumpsuit? What about him?"

"A couple of his cronies came by a few minutes ago and asked me if anyone has seen him in the casino tonight. Apparently, he went skiing today and never showed up to meet them for dinner in the Sagebrush Steakhouse."

Billy concentrated on his breathing as he slowly answered. "I haven't seen him Johnny. He's so damn loud, obnoxious, and demanding, I'm sure everyone would have noticed if he had shown up this evening, especially if he was still wearing that gnarly purple jumpsuit and that goofy court jester's hat he had on last night. You know, he stopped here yesterday right after skiing and played non-stop until midnight when they had to escort him to his room. He was shitfaced. Maybe he's pulling the same stunt tonight in one of the other casinos."

Johnny A. chuckled. "Yow. That's probably what happened. Well, if you do see him let me know."

"Will do." The Dark Thoughts whispered in the back of his mind. *"We won't be seeing Mr. Big Purple Tex in here ever again."*

As the night continued, Billy began to have trouble concentrating on his game. The re-emergence of The Dark Thoughts disturbed him. He had banished them for over a decade by creating a fantastic life for himself in Tahoe. That life was beginning to unravel though. In the last three months, he had lost both his fiancée and his best friend and mentor.

•••

Billy had been engaged to the hottest cocktail waitress at Harry's, Mimi Merridale. She left him at the end of summer, not in any traditional manner either. She had simply disappeared one day that past September while Billy was at work, taking everything she owned from the cabin on Needle Peak drive where they lived together. There was no note of explanation, and none of her friends had any idea what she had done either. She was just gone. Billy wanted to file a missing person report, but decided to wait a couple of days to see if she would come back, call, or something. One of her closest friends and co-workers, a cocktail waitress named Simone, finally told him on the third day that Mimi had contacted her and she was safe. He grilled Simone hard for more information but she was not forthcoming.

When Billy finally resorted to begging, Simone broke down and told him the crushing truth. "Billy, Mimi left you for someone else. He's a rich guy. You know that's what she always wanted."

Billy went into a dark place after that. The salve of paradise that he had used for so many years of his life in Tahoe began to lose its ability to temper his lurking anger, a dark part of his past and a carefully hidden part of his present that he thought he had finally put to rest by falling in love. He should have known better. He knew exactly when things began to go awry...

The previous spring, Billy had a stroke of luck one night after work while playing dollar video poker and hit a Royal Flush that paid just over eleven thousand dollars.

After buying the bar a round of drinks and tipping out the slot attendant and the bartender, he still had about ten thousand five hundred cash on him.

That night, Billy Stone's true stroke of luck came not in the form of the Royal Flush, but more so in a moment of clarity. He looked down at the wad of hundreds in his hand, thought about Mimi and their impending marriage, walked his ass straight out to the employee parking lot, jumped in his old beat up Wrangler, and made it home with the Royal Flush money still intact instead of gambling it back.

When Billy walked in the door that night, Mimi was sitting in front of the computer as usual, tracking her fake stock portfolio. She dreamed of being a day-trader. The dream was unrealistic because God used the blessings he gave to Mimi on her firm and curvaceous body, her pretty face, and her voracious sex drive, but somehow forgot to leave much for her brain. It was almost as if He had fashioned a perfect doll but only left room in the head cavity for two AAA batteries. When Billy came up behind her and let loose the shower of hundreds over her head, she squealed with delight. Clothes began to fly and Billy proceeded to have one of the most sexually extravagant nights of his life, thanks to that one moment of clarity. Something about rolling around in so many hundred dollar bills turned Mimi into a beast of love. That night she dragged Billy into every room in the house and let him have her any way he wanted, even giving him a little taste of the forbidden dark hole he had never been allowed to touch before. It seemed that the money had taken away all her inhibitions. Looking back, Billy realized how blind he had been when he had asked this woman to marry him.

Hours later, Billy lay in bed staring out of the east-facing window watching the morning shoo away the darkness, thanking God that he wasn't That Guy, sitting in the casino, still playing video poker and wondering what happened to his ten thousand dollars. As Mimi snuggled up close to him, he asked a fateful question that he realized upon further reflection was the trigger that blew up his whole blessed existence. "Baby, what should we do with the money?"

Without hesitation, and with a great deal of exuberance, Mimi, who was laying on her stomach, arched her back, stuck her ass in the air and gave him her best Marilyn Monroe impression. "Let's open up a stock trading account for me so that I can stop slinging booze to assholes in that accursed Harry's casino and make some real money."

Blinded by the powerful combination of love and smut, Billy was tempted to say yes to Mimi's dream of getting out of the casino. The clarity that saved him from blowing the money back in the first place came to his aid once again. He paused for a moment before answering her and tasted iron in his mouth. He had bitten his lip hard enough to draw blood.

"Don't you think it would be better if we saved it for the wedding or maybe even a new car?"

Mimi rolled over and sat up. The look on her face told him exactly how she felt about that idea. "You don't think I can do it, do you?" she screamed. "You think I'm fucking stupid!"

Billy tried his best to do some damage control. "Come on Baby, it's not that. It's just that right now this money could be spent on some more important things. We need another car and we're getting married soon. The wedding could cost ten grand alone."

Mimi stood up from the bed and began pulling some clothes out of the armoire. "We don't even have a date set for a wedding and you're the one who needs a new car. My car's fine, you selfish bastard!"

Billy stared at her as she put on her tennis shoes with more attitude than he could have imagined coming from the act of putting on tennis shoes. She was pissed. She stood up and walked out of the bedroom without so much as a parting word or even a glance in Billy's direction. The front door slammed, and he heard Mimi in "her" car screech out of the driveway. He muttered to himself, "It's my money anyway, bitch."

He went down to Carson City later that afternoon and bought himself a brand-new Jeep Commander, using the ten thousand cash and his Wrangler as a down payment.

•••

Billy snapped out of his painful fugue when out of the corner of his left eye he saw a players' card come flying in accompanied by a command: "Give me five thousand." As the card landed on the layout, Billy took a quick glance and realized that whoever threw the card was another Platinum player. He was getting sick of these guys.

Billy called out loud enough to be heard over the din. "Hey boss, I need a marker for five thousand dollars, Platinum player." He proceeded to pull chips out of the bankroll, putting together the five thousand in a good mix of denominations from twenty-five to five hundred dollar chips. This was where professionalism took over for dealers. Players of this caliber were important to the company and Billy knew that his treatment of a Platinum player reflected strongly on his abilities as a dealer. He had already checked the name on the player's card and proceeded with his own greeting. "How are you doing tonight Mr. Smith?"

Mr. Smith was preoccupied with telling his two buddies to get some chips and get in the game. If he heard Billy's greeting, he ignored it. His salt-and-pepper hair was freshly cut and impeccably styled, down to his trimmed goatee and plucked eyebrows. He wore designer clothing in shades of black and gray. He was one of those idiots that tucked his sweater into his slacks; west coast for sure. His fingernails were well manicured and he sported a deep tan. He also wore one of those ridiculously large watches that were popular these days; a subconscious effort to make up for something else that probably wasn't large. While staring at the watch on his left wrist, Billy also noticed that Mr. Smith did not wear a wedding ring. The tan line on his left ring finger told him that the ring existed but was left out of the equation for this trip. As Billy assessed Mr. Smith, a rumbling in the back of his mind left him feeling unsettled. The Dark Thoughts were emerging again.

Billy tried once again to engage Mr. Smith. "How are you doing today Mr. Smith? Welcome back to Harry's. I've got for you here a good mix of five hundred in twenty-five dollar chips, two thousand in one hundred dollar chips, and twenty-five hundred in five hundred dollar chips for a total of five thousand.

Mr. Smith ignored Billy and said "Just give it to me in all one hundred dollar chips.

The Dark Thoughts awoke in Billy's head. "*This guy is way over-confident. He thinks his fucking money will buy him into and out of everything. Kiss his ass for a few minutes and see if it leads you somewhere.*"

Billy was shaken to the core. He knew from his time in The Gulf War that The Dark Thoughts were insatiable in their hunger. Here they were, less than eight hours after the death of Big Purple Tex, identifying another target. He ignored them and concentrated on the task before him.

With a Platinum player on the game, all eyes were on him now. It was time to be a professional. Billy worked hard to maintain politeness. "Here's five thousand for you Mr. Smith, all in hundreds. All right, gentlemen, the best of luck to all of you."

Mr. Smith peered closely at Billy's nametag. "All right, Billy from San Diego, my friends here don't know how to play very well, so I want you to help them out...and ask your boss to get a waitress over here with a wine list from the steakhouse. We don't want to drink any of that shit you guys give away to everyone else."

Billy gritted his teeth while The Dark Thoughts offered their own response. *"Teach your own damn friends how to play the fucking game. You're just going to interrupt the lesson every time something comes up that you think you know about and they'll immediately turn their attention to you because they suck up to you."* Instead, Billy provided the appropriate response. "Absolutely. I'll help your friends out as we proceed. I'll also have Brian call the waitress station for you." He turned his attention to the two friends. "Okay guys. Put your cash down here on the layout in front of you so that I can make some change for you."

The Dark Thoughts had been correct in their assessment of Mr. Smith and his buddies. Billy spent about two minutes trying to explain the game to the two suck-ups that he nicknamed The Barnacles, and they weren't getting it because they weren't paying attention. Mr. Smith was bragging to them about some stock investments he had made that week and in listening to him, they were ignoring Billy at crucial points in the game. Billy explained to them the importance of the odds bet, but they never put it down once their point was established, as he suggested. The point was rolled, and Mr. Smith started right in on Billy. "Hey dealer, I thought I told you to explain the game to my friends. How come they don't have any odds?"

Billy tried his best to remain polite. "Sir, I just explained the odds to them and suggested that they put the bet down, but they ignored me."

Mr. Smith made an exasperated hissing sound and said to The Barnacles "This guy's no help, so just follow exactly what I do". He then looked at Billy and barked at him "Where's that waitress I asked for fifteen minutes ago?"

The Dark Thoughts had an answer for him. *"You've only been here for five fucking minutes you douche bag. How could you have asked for a waitress fifteen minutes ago?"*

"I'll check with my boss on that one as soon as he gets back over here." Billy wasn't in the mood to kiss enough ass to make this arrogant bastard even remotely happy.

When the waitress showed up with a wine list from the steakhouse, Billy saw that it was Simone from Brazil. Her cinnamon skin with those almond-shaped eyes framed by a swath of raven hair put most men into a trance. Then they were destroyed when they saw her ample cleavage. After Mimi left, Simone was the one most often chosen to handle special requests from Platinum players. As she approached, Mr. Smith looked her up and down, undressing her with his eyes. They stopped and stayed at her cleavage. He glanced at her nametag.

"Simone de Brazil. Como estas, mi corazon, mi cielo? Eres muy guapa." Simone rolled her eyes while Billy chuckled to himself. This nimrod was trying to impress a woman who spoke Portuguese with his Spanish. Simone bent her head down just enough to pull Mr. Smith's gaze away from her breasts and replied as professionally as she could. "I'm sorry sir, but I don't understand Spanish. I'm from Brazil and we speak Portuguese there. It's a little different. Here's your wine list. Let me take orders from the rest of the table while you look at it and I'll come right back to see what you want." Her accent was tantalizing.

Mr. Smith wasn't one to be kept waiting though; he started throwing his money around just as Billy had predicted. He pulled a twenty-five-dollar chip from his pile and handed it to Simone. "Here, sweetie, how about if you just stay here and suggest a good Cabernet for me and my friends?"

Simone had enough experience as a pit server to understand that Mr. Smith was hitting on her. She was also savvy enough to realize that for the rest of the evening, every time she brought something to this man, poured him more wine, or simply stopped by to check on him, she would get another chip. Whether it was a five, a twenty-five, or a hundred depended on how drunk Mr. Smith got, how horny he was, or how much he was winning. If she worked it right, she could make five hundred bucks off this guy before she went home. Mimi had been good at this game too. Some nights she came home with over a thousand dollars, grinning from ear to ear. She always talked about "working the whales" and took great pride in knowing how to get the most in tips out of these rich guys. Billy knew that he should have seen the gold digger signs early on, but he was blinded by what he thought was love.

Simone was good. She stroked Mr. Smith's ego through his pocketbook. "I'm sure that Harry's is comping this for you so I'll assume money is no object. The '98 Silver Oak is my favorite."

Mr. Smith immediately took what Simone said and the way she said it as an open door to hit on her. "Well, sweetie, if that's your favorite, how about if you and I go to dinner at this Sagebrush Steakhouse tomorrow night and we'll get two bottles of that '98 Silver Oak?"

Simone flashed her brilliant smile. "I'm sorry sir, the company frowns on employees dating customers, but how about if I just bring a bottle so you and your friends can try it? I'm sure you'll like it."

Mr. Smith wouldn't give up. "I'd like it more if I could share it with you."

Simone held her ground, but still spoke with that sultry accent that Billy was sure drove Mr. Smith nuts. "I'll be right back with your wine and three nice glasses. Good luck to you."

As she walked away, Mr. Smith took a good long hard look at her ass in the skimpy black velvet skirt that was her current uniform and said out loud to no one in particular, "I gotta get me some of that", eliciting ridiculous kiss-ass laughter from The Barnacles.

One of them played The Devil's Advocate. "What about that hot little wife you left at home?"

Mr. Smith laughed smugly as he replied. "She'll be there when I get back. Besides, she'll probably be on the computer the whole time we're here, trying to make a fortune by day-trading stocks. She's as dumb as a rock and thinks that she can figure out the market."

The other Barnacle laughed and chimed in. "She sure is hot though...probably a luxury model in the bedroom huh?"

Mr. Smith became even more smug as the conversation progressed. His chest puffed out so far, his tucked-in sweater came out of his pants to expose his hairy fat man-belly. "Oh yeah, blonde, blue eyes, heart-shaped tattoo on her ass, and a voracious sex drive when money is thrown her way." Billy sensed a familiarity in Mr. Smith's story that made him feel uneasy. He listened closely to the monologue. "When I met her, she told me that she dreamed of becoming a day-trader. She swore she could predict market fluctuations; buy low and sell high. All I had to do was romance her for a couple weeks, then tell her that I was in the market. Now I've got this bitch under my thumb. You guys should come by for some fun one night. I'm sure I could talk her into fucking both of you at the same time while I watched. She's a little sex machine. I just need to keep funding her day-trading account. She's fascinated by it but has no understanding of it whatsoever. She may as well bet sports, which is what she does on the weekends. She'll easily blow five or ten grand a week on college and pro football."

His story had an unsettling sense of familiarity to Billy. Mr. Smith continued. "You'd think that the excitement of winning would make her even hornier, but it's the exact opposite. On losing days, she makes sex an extravaganza. It's rough, vulgar, and physically challenging. She likes to bite .... hard enough to leave a mark."

The Dark Thoughts resounded in Billy's head. *"That's exactly how Mimi was. She was the same type of whore. Could this be the fucker who stole your fiancée? Listen up and find out more from this arrogant bastard!"*

Billy was rattled by the familiarity of Mr. Smith's story, but more so by the fact that The Dark Thoughts were awake and free in his mind, sharing their scathing opinion with him after a decade of silence. His iron grip on them had become tenuous. As Mr. Smith's story evolved, Billy was also beginning to lose his composure. His next break was in ten minutes. He could have called for an emergency break, but that process could have taken ten minutes depending on if an extra dealer was available or not. Instead, he stood there listening to the rest of the painful story.

Billy was having trouble concentrating on the game and had missed one roll of the dice. The stickperson wasn't paying attention either, and she started to send the dice out after a six rolled and Billy hadn't moved. The players on Billy's side of the game started freaking out. "Hey, where's my money for the six?" "Whoa, whoa, whoa! Six just rolled and I haven't been paid for my come bet!" "Hey, I haven't been paid yet either!" "Where's my money?" "What the hell is going on?"

Billy had faded away from reality, drowning in the pain of realization. He was gripping the rail of the game in front of him so hard that the veins on both of his hands were bulging out and dark purple. He tasted blood from biting the inside of his cheek. The Dark Thoughts were screaming incoherently in the back of his head about revenge and murder. He needed to snap out of this, and quick. He ignored all the players that were going nuts, put his hand out in front of Lori the stickperson in a gesture that said "stop", and asked her "What was the last roll?"

"I'm sorry Billy. It was a six. I was paying attention to the other dealer and I just assumed that because you were standing up straight that you were done first, like you usually are."

Billy stared at her, trying to regain his wits while ignoring the admonitions from all the players on his side. "It's okay Lori, I just lost myself there for a second. You said a six rolled?"

Lori looked like she felt responsible. "Yeah, six. I apologize again Billy."

Billy began methodically paying all the bets on six while ignoring the comments from the pissed off players. Mr. Smith, realizing that Billy was ignoring everyone's complaints, must have felt that it was his position to take up the complaining torch for the rest of the table. "Hey dammit,

I haven't been paid for my six yet either! You guys owe me three hundred and fifty bucks! What the hell is wrong with this place? Hey Billy from San Diego, do we need to get your boss over here to make sure we get paid properly?" He was standing right next to Billy, in the final spot to get paid. Billy felt a strong urge to reach into the middle portion of the bankroll, grab one of the pens that were there for signing paperwork, and in one swift backhanded move jam it straight into Mr. Smith's left temple. Once it was in, all it would take was a quick jerk either sideways, up, or down and he would fall over dead. Billy saw the scene taking place in his mind as he instead cut out three hundred fifty dollars on the layout, looked directly into the eyes of the man who he was sure had swiped away the love of his life on a whim and said "Do you want to press that six, sir, or do you want to get paid?" It never hurt so bad to suck it up in his life.

Mr. Smith's response held veiled threats. "I just want to fucking get paid the money that I'm owed for the six. Is that too much for a Platinum player to ask?"

Billy paid Mr. Smith and addressed the collective group of agitated players. "Sorry folks. We're not perfect around here and mistakes occur on occasion. We've fixed it though, and we're back on track. Let's gamble." He couldn't resist adding a scathing final remark. "And thanks for your patience."

Lori finally sent the dice out to the shooter again, and Mr. Smith threw in three one hundred dollar chips and said "Fuck it, after all that trouble, go ahead and press my six." Billy picked up the late bet and imagined reaching out with clawed fingers, digging into the soft tissue around Mr. Smith's jugular, and tearing it out with his bare hands. He could do it and watch this fucker bleed to death on the floor, but he wasn't ready to go to jail. He prayed for the next five minutes to pass quickly so that he could get away from all of the anger, anguish, conflict, and desire for vengeance.

The Barnacles had no clue concerning what had just gone down. They were more interested in the story that Mr. Smith had been telling about his newest trophy. One of them took up the conversation again. "So, did you give this bimbo the prenuptial schmeal?"

The other Barnacle laughed. "I hope so. This is your fifth wife in ten years isn't it?"

Mr. Smith puffed up again. "Oh yeah. She signed it immediately when I told her there was a quarter-million in it for her. She kind of looked it over but she obviously didn't know what she was reading, or she would have objected to the addendum that I put in about the day trading account."

"What addendum?" asked one of The Barnacles.

Mr. Smith grinned smugly, obviously pleased with himself. "If we divorce, she gets the two hundred fifty thousand minus any money of mine she may have lost in the stock account. I'll be able to write it all off as a loss when I file my taxes for the year. It's been only two months and she's already down almost a hundred grand. I'll probably dump her once she breaks two hundred, just so that she has a little bit of money to get her ass back to Tahoe and out of my hair."

The other Barnacle laughed. "So you found this one here? I had no idea."

"Yeah, she was actually a cocktail waitress in one of these casinos. I can't remember which one. I met her last summer at a wine tasting event at the casino across the street."

Billy's stomach clenched. He remembered that wine tasting dinner. Mimi had gone to it with her girlfriends and came home late. As the details of Mr. Smith's story came together, it was becoming undeniable that they were talking about his girl. He clenched his jaw and prayed for his break to come soon before he snapped.

Simone showed up with Mr. Smith's bottle of Silver Oak and three wine glasses from the Sagebrush Steakhouse. The bartender had already opened the bottle for her, but she poured a small taste for Mr. Smith anyway so that he could go through the ritual of making sure his wine was satisfactory. Through the whole process, he stared at Simone, lingering too long on her breasts and her legs. Billy could tell that she didn't like this, but she had enough grit and experience to maintain her professionalism to the end.

"How do you like it?" she asked.

Mr. Smith reached into his pile of chips, pulled out another twenty-five-dollar chip, and placed it on Simone's tray with a flourish. Then he leaned in close to her and said "I just love a woman who can pick out a great bottle of wine. Can't we go to dinner sometime, somewhere, Miss Simone?"

"I'm sorry Mr. Smith. It would not be very professional of me to date customers; although I'm flattered by your offer." Once again, she let her seductive accent flow through. "I'll pour these glasses full for you and your friends. You should let me know if you want more, because the bar in the steakhouse closes in forty-five minutes." As she split the bottle evenly between the three glasses, Mr. Smith stood there and stared at her butt.

When Simone was done pouring, Mr. Smith said “I’ll take two more bottles of this Silver Oak, Simone, but only if you bring them out to us.

Simone flashed him a brilliant smile. “I’ll be taking care of you for the rest of the night, sir.”

Mr. Smith then raised his glass to his friends and toasted. “To Simone.”

The Barnacles responded in unison. “To Simone.”

Simone acted like she was embarrassed. “Thanks guys. I’ll be back soon.” As she walked away, they all stared at her butt. Mr. Smith issued another toast. “...and to Mimi. May you both get to know her ass before it gets replaced.”

“Hear, hear” said The Barnacles.

Billy felt his stomach clench again as he heard the last toast. He didn’t want to believe that this was how he lost the woman he had been preparing to spend the rest of his life with, but there weren’t two Mimi’s like that in the world. That gold-digging wench had left him for this hunter of women. The Dark Thoughts whispered to him. *“Society would be better off without this scumbag. You could take him out, but you aren’t ready yet. You must prepare your arsenal.”* The urge to kill was gaining momentum.

Thankfully, Billy’s breaker finally showed up. As the dealers pushed around, Billy made the ultimate effort to stay calm, to listen to what The Dark Thoughts were saying. When he finally pushed out, he could barely make eye contact with his players, but he still managed to maintain his professionalism. “Good luck everyone. I’ll be back in twenty minutes.”

As he walked away, he heard Mr. Smith mutter to The Barnacles. “That guy looked like he was about to kill someone." They all laughed. They had no idea how close to true Mr. Smith's statement was.

Billy headed straight for the door that led outside to the west side of the building. Once outside, he looked around to make sure there was no one nearby, leaned over the railing, and vomited. "Seven, I'm out" he thought to himself. He walked back inside and headed straight to the Dealer Pencil.

Thankfully, the Pencil was his friend Christian. Outside of his full-time job as a pit boss, Christian was also an ordained minister. He was supposed to marry Mimi and Billy, so he knew Billy's anguish. He looked at Billy closely when he walked up. "You don't look good my friend."

"I don't feel too well either Christian. I just threw up outside. Do you think I could go home early?" Billy did not want to see Mr. Smith and his ass-sucking friends again. He might do something brash.

Christian frowned and looked at his computer screen. "I have two extra bodies at ten. Go ahead and get out of here. I'll give you an early out instead of a sick leave. Hope you feel better Billy."

Billy sighed. "Thanks Christian. You don't know how much I need to go."

CHAPTER 3

THE LURE OF TAHOE

The house on Needle Peak was a typical Tahoe cabin. It defined the lifestyle. Two blocks from the California Lodge at Heavenly and two miles from the casino core, it was the perfect spot for a casino worker and an active outdoor enthusiast.

As he walked around the house turning on all the lights, Billy thought about the decade he had spent there with his friend and mentor, and the year that he had spent there with his gold-digging fiancée. The walls of this home had seen so much over the years; the parties, the women, the mushroom trips, the extravagant dinners, the mad love-making, everything that was Billy's life for the last ten years. Now it would witness his evolution into a higher being; a man unafraid of his true calling in life, a purveyor of vigilante justice, a killer.

Billy knew he had to revisit the past he had spent so many years trying to forget. He needed to remember the special training he had received from the U.S. Marine Corps that had turned him into an efficient killer. He also remembered the compulsion of The Dark Thoughts when they first appeared in his mind during the liberation of Baghdad. He was a sniper at the time, charged with removing pockets of resistance as U.S. forces swept the city. Billy and his spotter, Elmer Maynigo, had been deadly and efficient. They removed all cells of resistance in the area, and just as Elmer was sure they had achieved their objective, Billy, compelled by The Dark Thoughts, grabbed Elmer's M-16 and began to shoot at the surrendering Iraqi troops. He didn't stop until Elmer warned him that they were drawing enemy fire. That day Billy Stone shot over a hundred retreating Iraqi soldiers. It was there that The Dark Thoughts asserted their control over Billy's psyche. After that day, he heeded their command without question, which led to the end of his military career.

Billy had stayed in Baghdad after the liberation to take part in Operation Desert Scorpion. He had no living relatives and no life outside of The Marines. He wanted to be a career soldier, but The Dark Thoughts ruined that plan during one of his first Force Recon missions. Billy led that mission, raiding a home on the outskirts of the city that intelligence believed was housing Hussein sympathizers. He had stormed into the kitchen of the home where four men, all wearing their Gutras, were playing cards. One of the men reached under the table, possibly for a gun, and on The Dark Thoughts' command, Billy shot them all.

Billy was tried for violation of the Military Rules of Engagement. His superiors wanted to make an example of him. His Marine JAG had been savvy enough to avoid a long-term sentence, but he did serve a few months in a U.S. military prison in Baghdad and later was court-marshaled and dishonorably discharged. His life and future as a Marine were over.

Upon Billy's arrival stateside in Arlington, the complete details of his dishonorable discharge were finally explained to him. He was to receive none of the benefits he had earned for five years of service to his country. There would be no more monthly paycheck, no assistance for college from the G.I. bill, no job placement assistance that was normally offered to U.S. military personnel, no pension upon retirement, and no veterans' health care benefits; essentially no help or assistance from the government in any way shape or form. He would be on parole for the next two years, and any violation of the terms of that parole would send him straight to jail. He was also stripped of his right to own a firearm for the rest of his life. The United States government was washing their hands of Sergeant William Stone Jr. He was now simply Billy Stone, civilian.

Thankfully, Billy had saved a portion of the money he earned during his service. He had close to forty thousand dollars in his bank account but essentially nothing else. He hoped it would be enough to survive on until he got a job and started a life. He was offered a ride to Dulles airport in Washington D.C., where he was unceremoniously dropped at the curb. He wanted to go back to the west coast, but he had no interest in being anywhere close to his home town of San Diego. There were too many painful memories there. The only person he knew in California was Elmer Maynigo. Elmer left Baghdad quickly after the war was over. His father had passed away during the war, and he went back to San Francisco to take over the family business. He told Billy before he left that if he ever needed work in the Bay Area to look him up. With no other compelling options, Billy chose to start there. He walked into the terminal, found the nearest pay phone, and placed a collect call to the number Elmer had given him over a year ago. He prayed it was still in service.

Elmer answered and immediately accepted the call. "Hey, bruddah Billy! How you be my old friend?" The flavor of his culture had crept back into him over the years. When Billy knew Elmer he spoke proper English and was an introvert. The Elmer he heard on the phone now was a different man. Regardless, he had nowhere else to turn, so he jumped right in.

"Hey Elmer, I'm stateside and I'm thinking about heading out west. I was wondering if your job offer with the family business was still out there". Billy prayed during the two seconds it took for Elmer to reply.

Elmer's tone reverted to the straightforward, serious voice that Billy recognized from the war. "Billy Stone, you once saved my life. You also helped me survive the U.S. Marines without going AWOL. You always have a place in my family business. When do you arrive? I'll come and pick you up".

Billy couldn't believe his luck. "Thank you my brother. I'll try to get a seat on American flight 420 from here in Dulles to SFO. It arrives at six-thirty in the evening your time. I should warn you, I'm out because of a dishonorable discharge".

The moment of silence on the other end made Billy nervous until Elmer cheerfully quipped back. "I already know about it bro. Don't worry about a thing. Brother Elmer's got you covered. I'll see you at the airport at six-thirty. Then we'll talk".

Billy breathed a sigh of relief. "Thanks Elmer. What is your family business anyway?"

Elmer's tone was even more serious this time. "Import, export".

True to his word, Elmer was waiting in baggage claim when Billy arrived. He gave Billy a bearhug in greeting. "Bruddah Billy, welcome home my friend"!

Billy was overwhelmed by the fact that someone was going out of their way to help him out. He choked up a bit when he thanked Elmer for offering him the chance to make a life for himself. "Thanks for believing in me, Elmer".

Elmer was fired up. "Hey man, let's go straight over to my warehouse and I'll introduce you to everyone who's important. My aunt Teresita owns an apartment complex in Burlingame, just south of San Fran, real close to my house. I called her up right before I came to pick you up and she has a studio available at a decent price for the South San Francisco area. We'll get you livin' the good life quickly. There's no place like the Bay Area.

As they pulled up to a large warehouse on the docks in South San Francisco, Elmer said "Don't worry about the lack of signage. All our business is conducted with outside clients. That's what makes it all safe." Billy wasn't sure what to make of that statement. He followed Elmer through a small, unobtrusive door into a scene out of a Hollywood movie.

The inside of the building was lit up like high noon. Halogen lamps lined the ceiling over row upon row of crates that were stacked at least thirty feet high. Forklifts moved about at random, carrying crates from one end of the building to the other. There was a lot of action at the far end of the building where Billy guessed the loading dock was located. Not one person, not even the guy by the door carrying an AK47, had even blinked when he and Elmer entered the building. Elmer led him to an area on the warehouse floor that was set up as an office, sans the walls or partitions that provided any sense of privacy. Billy looked at Elmer as he sat down at the largest of the five desks and asked him "So what exactly do you import and export, brother?"

Elmer once again gave Billy the forthright voice, but with a sharper more serious edge. "Drugs and guns, Billy. I made a few arms connections while we were in Baghdad and of course had numerous connections here in the Bay for the drug business. Now I just move product from one place to another. That's why I need someone to work with me, someone whom I can trust with my life. I'm working way too much, and I need a right-hand man to split the work with. You couldn't have called me at a more opportune time because my Lilly is pregnant with our first child and I shouldn't be working a hundred hours a week anymore. You're going to be me when I'm at home changing shitty diapers and watching DVD's of Sesame Street".

Billy couldn't believe what he was hearing. If anything was last on his list of possible futures, this was it. He would go straight to jail if he was caught doing anything this illegal. Even worse, he had no experience whatsoever in the trafficking of drugs and weapons. Outside of his non-conviction for murder, Billy was naïve to criminality.

"Elmer, you know I'll go straight to jail if I get in trouble for any of this". Billy's heart was racing.

Elmer replied, serious as ever. "Brother, once you're a part of this family, you'll be taken care of. We have attorneys. We'll get you out if anything happens. We'll cover your ass with any wrong turn you make, and you'll live well. You have the chance to be a modern-day king."

Billy answered Elmer with resignation. "I can't do it bro. I need to take a shot at living legit first. I have to fail at that before becoming a criminal."

Elmer looked at Billy with a saber-sharp gaze. "I thought you were different Billy. After seeing you coldly and efficiently kill all those people in Baghdad, I thought you had it in you to work with me, but I guess you're scared. Tell you what bro, take a couple of days to think about it. It's a pretty clean operation and no one has gotten into trouble in years."

Billy sighed. "Elmer, I do appreciate your offer, but I was discharged for killing some people I shouldn't have. I'm already starting out on thin ice. What may be a small infraction for you or anyone else that works here could very well land my ass in jail for a long time. I've got to be legit."

A dark look of understanding came over Elmer's face as he put his hand on Billy's shoulder. "That's heavy, my friend. I won't push you anymore. If you need any help in any way, or if you change your mind, I'm here for you." His grip tightened just enough to portray the seriousness of his next statement. "Of course, what you've seen here and the things I've said all have to die with you."

•••

Billy had no idea how difficult it would be to get a legitimate job with the black mark of a dishonorable discharge on his record. When he left Elmer at the warehouse, he took a cab straight to the nearest car dealership and bought himself a brand-new Jeep Wrangler. Next he went to a copy center and tried to come up with a resume. After listing his high school information and five years of military service, he barely filled half of one page.

Billy had learned so much in the military that just wasn't useful in the real world. He could track a man or even an animal through several different terrains. He could build more than ten different types of bombs and knew how to diffuse them all. He could kill a man with any of a hundred common household items, or snipe that same man dead in one shot from a thousand yards away. He knew how to administer drugs that were truth serums as well as those that incapacitated or killed. He understood battle strategies from the classical to the modern day and could apply any of them to a war situation. He knew how to survive for days in a bleak wilderness with little or no provisions. He could hike twenty miles a day without killing himself. The list went on and on. As formidable as his abilities were, none of it looked good on a resume, nor would those skills help him do anything such as sell a used car, manage an office, write a computer program, design a home, or anything else he would have liked to do for a living. The few job interviews that he did get bombed the minute the interviewer looked his name up in a computer and saw the dishonorable discharge next to it.

After a few months of fruitless job searching, Billy was entertaining the idea of going back to Elmer. He was tired, frustrated, and running out of money. His life was looking like another dead-end just like it had when his parents had died. He even tried to get a job as a sandwich maker at a local deli without using his military service as a reference. The owner had asked him what he had been doing for the last five years since graduating high school. Billy realized that the question would come up every time. He could not escape his past.

Billy was driving north on the 101 toward San Francisco after another frustrating day of searching for work when he began to despair. He felt like he had no choice but to become a drug runner for Elmer Maynigo. The idea of life as a criminal, no matter how lucrative, scared the hell out of him. He did not want to go to jail. He had seen firsthand what jail did to a man. His eyes began to well up with frustration. As he looked upwards to blink away his tears, he saw a billboard sign with a picture of Lake Tahoe on it. The words on the billboard spoke to him.

"Tired of the city, the traffic, and the pollution? Then come visit the pristine mountains of Lake Tahoe, America's Playground. Stay at Harry's Resort Hotel and Casino midweek for $49 a night. Take 101 N. to 80 E. then 50 E. straight into South Lake Tahoe."

Billy had been to Tahoe once as a teen-ager. The family had headed west toward San Diego upon departing from Fort Collins Colorado. They had taken the eighty into Tahoe through Truckee and had camped on the west shore in a beautiful spot close to the beach called Camp Richardson. Billy remembered that week more fondly than any other part of his past. Without even pondering what he would do when he got there or what the hell he was doing anyway, Billy took the 101 north into the City and got onto the Bay Bridge, which sent him east on highway 80, ultimately becoming 50 East just outside of Sacramento, up the western slope of the sierras, over echo summit, and down into the Tahoe basin. He was there in four hours and drove directly to the Stateline area and found Harry's. He wanted one of those $49 rooms.

Billy checked in to Harry's with nothing but his wallet and the clothes he wore. As he went down to the casino floor, his anticipation grew with the thought that there were games of chance to be played and fortunes waiting to be won. He had never gambled in a casino before. The lights and bells and yelling, screaming customers were all mesmerizing. Billy decided to try blackjack first, a game he had played frequently with the members of his platoon in Baghdad, especially when they were cooped up in their tents during sandstorms. Some seasoned veterans of the game had shown him the basic strategy for hitting and staying, so he felt like his knowledge would give him a better chance to win.

After stopping at the ATM for some cash, Billy walked around the pit until he found a game with a young and beautiful female dealer on it. This was his lucky table. Her nametag said "Janise, Chico Ca." Billy sat down and tried to be witty as he gave Janise his three hundred dollar bills. "Hey, Janise, how are things in Chico?"

Janise looked at him and rolled her eyes. "Probably the same as they were when I left from school two weeks ago." She didn't look too happy, nor did she interact well with any of her customers. Billy wondered if all dealers were bitter like this Janise girl from Chico. He lost his first three hands and was getting ready to move to another table when Grumpy Janise's relief came to give her a break. The young man looked to be about Billy's age and immediately brought some positive energy to the table. He greeted everyone and asked how they were all doing. He also got the whole table to give Grumpy Janise a round of applause upon her departure. He even whispered something in her ear that made her laugh before she walked away. This guy had it going on. His positive attitude radiated. Billy peered closely at his nametag. It said Richie, Santa Cruz.

Richie from Santa Cruz was both cocky and confident, and Billy could tell he knew how to walk the line between the two. He deftly, almost blatantly ignored the complaining customers and always had a positive comment for the winners. Anyone who tipped him was thanked graciously but not profusely; just enough to let the other players at the table know that tipping your blackjack dealer when winning was an integral part of the game. He gave out high-fives for blackjacks and felt the pain when someone busted. His positivity was infectious.

An older woman sitting in the center spot finally looked up at him and said "Wow, Richie. You seem like the only dealer in here that actually likes his job".

Without missing a beat while pitching out the next round of cards, Richie gave her a devilish smile and leaned in close to her, as if he were about to share a great secret. He spoke loud enough so that the other players could hear too. "I better like this job because I gave up a career in Architecture and Engineering so that I could have this life in Tahoe. Dealing is the perfect job for it too. I work at night and play during the day. Sometimes I work at night and party until it becomes day. This job is great because I work less than forty hours a week and my work never comes home with me. All I have to do is deal a perfect game of blackjack or craps and be able to put up with you guys while I'm doing it. As soon as I clock out, my life is mine." This brought a chuckle out of everyone at the table. This guy was damn good with his customers.

Richie's mention of a career in architecture and engineering struck a chord of memory for Billy. He had to ask. "Did you happen to study at Cal-Poly in San Luis Obispo?"

Richie looked up at him with some interest. "I sure did. How did you guess?"

"I wanted to go there after high school because it had one of the only programs on the west coast that taught both architecture and engineering."

Richie gave Billy a reassuring grin. "That it does, and one of the best in the nation as well. I did graduate from the program, but this place got a hold of me at the end of my junior year. My parents had been hinting to me that I needed to get a job and start bearing some of the cost of my education. At the time, I was going to be delivering pizzas and attending summer school. A sorority-girl friend of mine called me up one night and told me she had just gotten a job as a summer dealer here at Harry's and that I should go to the job placement center the next day and try to catch their human resources representative before she headed back to Tahoe. I dropped in on the poor woman the next day just as she was packing up to leave; she interviewed me on the spot without an appointment, and I got the job. That was a life-changing moment for me because after spending just two summers and two winter breaks living and working in Tahoe, I was hooked on the lifestyle. When I graduated, I had three job offers in my field and turned them all down to come back to Tahoe. I never wanted to live in a big city anyway, and that was pretty much the only option for a beginning architect or engineer. I just couldn't fathom the idea of working sixty or eighty hours a week and commuting at the same time. Now I live fifteen minutes from work. I work about thirty-five hours a week and I make a decent living. I'll never be rich, but I'm in paradise every moment of my life. It's one of those work to live, don't live to work situations."

"In the summer, my daily choices are mountain biking, hiking, kayaking, or the beach, all of which usually include a visit to The Beacon Bar and Grill at Camp Richardson for rum runners and live music in the afternoon. If I'm on the Nevada side I can do the same thing at Zephyr Cove. There's also camping, fishing, and golf, if you're a more sedentary person. In the winter, there's skiing, snowboarding, cross-country skiing, ice fishing, snowmobiling, and snowshoeing. Hell, I've even built an ice cave up in the mountains and camped in it. No matter what time of year it is, there's always someone here at work inviting you to join them for some sort of an excursion. This is a twenty-four-hour town, so there's always a party to be found after work if that's what you feel like doing. I don't ever sit around and watch television, and I don't sleep all day unless I partied all night the night before." The more Richie spoke about Tahoe life, the more Billy wanted to hear. After about an hour of hearing him preach about Tahoe, Billy had to ask a burning question.

"Hey Richie, what does it take to become a dealer?"

Richie flashed Billy a reassuring smile. "It takes almost nothing. Harry's likes to train their own, so if you apply just before they're getting ready to conduct a blackjack school, all you need is a clean record to be able to get a Nevada Gaming license. They call it a Sherriff's Card."

Billy's heart sank when he heard the words "clean record". "What do you mean by "clean record"?"

"That just means you can't have been convicted of a gaming related crime. You know, something like stealing or embezzling money from a casino, cheating, rigging slot machines, stealing chips, things like that. I suppose in this town it also helps to know someone that can get you an "in". You know what they say. It's not what you know, it's who you know."

This cat was a master at his trade. Billy looked around at the other tables. The other players were being obnoxious and rude to the dealers and those dealers looked miserable. Richie's customers were all having a good time, and he consistently managed to run off the rude ones who tried to get under his skin, either by ignoring them or by turning the other players against them. He actually stopped his game in the middle of a hand at one point when some drunk guy was verbally accosting him and asked the rest of the table "Do you guys want to hear this? You all came to have a good time, didn't you, not listen to people complaining about their crappy cards?" Everyone at the table agreed vehemently and the drunken idiot got up and left, mumbling something under his breath as he stumbled away that sounded a lot like "fuck you".

Richie looked at Billy and said "That right there is one of the biggest drawbacks to this job; the obnoxious drunks. If you can find some way to handle that, this job isn't all that bad."

Later, when Billy was the last customer on the table, Richie started telling him the more sordid stories about life in Tahoe. He leaned in closer to Billy as he dealt the cards, as if they were co-conspirators. "Now that we're no longer in mixed company, I'll tell you about the female scene here.

This town gets a huge new crop of young, beautiful, and fun-loving women every summer because all the casinos, restaurants, bars, and shops need extra help during the high season. Most of them recruit from the nearby colleges, but there is also an international program that brings in large groups of young people to work in the casinos. Male and female, they bring in some of the most beautiful, vibrant and outgoing youth from places like Poland, Costa Rica, Brazil, South Africa, Mexico, Korea, China...the list goes on forever, and most of the chicks in these groups are absolute babes. Now, if that isn't enough variety to satisfy the common man, add to your selection all the women that play on your game that take a liking to you. I've had women tell me their hotel room number more times than I care to remember. Some of them are ugly, some are hot, some are rusty old cougars, and others are into kinky shit, but they all want something from you. You have to be careful there because the casino does have rules against patronizing with the customers on property, but off property is your own business. Basically, if you like to hunt, Tahoe is a well-stocked private reserve. I don't know what line of work you're in now, but you seem interested in the job, so I'm just trying to let you know that the job is more of a vessel to an awesome life rather than an actual career. All you have to do is come into work regularly, and make them think that you have respect for their rules."

Billy was so mesmerized by Richie's sermon that he didn't even realize that he was sitting there speechless. In the moment of awkward silence that ensued, Richie dealt Billy a Blackjack and while paying his five-dollar bet seven dollars and fifty cents said "Hey man, if you ever want to survive as a gambler in this town, you've got to increase your bet while you're winning. You just won twelve hands in a row and bet five dollars every time."

Billy had no concern for the money. He looked up at Richie and had to ask. "Do you think I could land a job doing what you do?"

Richie flashed Billy a confident smile. "That's what I've been leading up to bro. If you're interested, you're here at the right time. I know that Harry's is having a blackjack school for the summer dealers. It starts next week. Now they may have all their predicted needs filled right now, but you never know if someone is going to drop out, or just not show up. They're counting on college students and people from other countries, many of whom will have changes in their agendas. On the note that I mentioned to you earlier about who you know versus what you know, just go into Harry's personnel office tomorrow when it opens and ask for Gwendolyn. I took her out last week and showed her the time of her life and then took her home and showed her an even better time. If you tell her I sent you, she might be willing to do you a favor. That is, if you don't have a job or a life tying you down somewhere else."

Billy was amazed. "Why would you do something like this for someone you don't know?

Richie laughed. "Because I can, and I want to see more cool dudes working here. Right now most of the guys that work here are a bunch of douchebags. We need some youth, some new blood."

Billy chuckled, but then looked at Richie apprehensively and asked him one more time. "What if I have a black mark on my resume?"

"Dude, like I told you before, as far as your gaming license is concerned, you can have a felony DUI on your record, domestic battery charges, manslaughter, anything, as long as you're clean right now and haven't ever committed a gaming-related crime. Anything else, hopefully my girl Gwendolyn can help you out by looking the other way, if you know what I mean."

As Billy stood up and started to gather up his chips, Richie assumed a more business-like voice. "Hey, when you leave a blackjack table, you should trade all of your five dollar chips for twenty-fives or hundreds. That way you have something easier to carry and the dealer keeps their smaller denomination chips in the tray. It's called "coloring up". Then you should tip your dealer if you've won. We earn most of our money from tips, not from what the company pays us. If you get this job, you'll see exactly what I mean. Also, if you get the job, come back in and find me tomorrow because I might need a roommate for the summer. We'll knock it down, bro."

Billy pushed his chips out to the center of the table and asked Richie, "What's an appropriate tip?"

As Richie counted Billy's winnings, he said "What you should have been doing is placing bets for the dealer, AKA me, on the front end of your betting circle. That way we could have won together. I could have made at least a hundred bucks off of you during your twelve-hand win streak if you were betting just a couple of bucks per hand for me, but this is probably your first time in a casino, isn't it?"

"Is it that visible?" Billy asked.

Richie from Santa Cruz smiled at Billy Stone as he called out to the pit boss "Coloring up five hundred and seventy-five dollars Boss, purple out." He pushed out a five-hundred-dollar chip and three twenty-five dollar chips in front of Billy and said "Yeah bro, you're still wet behind the ears and more nervous than you probably were during prom night, but a few weeks in this town and that'll change."

Billy didn't want to tell Richie that he never went to the prom. Instead, he handed him the spare seventy-five dollars and said "Is that enough?"

Richie picked up the three chips, tapped them on the edge of the tray making a loud rap, and said with great sincerity, "Thanks a lot; I'm sure your talk with Gwendolyn tomorrow will be positive."

The next morning, Billy walked into the human resources department of Harry's Resort Hotel and Casino and changed the course of his life. He found Gwendolyn immediately and walked up to her window with a blank application.

"Hi there. You're the woman I was sent to see."

Gwendolyn was young, cute, and a bit overweight. She wore loose but elegant clothes. Her demeanor was serious though; this was going to take some work. Billy smiled at her and said "I would like to try to get into your next blackjack school."

As the words came out of Billy's mouth, Gwendolyn was immediately shaking her head. "The current school is full, and the next one we will be conducting is in December."

Billy's first instinct was to give up and walk out, but he remembered that he had an ace to play. He tried to be as polite and forthright as possible. "A friend of mine named Richie from Santa Cruz told me to look for you. He said you might be able to help me. You're a lot prettier than his description."

Gwendolyn smiled and became lost in a faraway look. "Richie Wylde, what a gentleman; she giggled, and a stud too. That guy does daily what most of us would only dream of doing every now and then.

Billy laughed. "Yeah, I was impressed too; enough to try to get a job here as a dealer. Can you help me?"

Gwendolyn smiled at Billy. "If you're Richie's friend, I have a space for you. Two of the Brazilian girls that were supposed to be coming have backed out because their families planned a summer trip to Europe. I was saving those spaces as favors for friends, and you knowing Richie comes under that category. Just fill out the job application and I can get the ball rolling for you."

Billy reached across the counter and shook hands with Gwendolyn. "It's nice to meet you Miss, but I have a past with holes in it, and I can't submit a normal, thorough resume like most people want. I have four years of military service after high school until the present that I can't use on an application because I have a dishonorable discharge on my record. After that, I have nothing."

"Did you work in high school?" She asked.

Billy replied apprehensively; "Yes, I worked in my father's delicatessen, but it's out of business." This wasn't looking good.

Gwendolyn frowned, scratched her head, and rearranged her blouse so that her boobs were more revealed. "As a favor to Richie, I'll help you concoct a fake past. You've got to realize that this breaks down if you break down. If you don't screw up, they won't ever have to pull your application to see if you were hired correctly or not. Now, use your work at your father's deli, but extend the dates until 1999. Then come up with one of the local competitors and say you worked there until 2001. Then find the local Costco in San Diego and say you worked there until now; they keep poor employment records. The main thing I need from you is legitimate telephone numbers for each of these businesses. That way my ass is covered if you do anything stupid. Other than that, just go down to the Sherriff's office just across highway fifty from the Lakeside Inn and apply for your Douglas County Work Permit. If your record is clean, they'll fingerprint you and you'll bring back your temporary card to me and you'll be able to attend the blackjack school and become a dealer. Remember; I need those phone numbers on the job application to make it look legit. You tell Richie he owes me big time for this."

"I won't let you down Gwendolyn; neither will I let Richie down. Hell, if I get the job, he wants me to be his roommate."

Gwendolyn looked at Billy Stone up and down like he was a pork chop, licked her lips and laughed. "You two would be dangerous together."

Billy's fate was thus sealed. With Gwendolyn's help and a little bit of footwork on his part, he would attend his first day of blackjack school the next Monday.

Richie was true to his word when Billy came to find him that evening in the casino. He was on a busy craps game and didn't have much time to talk, but he told Billy to just meet him at the Upper Corner Lounge later that night around midnight.

"Congratulations on the beginning of your life in paradise. It's going to be more fun than you could ever imagine. Remember, it's not what you know, it's who you know. I'll meet you after work and show you your new place." Once again, through the whole conversation, Richie never missed a beat with the nine customers he had on his side of the craps game. Billy wondered if it truly came that easy.

Richie lived in a three-bedroom two-bath cabin with a two-car garage about two blocks from the California parking lot of Heavenly Ski Resort. It only took them five minutes to get there from the parking garage at Harry's.

As Richie showed Billy around the cabin, he discussed the financial details. "The rent here is only six hundred fifty bucks a month, which I'll split with you straight up the middle. I've been here for five years and already have deposit money set up so I don't even need that from you. The landlord hasn't raised the rent on this place since I've been here. That's because I have always taken care of any minor problems the place has had. It's a pretty old cabin and, as you can tell, a bit run-down. The dude that owns it is some sort of trust-fund brat that lives in Los Angeles. All he wants is the mortgage covered and to not be bothered. I've got the place furnished well. There's even a spare twin bed you can use. Of course, feel free to bring in anything you might have to add to the place. We can store a lot of things in one side of the garage."

Billy looked at Richie with a pang of shame. "I don't really own anything besides that Jeep. I've lived the last two weeks in a studio in the Bay Area and all the furniture belonged to my friend's aunt who owned the complex. I don't even have enough personal effects to make it worth my while to drive back."

Billy was once again starting his life over with nothing. The reality of his current situation made him want to hang his head. He must have done just that, because Richie walked over to him and put one arm around his shoulders. Billy tightened up a bit. He wasn't used to this kind of human contact from people he didn't know.

As Richie gave Billy a friendly squeeze, he said "Don't worry my friend. You'll have everything you need to exist here until you start receiving your tip money. That won't come until you finish blackjack school and start dealing. Then you'll be getting cash daily from the collective tip money earned the previous night you worked. Until then you'll only be making the minimum wage that the casino is paying you. Don't worry about paying rent until you start earning tokes. I can afford the six-fifty on my own anyway."

In his mind, Billy thanked God for once again providing for him during a time of great need. This Richie from Santa Cruz was like an angel sent to him to guide him through his initial entry into what seemed to be utopia. He shook Richie's hand and said "I don't know how to thank you enough. Since I got out, I've been floating around the Bay Area for the last couple months jobless, unable to find a job, and feeling like a complete loser. With your help I'm employed, I have a place to live, and a future to look forward to; all in a matter of thirty-six hours. I'm virtually speechless." Billy paused for a moment and looked around at the open-beam ceilings, the knotty-pine paneling, and the cheerily lit fireplace and wondered aloud. "If you can afford the rent by yourself, why are you getting a roommate?"

Richie chuckled. "When you landed two nights ago on my table, you looked like you had hit rock-bottom. I initially thought it was because you had gambled away your savings like everyone else that goes in there, but then when you became interested in my story and started asking about the job, I decided to help you out. I've lived here without a roommate a few times over the years and never really liked it. There's one college chick that needs a place for the summer, but I've tried that before and couldn't stand living with a woman. I would rather bring them home for one night and send them back the next day, if you know what I mean. You're young, in shape, and a handsome guy. Chasing skirt always works better if you have a partner. You know what I mean? I'll show you everything you need to know about life as a dealer in Tahoe, both good and bad. You'll love it. All I ask is that you respect my sleep and don't make any noise while I'm snoozin', and if you smoke, do it outside. I get enough of the shit on the job."

Billy frowned at the mention of smoking. "Don't worry about that. I've never smoked a day in my life."

Richie smiled and gave Billy a conspiratorial look. "Smoking pot is okay though. I do it regularly but I'll keep it in my room or outside if it bothers you. Harry's doesn't drug test but I heard a rumor that they're going to start mandatory testing for new-hires this fall, so if you've done anything illegal recently, you're getting in just in time."

Billy shook his head. "I've been pure as the driven snow for the last four years."

Richie chuckled at that. "Where have you been, in prison or something?"

The reminder that he could possibly have been in prison cast a dark look over Billy's face. He answered Richie's question with an unsettling seriousness. "Not prison. I've spent the last four years of my life in the Middle East as a Marine."

Richie stopped laughing and stared sadly at Billy. "It may as well have been prison, huh?"

•••

Billy was so busy and so overwhelmed with all the new things he was seeing and experiencing both in and out of work that he rarely thought about his past life or his dark desires. The Dark Thoughts hadn't spoken to him in quite a while. This was exactly what Billy needed. He felt happy and satisfied with his life for the first time since before his mother died. Instead of communing with The Dark Thoughts, he began to talk to God in his mind, thanking Him with every new revelation of beauty and fun in Tahoe for leading him to this paradise and for blessing him with a mentor/angel/friend in the form of a guy named Richie from Santa Cruz.

After Labor Day weekend, they said goodbye to all their college friends as they went back to school. Billy felt a pang of jealousy for having never experienced college life himself, but he was satisfied with the life he was developing now. Richie made sure they established continuing contact with their favorite sorority girls by giving them their phone number and offering them a place to stay for the Christmas holiday and any other three-day weekend they decided to come back to work. "This way, they think we're nice, but when they stay in our house, they will be partying with us and we'll have a great shot at hooking up again."

They spent most of that fall mountain biking as much as they could before the snow started to fly. It was a great time of year since they caught an "Indian Summer" where the warm weather lasted well into October. Since the tourists were gone, it felt like they had their Tahoe playground all to themselves. For the first time since San Diego, Billy was starting to feel like he had a home.

November rolled around and winter became imminent. Billy woke one morning to Richie poking him in the forehead with one finger.

"Hey dude, get up and get your first look at Winter Wonderland. It snowed a foot and a half late last night."

Billy felt a twinge of a hangover from his video poker/drinking session at the UCL after work the previous night. He didn't want to get out of bed. "Can it wait? I don't feel well."

Richie laughed again; that special laugh he used only on Billy. "I suppose it could wait, but remember what I told you about your gambling time cutting into the wonders that we can experience in our lives. You'll see something like this eventually but the first blanket of snow of the year is always the best. Now get up and check it out, revel in the glory for a moment or two, then you can go back to bed and feel miserable while I clear the driveway and then go cross-country skiing on the beach."

Billy walked down the stairs to the living room and saw that Richie had pulled the front window shades up high. Everything was bright white outside. From the pine trees that just yesterday were dark green to the ground as far as

Billy could see to the unplowed road in front of the house; it was all covered in a solid blanket of snow. The landscape looked like something out of a movie, or on a postcard, both surreal and majestic at the same time. Billy stood there at the window, staring out in awe.

Richie chucked him on the shoulder. "Just another wonder to convince you that there's no better place in the world to call home, eh bro? Do you still want to go back to bed?"

Billy submitted to Richie's excitement. "I guess not. Today is probably a good day to learn how to cross-country ski."

That day Billy learned how to use the snow blower to clear the driveway, then how to cruise around the snow-covered beach on a thin pair of skis that did nothing but slide sideways and make him fall. It was one of the best days of his life. Little did he know it would be followed by a night of great magnitude.

•••

It was twilight when Billy and Richie finished their cross-country ski trip up and down Nevada beach. Billy had a hard time initially with the thin fiberglass skis attached to his not-so-sturdy touring boots and spent most of the afternoon on his ass. Richie gave him patient instruction though, and by the end of the day he could go a hundred yards without going down. The sunset had been one for the ages, the sky ablaze in shades of orange, pink, purple that all faded to red. Billy was ready to get some food into his rumbling stomach and maybe go out and do some gambling and partying.

"Hey Richie, let's go eat at Latin Soul downstairs there at The Lakeside Inn, make a few sports bets, and maybe play some video poker afterwards."

Richie fixed Billy with an intense stare. "Not tonight brother. We're not going to eat until later. I'm going to introduce you to something that's going to change your life."

After a trip to the supermarket where Richie bought a spread of food that would put any wine-tasting event to shame, they went home and began to set up a feast. Billy was starving and wanted to dig in immediately, but Richie held him off. "You need to fast a little longer. No beer, no wine, no food until we get going. Stick with water for now. Go take a shower and get yourself into your most comfortable house clothes. We're staying in for the night."

Billy was beyond curious at this point. He had never seen Richie act so strange. "What's going on bro? Are there some girls coming over? Are we going to watch a killer movie? Are you cooking a gourmet meal for us? Come on man, tell me what's going on."

Richie just gave him a mischievous smile and said matter-of-factly "You'll find out soon."

When Billy came downstairs from his shower, the living room and kitchen were transformed into something that looked like the beginnings of a séance. There were burning candles everywhere, as well as a few strategically placed sticks of incense. All the electric lights and appliances were turned off. The feast was laid out on the coffee table. There was a cornucopia of deli foods, the kind that went with the four bottles of wine that were open and breathing. There were big bars of different kinds of chocolate, open and waiting to be devoured. A huge bowl of freshly cut fruit made Billy's stomach roar. He walked into the kitchen where Richie was doing something with the blender by candle light. "Hey bro, awesome spread. Are you surprising me with a couple of those Brazilian hotties to go with this meal?"

"Not tonight my friend." Richie's face looked eerie, shadowed in the light of the candle. He held up a rolled Ziploc baggie and let it slowly unroll. Billy couldn't tell what was inside.

Richie continued in a most serious tone. "Tonight, I'm going to introduce you to psilocybin. I'll be guiding you through your first mushroom trip."

Billy immediately didn't like Richie's idea. His fear of The Dark Thoughts made him even more apprehensive. They had been silent in his head ever since he came to Tahoe. He didn't know what combination of things had given him that solidity in keeping them shushed for over five months now, but he surely didn't want to do anything to disrupt it. "I don't think I can do that, Richie. I appreciate all the effort you've gone through to set up this feast and all, but I'm going to have to respectfully decline your offer. I'll eat the food though and watch you turn into a blubbering idiot."

Richie laughed heartily. He was laughing AT Billy. "Are you going to sit there and be exactly like all of those conservative bastards who have taught you everything you think you know in the past five years? Those people have completely bought in to the government's mantra that psychoactive drugs turn people into morons who can't exist cohesively in society. Granted, they are right in the sense that if not used properly, psycho actives can lead a person down a path in their mind that they can't return from, but they don't understand that when used with respect and an open mind, the trip will not only increase your understanding of life, but also your ability to see life situations clearly for what they truly are and to respond in a mindful manner. Doors of perception will open within your mind and your mindfulness will show you how to create a positive influence in the world. We're going to approach this mental expansion the same way the shamans did back in the tribal days. I will guide you through most of your trip, while you will be compelled to help me out during difficult periods of mine. We will both see and think things that are beyond our normal capacities of thought or vision. If we're lucky, each of us will bring back some important thought or conclusion from our trip. We aren't going to do what most idiots do and take some shrooms, go to the night club, and drink ourselves silly while everyone there laughs at us because we are obviously tripping. Nor will we go to Harry's, sit in front of a video poker machine, and watch the cards morph into flowers or legendary beasts. We'll stay here at home where we're safe and talk to each other, as we will be on the same wavelength, and we will not go out and interact with normal society until our trip is completely over. I have five CD's set on a random mix of music that will take you to faraway places within and outside of your mind. You will connect to this music now and this night for the rest of your life. I have a fractal graphics program running random shapes, patterns and colors on the computer that will engage you for quite a while if you let them. Don't worry Billy. Have I steered you wrong yet?"

That final question convinced Billy, because the answer was obvious. Richie had shown Billy how to live and how to live well, better than he could anywhere else and in any other capacity. At that moment, Billy knew that he trusted his roommate like a brother, and that he wouldn't say "no" to anything that Richie suggested. "All right Richie. It's against my better judgment, but if you're willing to guide me, I'll try it."

Richie's smile was wide and genuine. "I'm happy that you consciously choose to do this Billy. I would never force this on someone. If you don't go into a psychoactive experience with a positive mind set, it could become something terrible. It varies from trip to trip and could scar you for life; but if your attitude and mindset are positive, you'll come out of your trip fine and your life will be changed. I want to give you a gift my friend, one that I am a hundred percent sure will change your life."

"Okay, I'm in. What do we do?"

Richie began to drop caps and stems from the baggie into the blender. He examined a few and set them aside. "Those will be for another trip where we can't be that high." He then poured the rest of the bag into the blender and proceeded to add two cups of orange juice. Even stranger, he opened a bottle of 1000mg vitamin C and proceeded to drop about ten of them into the mix.

Over the roar of the blender, Richie explained what he was doing. "You can eat a few caps and stems and get a trip out of it, but it will take about forty-five minutes for the trip to start, and there's always the possibility that you will vomit the contents of your stomach, including the mushrooms, and the end of your trip will be nothing but you feeling sick and out of sorts. These things taste like shit because that's what they grow in. If you drink this orange juice smoothie, you won't taste them, you'll come on faster because the mushrooms are ground up, your peak will be longer due to the ten thousand milligrams of vitamin C I dropped in there, and your coming-down period will be longer and more pleasant. That's when we'll destroy this feast."

Billy stared at the whirring blender, apprehensive about stepping into the unknown. He prayed that the things he had done in Baghdad wouldn't rear their ugly heads while he was losing control of his faculties.

Richie handed him a tumbler glass full of frothing grey-orange liquid. "You're getting about a gram of mushrooms, which is strong for a first-timer, but you have me as a guide. I will not let you completely lose yourself. I'm taking about twice that amount. I know this concoction still smells bad, but just pinch your nose and put it down quick. You'll be able to keep it down just fine." He held up his glass to cheer. "Here's to the first day of the rest of your life, to your awakening."

Together, Richie and Billy slammed their orange juice, vitamin C, and psilocybin concoction. Then they stood there and stared at each other. After a moment of tension, Richie finally laughed and said "Let's turn on the music and sit down to wait for this thing to happen."

They sat and listened to an epic tune by Phillip Glass that Billy was sure had been the theme song for a civil war movie he had watched a few years ago. Richie kept his eyes closed and said nothing. The next song sounded like it was from a Hawaiian luau with the most beautiful female voices singing about riding on stars and staring at waves. Billy felt himself being transported by the music. He stared at the thin tendrils of smoke coming from the incense and swore that they moved sideways in synch with the luau song. The candle light was becoming blurry in the periphery of his vision.

Richie's voice pulled him back from wherever it was he was going. "Are you feeling it yet?"

"I think I am. I was just letting the music transport me somewhere tropical before I heard your voice."

"Good. You're feeling what I call "The Quickening". Like in the scene from the movie Highlander where Sean Connery assimilates the energy of the Highlander he has just killed, you are assimilating the energy of the psilocybin in the mushrooms. They are coming on for you. Embrace that quickening and don't be afraid of what you see or feel. Embrace it with all your curiosity. If you need to speak with me, by all means do, as I am supposed to be your guide, but if I tell you to lay off me for a moment, you must back off. We're coming into the most intense part of the trip, and it's best for you to experience it in your own mind. Also, stay indoors and don't go running off. That could be dangerous. You're perfectly safe in our cabin so just stay here."

Billy was already lost again in the music and the fractal graphics that were on the computer screen. It amazed him that one moment he was worrying about being hungry and now he was seeing everything around him in a whole new light while taking a voyage through his own mind aided by trippy music and two-dimensional graphics that became three-dimensional under the influence of these mushrooms. It was all quite difficult for Billy to assimilate, as everything he saw or heard was not what he expected it to be. His vision was more acute, but the images came to life and moved or danced to the background music that was also transporting Billy to another place, another culture, and another time.

When he got to the point where his fear of never being able to turn back was too much, Billy called out Richie's name. For a moment, there was no response and Billy began to think that he was going to end up mentally damaged just like they told him in his psychoactive drug lecture. Then Richie's voice came to him; a life preserver tossed from nowhere in the middle of a raging sea.

"You okay man? Hey Billy, what are you seeing right now?"

That simple question brought Billy back to reality enough to answer. "I'm in a place where the incense smoke dances for me like a woman would, but I can't seem to get anything else out of it. It just dances for me. The music has me somewhere in a deep forest, surrounded by indigenous peoples. They are telling me to leave, as I have brought great death to their people."

Richie's tone became more concerned at this point. "Hey bro, you aren't in a jungle and there are no people. You're right here in our home on Needle Peak Drive in South Lake Tahoe and you're with your roommate. There's no reason to be scared." Richie reached out and grabbed Billy's hand. "We're okay bro."

Billy was still somewhere else, except this time it wasn't the jungle with some indigenous people. He was suddenly in a small desert suburb of Baghdad. He was walking out of a villa where he had just shot and killed all the male members of the household. The only thing he knew about them was that their family name was Sadiq. It meant friend. Children and women were wailing from inside at the aftermath of Billy's lust for killing. The Dark Thoughts were once again reveling in the back of his mind.

"You were meant to kill Billy .... every moment of your life. You think you may have locked us in the farthest recesses of your mind, but we will always be there, and at some point, your control over the barriers will weaken. Then you will realize your true potential."

Richie was tripping hard at this point, but he knew that he had to snap out of it and help his roommate through whatever demons were attacking him during his own trip. Billy was on the floor in the fetal position and, mumbling something about killing innocents. Richie needed to pull him out of that funk immediately. As he reached down to turn Billy's face toward his, Billy's right hand shot out and took a firm grip on his throat. It felt like Billy could tear his larynx out with one twist. He could barely breathe. "Hey Billy! It's me, Richie. Your roommate. You're safe here. Whatever you're seeing isn't reality. You're in our cabin and you're safe. Don't forget that. Whatever you're seeing that's causing you this grief will go away if you just come back. Leave that place." He was choking from Billy's death grip on his larynx. Suddenly, the grip was released, and Billy lay there on the floor crying.

"I didn't mean to kill those guys in the villa. The Dark Thoughts told me to. There were four of them, probably brothers or cousins. They were playing a game of cards. They didn't look like insurgents, but The Dark Thoughts told me to kill them anyway. When one of them reached down, I thought he was going for a gun, so I shot them all. It turns out the guy was reaching for a bag of chips; but The Dark Thoughts told me to shoot them all so I shot them all." Billy was wracked with sobs.

Richie wondered if he was finally experiencing his first bad trip. He had heard others talk about "That one bad trip" but always figured his positive outlook on life would protect him from it, but here he was listening to a friend confessing to the taking of four men's lives. He knew Billy Stone had been a soldier. He figured he had even killed some men, but what he was hearing right now sounded like a serious psychological problem. He thought about his promise to Billy before the trip started. "I will guide you through this." It was time to keep that promise.

"Billy! Snap out of this funk. You are not in Baghdad anymore. You are no longer a Marine. You live here in paradise, Lake Tahoe, and I am your friend and roommate. I don't care about how many people you killed serving our country. The most important thing is that you served our country. We're like brothers man! I don't care about your past. It's probably nowhere near as sordid as mine. We have a great life here, and I'll never judge you for the things you did before I knew you. Now just exorcise those demons from your head and we'll start in on this feast."

By now Billy had his head in Richie's lap and was sobbing like a child. Richie held him until the sobbing stopped, then slapped him on the forehead. "Come on! Get that shit out of your head and let's proceed to the best part of the mushroom trip: the post-peak feast!"

In his mind, Billy spoke clearly to The Dark Thoughts. "You've tried to escape, but you weren't strong enough. I will keep you imprisoned for the rest of my waking days, and I will live a normal life." He looked up at his best friend, mentor, and roommate and said "Yes, let's eat .... and turn up that music some more. I want to enjoy this trip.

•••

Billy snapped out of his memories of a better time; a time gone by. He was alone now with only The Dark Thoughts and his evolution to keep him company. He had some research to do. Luckily for him, Richie had left all his belongings during his abrupt departure, including his computer. Billy sat down with a chilled bottle of Jagermeister and a shot glass, turned on the computer, got on the Internet, and began doing research on drugs that incapacitated humans and others that killed. He was going to need to call Elmer tomorrow to see about some acquisitions.

Billy woke up the next day around noon face down on the keyboard. The bottle of Jaeger was empty and the computer still showed the web page of the last site he had visited before he passed out. It was a Home Box Office site that was opened to the summary of the most highly viewed documentary the cable channel had ever aired: Confessions of a Mafia Hit Man.

The Iceman was the Mafia's most renowned killer. He had taken out over two hundred targets using numerous methods to kill. The particular portion of the story that Billy had passed out on spoke about The Iceman's use of cyanide as a killing agent. Billy had written the word down last on a list that he had been making. As he looked at the ten or more items he had on the list, he wondered if Elmer would be both willing and able to come up with the things he needed. His head was pounding and his mouth tasted like a cat had crapped in it.

It was cold outside, but the storm had let up some time in the wee hours of the morning and the sun was out. Billy shoveled two feet of snow off the deck while his coffee was brewing. Two feet on his deck meant three to four feet in the upper elevations, especially in the trees on Powder Bowl run. He was sure that no one would find Big Purple Tex until his friends finally reported him missing and requested a search party. Once the deck was clear, he sat out in the cold and sunshine with his coffee and called Elmer's number in South San Francisco.

Elmer was still his jovial self when he answered. "Bruddah Billy! How you be old friend? I haven't heard from you in over a year; ever since you moved that girl in with you. You married yet?"

Billy was saddened by Elmer's mention of Mimi. "No bro. That's over with. She left me about four months ago for some rich guy."

"Her loss bro. Good thing you live in a place full of young and exotic women. You gotta get back on the bike when you fall off, my friend."

Billy always loved Elmer's infectiously positive attitude. "We'll see my friend. This one threw me for a loop. Anyway, sorry to call you on a Sunday to talk about business, but I was wondering if you could get a few things for me."

Elmer laughed heartily. "You gonna go out and start partying again like you used to with that roommate of yours. What was his name...the guy who liked the mushrooms...Ricky or something like that?"

Billy was further saddened by Elmer's mention of Richie. "He's not around anymore either bro. Richie turned out to be a liar and a thief. He skipped town right before Mimi moved in with me. But yeah, I need some of those party favors and a few other things too." He began to read his shopping list of illegal and illicit substances to Elmer. When he finished, there was silence on the other end.

"You still there Elmer?"

"Ya brah. It doesn't sound like you want to have a party with some of this stuff. You're not planning to do something stupid, are you? You been talking to those voices in your head again?"

"No bro. I'm cool. I do want to do some partying, and the rest is for experimentation and self-protection from bears and such. Those voices have been shut down for years by the way. So, what do you think?"

"I can have everything on your list by tomorrow except for the cyanide. That one will take a few days. You got the cash to cover all this? It's going to be expensive."

"Yeah bro. I got that part covered. I'm off this Wednesday and Thursday. How about if I come down to see you Wednesday night?"

"You got it my friend. We'll have a little party and I'll have my wife cook up some of that Lumpia you like so much. Bring me a couple pounds of that Alpen Sierra mountain roasted coffee like you always do too."

"You got it. Jamaican Blue Mountain, right? I'll see you in a few days. Peace."

Billy was grateful to have a friend that could get him anything he wanted or needed from the black market. He was also thankful that Elmer didn't ask too many questions beyond his concern for his friend's well-being. Things were now being set into motion. Billy Stone would be ready for the next bane to society he was sure to encounter. The greater part of being a killer was preparation and knowledge. The rest was luck and nerve. Now that he had the largest chunk down, he prayed that the luck and the nerve would show up when he needed them.

CHAPTER 4

MR. VEGAS

It was the Thursday before Christmas. The week from Christmas Eve to New Year's Day was particularly tough on casino workers. The days were long, the days off were few and far between, and the crowd grew larger by the day, becoming more nasty and out of control as it culminated on New Year's Eve. Billy was never bothered by the heavy work detail during the holidays. It helped him forget the fact that even if he were free to do as he pleased during the holiday, he had nowhere to go and no one to see. This season though, he was particularly energized because of his new evolution, and he looked forward to all the craziness. He had faith that The Dark Thoughts would guide him to a higher state of existence in and amongst the chaos.

Billy knew this would be the last day of calm before the storm. Craps 301 was hooked up with one of the blackjack games. After each break, Billy spent twenty minutes dealing blackjack, then went to the craps game for an hour. It was good that the stint on blackjack was only for one round because the game was monotonous. Today though, the snap game had been a pleasant surprise as four of the five spots were taken by a group of young girls from San Francisco. They were all attractive and flirtatious, particularly the one on first base, a beautiful Asian woman named Hope. Billy had pushed through the game three times already tonight, and each time his cards were cold. He was giving away a lot of money. After Billy's second round, the girls were cheering his name, calling him their "lucky charm", and giving him high-fives. They were getting loose and having a great time. Billy was enjoying himself; and Hope had started to pay special attention to him, reaching out and rubbing his arm each time he gave her a blackjack, and telling him that she loved him each time she won a double-down hand. Her friends had started making innuendos about Billy being Hope's "lucky dealer". He hadn't dated or even been with a woman since Mimi had left him, and he was starting to think that it might be time to start that mending process. The stage was already being set as he dealt Hope another blackjack right after he had told her to take a chance and double her bet. Her friends were screaming, yelling, and giving high-fives around the table. She had stepped into the pit to try to give Billy a hug. Of course, this brought the pit boss over immediately. Billy was relieved when he heard the voice behind him say, "Now miss, you're going to have to wait until Billy gets off work before you do that again". It was Randy, one of the more fun-loving pit bosses at Harry's. He loved to joke around with customers and dealers alike, and he wasn't a hard case like some others could be. Randy loved to take part in casino shenanigans.

Not only did Randy have a good wit, he also had a savvy eye. As he helped Hope from inside the pit and back to her seat, he grabbed her left hand, held it up in the air, looked at Billy and said, "So Billy, what are you going to tell the guy that bought this rock when he sees his girl giving you hugs in the middle of the pit?'

Billy was taken aback as he saw a nice-sized diamond on Hope's ring finger. With all the hooting, hollering, high-fiving, and flirting going on, he had forgotten the number one rule when it came to women on the game: Always check the ring finger. A ring on the ring finger backed him off. He didn't want to get tangled up with any married women at work. Billy was angry with himself for getting caught up in all the attention he was receiving from this girl. He was also bummed that he couldn't allow this fun to go any further. The girlfriends came to his rescue though, as they all broke into hysterical laughter.

They all put out their left hand, and Billy saw that each girl had the exact same ring on her ring finger. One of the girls stopped laughing long enough to say "None of us are married. These aren't even diamonds, just cubic zirconium. We wear these when we go to Tahoe or Vegas together to keep away the douche bags."

Randy was laughing hard at these crazy girls, and he just had to put in his two cents worth on the subject. "So I take it you girls don't like men."

This brought out another round of laughter from Hope and her girlfriends. The blonde on third base chimed in. "Oh, we like men all right; quality men like Billy here." Billy felt a glimmer of hope in more ways than one. Hope had removed her ring, put it on her right ring finger, and was touching his arm again. Randy was giving her the stern "no touching" look, but nothing else. Right at that moment, Billy's relief came to push him out and send him over to the craps game.

All four girls started whining as Billy pushed off the game. "No Billy, please don't go. You're our lucky charm. Hope is going to miss you terribly. We love you."

Billy spread his deck on the layout. "Don't worry girls, this is my good friend Pablo, and hopefully he'll take good care of all of you. I'll be back here in an hour or so. I'm sure you'll all be here. If you do leave, stop by that craps game over there and say goodbye to me." He didn't want to miss out on his shot at Hope. They all handed him a few five dollar chips as he left.

As Billy walked out of the pit, Randy was standing there at the podium with a devious grin on his face. "If you don't land that one brother, I'm going to think that girl Mimi stole not only your heart but your balls as well."

"Thanks for helping me out Randy. Do your best to keep them there until I get back."

The next hour on the craps game was long for Billy. He kept looking over at the blackjack game to make sure his girls were still there. He knew they were getting drunk to the point where at any moment one of them could go off and do something stupid. He hoped that didn't happen before he got back there. Every now and then he heard a group scream come from their table that told him they were still winning. He also got an update from each dealer that came over to the craps game after their twenty-minute stint.

When Pablo pushed him off the stick, he whispered in Billy's ear. "Those girls are talking their friend on first base into getting with you when you get off work. What time did you start tonight?"

"Five o' clock. Maybe I should sign the early out list. With a little luck, I could be out of here before midnight."

Pablo laughed. "You better do that bro. You might end up with two of them. Let me and Luis know if you need backup."

"You got it bro. Hopefully, forty more minutes."

When he went on break, he stopped by the pencil to sign the early out list. "Hey Christian, how's it look tonight?"

Christian had his face buried in the computer from where he orchestrated the dealers. "Well bud, it doesn't look good for ten o'clock because they want to open that last craps game, but there's a good-sized push coming in at midnight, so that should work. That is, unless they call you off the floor before that to drive the limo."

"Oh damn! I didn't think about that. You sure you can't just sneak me out at ten?"

"Sorry my friend. I have twelve bodies coming in, eight to get out, and I need four for that craps game. Plus, the other on-call driver from day shift is getting pushed out at ten to take some high-roller to the airport in Reno. It looks like midnight."

Billy was disappointed. "All right Christian, thanks for being straight with me." Those girls would all be wasted by midnight, or they would be at the club in the casino across the street from Harry's and Billy would have to go chasing after Hope. If he was called to drive the limousine for some drunken high roller it would all be ruined anyway.

The on-call limo driver position was a coveted job. The company used four dealers, two from day shift and two from swing shift. If a big player asked for a limo ride out of the blue, one these dealers was pulled from their game and sent to drive the high roller to wherever they needed to go. Most often it was for a ride to the Reno airport or to the cat houses east of Carson City. This was Harrys' way of being able to oblige an unexpected request without hiring extra people for the transportation staff. It was a great gig financially because the on-call drivers were paid fifty dollars an hour plus whatever tips they might receive. A trip to the Reno airport generally yielded between one hundred and two hundred dollars for Billy. This was another one of the perks that Richie had hooked Billy up with while they were roommates. Billy had been an on-call driver for the last eight years. It was a lucrative side job but it could be a huge liability, especially in situation like tonight. Billy prayed that he didn't get the call on this night. At least it wasn't snowing.

After his break, Billy returned to the blackjack game and was thankful to see that Hope and her girlfriends were still there. All four gave a big cheer when they saw him. He could tell that they were more wasted than they were last hour, but they weren't sloppy yet. He wondered if they could make it to midnight. He tapped his buddy Luis on the shoulder to push him out and whispered in his ear. "What do you think man?"

Luis gave the girls a round of high-fives as they all gave him a round of fives, as in five dollar chips. "Thanks so much, ladies. Who loves you?'

They all fired back in unison. "You do Luis!"

Hope threw in her own addendum. "And we love Billy too!" They all responded affirmative.

Luis leaned close to Billy's ear as he pushed off the game and whispered. "I think Ling-Ling the Asian Goddess of Love wants to eat you like a pork chop dude. I'll take the blonde on third base if you need some backup."

Billy chuckled. "Get on the E.O. list bro. Christian said he could get us out at midnight".

Luis slapped Billy on the butt as he walked away. "I'm right behind you bro."

Hope was much more open and flirtatious than she had been an hour and twenty minutes ago. She stared deeply into Billy's eyes as he dealt the cards. It was a comfortable distraction. Her girlfriends were also working for her. They were dead set on getting her and Billy hooked up tonight. The risqué questions came from all sides.

"So Billy, do you like Asian girls?"

"Are you allowed to fraternize with customers when you're off work?"

"What time do you get off?"

"Are your friends Pablo and Luis single?"

"Do you like dancing? We're going to the club across the street soon."

Billy knew it was set now. All he had to do is plan something with these ladies and get that early out. "So, you girls are going to the club? It's almost ten-thirty, so it should be firing up over there in about an hour."

Hope gazed into his eyes with that dreamy look as he flicked the cards out. "Do you think you'll be able to meet us there Billy? How late do you have to work?"

The blonde friend on third base cut in. "Yeah Billy, hook up with us when you get off, and tell your friends Pablo and Luis to come too. I just love dark-skinned men." The girls all giggled like they were still in high school.

Billy grinned confidently. "I'm working on getting off around midnight, so if you girls promise you'll be there and not be hanging out with any of those "douche bags" that those rings protect you from, I'll come over. I'll even talk Luis and Pablo into coming with me just for you, dear." He looked straight at the blond on third base when he said this, eliciting giddy laughter from all of them.

Hope looked hopeful. "So, it's a date?"

Billy reached out and touched the back of her left hand. "Barring the most unforeseen circumstances, I'll be there by half past midnight looking for you, Miss Hope." This elicited a round of cat calls from Hope's girlfriends that caused her to blush.

At that moment, a large wad of cash came flying in from behind the two girls who were sitting in the middle of the game. It landed on the layout on top of Billy's cards. Billy looked up, irritated. A pear-shaped man in a sweat suit with stripes running down the sleeves and pant legs stood there staring at him. He had deep pock marks in his puffed face; a sure sign of a cocaine user. A player's card hung around his neck by a bungee cord; a sure sign of a regular gambler.

"No one's playing this spot are they? Gimme quarters and hundreds!" His voice dripped with a Jersey accent and attitude.

All night long the middle spot had remained unmolested. The girls were spread out well enough with their cocktails and their stacks of chips that most people walking by wouldn't even bother trying to worm their way into that last open spot, especially since it was obvious that they were all together and enjoying themselves as well. It had also helped that there were only four chairs at the table.

"...and get me another fuckin' chair. Don't they always have five chairs at every blackjack game? Down in Vegas all the casinos have at least five chairs on all of their games." He squinted at Billy's nametag. "What's wrong with your game, uhh Billy?" He looked around the table at the four girlfriends. "You beauties don't mind shiftin' around a bit, do youse? I'll make it worth your while. We'll have fun together and we'll take this guy for everything he's got in his tray."

Hope and her girlfriends all looked at each other and rolled their eyes. Then they looked at Billy as if he could somehow save them. As much as he wanted to, Billy couldn't deny an open spot to a player, much less one with a wad of cash that looked to be all hundred dollar bills. He gave the girls an apologetic look and ever so slightly shrugged his shoulders. As the two girls in the middle moved their chairs closer to the edges, Billy picked up the cash and began to count it, laying each bill down on the layout and turning it over so that the people manning the observation cameras could see both sides. The wad felt to be about five thousand dollars thick in his hand. This was going to take a minute. He breathed slowly while counting the money, trying to maintain composure. He didn't want to do anything to create a scene that would run off Hope and her girlfriends.

As he rolled the bills over one after another, Billy remembered his protocol and looked up at the man he had now nicknamed in his mind "Mr. Vegas". "How are you doing tonight, sir?"

He got the standard jack ass response. "Terrible. I've lost almost thirty grand in this shit hole since I got here yesterday and my girlfriend's down in Vegas cheating on me as we speak."

Billy continued counting the hundreds and fixed Mr. Vegas with a genuinely concerned look. "I'm sorry I asked." He then flashed a quick glance at Hope and winked at her. She smirked and almost choked on her drink in mid-sip.

Mr. Vegas went on with his obnoxious rant. "Have you forgotten that I still need a chair? And how long has it been since the waitress has been around? I need some scotch and a cigar." He looked over at the no smoking sign on the table. "While you're at it, tell your boss to make this a smoking game. I've got my Gold card here. I'll be a Platinum player soon. I'm surprised I haven't gotten there already but your pit bosses are terrible at tracking my action." He tossed his card in, messing up a few of the neat stacks of hundreds Billy had just laid out on the table.

Billy put the card off to the side, slowly straightened out the stacks of bills, and called out to Randy. "Changing five thousand cash, Five-Star player!" He whispered in Randy's ear when he came over to witness the transaction. "We've got a real stinker here, and he wants a chair and cocktail waitress yesterday."

Randy looked at Mr. Vegas' card and greeted him by his real name. "How are you tonight, Mr. Kurchstein?"

Mr. Vegas hit Randy with the same bad attitude he had given to Billy moments ago. "I'm terrible. Your casino sucks, I've already lost over forty thousand bucks, I don't have a cocktail, and I don't have a chair. What's wrong with this place? I should have stayed in Vegas. They take care of me there."

Now it was Randy's turn to bite his tongue and maintain his professionalism. "Don't you worry sir; I'll get you a chair right away and I'll call the waitress station. What are you drinking?"

No response came from Mr. Vegas as he was searching through the pockets of his sweat suit. He pulled out a handful of cigars.

Billy whispered in Randy's ear again. "He said something about scotch, and he wants this to be a smoking game, as you can see." He stared in disgust at the three huge cigars that Mr. Vegas had put on the table.

Randy whispered back into Billy's left ear. "Sorry bro, I'm going to have to do it."

He then turned his attention to Mr. Vegas. "Sir, what kind of scotch are you drinking? I'll call the waitress station for you."

Mr. Vegas was oblivious to anything that Randy was saying, caught up in his own bitterness. "Hey pit boss, where's my damn chair? ....and where's my damn scotch? I want this game to be a smoking game as well and change the limit to a hundred-dollar minimum but grandfather these pretty girls in at whatever they're betting now. We're going to have a good time if you guys don't fuck it up. So far you're not doing very well. Come on!" He started snapping his fingers in the air.

As Billy continued counting the wad of hundreds and the girls sat there looking disgusted, The Dark Thoughts suddenly came to life again in Billy's head. *"You've already fucked it up with your jackass attitude, Mr. Vegas. There are some people who are a bane to society by their mere existence."*

This time Billy didn't try to quiet The Dark Thoughts like he always had before. Instead, he embraced their presence in the back of his mind.

Randy was getting irritated with Mr. Vegas and his attitude as well. "Sir, if you want a game with a hundred-dollar minimum, you should try our high limit blackjack room just over there next to the high limit slots. There are also some fifty dollar games on the front line over there by the Sagebrush Steakhouse."

This didn't sit well with Mr. Vegas. "You listen here...." He squinted at Randy's nametag. "...Randy. I'm buying in for five thousand cash and I've already lost almost fifty thousand in this shithole you guys call a casino. If I were in Vegas right now, they'd have the limit sign and the damn smoking sign changed, I'd have a chair to sit in, there would be a waitress standing right here, and you'd be kissing my ass. You guys are all a bunch of Hillbillies up here. I want to talk to your shift manager, now!"

Billy noted that the amount Mr. Vegas said he lost went upward with every outburst. He may not have lost anything yet.

Now it was Randy's turn to maintain some professionalism. "Sir, I'm going to get you a chair right now. If you'll tell me what kind of scotch you like, I'll call the waitress station and have one of the girls bring you some. I'll take away the no smoking sign and get you an ashtray as well. Then I'll call my shift manager and see if I can give you your hundred-dollar game. Now what do you want to drink?"

Mr. Vegas calmed down a little, but Billy could tell he was still irritated. "I only drink the best scotch. You guys probably don't have Macallan like they do in Vegas, so gimme Johnny Walker Blue."

Billy hated it when players compared Tahoe to Vegas. Half the time what they said was made up bullshit anyway, but it was every player's Swan Song when they weren't happy about their gaming experience in Tahoe. Everything was better in Vegas. Billy was sure that when they were in Vegas, these same players complained that everything was better in Tahoe. He kept counting the hundred dollar bills.

Randy brought Mr. Vegas a chair and tried to placate him a bit. "Here's your chair sir, and I'll have the waitress bring you a cutter for your cigars along with some Johnny Walker Blue. Good luck to you."

Billy finished counting the money and looked up at Mr. Vegas' pock-marked face. "You have forty-seven hundred here sir."

Mr. Vegas' face turned a deeper shade of red within seconds. "I gave you five thousand! Where's the other three hundred dollars?"

Billy stared so hard into Mr. Vegas' eyes, hard enough to make him flinch. "This is what you gave me sir, and you watched me count it out five bills at a time. Forty-seven hundred is all that's there." All four girls nodded in agreement.

Mr. Vegas wouldn't back down. "Count it again. Maybe some of the bills stuck together." Hope and her friends rolled their eyes again.

Now Billy was embarrassed. He was starting to get angry too. The Dark Thoughts mused in the back of his mind. *"A coke snorting gambler from Las Vegas, dressed like a pimp, lying about how much money he's lost and who knows what else? Rude, demanding, and sexist. A definite bane to society. Engage."*

This time though, Billy chose to ignore The Dark Thoughts. Hopefully, he had something better to do this evening with Hope and her friends. He stayed in good dealer mode, picked up the wad of hundreds, and proceeded to slowly count them over again, giving each one a slight twist to make sure none of them were stuck together.

While Billy was re-counting the money, Mr. Vegas turned his attention to Hope and her friends. "So, where are you beauties from?"

There was an awkward silence as none of the girls wanted to answer. Finally, Blondie spoke up from third base. “We’re all from the Bay Area.”

Mr. Vegas smirked. “You mean the Gay Area? I’ve heard about San Francisco. You girls don’t look like carpet munchers to me.” He laughed heartily at his own joke. The girls didn’t.

Instead, they all held out their left hands in unison while Blondie stated very matter-of-factly; “We’re all married, and did you know that Las Vegas is rapidly approaching San Francisco and New York in the category of highest number of homosexuals per capita? The odds are already one in eight that you could be one of them.” This time the girls laughed while Billy stifled his own chuckle.

Mr. Vegas wasn’t the least bit fazed by Blondie’s insult. “Well, I assure you girls that I’m not one of them. I have a girlfriend who’s a stripper at one of the hottest clubs down there; although the little cunt is probably cheating on me in my own condo as we speak. I’m thinking of going home a day early just to catch her in the act so I can shoot her and her lesbian lover both in the head. Or, if I’m lucky, maybe they’ll invite me in for a threesome. Sometimes great things happen if you’ve got enough coke on you.”

Hope and her friends looked disgusted. Billy could tell they were getting close to leaving. He hoped that their plans for later in the evening wouldn’t be changing. He finished counting Mr. Vegas’ money for the second time and once again there was forty-seven hundred dollars. “All right, it’s still four thousand seven hundred dollars. Do you want some twenty-five dollar chips in that mix?”

"Hell no! Just give me hundreds. I still don't know what happened to that other three hundred. Are you sure you counted it right this time?"

"One hundred percent sir." He proceeded to cut out forty-seven black chips on the layout next to the pile of bills, then called out to Randy; "Change forty-seven hundred, black going out! There you go sir; four thousand seven hundred in hundred dollar chips."

As soon as the chips were in front of him, Mr. Vegas picked five of them off the top and tossed them back at Billy. "Now gimme five hundred bucks in quarters so I can share with my married girlfriends here." Billy had to bite the inside of his cheek again. The scar tissue was building up. As he pushed out twenty quarter chips to Mr. Vegas, The Dark Thoughts started in again. *"This guy is a scumbag drug dealer who corrupts people with cocaine. He doesn't give a shit about anything but his own desires. There are those in society who need to be removed. Engage."*

Just then, Pablo showed up from his break to send Billy over to the craps game. The girls looked forlorn when Billy pushed off the game, their previous energy deflated by the scene that had just gone down. He tried to give them a cheery smile. "Good luck girls. If I don't see you here when I come back, we'll proceed with our previous plan okay?" He then leaned into Pablo's ear and gave him the run down on Mr. Vegas. "This dude in the middle just bought in for forty-seven hundred bucks. He's a Gold player but thinks he's a Platinum; arrogant and demanding. He's waiting for Randy to change the limit to a hundred-dollar minimum. If he runs the girls off, which I'm sure will happen, send them by the craps game. Good luck with this one bro. Be patient." He weakly waved his hand in Mr. Vegas' direction and said "Good luck."

Mr. Vegas didn't even acknowledge Billy as he left. He was busy slipping a twenty-five-dollar chip under each girl's bet. "Come on girls; let's take this guy Pablo for all he's got! Stick around and party with me and I'll make your night very profitable."

Billy looked over his shoulder at Hope as he walked away. "Don't leave without stopping by the craps game to let me know what you're doing." She smiled at him and put her thumb up, but she looked nauseated nonetheless.

While pushing into the stickman's position on the craps game, Billy whispered in Luis' ear. "Be careful when you get over to that blackjack game. We just had a real piece of work land in the middle seat; thinks he's some big hotshot from Vegas."

Luis joked back. "Piece of what? I'll push in there and destroy his ass. Piece of shit." Billy couldn't help but laugh. He glanced at his watch. It was twenty 'til eleven. Hopefully only an hour and twenty minutes to go, and only one more round with Mr. Vegas, unless Luis ran him off before that.

When Billy's twenty minutes on the stick were up, Pablo came over to push him out and gave him the bad news. "That jackass from Vegas ran the girls off about ten minutes ago. Did they come by the game?"

"No, what the hell happened?"

"Sorry I couldn't keep them there bro, but that idiot started talking dirty to them and was basically propositioning all of them to come up to his hotel room and do a bunch of coke or something, and then of course some other things too. He's a total shit-pig. The blonde chick on third base told him to go do a big fat line and fuck himself. He didn't take that very well and started talking some shit about his stripper girlfriend in Vegas and how he thought she was cheating on him with another woman. Then he started talking about going back home early to try to catch her cheating and all this other shit about wanting to shoot her. The guy is fucking nuts."

Billy pushed around to the inside base of the craps game and continued the conversation with Pablo, all the while efficiently booking and setting up bets for the eight people on his side of the game. "Yeah, he was talking all that whacko shit while I was over there too. So how did he finally run them off?"

Pablo looked apologetic when he answered. "I sent them myself. But I did tell them to stop by this game and talk to you. I basically told your friend Hope that I was going to destroy the game and that they shouldn't be there to lose back all the money they had won. Once they left, it was just me and him, so I shuffled up the cards, threw in a few extra shuffles, and luckily changed the cards to my favor. I took that jackass for his whole forty-seven hundred plus five thousand more in ten minutes."

Billy smiled at that. "Well, good job on that part. Hopefully Luis will go in there and drive the dagger in. Now we have to figure out what happened to the girls." He thought silently to himself, "Score another one for the dealers."

The next twenty minutes went excruciatingly slow for Billy. He looked all over the casino floor as far he could see from where he was standing in search of some sign of Hope. He was beginning to think he had lost her when he moved over to the second base spot to push Luis out for his break. Before leaving, he leaned in close and said "There's your little Ling Ling."

Billy felt a flash of hope as he pushed in and sure enough, there she was standing just outside of the game, peering between two old guys who were wearing World War Two Veteran hats. She waved at him.

"Hey you! We're downstairs in the Mexican restaurant getting some food and having margaritas but we'll be in the club by midnight. See you there?"

Relief washed over Billy like a cool breeze. "Hey you back! I should be off around midnight unless something goes very wrong, so I'll just change quickly and meet you girls over there. Tell your friends that Pablo and Luis are coming as well."

Hope flashed him a brilliant smile. "Very cool. We'll see you in about an hour."

The two old Veterans were chuckling at Billy and one of them quipped, "You make us feel young again son. Good luck." Billy just smiled. Forty minutes until midnight.

•••

When the next push came around, a new dealer was pushing in on the stick on his game. It was a young Pilipino guy named Franklin. He gave Billy a bored look as he pushed in and said "Hey man, I think you're done."

Billy was pleasantly surprised. Not only was he getting his early out, but he was getting it twenty minutes earlier than expected. Maybe he would head straight down to the restaurant and see if the girls were still there and offer to pay for dinner. He wished everyone on the game good luck, cleared his hands, and headed straight over to Christian at the pencil. As he walked into the pit, he clapped Christian on the shoulder and said "Thanks my friend. You're aiding me in a date with four attractive young women."

Christian had a grim look on his face. Billy didn't like that look at all.

"Sorry bud, but some idiot asked for a limo. He wants to catch the 2 a.m. red-eye to Las Vegas. They've got the car running down in valet already with the guy waiting inside so you've got to haul ass, get your uniform changed, and get down there."

Billy was crushed. All his hard work, the excitement of attraction, the thrill of the chase, the plan coming together, the hope of beginning a relationship, or at the very least having a wild and promiscuous night, all lost because some fucking moron wanted to leave town at the last minute and head back to Vegas. The Dark Thoughts began to whisper in the back of his mind. *"Aren't you getting tired of having people mess up your life to satisfy their own selfish desires?"*

Billy pondered what The Dark Thoughts were hinting at as he went downstairs to his locker to get his black pea jacket and Greek fisherman's hat. It wasn't a specific costume, but it was what Billy had worn to drive the limo ever since he started the job. He thought it made him look like a driver. The pea-coat also had numerous large pockets inside and out. This made it convenient for him to carry certain things that he might need for the drive. Sometimes he brought a flask filled with Jagermeister, which he sipped at while driving. Other times he brought his pinch-hitter and smoked pot if the client was one of those that kept the interior window closed and didn't want to have anything to do with the driver. Tonight, he packed a small attaché that he had created with some of the things he had purchased from Elmer. It contained four small vials of GHB in varying doses, two medical syringes, a two-gram vial of cocaine, a one-gram vial of heroin, a small metal container that served as a cooking spoon, two ounces of liquid ether, five hits of acid, two hits of PCP, a lighter, and a two-ounce spray can of hydrogenated cyanide. He was ready for the next time the Dark Thoughts gave orders.

Billy checked with the valet captain Neil before heading over to the car. Neil was on the run as usual during the midnight rush and gave him the rundown quickly. "This one's a real asshole; been complaining from the moment he got down here. Gold player. Says he lost sixty grand here in the last two days. He wants to catch the 2 a.m. flight to Vegas so you need push it. He's got one bag that I already put in the trunk. He stiffed me by the way, and he's drunker than shit. Smells like the bottom of a scotch barrel. Name's Kurchstein if you care to try to talk to him."

"I'll be damned", Billy thought to himself. Mr. Vegas had succeeded in ruining his night after all.

The moment Billy sat in the driver's seat of the limo, he heard the angry voice with that irritating Jersey accent over the intercom. "It's about damn time you showed up! I need to catch the red-eye to Vegas and we only have an hour and a half so get your ass movin'!" The interior window rolled down and Billy stared through the rear-view mirror at the same pock-marked face he had stared down over an hour ago.

"And before we go, I want you to pour me a drink of something better than the craps you've got in the bar back here. I know you guys all keep a stash of the good stuff in the trunk for your "better" customers. Well lemme tell ya, I just lost seventy-five grand in two days in this shit hole they call Harry's Casino, so you better get out the good shit. I want scotch, and not this rotgut Glenleavitt that I'm staring at back here." He stuck a double rocks glass through the partition and barked. "Straight up, and to the top, and not a drop less of the best scotch you've got stashed back there. Pour me a drink now and let's get our asses on the road."

The Dark Thoughts appeared cheerily in Billy's mind. *"Why yes Billy. Why don't you pour that man a straight up double of the best stuff you've got? Make it a double-double."*

Billy stared hard at Mr. Vegas through the rear-view mirror; hard enough to make him look away. "Scotch huh? You're probably a Macallan man but since they don't serve it for free here, you probably drank Glenfiddich or Johnny Walker Blue."

Mr. Vegas still didn't recognize that Billy had been his dealer less than two hours ago. "Yeah, it was Johnny Blue. At least the waitress kept me going while I was playing. The dealers and the pit bosses are all rude and I'm sure they are all cheating. I swear one of them pocketed three hundred from me when I wasn't looking....and they're all shuffling up the cards the minute they start losing to someone. The average player doesn't stand a chance. That's why I don't tip any of them, because I know they're all out to get me."

Billy pulled his cap a little bit further over his eyes, turned around, took the glass from Mr. Vegas' sausage link fingers, and carried it around to the trunk of the limo. The air in the trunk had the stale odor of cigar and cigarette smoke. The man's suitcase smelled like a dirty ashtray. Billy sifted through a milk case full of premium blends of whiskey, scotch, cognac, vodka, and gin until he saw the familiar short but stout bottle with the Johnny Walker symbol in blue on the front. The Dark Thoughts warned him. "*You better use the double dose.*" He pulled out the attaché case, selected a GHB vial that contained two ounces of the date rape drug, and topped off the double Johnny Walker Blue.

GHB, or Gamma Hydroxy Butyrate, was essentially liquid Rohypnol, the date-rape drug. It served to multiply the intoxicating effects of alcohol. A shot of GHB taken alone caused the recipient to feel like they had just downed four or five shots of some distilled spirit, a whole bottle of wine, or a six-pack of beer. Any subsequent cocktails consumed along with the drug each served to intoxicate the drinker quite rapidly until they finally blacked out. The drug was colorless and odorless. It was also an amnesiac which made it a favorite amongst predators. A shot of GHB could be poured right into any drink and the process would begin immediately. The Dark Thoughts were whispering to Billy. "*Be a predator.*"

Billy came back around to the front of the limo and carefully opened the driver's side door. He was once again assaulted by Mr. Vegas' obnoxious voice.

"How fuckin' long does it take a person to pour one damn drink? Did you at least bring the bottle with you so you don't have to pull over when I need another one?"

Billy handed him the glass that was filled almost to the rim. "Be careful, sir. You don't want to spill any of the good stuff. I'll go back and get that bottle for you."

Mr. Vegas took the drink and downed a third of in one gulp. "I'll spill whatever the fuck I want to spill! Now hurry the hell up and let's get out of here. I don't want to miss my flight. I'm going to catch that cunt girlfriend of mine red-handed. She doesn't expect me back until Christmas day. Now haul ass!"

Billy remained smooth and professional. "Absolutely, sir. Right away." As he listened to Mr. Vegas complain loud and long about how much he hated Harry's casino and Tahoe in general, The Dark Thoughts spoke to him as well. *"You know we're not going to Reno. We must remove this bane."*

Mr. Vegas didn't make it much further past the Cave Rock tunnel on the east shore of the lake. His speech slurred more and more as he polished off the last of his special cocktail. Every few minutes the intercom would come on and he would accost Billy again about the time. "Speed it up, damn it! I gotta make that flight to Vegas! Can't you go any fucking faster?" As he got further into his drink, the ramblings became more and more incomprehensible. "Gotta catch that bitch .... stripper whore .... kill her and her dike girlfriend .... probably cheating on me in my own bed right now.... snortin' up all my goddamn coke .... cunt .... whore .... kill her too ...."

As they began the final ascent to Spooner Summit which would lead them out of the Tahoe basin, Billy heard nothing over the intercom but loud snoring. Mr. Vegas had passed out with his finger on the intercom button. Just to make sure his cargo was truly passed out, and to get the man's finger off the button, Billy hit the brakes hard. He heard a loud thump from the back of the limo as the intercom cut out. He waited for the intercom to come back on and to hear that obnoxious voice complaining about his driving. Nothing but silence for the few minutes it took to reach the summit. He continued over the hill on highway 50 and headed down toward Carson City, sure that Mr. Vegas would be out for at least twelve hours. He spoke out loud to no one in particular, or perhaps to The Dark Thoughts. "What now?" The cab of the limousine was silent, as was Billy's mind.

Highway 50 east from the top of Spooner Summit ended at highway 395 just south of Carson City. It would pick up again on the north side of downtown Carson at William street. From there it headed out east toward the whorehouses at Moundhouse, then Dayton, Lake Lahontan, Fallon, and Virginia City before continuing out into the barren Nevada desert and ultimately ending in Ocean City Maryland on the other side of the country. To get to Reno, Billy had to stay on highway 395 headed north through Carson City. The Dark Thoughts were right; Mr. Vegas needed to be eliminated. Billy was sure that he wouldn't be on the red-eye to Sin City that night. What he wasn't sure of though, was what would happen instead. As he drove slowly through downtown Carson City past the capital building, The Carson Station casino, The Carson Nugget, and Cactus Jack's, he waited expectantly for a sign or an idea.

Outside of the downtown area, Carson City was just a town of strip malls. Billy stared at the passing sandwich shops, furniture stores, motels, gas stations and pawn shops. He mused at how bleak existence would be if he lived here instead of Tahoe, merely thirty miles away. The Dark

Thoughts mused along with him. *"Nothing here but strip malls, abandoned silver mines, and whorehouses, all out in the middle of the desert."*

Just then, Billy looked up at the traffic lights and saw the highway junction sign for highway 50 east at William Street. That last statement by The Dark Thoughts echoed in his mind. "Abandoned silver mines and whorehouses..." Richie had taken him out into the desert somewhere around Moundhouse once to show him some of the old silver mines. There were hundreds of them out there; relics of a lost era. He remembered Richie's warning speech as they approached one of the mines. "Be careful bro. Most of these things are people proofed by the Nevada Bureau of Land Management. They remove the makeshift ladders that access the shafts and cover the holes with some sort of chain link fencing material. Kids still come out here all the time and vandalize some of their work. They remove the coverings and throw shit down the shafts just for fun. You could accidentally fall down one of these shafts and you wouldn't be able to get out unless someone had a long rope and a means of securing one end of it. If you were by yourself, there would be no way out. No one would be able to hear you cry for help out here either." He had taken Billy to one of the cat houses after the mine visit on the premise that you couldn't go east of Carson without visiting a house of ill repute.

The Dark Thoughts echoed in Billy's mind. *"Abandoned mines and whorehouses."*

The William street sign pulled hard at Billy's attention, compelling him. He put on the right turn signal and headed the limo east on highway 50. Billy wondered what he was doing. He was in a white stretch limo driving around the desert east of Carson City. There could be only one place that he would be going. He checked his watch. It was just past one a.m. Billy still wasn't sure what to do. The ideas weren't falling into his lap like they did with Big Purple Tex. He currently had an incapacitated customer passed out in the back of his limo and he had to figure out what to do with him and how to hide the body. He needed help.

The Dark Thoughts came to his rescue with a precise and truthful statement. *"All degenerate gamblers ultimately want to come to one of these places to see what their money can buy. They usually find out that it will cost them much more than they are willing to pay, but the lure of forbidden excitement is overwhelming, and they pay anyway. It makes you wonder. What is more powerful? The pussy, or the dollar? They dance and battle with each other every night out here under the endless desert sky, but who really wins?"*

Billy made a decision. It was time to execute. He would call back to dispatch to set up a viable story. He pulled out his cell phone and dialed the main operator at Harry's. "Hi, Jeannie, this is Billy Stone; can you please connect me to dispatch?" He knew the call would be recorded. The line came alive again. "This is Travens from dispatch. What you got bruddah Billy?"

Vince Travens was a home-grown product of the Hawaiian Islands. He appeared as white as they came, since his family was part of the indigenous Portuguese population on the island. He still had that sing-song Hawaiian accent. He was the perfect guy for Billy to tell his story to.

"Hey bruddah, I got this cargo that was dead set on making the 2 a.m. red-eye to Vegas from Reno, and the dude is pau in the head. I'm almost in Reno and now he wants me to take him to one of the hooker joints out there east of Carson. He just wants me to drop him off and says he'll get them to take him to the airport in the morning.

Vince acted like he had heard this before. "Yah brah. Just take him wherever he wants. Make sure he gets his suitcase when you drop him. That way we no longer have any responsibility for him or anything he does after you leave him."

Billy wove the lie a little bit tighter. "Okay brah. I'm almost in Reno right now, so it's going to take me about an hour to get there and maybe a little bit longer to get rid of him. I might not get back to South Shore until about four a.m."

Vince acted like it was no big deal. "I'll still be here, Haole. I'm working graveyard you know?"

Billy had a story in place now. He was getting close to Moundhouse, which meant he had about an hour and fifteen minutes to come up with a way to remove the bane to society he called Mr. Vegas before his story became questionable.

He saw the huge blinking neon right turn arrow appear over the horizon, directing all men to three establishments where they could spend their money, hard-earned or not, to satisfy their dirtiest needs. The Kit Kat Club, The Moonlight Bunny Ranch, and The Pink Flamingo were all down this road.

Billy drove slowly, wondering what to do next. If he was going to pull this off without getting caught, he needed to think like a killer, execute like a professional, and have nerves of steel. He didn't feel like he was doing any of those things. He needed help, and so far, The Dark Thoughts weren't coming through.

As he drove slowly past the first house of ill repute, The Kit Kat Club, he remembered that this was where Richie had taken him over six years ago. It was the last time that he had paid for sex, and Richie was the one who paid. Billy remembered being nervous for some unexplainable reason. While in the military, he had paid for sex everywhere he went. He never had the time or the means to establish a real relationship, so prostitutes were the only answer. It felt dirty to him once it wasn't necessary. Of course, he didn't tell Richie that; he just voiced some concern over seeing someone he might know or having the information leak out somehow that he had been there.

Richie had assured Billy with another one of his lectures. "Hey man, how do you think these places have thrived here for over a century? On confidentiality, that's how. Back in the day, everyone came here; the chief of police, the Mayor, the local doctor, legitimate business owners. The people that run these places know that they can't remember a single face. If they're ever questioned, they never recall details, or they give vague answers. Identities are safe in these places bro. Your credit card even gets charged to a legitimate business name. Don't worry about a thing." Convinced, Billy had done it, but he had felt unclean afterward and never returned. The idea of confidentiality had stuck in his mind.

While Billy pondered how strong that confidentiality truly was, The Dark Thoughts once again repeated the mantra of the evening. *"Abandoned mines and whorehouses."*

Billy started to see a plan. He pulled in to the gravel parking lot of the next place down the road and parked the limo as far away from the front doors as possible. The Moonlight Bunny Ranch was just a bunch of trailers lined up outside of one main building that looked more like a double wide. The whole property was surrounded by eight-foot tall cyclone fencing. He wasn't sure how busy these places got, but it looked to him like there were about ten cars in the parking lot...ten people that were questionable in their confidentiality.

He turned the lights off and cut the engine, then stepped out of the limo and came around to the passenger door that faced away from the establishment so that no one would stumble out and accidentally see what he was doing. Upon opening the door, he saw Mr. Vegas laying on the floor in the fetal position, snoring. Billy put on a pair of rubber gloves, which he now kept on his person all the time, reached down and pulled the body up to a seated position close to the door. The movement failed to waken him. He reeked like scotch and cigar smoke. Billy then removed Mr. Vegas' striped sweat suit top and put it on over his own t-shirt. He had left the pea coat in the front. He reached into Mr. Vegas' sweatpants pocket and found his wallet. It was stuffed with a bunch of credit card receipts for cash advances and about nine hundred cash. Curious, Billy looked though the receipts and concluded that Mr. Vegas had only taken close to twenty thousand in cash advances off the card in the last two days. There was no way he could have lost the seventy-five thousand dollars he claimed to have lost at Harry's. Billy thought about taking the cash, but he only needed the credit card. He wanted a paper trail in case the confidentiality broke down. Before closing the limo, he reached into the front seat and grabbed one of the smaller vials of GHB out of the attaché case and slipped it into his pants pocket. He walked across the parking lot wearing Mr. Vegas' smelly striped sweat suit top with the black taxi cab driver's hat pulled low over his brow, walked up to the front door of the double-wide, and rang the bell.

The small peep door opened enough to reveal a pair of dark brown female eyes. Her voice was muffled by the closed door. "You lookin' for some entertainment honey?"

Billy took a deep breath. *Nerves of steel.* "Yes ma'am, I sure am."

The peep door closed and the main door was opened by a large black woman in a purple Mumu who was probably the madam. She led him down a dimly lit hallway and called out ahead of her "Ladies, we have company."

The hallway opened into a decent sized but poorly lit lounge area that was furnished with old couches and love seats. There was a big screen television against one wall and the other side of the room had a bar that went across the whole back side of the trailer. There were a handful of men at the bar, each with a girl or two in lingerie sitting close, most likely trying to work up a deal. The bartender was one of the largest men Billy had ever seen. He had to be at least six and a half feet tall and looked like he wrestled bears for a living. He most likely served as the bouncer too. Billy was sure the guy had a few guns behind the bar and probably a few friends within calling distance if he ever actually needed backup. The available girls were lining up by the first couch as Billy entered. The madam whispered in his ear as they approached the girls. "You pick out one you like. You're welcome to take a few minutes and chat them up, but don't you dilly dally. Time is money here. Once you find one you like, strike a deal with her and come see me down there at the end of the bar so we can work out payment. Here's a menu of the standard stuff and what it costs. If you want stuff that's off the menu, the price goes up substantially. Now what shall I say your name is?"

Billy hesitated for an instant, taken aback by that request. He quickly recovered though. "You can call me Mr. Vegas."

The madam chuckled as if she had heard that name before. "Okay girls, say hi to "Mr. Vegas" here." She winked at Billy and said "Come see me when you get a deal set up. Remember, you have to pay first."

Billy walked down the line of hookers and each of the girls introduced themselves as he passed by. He knew they were all using fake names. A blonde girl called herself Misty. A Latina introduced herself as Louise. The Asian girl in the bunch actually called herself Ling-Ling. Billy wasn't looking for any special look or flavor. He peered into each woman's eyes and tried to determine which girl was the most wasted. He hit pay dirt with the last one. She introduced herself as Leilani and Billy could barely understand what she said, she was so out there on something. She was beautiful though, probably a mix of black and island parents. He stopped in front of her, put out his hand to shake hers, and said "Hi, I'm Mr. Vegas."

Leilani laughed drunkenly and quipped back at him. "Yeah, Mr. Vegas; and I'm Leilani from Maui." She laughed so hard that Billy thought he saw snot coming out of her nose. This was the one.

Billy opened the menu and asked “Are these prices negotiable?”

As the other girls started to disperse, two of them stopped by and warned Billy, “Hey Mr. Vegas, you’re taking a chance with that one. She’s been drinking and partying with four Mexican brothers for the last six hours. She might not make it for one more.”

“I’m willing if she is; as long as there’s a shower in the room”. The other girls walked away and gave Billy a look of disgust. He turned his attention once again to Leilani and the menu. “The price for this “Chocolate Highway Tour” seems a little steep. Could you throw in a “Deep Throat” for free?”

Not looking at Billy she mumbled something that sounded like “small print” and began laughing that wasted laugh again. Once she got a hold of herself, she chuckled at Billy and slurred “You’re new at this, aren’t you? Check the small print at the bottom where it says how much extra it costs you each time you get off. Is it still two hundred bucks each time? I’ll tell you what, young man, just because I like you, I’ll give you that whole package for the cost of the Chocolate Highway. You can bet your ass I’ll have to take a shower before that one, so go over there and talk to nurse Etta and her purple Mumu and let’s get going.

As Billy approached the desk at the far end of the bar where the Madam sat, he pulled out Mr. Vegas’ credit card and handed it to her. “One Chocolate Highway Tour please.”

Etta gave him a stern look. “That girl may not go the distance before she passes out....and there’s no refunds. I don’t want anyone doing anything creepy to my girls if they black out.”

She looked at the name on the credit card. "Kurchstein .... you've been around here before, haven't you?"

Billy threw in his best Jersey accent. "Yes I have, Miss Etta, and I was hopin' you'd fuhget about it each freakin' time."

"I always forget young man, but if I need to, I always remember."

Miss Etta's statement was a bit cryptic and it almost backed Billy off, but he had faith in the strength of the plan he was formulating. He needed to move quickly though. He still had to deal with the real Mr. Vegas. As he walked the length of the bar back to Leilani, he stopped and asked the bartender for a glass of water.

His voice was deep and gravelly. "If you're headin' back to a room, you can't have a glass, but I'll give you a bottled one. We don't want any of our girls getting cut, either by accident, or on purpose."

Billy grabbed Leilani by her upper left arm so she wouldn't fall over while she walked to the hallway where the trailers were all lined up. "Let's get you that shower now dear." The room they entered was taken up completely by a king-sized bed. Enough floor space was left for the entry door and the bathroom door to be opened. Leilani stumbled in, fell onto the bed, and removed her clothes. As she reached over to start on Billy, he stopped her and said "How about that shower? I'll wait out here."

She giggled and stumbled her way into the cramped bathroom. Before shutting the door, she slurred again "You get yourself ready too, Buster." She threw him a handful of condoms. "Put on that unlubricated one first for your Deep Throat. You'll use the extra lubricated one for your Chocolate

Highway. Use the third one to shove the other two used ones into because you'll have to take them out yourself. If they find the condoms full of come in here when we're done, they'll want to charge me for each one. Comprende?"

Billy knew it wouldn't ever come to that. He needed to get out of there soon. Time was starting to get tight. Leilani mumbled incoherent words to him while she showered. This gave Billy the opportunity to drink down over half of his bottled water and add an ounce from the GHB vial to it. As Leilani blabbed on about how many guys liked her chocolate highway, Billy stepped into the bathroom and dangled the bottled water over the shower door. "Hey, you want the rest of this?"

"Oh thanks, you're a sweetheart." She grabbed the bottle and downed what was left of it. "I drank almost a whole bottle of tequila earlier so I'm thirsty. I'm sure glad I can handle that shit." Billy wasn't sure she could.

The shower went on for another five minutes. As Billy sat on the edge of the king-size bed that reeked of cheap perfume and must have seen thousands of different men, he began to worry that the GHB had already taken Leilani down. He couldn't afford to have a dosed and drowned hooker to deal with. She finally stepped out of the bathroom and Billy could see that the drug had taken effect. Her eyes were blank but almost completely dilated and she could barely stand up. She pointed her finger at him, said "How come your clothes aren't off?" and passed out face first on the bed.

Billy stood up, put on the rubber gloves again, put the condoms in the pocket of Mr. Vegas' sweat suit jacket, reached in the shower to retrieve the empty water bottle, and wiped down the knobs on both the bathroom door and the entry door. He then moved Leilani's limp body around to a comfortable position on the bed, covered her up, and headed back to the main trailer. She wouldn't remember a thing when she woke up in the morning.

Miss Etta was waiting for Billy in the lounge and came right up to him when he walked in.

"What happened mister? Is she okay? I swear if you've done anything to her you won't make it out of the parking lot alive!"

Billy spoke to her as reassuringly as he could. "Now don't you worry yourself sick Miss Etta. She did pass out after showering. I laid her down on the bed and put a blanket over her. She probably won't get up until tomorrow morning. I should ask you for a refund, as we didn't complete the terms of our business, but instead, I'll just let you owe me one and come back some other time. All of this of course with your extreme confidentiality."

Miss Etta looked relieved that her girl was all right and that Billy wasn't screaming and yelling for another girl. "You come back any time you want, Mr. K.; I'll hook you up."

"That's Mr. Vegas to you Miss Etta." The paper trail was set. Now to dispose of the body.

Billy walked out of the double wide and wondered how strong the confidentiality of these places truly was. A quick glance at his watch told him that it was almost 2 a.m. He crunched slowly across the gravel parking lot, went around to the driver's side of the limo and slipped in the back door, laying low just in case the cat house had some high-tech outside observation. Then he slithered though the partition and sat in the driver's seat. There he removed Mr. Vegas' smelly sweat suit top and put on the pea-coat. He had told Vinny that he would be returning around 4 a.m. This gave him just over an hour to dispose of Mr. Vegas. The Dark Thoughts spoke assuredly in the back of his mind. *"Nothing but whorehouses and abandoned silver mines out here."*

Billy slowly cruised the Harry's limousine back out toward highway 50. Instead of turning left to head back to Carson, he turned right and headed east toward Dayton, toward a place he remembered visiting with Richie six years ago. He was looking for a sign on the corner of one of the side streets, a sign he remembered vividly because it had said "Tumbleweed Trailer Park" and had a picture of a tumbleweed bouncing over a trailer. Sure enough, he saw the sign on the left hand side of the highway about three miles up. It appeared much more worn since he had last seen it, but the picture was still there. He turned left.

As Billy drove past the lonely Tumbleweed Trailer Park, it was as if time had stood still and progress had been denied by the ever-present sagebrush. There on the left, across from the trailer park, was the old junkyard. After that, nothing. *"Nothing but abandoned silver mines out here in the high desert on the eastern slope of the Sierras."*

The pavement ended about three miles past the junkyard and became a dirt road. Billy was thankful that the heavy snows up in Tahoe hadn't had a lasting effect on the roads down here at 4500 feet. There was no visible snow, but the dirt road was wet and full of potholes. Billy would have to stop in Carson at the nearest self-serve car wash if he had the time. He remembered having driven with Richie to a clearing on the right where there was a loop of old mineshafts close together in one area. The terrain was flat, so the limo should be able to make it to the clearing. He just hoped that the cover on one of those old shafts had been taken apart by some bored teen-agers or maybe some drunken thrill seekers. If they were all untouched, he would have a problem, as the only tool he had that could possibly do some damage was the tire iron for the spare.

Luckily, Billy found the clearing about a half mile up the road. He pulled the limo up directly in front of the first mine shaft he saw, put it in park, and stepped out to look at it by the light of the limo's headlamps. The ten-foot square cover of cyclone fencing material looked like it was still intact. Closer inspection revealed that the piece was held down by five or six small boulders, as if some people had gone out there and torn it up, but wanted to save the access for a later date.

This could work. If those people returned, the stench of decay would keep them from going down that hole anyway. Either that or the rats would take care of business long before the humans returned. Billy began moving boulders.

The boulders were heavy enough for one person to make the work difficult. One wrong step, and he would be the one in the bottom of an abandoned mine shaft in the high desert east of Carson City. Once the chain link fencing was freed and pulled aside, Billy looked at his watch. It was 2:35. He should have been in his bed at home on Needle Peak drive with Hope having some good old fashioned fun. Instead, he was out here in the sagebrush with Mr. Vegas. This was where the man paid.

Billy had to move quickly so that he could stick with his four a.m. ETA at Harry's. He didn't want any suspicious minds seeing a timeline that didn't jibe with his story. He had ten minutes to get this done. He put the rubber gloves back on. In the back of the limo, he searched Mr. Vegas' pants pockets and found his cell phone, from which he removed the battery and replaced the useless phone back into the front pocket of the sweat suit. Then he dragged Mr. Vegas' limp body by one ankle out of the limo and over to the open hole, and unceremoniously dumped it down the mine shaft. Mr. Vegas hit the side of the shaft three or four times before one final THUNK! Then Billy sent the suitcase down, followed by the striped sweat suit top and the double rocks glass that once contained "The Good Stuff".

Billy stood at the edge of the shaft, bathed in the light of the limo's headlamps, staring down into the darkness where he knew Mr. Vegas' still living but battered body lay, and vented his frustration. "You ruined my night of hope, simply by your own lecherous, demanding existence. You accused me of stealing from you, and of cheating you. You belittled me, my co-workers, and the girls I was trying to pick up on. You lied and complained like it was your right, and you threatened to kill two women that I don't even know. Worst of all, you stiffed my valet captain when he loaded your bag into my limo. Seven, you're out." Billy spat down the hole then pulled the chain link fencing back over it and secured the boulders in place. He carefully backed the limo around and headed back down the muddy road toward highway 50. He looked at his watch. It was 3 a.m. He had just enough time to clean the sides and undercarriage of the limo at the self-serve car wash and then drive back to Stateline. If he pushed it, he might get there ten minutes early. All bases were covered.

"And that's the end of that." Billy wasn't sure if he had said it, or if The Dark Thoughts were sounding off. He was sure that at this point it didn't matter.

•••

Mr. Vegas woke to pain. He had no idea where he was. The pain in his right ankle was excruciating. He couldn't move his left shoulder as it was completely out of socket. He was bruised, cut, and bleeding, although he couldn't tell that because it was pitch black dark. The last thing he remembered was drinking scotch in the back of a Harry's limousine while heading to the Reno airport. Then he remembered the limo driver's face as he had handed him the double Johnny Walker Blue. It was the same guy: The dealer that had swiped three hundred bucks from him on the blackjack table.

"That mother fucker drugged me! I'll kill the son of a bitch!"

He tried to shift his body around in an attempt to stand up, but the pain in his leg and shoulder were unbearable. He had no idea where he was or what kind of hole he was in. He screamed out in agony. "Where the fuck am I? Someone help! Anyone, please, get me the fuck out of here!"

Silence.

Mr. Vegas thought his screams fell on deaf ears until he heard a light skittering sound that surrounded him; then a collective animal-like hiss.

Rats.

For the next few hours, Mr. Vegas' screams of agony did fall on deaf ears.

CHAPTER 5

MR. THIGHS-FOR-ARMS

New Year's Eve arrived on the winds of a heavy Sierra storm. Traffic was a mess all day on the 30th as skiers, partiers, and revelers crawled up the western Sierra slope from the San Francisco Bay area, Sacramento, and everywhere else in California they were trying to escape from. Customers were stressed, angry and complaining. Billy was hard pressed to be on his best behavior. The Dark Thoughts were hungry.

It had already been a long and difficult week. Billy had worked every day since the 23rd of December, and the last three had been ten hours or more. He knew that this night could very well be twelve hours. New Year's Eve at Stateline in South Lake Tahoe was one of the most popular events on the west coast. The casino corridor was closed to traffic, and the revelers poured out onto the highway at midnight to celebrate. It was in fact a contained free-for-all where women were fondled, beer was thrown, fights broke out, police were taunted, and ultimately some idiot every year took his clothes off and climbed up the traffic light pole at Stateline bare naked. Billy never understood why anyone would call any of it fun, but rain or shine, snow or bitter cold, the monster crowd religiously arrived to partake in the "fantastic" New Year's Eve celebration in South Lake Tahoe.

All things considered, Billy was in a good mood as he slowly cruised the Commander through the side streets that led to the Loop road, which went around the back side of all the casinos. He hadn't heard a word about Mr. Vegas in over a week, and he figured he wouldn't until the guy's coke-head lesbian girlfriend finally ran out of the evil white powder he had been supplying her with and decided to look for him. She might not even say a word to anyone and just move on to the next dealer. It was possible that she didn't even know he was in Tahoe eight days ago.

Billy was satisfied with the tactical and efficient way he had handled Mr. Vegas. Of course, The Dark Thoughts had done more than their share, but he was impressed by how they could work together to formulate a plan, reacting to the situation as it evolved and acting upon it in a precise manner without the use of a gun or a knife or anything that would scream of murder. Mr. Vegas was simply one of the many unsolved disappearances that occurred every year in Nevada. Billy reveled in the thought that he had removed another bane to society; The Dark Thoughts reveled in the kill.

Billy decided to call Hope on his way to work. She had left her phone number with Luis that night in the club after he apologized to her for Billy's absence. Maybe she was interested. Her enthusiasm upon answering told him yes. "Billy from Tahoe! I thought you weren't interested when you didn't show up at the club the other night."

"Quite the contrary, young lady. I actually was called to drive some drunken high roller to the Reno airport." He left out any mention of Mr. Vegas.

Hope was readily forgiving and even a bit flirtatious in her response. "You'll have to make it up to me sometime; just you and me."

Billy jumped at the opportunity. "How about Martin Luther King weekend? It'll be crazy in the casinos, and probably a madhouse on the slopes as well, but I'm sure we can figure something out."

She gave him the same flirtatious response she had been giving him on the blackjack table a week ago. "I won't be going to either of those places if I come up to visit you Billy."

"Then it's a date. If it doesn't bother you, you can stay at my place. I have a spare bedroom since the last two roommates I had disappeared on me."

Hope was refreshingly straight-forward with him. "If you play your cards right Billy, it won't matter if you have an extra room. I'll get there Friday afternoon so we can visit a little before you go to work."

It was nice to have hope for the future. Billy's spirits were enlightened on this dreadful day of work. Twelve hours to go .... eleven if he was lucky.

The snow had let up for a moment after Billy parked in the employee garage, so he walked outside and entered through the rear of the building. He walked through the bustle of dealers in the locker-laden hallway getting ready for their long evening. The girls were all putting on extra makeup and sprinkling glitter on their faces, necks, and cleavage. The air was thick with perfume and the hair was thick with hairspray.

Most of the guys didn't give a shit about how they looked but a handful, Billy being one of them, had to wear white ruffled tuxedo shirts with royal blue cumber buns and matching bow ties. They would be dealing to a special party of high rollers in the convention center on the second floor. A small European style casino was set up in the lounge outside of one of the convention rooms with two craps games, ten blackjack games, a Baccarat game, and two Poker Pai Gow games, all of which had a one-hundred-dollar minimum bet. Harry's only used their best dealers for this event, and Billy was lucky enough to have been on this list for the last five years. The 'upstairs party' usually dispersed around 2 a.m. and then those dealers who had been enjoying an easy night were sent down into the chaos of the main casino floor to do battle with the uncivilized masses to finish off their shift.

•••

The second floor was where Billy found himself nine hours into his shift, closing the last craps game and praying that by some miracle there would be a lull in the need for bodies downstairs and he might get lucky and be off with only nine hours on New Year's Eve. No such luck was to be had at this juncture in the evening. Brian Seran hung up the phone in the middle of their makeshift pit. "All right Billy, let's close this game up and head down to craps 301, our home away from home. There are still a few day shifters to get off."

Billy was bummed. "Day shifters? Damn Brian! I was hoping we would slip through the cracks, get off with nine hours and be up at the UCL sipping Jager shots within the half hour."

Brian chuckled. "That would be great my friend, but once again the scheduler dropped the ball and made them top-heavy on dayshift. I think they were basically scheduling with the expectation that everyone would work twelve hours today."

Billy laughed. "You know Brian, it's no different from any other year. If it wasn't against the law to work employees more than twelve hours without their consent, they would probably work us fourteen or sixteen hours. Instead, they just factor us in for the most they can before it starts costing them too much to hold us. It looks like I'll be here 'til five in the morning."

While going down the escalator from the convention center to the casino floor, Billy and Brian watched the chaos slowly unfold before them. The place was still wall to wall with people and everyone was wasted. There was trash everywhere on the floor. A bunch of underage kids were sitting on the floor against the wall at the bottom of the escalators, cheering on one of their friends who was vomiting over by the vending machine. Drunk people leaned on each other everywhere, blowing their plastic party horns and screaming at the top of their lungs. The aisle way between the California Bar and the craps pit was packed solid with people, seemingly impassable.

When they got to the bottom of the escalator, Billy turned to Brian and said "I'll lead, but stay close behind me and hang on to my shirt because I'm not stopping for anything." Brian nodded affirmative and grabbed a handful of Billy's shirt from behind.

Like all dealers, Billy was well versed in the art of slipping through a dense crowd. He knew that if he used too much force, someone was going to get pissed off and try to start a fight or make a scene. If he was too timid, he could end up in a purgatory state where he couldn't move because the other people trying to get through were now moving around him. He also couldn't try to squeeze through spaces that were too tight because of the possibility of getting someone's watch or other jewelry hooked on part of his clothes. He remembered one year when some young girl's bracelet had somehow gotten attached to his belt buckle and he had almost dragged her into the pit before she finally twisted her hand around, cupped his balls, and whispered in his ear "I don't have a place to stay tonight. When are you off work?" A whole craps game had stopped dead in its tracks as everyone watched Billy trying to disengage his unwanted cargo. He received a standing ovation for that one.

Billy moved forcefully but deftly through the crowd toward craps 301 with Brian in tow. He placed his hand lightly on the shoulders of the people that he had to move one way or another and kept repeating "Excuse me. Pardon me. Coming through." A drunk girl blew a cardboard horn in his face. Another one almost fell backwards into him as he slipped by her and her friends standing in a huge circle in the middle of the aisle. Her drink spilled on the sleeve of his shirt. The next girl he got too close to grabbed the back of his head and shoved his face into her cleavage for some strange reason.

Brian was laughing at him as they slipped past the velvet ropes that sectioned off the inside of the craps pit and into relative sanctity. "Dude, I'm surprised you didn't stop for a longer taste of those melons."

Billy shook his head. "She had a serious case of B.O." He looked at his watch. It was five minutes 'til two in the morning and the crowd hadn't diminished a bit. He walked over to craps 301 and reviewed the situation. The game was full and two or three people deep. At least it was a twenty-five-dollar game. One side of the game was taken up mostly by the same players he had just been dealing to upstairs. They all still had on their tuxedos and evening gowns, and somewhere between there and here they had all acquired goofy cardboard hats that said "Harry's New Year's Eve 2005" and some big stinky cigars. Even some of the women were puffing away. The cigars were irritating but at least that side of the game would be civilized. The other side of the game though was quite the opposite. It was the typical situation that Billy saw on a craps game during every holiday weekend: A bunch of punks with twenty-five-dollar line bets and no odds, all swearing to no end and waving their hands around flashing gang signs every time they won a field bet or a line bet. This group was basically taking up space on the game for lack of anything better to do. Billy could tell by the way they were dressed and the way they spoke that they were from the hood. They all wore brand new hats that represented their favorite sports team, in the current style with the brim flat, offset to one side of the head, the price tag still hanging down from the side. Most of them wore baggy pants that hung down halfway over their butt cheeks with bunched up boxers sticking out the top. They also wore shiny necklaces and big sparkling watches; something they liked to call "Bling". This group was particularly obnoxious because every time they won a bet they pointed at it and screamed at top of their lungs "Pay me bitch!" Billy was surprised that the boss on the game was allowing this absurd behavior until he looked down and saw that it was spineless Will. At least Brian would be replacing him and they could work on culling the disrespect that permeated from this group of thugs.

Billy looked over at the main craps pit boss and said "Where do you want me? I'm in an hour but I guess that doesn't matter."

Johnny A. looked at him and frowned. “Sorry Billy, but I gotta work you another hour. Take the pole and tell Susan to go home.”

Billy had to squeeze back through the crowd to get around to the outside of the craps game. Then he had to back away two young girls that were practically draped over Susan’s back so that he could push in and get her out of there. The girls were yapping something about how rude he was but he just ignored them and whispered in Susan’s ear “I envy you young lady. You get to go home.”

Susan sounded exasperated. “Thank God. Okay, the shooter is three to the right. Also, watch out for all these guys on the left. They’re making late field bets and their swearing is out of control. I can’t believe that Will isn’t doing anything about it, but I guess it’s because he’s kind of a wuss anyway. And keep an eye on the skinny guy with the gold teeth two to your left; he’s been putting only ten dollars in the field quite regularly. We just started no betting him and getting on him to make sure he puts twenty-five. He’s buddies with this huge dude just to the left of me so watch what you say about him because the guy seems like he wants to rip someone’s head off. Good luck.”

“Huge dude” didn’t even begin to describe the guy to Billy’s left. About six feet four inches tall, he wore his brand-new Oakland Raiders cap backwards and had on a white t-shirt that was probably two sizes too small. His arms were the size of a normal man’s thighs. This guy was obviously on some sort of steroids. He had a tattoo on his right arm that depicted three sevens lined up in a row just like they would be on a slot machine. He looked like he could crush someone's skull with his bare hands. The name "Mr. Thighs For Arms" immediately popped into Billy's head.

Billy said goodbye to Susan and quickly sent the dice out to the shooter. He could feel Mr. Thighs For Arms leaning in on him as the dice were totaling. Billy called the dice when they landed. "Nine, a field roll."

Mr. Thighs For Arms exploded when the dice totaled and screamed in Billy's left ear at the top of his lungs; "Niiiiine! Pay me you bitch!" He looked rabid.

Billy immediately raised his left hand in a wide sweeping motion to cover his left ear. His hand got so close the guy's face that it made him flinch backward. He immediately turned and looked across the game at Brian Seran and said, "Are you ready to start taking care of this?"

Brian just smiled and said "Start the process."

Billy and Brian had spent hours over the years sitting up at the UCL after work drinking and talking about problem customers and what it would take to deal with them and yet remain in the realm of professionalism and not get into trouble. What they came up with was to be consistent with their story when there was an incident with a customer. If they both had the same depiction of how it went down, true or not, it would be believable.

Billy turned to Mr. Thighs For Arms, leaned right into him and got in his face. "Hey man, you need to stop screaming into my left ear and you should also stop saying "Pay me bitch" when you win. You'll get paid when it's your turn to get paid, and there's no need to refer to anyone on this game as "bitch"."

Mr. Thighs For Arms stepped back from the game with his monster arms spread wide, veins bulging everywhere, and said “What the FUCK!?” His fake diamond necklace pendant with two capitol J’s bounced off his protruding abs.

Billy stared at him for about ten seconds and finally said “Hey man, the language you’re using right now will eventually get you kicked out of here. No one here is a bitch and no one is going to put up with that kind of language. You’d best start cleaning it up right now before you get escorted out.”

Mr. Thighs For Arms stared at Billy, then started complaining. “Hey man, why you trying to ruin my fun? I’m just trying to have a good time on your craps game here and you” he peered at Billy’s nametag “Billy from San Fucking Diego, are ruining my fun. What the Fuck?”

At this juncture Brian Seran cut in to the exchange and gave Mr. Thighs For Arms the supervisors’ rendition of the rules regarding his actions. “Excuse me sir. We want you to have a good time here at Harry’s but our house policy draws the line at dropping those “F-Bombs”, and we definitely won’t put up with you or any of your friends screaming “Pay me bitch” to any of our dealers. If you can refrain from those two things, then I think you can have a good time here at Harry’s, but if you can’t, you WILL be asked to leave.”

Mr. Thighs For Arms had no interest in trying to work with Brian or anyone else on his behavior. He grabbed the chips he had left in the rail in front of him and said out loud “FUCK THIS PLACE!” and walked away. He left a twenty-five-dollar line bet and a fifty-dollar field bet on the table. Brian told the base dealer to lock that money up. That problem was solved. Billy liked working with Brian Seran.

The next problem that Billy needed to address was the two girls standing directly behind him. They were leaning in and looking over his shoulder every time the dice were rolled. They both reeked of cigarettes and alcohol and were draped over him like a cheap suit each time the shooter threw the dice. They were screaming like banshees directly in his ear and he could barely move enough to maneuver the stick correctly. One of them had already spilled some of her drink on his shoes. He turned around once while the dice were out and asked them succinctly but politely to give him some room. The girls just scoffed at him and made more colorful comments about how rude he was.

The drunken bimbos continued to lean on Billy's back as he tried to keep the dice moving. He glanced over his shoulder at one point and saw that the chick on his left side was holding a pink-colored drink; maybe a watered-down version of a Cosmopolitan. The next time he was ready to send the dice out of the middle, they were already leaning on him. This gave him an opportunity to abruptly stand up straight while at the same time throwing his left elbow behind him in what looked like an attempt to get ready to send the dice to the shooter. That well-placed elbow nailed the Bimbo right in her Cosmo and the whole thing spilled all over her beige-colored top and her jeans. She squeaked "fuck!", and turned away from the game to survey the damage. Billy glanced back, saw the bright pink stain all over her top and smiled.

She ranted as she walked away: "You fuckers are gonna pay for my new shirt, and I'm gonna sue you for more. You can't do that to a customer!"

Billy just smirked as he watched her stumble off and thought to himself "Seven, you're out, bitch."

As his twenty minutes on the stick was coming to an end, Billy looked out over the crowd that had not diminished at all and saw Luis headed his way. He was happy to have another friend on the game instead of some of those other lame dealers. A craps crew had to be aggressive but professional in order to maintain some sense of decorum on their table on New Year's Eve. Some dealers could barely keep their head above water, but Luis knew his stuff. Billy watched Luis cut through the crowd and go directly into the craps pit. He began talking to Johnny A. about something while pointing over in the direction of the California bar. Billy followed Luis' finger with his eyes and saw Mr. Thighs For Arms standing at the end of the California bar, cracking the knuckles on both of his gigantic hands.

Luis and Johnny A were still deep in conversation when Billy's relief came to push him to the base of Craps 301. Johnny motioned him to come over to them at the podium instead of pushing in to the game.

"What's going on guys?" He fully expected to hear something concerning Big Purple Tex or Mr. Vegas. He wasn't surprised though when they started talking to him about Mr. Thighs-For-Arms.

Luis started in with his explanation. "Hey bro, I was coming back from break and was told to give you a break on 301. As I walked past the Cali Bar, I saw that guy with the three sevens tattooed on his right bicep. I had dealt to him earlier so I decided to be nice and I just said "hey, what's up?" He stood there staring at me with a blank look on his face while cracking the knuckles on both of those meat hooks of his and said to me; "I'm waiting for your friend Billy to go on break. I'm going to crack his skull." I just about shit, then

I went directly into the pit to tell Johnny A. about this crazy fuck."

Johnny A. continued the run-down. "They're working on surrounding him with security guards right now and they'll throw him out. You won't have to see him again tonight and hopefully won't encounter him again. What did you do to piss him off?"

Instead of answering the question, Billy stared in Mr. Thighs-For-Arms' direction and saw that he was being cautiously surrounded by security guards as Johnny A. spoke. He watched the security supervisor approach the man along with two other guards. There were at least three others waiting in proximity.

The security supervisor had an animated talk with Mr. Thighs-For-Arms, then three of the six guards began to escort him out of the building. He appeared to be going peacefully, then suddenly he looked back over his shoulder and caught Billy's eye; giving him a look that meant they weren't done. Billy felt a small chill go down his back. If he encountered this man again, it wouldn't be pretty.

Billy stared intensely at Mr. Thighs For Arms and his escorts moving through the throng of people toward the Stateline entrance. Everything faded from his perception except for that block of a head encased in the backwards Raiders hat and those pumped-up arms that bulged heinously out of the sleeves of his too-small white t-shirt. Everything around him ceased to exist. He stared at Mr. Thighs For Arms and thought to himself, "That son-of-a-bitch might have gotten me if Luis hadn't walked by the guy when he did. Amazing."

The Dark Thoughts resounded in his mind. *"If you ever encounter that bane again, you're going to have to kill him."*

The sound of Johnny A.'s voice in his left ear pulled Billy out of his fugue. "Hey Billy, now that that's taken care of, I need you to push in on the right base of your game for fifteen minutes, then I'll be able to get you a break."

Billy watched for a few seconds more as the three security guards held the door open for Mr. Thighs For Arms. He turned his Raiders cap around and tipped it to them with his middle finger clearly exposed on the brim. They didn't even notice the slight.

"All right Johnny. Thanks for having my back on that one. I think that dude could have crushed my skull like a melon." Johnny laughed as Billy pushed in on the side of the game where all of Mr. Thighs For Arms' friends were playing.

His hoodlum buddies all began sounding off; "Hey man, that's not very fuckin' cool." "Dude, J. J.'s the last guy you want to piss off."

Right then Mr. Gold Teeth's cell phone began to ring. He answered it without backing away from the table and began talking.

Billy immediately got on the guy. "Hey man, you can't use your phone while you're at the table. You have to step away to take that call." Mr. Gold Teeth just flashed Billy an evil golden grin and kept talking.

As Brian Seran stood up to get the kid to back off the game, he clicked his phone shut and gave Billy a deadly look. "Hey dealer, you just had my friend thrown out of your casino. He won't fuckin' take kindly to that. In fact, he will look for you, find you, and then he'll fuck you up."

Billy felt a twinge of anxiety from this statement but held his ground. “Hey man, your friend crossed the line and threatened to do me bodily harm while speaking to one of my co-workers. We don’t mess around when it comes to threats of harm or even threats like the ones that are coming out of your mouth. He’s been eighty-sixed from this place and all other Harry’s affiliated properties for at least six months. You could be next.”

One of the other thugs stepped into the conversation. “It don’t matter if you kick J. J. out of here dude. He’s a bad-ass son-of-a bitch, and tenacious too; like a pit bull. He will look for you, he will find you, and he will get you. You should be scared.”

The Dark Thoughts shared their opinion, echoing in Billy’s mind. *“You have the skills and the training to take out anyone, no matter their size, strength, or weight. You know how to grapple and pummel. You understand and can apply the precepts of Kung Fu and Ju-Jitsu to a man three times your size. These threats are meaningless.”* Billy did not fear Mr. Thighs For Arms; he only pitied the kid for being such an untrained bully, jacked up on steroids, running around with this bunch of misled youth, none of whom could truly figure out what to do if they were actually attacked by someone in a quick and deadly manner. Unless they were carrying guns, they would all go down within minutes. Of course, this wouldn’t happen on the casino floor at three in the morning on New Year’s Day. Protocol still had to be maintained. Billy remained calm as he stared down this group of punks who were basically threatening him and his well-being.

Brian Seran, on the other hand, had seen and heard enough from these guys. He snatched the dice up just as the stick person was getting ready to send them out, abruptly bringing the game to a halt and getting the attention of every player. He then proceeded to wave his hand across Billy's side of the table, indicating each one of the thugs that Mr. Thighs For Arms was affiliated with. "That's it guys. All of you can pick up your money, leave this game, and go gamble somewhere else. You've all threatened one of my dealers and Harry's doesn't put up with that kind of behavior. The line has been crossed and now it's time for you to leave before you end up getting escorted out of here and eighty-sixed like your friend. Now move it! Grab your chips and leave."

Mr. Gold Teeth stood his ground and scoffed at Brian. He flashed some sort of gang sign and said, "Hey mother fucker, you don't have enough security guards to take us all out. You're making a dangerous call fool."

Billy thought that Brian's Italian temper was about to rear its ugly head and start some real trouble, but Brian kept his cool. He set the dice back down in the middle of the layout, leaned across the table on closed fists until he was right in Mr. Gold Teeth's face, and fixed the punk with a stone-cold stare. "If we have to throw you and your punk-ass friends out of here, it won't be our security guards doing it. There's over two hundred Douglas County Sheriffs in the area that can be here in less than three minutes. They'll take you and all your buddies to the temporary holding pens they have set up in the parking lot down at The High Sierra Casino and lock you in there until the paddy wagon comes to take you to jail. It's snowing hard out there, and none of you morons are wearing jackets. They won't give a shit if you're freezing to death because you're law-breakers. You could be out there handcuffed, frozen and getting snowed on for hours. The choice is yours; you can all leave now and not come back, or you can take your chances with plan B. You make the call."

Mr. Gold Teeth had initially flinched at Brian's mention of the sheriffs. Then he reverted to every angry customer's last resort: Indignation. He looked at Brian's nametag and sneered. "Okay Mr. Brian Seran. If you guys don't want our fuckin' business, we'll take our money somewhere else, but I want to talk to your manager first."

Brian, still leaning across the layout on his clenched fists, smiled and shook his head slowly back and forth. "I gave you your options son. Now you and your friends pack it up and go before I get the sheriffs involved. I don't want to see any of you guys anywhere in here again."

Mr. Gold Teeth finally got the picture, but he wasn't going to leave without incident. He picked up his chips and motioned to the rest of his posse. "This place doesn't want our money! Let's get the fuck out of here and go somewhere where they want some business." The rest of the thugs began gathering up their money and muttering expletives under their breath or out loud. "Fuck this place!" "Y'all are a bunch of rude mother fuckers anyway." "Pinches putos!" "This casino sucks. We're going across the street."

Mr. Gold Teeth took one final jab before he walked away. He pointed his middle finger at Brian and said "I don't forget a name, Brian Seran." Then he pointed the same offensive digit at Billy. "...and my friend J.J. doesn't forget a face. You better watch your back fool."

As Billy and Brian both stood there watching the boys from the hood walk away muttering their swear words and flashing their signs, the rest of the table began to applaud. Apparently the black-tie and evening gown folks were fed up with the punks too. Brian took a bow and said to the stickperson, "Now that we've taken out the trash, it's time for these folks to have some fun. Let's get a roll!" The crowd erupted in more applause.

Billy leaned in close to Brian and whispered to him. "Thanks for having my back bro. I'll buy you a drink at the UCL after work and we'll go over the details of our story just in case something comes of this."

Brian laughed. "I want two shots of Patron and a beer for that one, friend."

All the spots that were vacated by Mr. Gold Teeth and his thug friends were already taken up again with customers waiting to buy in. While Billy exchanged hundred dollar bills for stacks of chips, he looked at his watch. It was almost three a.m. He was about to start his eleventh hour.

•••

The crowd was thinning out around four in the morning, but all the craps games were still going strong. Billy was figuring he would have to work a solid twelve hours when a dealer tapped him on the shoulder. It was J.D., an old graveyard dinosaur who had been working at Harry's for about thirty years. He surveyed the game and the crowd and muttered something that only Billy could hear. "Hey kid, you were supposed to run all these fuckers off before I got here. Now I have to do some work, dammit!"

Billy chuckled. “Good morning to you too J.D. I’m usually already at the UCL and into my third shot when I see you. Does this mean I’m out of here?”

“It sure does kid. You were one of the lucky ones. They just finished getting the four o’ clockers out of here when I got to the pencil. Go up there and have a shot of whiskey or two on me.” He handed Billy a couple of free drink coupons. They were called “drink tokes” in the business and were hard to come by these days, but J.D. always seemed to have a few on hand.

Billy grinned. “Hey, thanks Pops. I’m sure you’ll be back to standing around doing nothing within a few hours.” He then turned to Brian and shook his hand. “Happy New Year, brother. I’ll see you at the bar.”

As Billy walked out of the pit, for some strange reason he heard Mr. Gold Teeth’s voice echoing in his head. “...and my friend J.J. doesn’t forget a face. You better watch your back fool.” A feeling of uneasiness washed over him, like a cold wind blowing through aching bones. This night was his eleventh New Year’s Eve at Harry’s. He wasn’t sure how many more he could handle. He went downstairs to his locker, grabbed his jacket, hat, and gloves, and headed back upstairs to do some partying of his own. It had been a long, strenuous night; Jagermeister was calling him.

Paulie was still tending the bar when Billy arrived at the UCL. He must have seen Billy coming because he already had a shot of Jager and a beer sitting on the bar in front of an “occupied” sign. He still had that fantastic grin going even after so many hours of work. Billy didn’t know how the guy did it. He would have to sit Paulie down and beg for his secret someday if he was ever going to make it much longer in the casino business.

Paulie reached out and shook Billy's hand. "Happy New Year my friend! I saved this spot just for you. How many hours was it this year?"

Billy sat down and handed Paulie a ten-dollar bill. "Happy New Year old friend. Lock that up before I lose it in this damn machine. I got lucky and slipped out with just over eleven hours. My life was only threatened twice tonight; once by a guy with arms bigger than my thighs and once by his punk-ass thug friends after we eighty-sixed him. How about you, buddy? You must be over ten hours back there by now."

"My night has been fairly smooth, and I'm only in my ninth hour right now since they brought me in two hours late. It's been profitable too. There were four royal flushes at this bar tonight and the winners tipped over six hundred."

Billy smiled at Paulie's good fortune. "Good for you bro. I'm sure all the employees that stop by in the next two hours will round things out quite nicely for you."

The UCL was always a hub of activity for employees after their long grueling New Year's Eve. The wee hours of the morning were party time for dealers, pit bosses, slot personnel, cocktail waitresses, and bartenders. The regulars like Billy were always there, but people who normally didn't gamble or drink after work would show up just to blow off some steam. It was a bonding process for a group that had just been through a relative war. Group pictures were taken as people kissed and hugged, toasting the New Year as casino employees did, four or five hours after the fact.

Close to six in the morning, the late-night workers' party was beginning to disperse. Everyone had to be back to work early that afternoon. Billy felt good as he walked out. He had survived another New Year's Eve relatively unscathed. Some of his fellow dealers hadn't fared so well that evening: One woman had been pissed on by a drunken twenty-one year old from underneath her black jack game. The guy had just pulled it out while seated and shot it all over her shins and feet. One of the craps dealers had a young girl throw up all over his left side while he was on the stick. The managers wouldn't let him go home; instead, they made him to go down to wardrobe and get a temporary shirt and pants. Another woman had an angry Asian man throw a hundred-dollar chip that hit her in the face. This sharing of the horror stories was another part of the bonding process. Billy felt relieved that he had only had his life threatened. He would probably be out of a job right now if any of those other things had happened to him.

Billy decided to stop by the sports book on the way out to get the updated lines for the upcoming bowl games, so he chose to exit through the hotel lobby and valet instead of going straight into the parking garage from the UCL along with everyone else. He would have to brave the snow that had been falling steadily for hours, but the cold air would sharpen his senses for the short ride home. He planned to take the back roads to avoid any possible strokes of bad luck while he was buzzed. He took the escalator down into the lobby and surveyed the aftermath from the evening as he descended. There were a handful of drunks waiting by the fountain in front of the entrance doors for valet to bring their cars to them. Two cleaning people walked around with vacuums strapped to their backs, sucking up glitter, cigarette ashes, and everything else that had been thrown on the floor.

Another one picked up cardboard horns and hats, plastic cups, and aluminum ashtrays that were scattered everywhere. Some drunken idiot was arguing loudly with the poor girl at the hotel registration desk about a room that he hadn't claimed the night before that was given away to someone else. It was a typical post-New Year's Eve mess. When Billy stepped off the escalator and turned toward the exit doors at valet, he saw something out of the corner of his eye that sent a burning chill down his spine.

There was Mr. Thighs For Arms, sitting on an olive green velvet chair with his head in both hands, staring at the ground. He still wore the backwards Raiders cap and the extra tight white t-shirt. He looked like he was talking to himself. Billy had a sinking feeling that bad luck was now paying him back for what he had done to Mr. Big Purple Tex and Mr. Vegas. He hoped to slip out the front doors before the guy looked up.

Billy stepped out into the bitter cold. The wind blew snow sideways outside of the protective overhang that covered the valet area. The door he had just exited swung back toward its normal closed position and Billy wasn't shocked to see a quick reflection of an oversized bicep and three sevens lined up across it. Mr. Thighs For Arms must have looked up at just the right time; or perhaps just the wrong time. Billy scanned the valet area, hoping to see at least one security guard: No luck there. He looked to his right and saw the only two valet attendants in the area engaged with a drunken couple who were arguing over who was going to try to drive home. There was no one else to be seen in the area, so Billy figured he would have to handle Mr. Thighs For Arms on his own.

As soon as the words "on my own" flashed through Billy's mind, The Dark Thoughts awoke with a vehemence that made him start. *"On your own is the best way right now. This idiot is not only a bane to everyone he gets angry at in his steroidal rage, but he's also a bane to your personal existence; a threat to your life. You can live the rest of your days constantly looking over your shoulder, or you can eliminate the problem right now. How many others do you think are looking over their shoulders, living in fear because of this thug?"*

Billy looked once over his shoulder and saw that Mr. Thighs For Arms was actually following him as he walked out into the storm. He quickened his pace while he put on his snow hat and driving gloves, pondering what to do. The snow in the parking lot had blown in drifts up to three feet high. He was currently carving a path through about a foot of powder over ice. The exit road was thrashed from not being plowed enough and too many cars going over it through the course of the evening. He looked back again and saw Mr. Thighs For Arms slip and fall down. He got right back up though and continued plodding in Billy's direction, muttering something that sounded a lot like "I'm gonna fuck you up!"

As he strode quickly but steadily though the shin-deep snow, Billy thought about his options. He could turn around and beat the shit out of Mr. Thighs For Arms, but that would definitely get security or even the sheriffs involved. It could also mean a mandatory drug test if he was sent to the hospital, which Billy knew he would fail. That option would most likely result in the loss of his job, which he wasn't ready for yet. Another option would be to lure his prey into the parking garage, take him out there, and throw the body into one of the concrete planters that hung over the outside edge of each level. If the winter was cold enough, the body might not be found for weeks. That plan was flawed because Billy wasn't 100% sure that the security cameras in the garage weren't operational. There was also the chance of a random person passing by, which also ruined the idea of taking him out in the stairwell. He kept walking toward the parking garage, still undecided. Mr. Thighs For Arms was about thirty yards behind him, mumbling something about ruining his night. He sounded wasted.

Billy was still undecided when he reached a corner where he would have to either to head toward the parking structure or out into the east parking lot. He felt some pangs of anxiety, unsure what to do. Something was sure to happen momentarily. The Dark Thoughts came to the rescue. *"The old Ford pickup is probably still parked outside in front of the parking structure."*

That was it! Billy turned left and headed toward the east side of the parking structure. There was a line of parking spots against the shear wall on the outside of the concrete garage structure. It was right by the garage entrance, so Billy drove by it almost every day that he didn't use valet. Someone had parked an old Ford pickup truck in the last spot on the far end of the row and left it there for at least a month now. Billy had watched that truck get covered in snow one day and thaw out three days later a few times in the last month. It was backed in to what was essentially a corner with the five-story shear wall of the parking structure at its back and a concrete buttress wall on its right side. Billy had noticed when he drove in to start his shift that the old Ford was fully covered in snow. That was thirteen hours ago. He knew that a camera was positioned on one of the upper floors of the parking structure, but he had seen the view before at one of the video monitors at the security station. It looked out over the east parking lot, but couldn't see the line of cars parked directly under it. He quickened his pace, concentrating on walking flat-footed instead of heel to toe to reduce his chances of slipping. He had to get to the old Ford before engaging.

Somehow, Mr. Thighs For Arms sensed Billy's urgency and miraculously stepped up his own pace. The gap between them began to close. He began to yell out at Billy from twenty yards back. "I'm gonna fuck you up dealer! No one talks to me like you did in there and no one gets me kicked out without paying a steep price! It's time to pay up bitch!"

Billy shuffled around the corner of the parking structure and was relieved to see the old Ford still sitting at the end of the lane, barely visible through the snow that covered it. He quickly surveyed the east parking lot, making sure there was no one around to see what he was about to do. Not a soul was in sight. He thought about basic training, where they had told him during hand to hand combat training "Use your opponent's momentum against him. You can break a man's bone with his own body weight if you move him in the right direction." He then thought about his close quarters grappling and pummeling training and devised his plan. As he approached the old Ford pickup, he reached into the pocket of his Pea Jacket, as if fumbling for his keys. He then stepped in between the old Ford pickup and the car that was parked next to it. The snow between them was at least three feet deep. Mr. Thighs For Arms had closed the gap and was standing by the front bumper of the old Ford, only three feet from Billy. He was so wasted, it looked to Billy like the man was bleeding from his eyeballs. As Billy faced him, he roared "I'm gonna fuck you up dealer!"

Time slowed like it always did. Mr. Thighs For Arms rushed. Billy saw the animal rage in the man's face as he launched himself forward. He saw the blood red eyes, the hatred, and the ignorance all at once. He saw snowflakes touch lightly down on the still backwards Raiders cap and fade into the black. He saw the bulging right bicep and the three sevens lined up to depict a winner. Today, Mr. Thighs For Arms would be a loser. Billy turned his body, pressing it flat against the truck and let his opponent pass right by him. Without Billy's body to stop him, the man's momentum was now carrying him directly toward the concrete shear wall. Billy reached out with his gloved right hand as Mr. Thighs For Arms went by him and clamped that hand on the back of his neck. Momentum was on Billy's side now, and with two easy steps, the Raiders cap met with concrete shear wall. It made the same sound that Big Purple Tex's goofball court jester hat had made when it hit that tree up on Heavenly. It was the sound of a skull cracking open.

Billy held tightly to Mr. Thighs For Arms' neck and quickly pulled his head away from the concrete wall. There was only a small blood stain where the skin on his forehead had broken open on impact, but Billy could see blood coming out of the young man's ears and mouth. He quickly reached his left hand under his crotch and lifted him up, then heaved the body into the back of the old Ford pickup. It disappeared in the three feet of powder that had accumulated overnight. The way the snow was still falling, the indentation of the body would soon be covered up. Billy concentrated on his breathing as he took a few handfuls of snow and wiped the blood off the concrete wall. It wasn't a perfect cleansing, but he was pretty sure that Mr. Thighs For Arms wouldn't be found for days, perhaps weeks. With a little luck, the owner of the old Ford Pickup would come by before the snow melted out of the bed and drive off, not even knowing that he was transporting a dead body to wherever the old Ford pickup called home. Regardless, Billy was sure that nothing at this scene would connect him to the death of Mr. Thighs For Arms.

As he walked around to the northeast stairwell of the parking structure, Billy muttered to himself. "Seven, you're out J.J. You've been paid bitch!"

CHAPTER 6

MR. DETECTIVE

Deputy Mike Westwood sat at [illegible]en table and stared at the unopened bottl[illegible] honey-colored liquid called to him [illegible] shaped vessel. There was a time, not to[illegible] Westwood had considered Crown Royal t[illegible] of the Gods, a magical potion that washed away all [illegible] worries. He knew now that it was in truth a pois[illegible]ous concoction of the devil that ruined lives.

He looked around the dreary one-bedroom condo and wondered out loud to himself. “What the hell am I doing here?” The question echoed in the high ceiling of the cracker box that he now called home. No answer came, not even from the bottle of Canadian whiskey that often spoke to him these days. He frowned at the bottle, muttered “Damn Canadians” and stared out the kitchen window at the feet of snow that he would have to shovel just to carve a small path from his front door and down thirty-two stairs to where his old Subaru was parked on Tramway drive. Then he would have to dig the car out so that he could head down the mountain for the pre-shift briefing at the Valley Station in Minden.

Westwood lived on the top of Kingsbury Grade, where the snow fell twice as heavy as it did at lake level. The condos and apartments on this giant ridgeline were all built close together and stacked up to three stories high. There were few carports, fewer garages, and thousands of stairs. Most of the places were winter vacation rentals for skiers due to their proximity to the Nevada side of Heavenly Valley ski resort. In the summer, they were rented out to college students and young foreigners that came to work in the casinos. Mike's rent was cheap because he had been willing to sign a one-year lease on one of the worst units available. He never would have done it had he known the severity of the winter up here. Last October it looked like a wonderful place to start his new life. In winter it was hell. He missed Vegas.

Westwood stopped short on that thought and chastised himself for thinking so absurdly. Las Vegas was the place where he had ruined himself. His old life was there, one that he could never return to. The bottle of Crown called out to him. He wondered why he had kept it around after the incident. Besides his clothes, it was the only thing he brought with him to Tahoe when he was exiled from The City of Sin. It was a symbol of his previous life; a constant reminder of what Mike Westwood had become and what he had done. It was a tangible reminder of how he had destroyed his life.

•••

Mike was a hard-working and successful homicide detective for the Las Vegas Metro Police Department throughout most of the nineties. He started out as a young beat cop working the graveyard shift and quickly worked his way into investigations. He had gotten himself under the wing of a good mentor, Investigator Jim Forvers, who was now Captain James Forvers, the head of the Vegas Metro homicide unit. Mike rode his mentor's coat tails during his rise through the ranks and there had even been talk that he was being primed as Forvers' worthy replacement if the old man ever decided to retire or die. He was one of the most tenacious investigators in the unit, putting in long hours to prove his worth and quell the musings of those who felt that he was given special treatment by his friend who had become their Captain.

Over the years, Mike had solved numerous high-profile cases with unwavering diligence and creative intelligence. By the turn of the millennium, it was finally understood throughout the department that he had earned his position of favor. He had finally earned the respect of his co-workers.

One of the first things Jim Forvers did upon his promotion to Captain of the force was to promote Mike to Lieutenant, thus making him the lead investigator on all cases he took. That was when the downward spiral began.

Mike's promotion finally made him financially able to think about starting a family. Las Vegas was going nuts. It was the most rapidly growing city in America. After buying a 2800 square foot home complete with all the upgrades and an outdoor pool, he went out and bought a two-carat diamond ring for Rennie, his girlfriend of eight years.

Rennie was a blackjack dealer at The Mirage. She made a decent living, but couldn't stand the customers. She had been hinting to Mike for at least two years now that she wanted more in life. She looked a little perturbed when he showed up outside of her game and asked her if she would be off soon. She probably thought it was just another booty call. He told her he would wait for her at the nearest bar.

Mike didn't know it at the time, but waiting for Rennie at that bar was the most crucially damning decision of his life.

Like all bars in all casinos, The Long Bar at The Mirage had video poker machines built into it so that every person who sat down had a game right in their face. While Mike was waiting for Rennie, he put a twenty into the machine in front of him and started playing to kill time. The bartender came by and offered him a free drink. He ordered Crown Royal on the rocks; after all, he was a king celebrating the purchase of his first castle. He sipped his Crown Royal and watched Rennie as she deftly but professionally evaded the flirtatious advances of the four drunken golfers she was dealing to.

Mike hadn't been paying close attention to the hands of video poker he was playing. He was instead watching Rennie and imagining how he would ask her to marry him when the bartender said "Hey man, you've got four to the royal flush and you still get to draw!" Mike looked down and saw that he had been dealt a king, queen, jack, and ten of spades along with a two of hearts. The bartender was excited. "Dude, the progressive royal jackpot is pretty high. It's worth over eight thousand dollars right now. Plus, since your straight is open-ended, you could draw the nine of spades and still get the straight flush which is worth over two thousand. Damn man! Let's see it!"

The sudden rush of excitement was like an injection of heroin for Mike Westwood. He pressed the hold button on each of the four spades, then held his hand over the draw button and hesitated, looking up at the bartender, who seemed more excited than he was. He winked at the guy, said "Good luck to me", and slapped the button. The bartender let out a loud cheer when the ace of spades popped up. The machine immediately began playing a loud, happy tune. Everyone at the bar began to look around to see who the lucky jackpot winner was. Mike sat there dumbfounded, staring at the spade royal flush in front of him. He felt numb and on fire, both at the same time. The bartender snapped him out of his funk by offering him a high-five and another shot of Crown Royal. "Congratulations man! You just won eight thousand three hundred and change!" Mike couldn't believe his fortune; an eight-thousand-dollar jackpot on the night he was going to ask his girlfriend to marry him. He had no idea at the time that this jackpot would cost him ten times that amount, and more.

Rennie finally got pushed out to go home and let out a squeal when she saw what he had won. She immediately set in on him about the casino etiquette for Royal Flush winners. "Hey Baby, don't forget to give the slot attendant at least a bill and maybe two for the bartender. It would probably be good if you bought a round of drinks for the other players at the bar since you swiped a royal from all of them."

Mike took care of the tipping, then said to Rennie "Let's get out of here."

Rennie was confused. Don't you want to go out and party? You just hit an eight-thousand-dollar Royal Flush."

Mike flashed Rennie that confident smile of a winner. "I've got something to show you, Sweetheart. It's a surprise."

When they pulled into the driveway of Mike's new home, Rennie was still confused about what was going on. "Are you watching someone's house for the weekend? Do they have a hot tub? Mike, are you planning to take advantage of me in your friends' hot tub, because if that's what you're planning, you better think twice buddy."

Westwood just laughed, gallantly opened the passenger's door for her, and led her to the front door. When they walked in, Rennie still looked confused as she stared around at the empty house. “What is this Mike? It looks like a brand-new home.”

Mike smiled as he walked her into the living room. “It is a brand-new home. It’s mine. I bought it today. I also bought this.” He stood Rennie right in front of the fireplace mantle.

Rennie saw the small black velvet box on the mantle and gasped “Is that....?”

Mike knelt on one knee behind Rennie as she reached for the box. When she turned around, she had tears in her eyes. He took her free hand in both of his and squeezed it tight. “Rennie, I bought a new home and a two-carat diamond ring today. I was wondering if you would like to share them with me for the rest of your life.”

The look of joy on Rennie’s face melted him. Without even opening the box to look at the ring, she just threw her arms around him and said “If you’re asking me to marry you, I say yes! Even without the house and the ring, I love you Mike Westwood. I never thought you would do this. Yes! I will share this home and this ring with you, and everything else that comes with it. I love you Baby!”

For at least one night in his life, Mike Westwood truly was King of the World.

•••

Mike didn’t do a very thorough job shoveling his stairs this morning. It was the first of January and it had snowed heavily since New Year’s Eve. The storm had broken in the early morning hours, but another front was expected to arrive around noon. There were at least four feet of snow on the thirty-two steps leading down to his car. He cursed through a plume of frozen breath, lit up a cigarette, and began to carve a foot-wide path toward his car. He wondered to himself "How in the fuck do these people do this?" He would have traded this shit for a 118 degree Vegas summer day in an instant.

An hour later, the path was cut, the car was cleared, and an exit hole was cut out of the berm that the snowplow driver had left on the edge of Tramway Drive behind all the parked cars. Mike started his old Subaru wagon and left it warming up while he headed back into the house to change out of his sweaty shoveling clothes and into his work clothes. His cell phone rang the moment he walked in the door. He rushed in to take the call and swore as he tracked snow all over the carpet in his living room. It was seventies-style brown shag; so it didn't really matter, but the place would now smell rotten when he got home. The caller ID on the front of his phone showed that it was someone from dispatch. He probably wouldn't be going to Minden today. He remembered the lady's name from the dispatch office as he answered. "Hello Clarice. How are you on this fine snowy morning?"

Clarice was cold, like everyone else he worked with. They all knew what he had done and why he was working with them instead of in Vegas. No one he worked with was very happy about the fact that he had come in from nowhere last October and was immediately given a coveted spot on day shift. Most newcomers had to start on graveyard. "Deputy Westwood, you need to go the Stateline office up there at the lake and conduct a follow-up interview; someone who claims their friend has gone missing since New Year's Eve. Since the weather might be bad later, Under Sergeant Swan says for you to work up there for the rest of the day."

Mike was irritated not only by her cold tone, but also by the fact that he had to take a deposition on a missing person. He was still not accustomed to the idea that he was no longer a detective, but just a deputy with no seniority who often ended up working one of the lake beats. Beat selection was given out by seniority during the daily briefing. No one wanted beat one or beat three in the winter because that was Stateline. Working up at the Lake was a pain in the ass because of all the trouble generated by the casinos. It was even more disrespectful when he wasn't even given the choice and was just told to go there. "You got it Clarice. Have yourself a nice day." He hung up and added "Bitch."

Mike left his crappy snowbound studio, got into his crappy used Subaru, and slowly drove down the Tahoe side of Kingsbury Grade to his crappy job. He wondered to himself if he might have been better off if he had just let them fire him from Vegas Metro and gone on to try something outside of law enforcement.

•••

After a fantastic Vegas-style wedding, Mike and Rennie Westwood settled in to their new married life. Mike worked long hours to establish himself worthy of his promotion, and Rennie didn't mind because she was putting in long hours herself getting things together for a boutique that she wanted to open on the Strip. In building their new life, they had become accustomed to not seeing much of each other. Once the boutique was up and running, Rennie was often gone for more hours in the day than Mike.

Mike never liked coming home to an empty house, so on the nights that he knew Rennie would be home late, he started going to the casinos to kill a little time by playing video poker. He had been bitten by the bug that night at The Mirage when he hit his royal flush. He wanted more. His gambling addiction started with the same twisted logic that most gamblers used. Even though the eight thousand bucks from his jackpot had been spent last year on things for their new home and tertiary start-up costs for Rennie's boutique, he still figured he had eight thousand to blow back into those video poker machines. Like a fool, he also figured that he would win again. Thus the addiction grew, and along with it, an addiction to Crown Royal Canadian whiskey. Since drinks were free while he played, Mike regularly ordered Crown on the rocks. By the time he was deep into his addictions, his bartenders knew what to pour the minute he sat down and just kept pouring until Mike stumbled away wasted after losing another five hundred dollars, his daily limit from the ATM.

Some nights, Mike won; either a couple four-of-a-kinds or an occasional straight flush, but for the most part, he lost. Soon he was in deeper than the original eight-thousand-dollar jackpot he had won at The Mirage. He was coming home later each time he gambled, smelling of cigarette smoke and alcohol. He began to show up late for work, always with an excuse. Rennie was becoming irritated and questioning. So was Captain James Forvers.

Money was tight because Mike's video poker habit had drained their savings account. Rennie had gotten pregnant and had a miscarriage on a night that Mike was out late gambling. She couldn't devote any time to the boutique and ended up selling it to her assistant manager to help pay off their medical bills. She blamed Mike for the loss of her business and became cold to him. They hardly spoke to each other, rarely slept in the same bed together, and had no sexual relations whatsoever.

Mike Westwood's life was turning into something that he no longer wanted to come home to. When he was at home, he drank heavily after Rennie went to sleep. He was showing up to work with a hangover quite regularly. The gambler's mentality crept back into his mind, and he foolishly began to think that things could be made right if he just hit another one of those royal flushes. The pull of the video poker machines was too much for him. He joined a local gym and told Rennie that he needed to start exercising. Then he started leaving work early so that he could go play some video poker for a while before Rennie expected him home. Just before coming home, he would stop at the gym and shower so that he didn't smell like a casino when he returned. He started doing his own laundry so that Rennie wouldn't smell the smoke on his clothes. He had a perfect plan in place; now all he needed was that elusive royal flush.

The weeks went by. Mike made a few lame attempts to make love to Rennie on the rare nights that he wasn't out late gambling. She continued to reject him. He needed to hit something big to make everything right again, but the royal flush never came. Mike had signed up for a few of the many credit card offers he received in the mail and was taking cash advances off those to finance his gambling. Soon, one card was maxed out at twenty thousand and another was eclipsing ten. He opened a checking account through a local credit union to pay those bills himself and had them sent to a post office box across town. Rennie had no idea what he was doing. He needed to hit at least two or three royal flushes just to get even on the credit cards. He began to leave work earlier each day and was pushing the bubble of late arrival on the home end as well. The video poker was consuming him.

•••

Westwood slowly approached the bottom of Kingsbury Grade at highway 50. Even though it was almost freezing outside, he kept the window open a couple inches to air the car out while he smoked. He could hear the busy sounds of snow removal all around him. Tractors, Bobcats, and snow blowers were all at work clearing parking lots and cutting access openings for driveways.

Mike turned right on to highway 50, then took the next right and pulled into the public parking garage that was in front of the Douglas County Sheriff's Station at Stateline. He walked in through the glass doors in the front of the station because he still wasn't too familiar with the building and recognized the woman sitting at a reception desk behind a closed window. "Hey Bobbie. I'm Mike Westwood. Remember me? I'm here to take a missing person deposition then I'm supposed to stay here and work for the rest of the day."

Bobbie frowned at him. "Put out that cigarette. There's no smoking allowed in the building. Your guy is sitting at that table in the front lobby. He's been waiting for over an hour."

Mike stepped outside to get rid of his cigarette and wondered if all the women that worked for the Douglas County Sheriff's Department were this bitchy. He apologized when he walked back in. "Sorry I'm late. It takes a while to shovel thirty-two stairs, then my car, then the berm. I live at the top."

Bobbie wasn't impressed. "Tell that to your interviewee. I don't give a shit."

The kid waiting in the lobby looked like a train wreck. His eyes were red and his pupils were dilated. Mike guessed a combination of too much drinking and too many party drugs. He reeked of B.O. and marijuana and was constantly scratching himself. He wore a Los Angeles Lakers cap that still had the price tag attached to it. His front teeth were capped in gold.

"How you doin' there bud? My name is Deputy Mike Westwood. I hear that one of your friends has disappeared on you. First things first, I need to know some pertinent pieces of information. Is there any way your friend could have headed back home without telling you?"

Mr. Gold Teeth just scratched his scalp the same way that all the meth addicts did, trying to maintain his cool but needing to get high again, soon. "Hey Mother Fucker, my friend rode up with me from Hayward and there's no way in hell that he would have left me. I have the fuckin' car keys."

Mike kept his calm, which was necessary when dealing with punks that were whacked out on drugs. "What was your name again young man?"

"Why do you need to know my name? I'm not the one who's fucking missing. It's my friend J.J."

Mike stared at this messed up kid, feeling sorry for him. "Hey man, things need to be done a certain way around here. If we're going to file a missing person's report, there must be a name on it; someone to declare that the person is definitely missing. Now I need to see your driver's license."

Mr. Gold Teeth stared at Mike, grinding his teeth. He kept his eyes glued on him, staring him down as he slowly pulled on the silver chain that ran from the belt loop of his oversized jeans to the wallet that was stuffed into his back pocket. He flipped open that wallet, used one thumb to remove his license, and flicked it across the table to Mike.

Mike looked at the California driver's license. It was expired, but the photo was definitely the same kid in front of him without the gold caps on his crooked teeth. The name said Maurice De La Cruz. "Okay Maurice from Hayward California, I need your friend's full name, an address if you've got it, and maybe his home phone number so that we can try to call there and see if he went back to Hayward without you."

Maurice had one hand under the Lakers cap, scratching away nervously. "Hey man, I already told you that J.J. would not fucking leave without me. ...and my name is Mo. Just call me Mo alright?"

"Okay .... Mo, what is your missing friend's full name?"

"J.J. West." More scratching.

"Listen son, I'm pretty sure the initials J and J stand for something else. I need his full real name."

"His real name is Jeremiah. I don't know what the fuck the second J stands for. I've just known him as J.J." More scratching, this time in his crotch.

Mike thought to himself, “What a poor, disgusting individual.” “Okay; Jeremiah J. West. ...and he’s from Hayward too?”

“No damn it, he’s from fucking Fremont.” Another attempted stare down.

Mike was getting tired of this punk and his attitude. “How about your friend’s home telephone number? Does he live with his parents or on his own?”

“J.J. still lives at home, but I’ve never called him there. His mom’s a fuckin’ beyotch. I just call him on his cell phone.”

“When was the last time you tried to call him on his cell?”

“I tried right before I called you fuckers this morning to report him missing. Are you gonna sit here all day and ask me a bunch of stupid fuckin’ questions or is your sorry ass gonna do somethin’ to try to find him?”

Mike’s patience was starting to wear thin. “Listen here, punk! I need certain information about your friend to get the ball rolling. Now if you keep talking to me the way that you are, I’ll end this conversation right now and make you come back when you’re sober, which by the looks of you will probably be never. You need to answer my questions straight forward and politely so that I can file this report and put the wheels in motion. Now when did you last see J.J.?”

Mike’s lecture cowed the kid. He no longer looked so tough, only sad. “New Year’s Eve in Harry’s casino at the craps table.”

“Approximately what time?”

"Oh man, I don't know...about three in the morning. Some asshole dealer from San Diego got him kicked out of there. Said J.J. threatened him."

The story was beginning to sound very typical. "Were you guys up here with anyone else?"

"Yeah, there's about eight of us."

"Has anyone else in your group seen or heard from him since then?"

"Nope."

"Where are you guys staying?"

"Well, we were staying at the Ace High motel right down the road from Harry's but the fuckers kicked us out last night for being too noisy. We would have left to go home then but we still hadn't heard from J.J. We all just figured he hooked up with some chick and would show back up at the motel. Once they booted us, I got worried that he wouldn't be able to find us if he lost his cell phone or the battery was dead or somethin'. I've called his ass about twenty times since then."

Mike scratched a few more words on his note pad then looked up at the punk who now simply looked like a kid about ready to cry. "Listen son, I'm going to fill out the Missing Person report now, then I'll enter his info into NCIC. I'll also fax it over to the Freemont and Hayward police departments so that they know what's going on. I need a physical description of J.J. and I'll have dispatch broadcast the info. Before I do that though, I should have them contact J.J's mother. Do you know her first name?"

The punk attitude came back at the mention of his friend's mother. "Like I told you before mister, I can't stand that bitch. I never talk to her and she don't talk to me."

Mike tried to stay patient. After all those years in Vegas Metro, he still couldn't stand dealing with people that were whacked out on crank. Their emotions were way too volatile. "This one is important Mo. It's essential that someone try to contact her to at least find out if J.J. somehow got home without you."

Maurice started to lose his cool again. "Man, all you fuckin' pigs are all the same. You mother fuckers aren't even going to try to look for my friend. Just file your damn paperwork and do nothing. You're so fuckin' typical! All right, that bitch that calls herself J.J.'s mom is named Lydia. Why don't you call her sorry ass up and tell her that her son is missing and he ain't never comin' back! Man, fuck this shit and fuck you pig! I'm outta here!" With that, Maurice De La Cruz slammed open the door of the lobby and stormed outside.

Mike sat there and thought about how he had gotten himself into this lousy life of digging himself and his car out of piles of snow and interviewing gang-banger drug addicts. He was paying the price of his addictions.

•••

The bad night finally came. It had started as a pretty good night. Mike left work an hour early after quickly typing up a shoddy report on a shooting murder case he had finished up that week. He decided to go try his luck at The Rio, a casino just off the strip that was owned by Harrah's Entertainment. He normally shied away from the big corporate places because he figured their slots were tighter, but he hadn't had any luck in any of the dumps downtown, so he decided to change it up a little. He sat down at the first bar he saw upon walking through the main entrance of The Rio and put two hundred dollars into the dollar video poker machine. The bartender came over and offered him the customary free drink. As usual, he ordered Crown on the rocks. He decided to come out strong and tipped the girl five bucks immediately so that his drinks would flow well.

Like any seasoned video poker player, Mike didn't miss a beat in his playing. He pressed the deal button to get his first five cards dealt while he looked down quickly to locate a fiver in his wallet. The bartender, a young and very attractive blonde named Gina, let out a small squeak as his cards were dealt. The machine immediately started playing that happy tune that Mike had been longing to hear for more than three years now. He had been dealt a royal flush, once again in spades, just like his big win at the Mirage. Gina began to clap, squealed a little more, and offered him a high-five. He slapped her open hand and looked at the number at the top of the payout schedule on his screen. It was worth twelve thousand five hundred thirteen dollars and some change. He couldn't believe his luck! Twelve grand would knock out one of the credit cards that he was hiding from Rennie and get him started on the other one that he had maxed out at twenty grand. All he could think about was how he would get his life back on track if he could just pop that royal one more time.

After tipping the slot person a hundred dollars and giving the delighted Gina two hundred, Mike had twelve thousand and change in cash plus a little less than two hundred credits on his machine. Gina had just poured him a triple Crown on the rocks and was taking orders from the rest of the patrons at the bar for the round that he had offered to buy for everyone. The people at the bar were congratulating him and thanking him for the free drinks. He was king again. He figured he would stay at his lucky machine and play a while longer until his credits ran out, mentally setting his stopping point at twelve thousand even. This gave him about three hundred dollars to try to hit something big again. He was sure he could do it.

Winning was a drug. It made Mike warm inside and confident at the same time. Gina the bartender became more and more flirtatious as he started tipping her twenty bucks for every Crown on the rocks she poured for him. He hit a four of a kind in aces with a low card kicker as the fifth card that was worth a thousand dollars. He just knew he would hit another royal. This was his lucky night. The Crown kept flowing and Mike kept playing his "lucky" machine. He fell into a mesmerized funk where for a while he saw nothing but the cards popping up on the video screen in front of him. He was playing fast and efficient, not even bothering to look up when Gina brought him another shot of Crown. He lost track of how much he had to drink after about the fifth shot. His frustration began to build as he quickly blew back the thousand credits he had won from the four aces. He suddenly stopped and realized that he only had fifty credits left; only ten more hands to hit that second royal flush. He was quite drunk and had completely lost track of the time. He had missed dinner again. Rennie would be furious. He wondered if she would be a little more amicable if he walked in the house with the twelve thousand cash, but then remembered that he couldn't tell her about it; it had to go to the credit card. He began to feel a sense of panic.

Mike's fifty credits disappeared in a matter of minutes, bringing him to the crucial decision-making point that all gamblers reach after cashing out a jackpot. He was still high from the buzz of winning. He was also drunk, which severely affected his ability to make the wise decision and leave with the twelve thousand cash. His two buzzes together were stronger than wisdom, and he pulled out five hundred dollars from one of his coat pockets. The addict in him said "Just this and I'll leave when I get up a thousand." The alcoholic in him said "Just one last double Crown on the rocks, and I'll be sure to drive extra safe on the way home."

Neither one of the predictions made by Mike's addictions came true. The five hundred disappeared in a matter of thirty minutes. The "last" double turned into three more once he started losing. Soon he was into his machine for two thousand of the cash in his pocket. He vaguely remembered counseling himself at some point during his fall from grace to at least get out of there with the ten grand. That was before he stumbled into the high limit slot area, sat down at a bar that had five-dollar video poker machines, and fed the machine in front of him fifty of his hundred dollar bills. He had two hundred hands to try to hit something decent. Four aces with a kicker was worth eight thousand dollars on this machine.

The bartender hesitated a moment when Mike slurred out his order for another double Crown on the rocks but then complied when he saw the thousand credits on his machine. It was probably Mike's tenth drink so far, but he had lost count at the other bar.

This machine was just as cold and stingy as the one Mike had left at the dollar bar, and soon his credits were down to nothing. At some point during the loss of five thousand dollars, he had started swearing at his machine and pounding the buttons with unnecessary force. He also began to bark at the bartender who had been avoiding him by staying at the far end of the bar. When the last hand of his first five thousand came up a loser, Mike yelled across the bar "Hey damn it! I just lost five thousand bucks at this bar! What does it take to get another fucking drink around here?" This of course brought on a visit from the Rio's beverage supervisor and a security guard whose neck looked like that of a Pit Bull. He stood behind Mike and out of his peripheral vision while the beverage supervisor introduced himself and went into a practiced speech about wanting to take care of customers but not wanting to bury them.

Mike couldn't believe it; he was getting cut off from drinking alcohol even though he was sitting at a five-dollar machine that he had just pumped full of thousands of his dollars. When he tried to argue with the guy though, he couldn't speak straight enough to even plead his case. The supervisor then offered him a room or a cab ride home. In his drunken anger, Mike was barely able to slur the words "Go fuck yourself "as he turned his back on the man and started putting his last five thousand dollars into his machine. The beverage supervisor said something to him about coffee, tea, water, or soda and walked away while Mike flipped him the bird. The bartender placed two bottled waters in front of Mike and slithered down to the other end of the bar again.

It took Mike three more hours to give the rest of his jackpot back to The Rio. He hit a couple four-of-a-kinds that gave him some momentary hope and an extra two thousand credits, but he was so drunk that he was getting sloppy with his play, not making the proper holds, and simply trying for a royal or a straight flush. Once the credits were all gone, he was too defeated to even be angry. After hours of drinking nothing but water, he was still so drunk that he couldn't walk straight when he left the casino to find his car in the parking garage. It was almost midnight. Rennie would surely be livid.

The last thing Mike remembered upon leaving the Rio parking garage was sideswiping one of the columns on the down ramp between the third and second floors. Luckily, no one had been around to witness his erratic driving. Looking back, he wished that someone had been around to see him driving like a drunken idiot to possibly stop the events of that evening from unfolding. He didn't remember turning out of the Rio's parking garage onto Flamingo road and taking the 15 south to get on the 215 to Green Valley at the juncture. He didn't remember stopping at the liquor store in the strip mall just outside of his neighborhood, nor did he remember purchasing a bottle of Crown Royal with his last forty dollars. He vaguely remembered Rennie's rage when he arrived home, drunk to the point of being unable to walk without falling down. After that, he remembered nothing.

The next morning, Mike woke up in a private holding cell in the station with a pounding headache and the feeling that a cat had shit in his mouth. He looked at the desk outside of his cell and saw his friend, mentor, and captain staring intently at him with a look of pity on his face. A wave of shame washed over him. He was sure that he had been pulled over for a DUI on his way home last night. He also felt relieved to see Jim there, as he knew that the department took care of its own when it came to these types of transgressions.

Mike immediately began to apologize. “Hey Jim, I’m sorry if I got out of hand last night. I promise you it won’t happen again. I’ve been having some personal problems lately and you know...”

Jim Forvers raised one hand up, signaling Mike to stop. “Mike, you pulled your gun on your wife last night, or so she claims. The problem is a lot bigger than you think. She’s already filed a restraining order against you.”

Mike’s heart sank with those words. He couldn’t believe what he was hearing. “What do you mean I pulled my gun on my wife last night? I would never do something like that!”

“She says that’s what you did. Rennie claims that you came home around one o’clock in the morning so drunk you were unable to stand up, and when she locked you out of the house, you pulled your gun out and threatened to shoot her if she didn’t let you in. Then she called 911. Do you remember any of this?”

Mike sat there staring at the floor, his head pounding even harder than before. He wanted to cry. He looked up at his boss. “I really don’t remember anything from last night since I left The Rio.”

“What the hell were you thinking Mike?”

Mike hung his head in shame. This time he really did start to cry. “Jim, I’ve been ruining my life ever since I got married. I’ve dumped most of my money into various video poker machines throughout the city. I owe over thirty thousand dollars on credit cards that Rennie doesn’t even know about. On top of that I’ve become a heavy drinker; it kind of goes hand in hand with the gambling. My wife can’t stand to be around me anymore and she would probably divorce me if she knew how bad it actually was, how bad it actually is. ...and now this. Yes, Jim; I was shitfaced last night and I drove home while blacked out. What a piece of shit I've become! I should stay here in jail."

Jim stood up and opened the cell, letting Mike out. "We're going to do our best to not let that happen, Mike. You know as well as I do that this department takes care of its own. I need to know if you remember encountering anyone who might be able to testify that you left The Rio drunk last night."

Mike sighed. "Yeah, I was cut off by the beverage manager at some point in the night. I don't remember when. Then there were the two bartenders. The first one was a young girl; Gina, I think. I don't remember the name of the guy at the bar where I got cut off. Shit! They could really mess things up if they testify."

Jim gave Mike a grim smile. "We're going to do our best to not let this get to court. Your wife is claiming that you pulled your gun on her, but no one in the area reports hearing any shots fired. We're trying to convince Rennie to calm down, think rationally, and not ruin your life by going forward with this. This incident could be bad for the department and will definitely be a career killer for you. We're trying to back her off." You're also in some trouble with Internal Affairs. They claim to have witnesses that will testify that you took monetary bribes from them. That one doesn't look good at all for you unless you are a hundred percent sure that their sources are wrong. We were able to obtain a list of those sources so that you can check their level of believability."

Mike stared at the floor, ashamed that he was having this conversation with the man who mentored him, who had faith in him. "So what's my bail? I don't think I can call Rennie for help, but someone should be able to get me out."

"Don't worry about that Mikey. We put you in here for public drunkenness. There's no bail if you're sober. Your immediate problem though, is that with the restraining order Rennie has filed, you can't go home. My wife Claire has been kind enough to let you stay with us until you work something out."

The last thing Mike Westwood wanted to do was spend the evening with his boss and his boss' wife. He knew he had enough comp dollars to get a free room in at least six different casinos on The Strip or downtown. He had to get out of there and think for a while, maybe just play a little bit of video poker to take the edge off. He didn't realize it, but he was jumping right back into the same routine that caused him all this trouble in the first place.

"Thanks for the offer Jim, but I'm just going to stay down at The Mandalay Bay tonight. I don't want to inconvenience you or Claire. Tell her I said thanks and that I deeply appreciate her offer. I need to try to smooth things out with Rennie before I do anything else.

Rennie had no interest in talking to Mike. After filing her restraining order so that he couldn't come within 500 feet of her at any time, she had also filed divorce papers. She wanted the house and for Mike to walk away, nothing else.

That hardly seemed fair to Mike that Rennie would get the home that he had bought. He was prepared to fight the issue and was in the process of procuring one of the best divorce attorneys in Clark County the next day when Jim

Forvers called him on his cell phone. “Hey Mike, we’ve got problems. IA is pushing hard with their case. They want to use you as an example. Rennie wants you to agree to her divorce terms so bad, that she’s threatening to tell the press about your gun-pulling incident. If that happens, your career here in Vegas is over. If you think you can get beyond those two, you’re out of your mind. Then there’s the drinking and gambling. You’re burying yourself Mike. Not only do you desperately need to quit your destructive routine, you need to get the hell out of here and get your shit together. I’m going to have to fire you, Mike.

Mike was astounded. He didn’t think that his boss or anyone else could strip him of his good job, but it was happening right under his partially blinded eyes. “Come on Jim! You know as well as I do that this incident will diffuse itself if left alone. Give me a break!”

Jim didn’t waver the whole time he spoke to Mike. “I have to fire you, my friend. There’s no way around it. There’s one thing I can offer to try to help you though. I’ll call in a favor from an old buddy of mine who lives close to South Lake Tahoe. He’s the Captain of the Douglas County Sheriff’s Department. That’s still Nevada, Mike. It’s a beautiful area, and it has two of the best programs in the state for recovering alcoholics and gamblers. You have some problems that you can’t control. The things you’ve done here in Las Vegas have ruined your life and your career here. From a departmental standpoint, I need to get you off my squad and the hell out of Clark County so that both Rennie and Internal Affairs get off my back. You won’t know anyone in Tahoe, so you can concentrate fully on curbing your addictions and getting your shit back together, then maybe in a year or so, you can return here and try to continue your career. Until then, I can get you on as a Deputy Sheriff for Douglas County. You can take it or leave it my friend. If you take it, you might get your shit together and you might be able to return to your same position as investigator here in Vegas. If you reject it, I'm going to have to fire you anyway. You might end up a private Dick somewhere, working for bored housewives who think their husband is cheating on them, and you'll still have your addictions. You choose, my friend; and choose wisely, because you are in an extremely precarious position as it stands right now."

As much as he didn't want to leave Las Vegas, Mike understood the reality of Jim Forvers' suggestions and took him up on his offer. Thus, he found himself shoveling snow, disrespected, and unhappy. The only good thing about his acceptance of this job was that he no longer gambled, nor did he drink anymore. The help programs had worked. It was too bad he hated the rest of his life. He needed to investigate something, soon.

CHAPTER 7

FIRST CONTACT

"Back to the lake again." Mike Westwood thought to himself as he drove over Daggett summit and into the Tahoe basin for the third time this week. It seemed absurd that he was in this same spot on Kingsbury Grade heading the other direction almost two hours ago. If they were going to give him one of the lake beats every day, the least they could do was let him drive down to the Lake substation and get one of the patrol cars there. Instead, he had to drive eight miles down the back side of Kingsbury and into Minden every morning for his pre-shift briefing, only to be told that he was heading back to Tahoe for the day. The beat assignments were supposed to be random and somewhat fair in distribution, but Mike was sure he was given the lake beats more than anyone else on his shift. He was also sure the Undersheriff, Steve Swan, had it out for him due to his "preferential" hiring; thus, the unfair assignments. He thought of complaining to Captain Vanderwaal, but the man had done enough for him already by taking him on. Mike didn't want to push the limits of the favor Jim Forvers had called in for him.

It was bitter cold, but at least it wasn't snowing today. The sun shone brightly in the freezing February morning. A light dusting of snow the night before left the pines cloaked in white, sparkling in the steel blue morning sky. The scene was surreal in its perfection, like something from a Lake Tahoe postcard. Mike knew he should consider himself lucky to be surrounded by such beauty. Hell, he should consider himself lucky to still even have a job, but he hated the cold, and he was tired of shoveling snow. He missed the oven warmth of Las Vegas. After a mere four months, this Deputy Sheriff bullshit was already mundane. He missed the action and the challenge of being an investigator.

Mike wanted to go back home to Vegas in the worst way, but he knew he was stuck here in Douglas County for another eight months, possibly longer. Jim Forvers had told him that he needed to be gone for at least a year to let the incident with Rennie blow over. Hopefully Internal Affairs would forget about him as well. Mike prayed daily that a year was all it would take. Until then, he would continue driving around Douglas County taking care of domestic disputes, hauling drunks out of the casinos, helping tourists who didn't know how to drive in the snow get their rental cars unstuck, and taking depositions for missing people who most likely weren't missing. The boredom alone was going to drive him to drink and gamble again.

Mike slowly snaked his way down the windy two-lane road that was state route 207 and watched the oncoming traffic creep up the hill. The skiers and snowboarders were heading up to Heavenly Ski Resort for what was going to be a perfect day on the mountain while he was heading down for what was going to be a shitty day at the lake. He thought to himself for probably the thousandth time "At least I have a job." He was getting tired of that thought. About midway down the mountain, his first call came in from dispatch. Of course, it was a missing person. "Think not of that which you fear" Mike thought to himself as he listened to the details: Stanley Kurchstein, currently of Las Vegas, was reported missing by a woman who claimed to be his girlfriend. According to the woman, the reason she called Douglas County instead of Clark County was that he had taken a gambling trip to Lake Tahoe the week before Christmas and hadn't returned. She was positive he had been staying at Harry's at Stateline. When questioned why she hadn't reported the situation earlier, she started going off about how the Bastard had disappeared on her for weeks at a time, but never this long. She hadn't seen him in over six weeks. Mike's job was to go to the casino and find out what records, if any, they had of his visit last December. His contact at Harry's was the day shift games manager, Mel Morales. "Just go into Harry's, pick up any courtesy phone, and ask the operator for the games manager on duty" said the dispatcher.

Mike sighed as he turned left at the bottom of Kingsbury Grade and headed toward Harry's. This was going to be another boring task. The guy was probably down in Vegas somewhere trying to avoid the girlfriend who most likely wasn't even a girlfriend in his mind. He would get this Kurchstein character's cell phone number and leave him a message letting him know that his "girlfriend" had reported him missing. Once Kurchstein called back to say that he wasn't missing and that he was just avoiding some psycho chick he slept with a few times, the situation would be resolved and Mike will have wasted more of his time on another meaningless call. "At least I have a job" he thought to himself for the thousand and first time as he parked his patrol car in the bus center just outside of Harry's main lobby.

Mike felt the old rush as he stepped off the escalator from the lobby and onto Harry's casino floor. He still burned with the desire to walk up to the first bar he saw, slip a hundred into the bill acceptor of the video poker machine, and order a double Crown Royal on the rocks. He tried to counsel himself. "You haven't gambled or drank for over five months now Mike. Fight the feeling. Let it go." He had work to do anyway. He looked around until he saw a courtesy phone hanging on a column next to an empty blackjack pit.

The operator had a practiced drawl. "Welcome to Harry's Resort Hotel and Casino. How may I direct your call?"

"Mel Morales, games shift manager on duty please."

She gave him the other half of the rehearsed saying that she had probably repeated thousands of times. "You have a nice day sir and thank you for choosing Harry's for your gaming enjoyment."

"I didn't choose this dump for any enjoyment whatsoever" Mike thought to himself as the recorded Harry's commercial told him about their seven fabulous restaurants.

The commercial abruptly cut out and a husky voice on the other end said "This is Mel Morales, games manager. How may I help you?" He sounded young on the phone.

Mike wondered if he was going to be dealing with one of those Harvard graduates that casinos everywhere were hiring these days. "Hello Mr. Morales. This is Deputy Mike Westwood from Douglas County. I was told you were my contact for some information on a possible missing person whom we received a call on today."

"Ah yes. I was told you would be coming, Deputy. What was the guy's name? Kurchstein?"

"That's the one" Mike answered. "Where do you want me to meet you?"

"Don't worry Deputy. I can see that you're calling from the phone that's over by pit six. I'll come to you. Just wait right there."

Mike hung up and leaned against the column. The lights and the noise brought back all the old feelings he had been trying to bury since he had come to Tahoe. He felt like a man dying of thirst in the middle of the ocean, surrounded by water he couldn't drink. He was thinking that he might have to attend another G.A. meeting tonight when the strangest looking woman walked up to him and stuck her hand out to shake his. She wore a rust-colored retro seventies three-piece suit. Her hair was classic eighties: Shaved high and tight on the sides with a shoulder length mullet hanging down the back. Her grip was firm, her voice deep, for a woman. "Deputy Westwood, I'm Melanie Morales, the day shift games manager. Nice to meet you."

Mike flushed with embarrassment. "Nice to meet you Mel. I apologize for calling you mister on the phone."

Melanie laughed. "Don't worry about it Deputy. I've been called worse by better."

Mike wasn't sure if she was joking or not so he cut straight to his business. "We received a call today from a gal in Las Vegas who reported a Mr. Stan Kurchstein missing since the week before Christmas. She claims to be his live-in girlfriend and said that he had come to Tahoe on a four-day gambling trip. Says he was staying at Harry's. Do you think you could access some information on him for that week?"

Mel smirked when she heard the name. “Stan Kurchstein. I remember him. What a rotten son-of-a-bitch; demanding, argumentative, and rude to the whole staff, from the V.I.P. hosts all the way down to the maids. Yeah, he was here that week. Follow me upstairs to my office so we can access the data base. I can’t legally share any information with you concerning his gambling habits or his monetary situation, but I can tell you when he checked in, when he checked out, and whether, or not we made any travel arrangements for him. Follow me.” They walked toward the sports book and took the elevator up one floor to the convention level. Mike was relieved to escape the myriad of lights and sounds of the casino floor. It was quiet on the second floor.

As they walked down a hallway lined with office doors, Mel made idle chatter. “I bet you’ve never seen an openly gay female shift manager, have you?”

Mike grimaced behind her. He was glad she couldn’t see his face. “Can’t say that I have, Miss Morales. From the sound of your voice on the phone, I was expecting a snot-nosed Ivy League grad who didn’t know the first thing about gaming.”

Mel laughed heartily as she stopped in front of one of the office doors. The sign on it simply read GAMES. “Yeah, people like me who worked their way up from dealing are becoming a thing of the past. The Old School is slowly disappearing. It’s sad really. It takes away some of the mystique of the business. She waved her hand toward the large oak desk inside. “Everything is done on computers now, with half the shit outsourced to some headquarters in a state that doesn’t even allow gaming. Have a seat Deputy.

Let's see what we can find on this bastard." Mike was beginning to like this gal.

"Okay Deputy Westwood, here he is: Stanley Kurchstein showed up at Harry's unannounced on the 20th of December and asked to be comped a free room for four nights. He told the host assigned to him that he was a regular high roller at numerous joints in Vegas but couldn't produce a player's card from any of the places he mentioned. He also said he had seventy-five grand cash that he would keep in the safe in his room and that he planned to gamble with it. The host agreed to let him get the room if he charged it to his credit card and maintained at least six hours of play each day while maintaining a required average bet, his room and meals would be comped for the whole trip. Kurchstein did maintain the required level of play for those three days, and he was losing substantially, so the casino was going to foot the bill. He was supposed to stay through Christmas Eve and take a flight back to Las Vegas that evening, which we were paying for. On the evening of December 23rd though, he had a pretty bad streak on the blackjack games and decided to go home immediately. The notes in his file show that he asked for a limousine ride from Harry's to the Reno International Airport just before midnight on the 23rd. He was planning to catch the 2 a.m. red-eye; the last flight from Reno to Vegas for the day, or the first, depending on how you look at it. He checked out right at midnight and was off in an on-call limo at approximately 12:25 a.m. the morning of the 24th."

Melanie tapped away some more at the computer. "They pulled one of the on-call limo drivers from the pit to drive Kurchstein. Billy Stone. He's one of our best both at craps and driving the limo. I'll have to talk with the guys in dispatch to see if they still have their correspondence records from that evening so we can see when Kurchstein was dropped at the airport. I can get those records for you later this afternoon Deputy, so why don't you come back around three o'clock?"

Mike was curious about the driver, Billy Stone. "Would it be possible to talk to the driver for a few minutes? He might be able to give some insight on Kurchstein's mindset during the ride."

Melanie Morales stared hard at Mike for a long moment. "You know Deputy, we normally make you guys show up with proper paper work if you want to question one of our staff, but I'll give you fifteen minutes with him before his shift in one of our holding rooms, and I must be present the whole time."

She tapped around on the computer for another minute then grinned. "Billy has a four o' clock start today, so I'll have the pencil send him directly to the holding room. He'll be going to a craps game at twenty after the hour, so you'll have fifteen minutes. When I say it's time for him to get back on the casino floor though, that's it."

Mike nodded in agreement. "Don't forget those dispatch logs either."

Melanie stood up and ushered Mike out of her office. "Don't worry Deputy, I'll have that too. Now follow me downstairs and I'll show you where you can meet me no later than three forty-five this afternoon."

•••

The meeting place was a small room that Harry's security used as a holding room for anyone who was being transferred to the Douglas County jail. Mike had seen the same room in numerous casinos throughout Las Vegas. It had the same two metal chairs on one wall facing the same nondescript metal desk. The furniture was bolted to the floor so that the crazy people on crazy drugs couldn't use any of it as a weapon. A ceiling camera hung over the desk and pointed directly at the chairs. Mike had sat in one of those chairs in one of those rooms in the Continental Club in downtown Vegas on one of his bad nights.

Mike didn't want this Billy Stone guy to be uneasy with being questioned, so he suggested that he and Melanie sit in the chairs and let Stone lean against the desk, thus creating a less hostile situation for him. Melanie placed a folder full of papers on the desk. "These are the notes from the dispatch log from the night of the twenty third and the morning of the twenty fourth." She glanced at her watch. "It's four o'clock deputy, Billy should be here any moment now. Remember, when I say it's time for him to return to his game, you stop, say thank you, and that's it. I need my dealers working, not answering questions about some guy who probably isn't really missing."

Mike was impressed that she saw the situation the same way he did. He didn't mind the power play over "her" dealer either. "I'll stop the minute you say so Mel."

They waited in silence.

•••

Billy walked onto the casino floor the Friday before St. Valentine's Day with a jovial spring in his step. Hope was going to be in Tahoe for the weekend with her girlfriends. They called this trip "The Anti-Valentine's trip for women who don't need a Valentine trip." The only difference was that this time Hope would stay an extra day and she and Billy would celebrate together on St. Valentine's Day itself, which was Monday. It was only their second date, but he already had plans to do it up in style, just like Richie had taught him. She was to meet him at his place, where he planned to have wine, fruit, brie cheese, and crackers on the front deck during sunset. Then they had reservations at the best restaurant in all of Tahoe, Café Fiore, which was right down the hill from Billy's cabin. With any luck and a little bit of charm, he could entice Hope into coming back to the cabin after dinner for some slow dancing. If he got that far, Billy knew that clothes would be flying soon. He was excited to see what this girl Hope from San Francisco was all about. He was still reveling in the death of that punk, Mr. Thighs-For-Arms, and The Dark Thoughts were hungering for more. He felt more alive than he had in months. Billy Stone was evolving, and he liked what he was becoming.

Billy walked into the main pit fully expecting to be sent to craps 301, the main game. The day shift pencil frowned at him as he approached. "Hey Stone, Melanie Morales wants to see you in the holding room next to the employee entrance that goes down to the cafeteria. There's a Douglas County Sherriff with her, wants to ask you some questions. You know where I'm talking about?"

Billy laughed and tried to remain calm. His mind was already racing with questions. "Oh I know exactly where you're talking about Joe. They had me handcuffed in there last week."

Joe grunted at Billy's lame joke. "Just go straight to the craps game when they're done with you. That is, unless they take you somewhere else." He laughed at his own lame joke.

Billy was freaking out, sure that they were going to ask him about Big Purple Tex, Mr. Vegas, Mr. Thighs-For-Arms, or perhaps all three. The thought of going to jail for murder still scared the shit out of him.

The Dark Thoughts suddenly appeared in his mind. The voice was stern but calm. *"This is the first true test of your ability to live with what you've done, what you've become. Your stories are air tight. You didn't see Chas Wellington since the night he played on your game and got escorted to his room by security. You don't go on the mountain on weekends and haven't done so in over ten years. You dropped Stan Kurchstein off at The Pink Flamingo after almost driving him all the way to Reno, only to be told by the jackass to turn around and take him to the whore house. The mileage on the limo and the times on your dispatch calls should match that description closely. Any investigator will hit a dead end once they start asking questions inside the cat house. Nurse Etta maintains the utmost confidentiality. The last time anyone knows you saw that punk with the tattooed sevens on his monster arm was New Year's Day at three in the morning when he was escorted out by security. You grabbed his head and his body that morning with gloved hands. There won't be any prints. Stay calm Billy. Tell this Sherriff the truth he needs to know and nothing else; because for all intents and purposes, there is nothing else to tell."*

Billy practiced his breathing exercises as he approached the blank door that led into the short hallway that accessed the three holding rooms. He knocked on the first door and tried to maintain an air of calmness and serenity.

•••

Mike Westwood tried to visually take in as much of Billy Stone as he could before Melanie introduced him. He was fit but gnarled, like an old tree. His demeanor was solid and respectful, most likely military. He exuded an outer appearance of calmness, but Mike could see the muscles on either side of his jaw flexing. He gave Melanie an embrace and smiled. "You're lookin' good Mel. How's your wife, Heather?" He was smooth. Melanie smiled at Billy and introduced him to Mike. His grip was quick and vice-like. That hand could crush a person's larynx. Billy stood in front of the desk and folded his hands behind his back as if he were at attention. Definitely military at some point. He was staring directly into Mike's eyes, unflinching. Mike stared back, nervous.

Mel read the tension and broke the ice. "Billy, Deputy Westwood here received a missing person call today on a guy you drove to the Reno airport in the early morning last Christmas Eve.

Mike watched Billy's eyes closely as he began to answer. He didn't see any of the telltale signs that someone was lying: The nervous tick in the jaw, the inability to look directly in the eye, nor the standard averting of the eyes upward and to the right. Billy looked straight into Mike Westwood's eyes, and disturbingly, straight through them. His steel blue eyes appeared distant, definitely not there; but at the same time, Mike felt as if they bored right into his soul. "Yeah, I remember Stan Kurchstein. He was already wasted when I got to the limo, but he insisted that I pour him a rocks glass full of Johnny Walker Blue because he didn't want drink any of that "swill we were serving to the common people". Then he bitched at me to hurry up because he wanted to catch the two o' clock red-eye to Vegas. He also said something about wanting to catch his coke-whore girlfriend cheating on him with another girl." Mel snickered at that one.

Billy paused for a moment, as if for effect. Mike thought he muttered something to himself under his breath. Then he continued his story, but now those steel blues were blank. "So we get almost into Reno, you know, right around the Mt. Rose Highway junction, and I'm merging into the right-hand lane to stay on 395 north and head toward the airport, and out of the blue he rolls down the interior window and says "You know what driver? Fuck that freeloadin' coke whore and her gay lover! Take me back to Carson; we're going to the whore houses!" I asked if he was sure he wanted to miss this flight since Harry's was paying for it and wouldn't pay for another one. He laughed at me and said that he'll spend enough at the cat house tonight that they would pay for his morning flight and drive him to the airport themselves."

Billy then locked Mike's gaze with his and held him there. "So I turned the limo around, drove back to Carson City, and took Stan Kurchstein to the nearest whore house. When I called Vinny here in dispatch to let him know what was going on, he told me to make sure he had his suitcase and all his personal belongings. That way, we will have washed our hands of Stan Kurchstein. He had me stop at The

Pink Flamingo. I unloaded his suitcase, which he carried to the front door of the trailer, and he disappeared inside."

Billy's eyes slowly came back into focus. He was still staring intently at Mike. "That's about it Deputy Westwood. Maybe someone inside The Pink Flamingo knows what happened after I dropped Kurchstein off. Me? I went home and got drunk. Is there anything else I can help you with?"

Billy was smiling at Mike at this point, but his look was full of disdain. Before Mike could answer his question, Melanie Morales cut in and said "That's it boys. Time's up. You need to get back to your craps game Billy. Push into the pole and you'll be in the regular rotation. Thanks for your help. I'm sure the information you've given Deputy Westwood is invaluable. Don't you think so Deputy?"

Mike was distracted as he answered. He was watching Billy Stone's facial expression, trying to see any signs of nervousness or lying. What he saw instead was the disdain. He wasn't sure if that look was for him or for Stan Kurchstein. "Yes Melanie, of course. This information gives me an idea of what happened and where to look next." He turned to Billy and extended his hand. "Thank you for your time Mr. Stone."

Billy's grip was hard enough to break bones, but he let go quickly. "If you need anything else Sherriff, just let me know." He was confident. Something about Billy Stone made Mike Westwood's investigator's radar go nuts. The guy wasn't what he appeared to be.

CHAPTER 8

MR. LOCAL ASSHOLE

The wind rattled the windows in the cabin on Needle Peak with conviction late in the afternoon on the last Friday in March. A day that had started with so much promise had slowly degenerated into a dark, overcast, bitter cold thing that foretold the return of Old Man Winter at least one more time before spring took hold. Billy had spent this day back-country skiing around the rugged saw-tooth mountains of the Carson Range, which surrounded Hope Valley, an area just south and west of Lake Tahoe. With more than fifty lakes within a hundred-mile radius of Hope Valley, numerous mountain biking and hiking trails, and the west fork of the Carson River running through, the area was a Mecca for outdoor enthusiasts of all types, both in summer and winter.

Today Billy had tried to ascend Carson Pass on back country skis from the Kirkwood ski resort area and drop down to Round Lake, which was just below and northeast of the pass. He reached the ridge line around noon and saw a massive front of storm clouds built up over the Western Sierras and Desolation Wilderness. The wind was blowing hard, which made him decide to turn around and call it a short day. On this day, Billy hadn't told anyone where he was going. If he were to get lost, no one would come looking for him in time.

Thus, he instead found himself sitting in front of the television at home with a warm fire burning, scanning the local Reno station for a weather report, and trying to keep the Dark Thoughts at bay. Like a premonition, they were rolling violently in his head, reminiscent of the dark clouds of today's storm that was now surging into the Tahoe basin. The fatigue of the day finally caught up to him and he dozed off.

Dreams crept onto Billy's mind as he napped; dreams of a better time less than a year ago when he thought his life in Tahoe was perfect. He dreamed of Richie, his best friend and mentor, and all that they had experienced together in a decade of friendship. He dreamed of Mimi, the hottest waitress at Harry's; the woman he was lucky enough to land with charm, diligence, and a courtship that would have melted the heart of any woman. He was king of the world back then, but reality existed in this dream just like it did in life, and Richie disappeared into thin air while Mimi was stolen from him by Mr. fucking Smith. Once again, he was left with nothing and no one.

An obnoxious voice on the television snapped Billy back to the present. His palms were sweating from his trip back to where it all began to unravel and he felt the pain of loss like poison burning through his veins. He needed to shake off this fugue that had overcome him, but the irritating voice coming from the 50-inch screen wouldn't free him. He looked up and he saw a familiar face in a commercial, a face that made the Dark Thoughts swirl angrily in his head again. It was Mr. Local Asshole.

Mr. Local Asshole was the Harry's employees' secret name for Joe Benton. He owned a couple of car dealerships down in the Carson valley, one of which was the largest Subaru dealership in Northern Nevada. Benton had bought his first Subaru dealership back in the mid 90's, right before the ever-popular Outback and Impreza hit the market and Subaru sales skyrocketed. In the last ten years, he had ridden that popularity straight to the bank. In today's commercial, he was pushing Subaru's again in one of those cheesy ordeals that has always been the genre for local car dealerships: Here's Mr. Asshole standing in front of the sales office next to a bright red Outback Sport, wearing an obnoxious looking rancher's hat, holding a young girl of maybe five years in one arm, with the other arm around some old lady. "Hey y'all, come on down to Local Joe's Subaru here in the beautiful Carson Valley and say "Hi" to my daughter and my Grandma, and we'll give you a brand-new Outback at just five hundred dollars above cost! Get down here quick before I call the police on all these kind folks that are practically stealing from me!"

The Dark Thoughts swirled even harder in Billy's head as Mr. Asshole's voice faded into oblivion. "The manufacturer has told me to move all merchandise before the end of the year...........great deals on ALL Subarus............Millie and Grandma say bye bye.............1.9 % financing......" Billy stared at the face on the television screen and realized that it was the last Friday of the month; the day that Mr. Local Asshole religiously came up to Harry's and made everyone's life hell for an entire evening.

Joe Benton was what the casino referred to as a Pattern Gambler. Pattern Gamblers had the same casino experience each time they came to gamble. Mr. Local Asshole's pattern was something more like a war waged on the casino staff. He did the same thing each time he came to Harry's, and every aspect of his visit was laced with behavior issues, foul language, threats of never returning, and the general abuse of everyone from the cashiers to the wait staff in the restaurant to the pit bosses, and especially the dealers. On the last Friday of each month he took his top ten salesmen for that month out to dinner at The Sagebrush Steakhouse, the best restaurant in the casino. Like most car salesmen, the group was loud, obnoxious, aggressive, and rude. They smoked cigars in the restaurant, complained about the service, sent back good bottles of wine claiming "This shit tastes like vinegar", and made lewd and suggestive comments to the female wait staff. All of this was of course overseen, funded, encouraged and laughed at by Joe Benton.

Once dinner was over though, the salesmen were excused to go do as they please while Mr. Local Asshole went directly to the high limit blackjack area and commenced to abuse the dealers and pit bosses for the next six or eight hours. His game was blackjack, and he generally played one to five thousand dollars per hand on one to three hands. At any time he could risk up to fifteen thousand dollars on the outcome of a single hand. His play was angry. He cursed every bad hand he received, cursed the dealer for handing it out, cursed the pit boss for standing too close to the game, yelled at the cocktail waitress for approaching him in the middle of a hand, verbally abused other players that tried to enter the game, and was simply unhappy about everything. The only reason that Mr. Local Asshole was allowed to live out this sick personal fantasy, or hell as it truly was, was that he was a terrible blackjack player and had lost over five hundred thousand dollars to Harry's casino every year for the last six years, all on the last Friday of every month.

Billy shook off the bad vibe he was getting from thoughts of Mr. Local Asshole and stood up from the couch to get ready for work. He was running late. A quick Marine-style shower-and-shave and he was out the door and in the Commander, just as the snowflakes started to fall. The snow was light but it was coming in sideways, indicating a wind-driven storm that Billy was sure would only get worse as the night progressed. Travel-wise this was no problem, as Billy had the Commander equipped with studded snow tires every winter. This was excessive for any four-wheel-drive vehicle, but Billy felt safer this way. Also, he would never have to chain up. Of course, if a four-wheel-drive needed chains, it shouldn't be on the road anyway. Billy liked to feel safer though, knowing that his car could handle any conditions better than all other cars out on the road. The worst enemy in bad weather was always the other driver; therefore, he felt that it was best to equip his own vehicle accordingly. He took the back roads to work, arrived at five minutes 'til the hour, and headed straight up to the casino floor.

As he walked by the Sagebrush Steakhouse, Billy heard some commotion, so he poked his head in to see if it was Mr. Local Asshole and his cronies. There they were in the center of the restaurant, beneath a hovering cloud of cigar smoke.

"Hey Billy". It was Paul, the Maitre'D of the restaurant. "How you doing tonight bro?"

"Hey Paulie" Billy said without taking his eyes off the shit show in the middle of the restaurant, "looks like you've got your hands full."

"Last Friday of every month for six years running now. I wish they would go bother someone else."

Billy's curiosity overcame propriety and he had to ask, "Do they tip at all?"

"Nothing more than the required 18 percent that's added in on parties of eight or more." Paul was now staring at the repugnant bunch as well. "You know their ringleader there, Mr. Local Asshole?" Joe Benton was pulling hard on a huge cigar at this moment, stoking up the cherry and creating a monstrous cloud of smoke, drawing nauseated looks from the nearby patrons.

"I've never had the displeasure of dealing to him. He's Blackjack only and I rarely deal cards anymore. Thank God because I've heard nothing but bad things about the guy. I'll see ya around Paulie, try to make the best of it. Peace." As Billy turned to head out of the restaurant, he took one last look over his shoulder at Mr. Asshole and once again felt a push in the back of his mind from The Dark Thoughts. He reminded himself to try to be extra good tonight.

Craps 301 had no players when Billy walked up, which was fine with him. It looked like they had just opened another craps game and raised the limit on 301 to ten dollars. The mass exodus to the five-dollar game would leave Billy's game dead until the other one became two deep with people waiting to play and a few brave souls decided to spend ten bucks. The first twenty minutes of the shift came and went without incident. Brian Seran sat down for a moment, stared at them, and said "This must be the best craps crew in all of Northern Nevada."

Pablo piped in before he left to take his break. “How about the whole state? We’re better than those old dinosaurs down in Vegas!”

Brian fired back. “I don’t know. I heard that any given crew at The Palace has over 150 years of craps dealing experience between them.”

Billy laughed, “Those guys are just a bunch of grumpy old bastards with no customer service skills whatsoever.”

Brian replied sagely, “They might be grumpy, but rumor has it they make three times more in tips as any crew up here.”

Billy had the final word; “Yeah, but they gotta live in Vegas, and that will make anyone grumpy.”

The next couple hours went by without incident and Billy forgot about Mr. Local Asshole. The game was busy, but not crazy, and no one was irritating him. He was starting to get into a groove with the customers on his side of the game. They were all tipping well and having fun. Billy was beginning to actually enjoy himself when a dealer tapped him on the shoulder to push him off the game. He glanced at his watch. It was ten o’ clock, too early to be going home on a Friday night. This could only mean trouble.

The new dealer was Big Jimmy B., the class clown of the craps pit. “Go see Steph Bartopholis in the High Limit room.”

Coming from Big Jimmy, Billy was sure this was a joke. “You go straight to hell” Billy replied, laughing as he said it.

“It’s no joke dude, they want you over there now.” Billy knew it had to be trouble.

As he walked toward the High Limit table games area, he could see Steph standing at the podium in the pit talking to John Hughes, the shift manager. Everyone referred to him as

"Johnny Nine", as he was missing the index finger on his right hand due to an old construction accident. His nub served him well in his managerial capacity though, especially with angry players. Every time he offered his handshake, the recipient felt the nub and was immediately knocked off guard. Johnny Nine always had the upper hand when he started a discussion. His presence in a spot to which Billy was heading for an unknown reason could only mean trouble. He would probably have to shake the nub. He practiced his breathing while walking across the casino floor.

Billy walked into the High Limit pit, steeled himself, and said "Hey Nine, hey Steph." He tried to remain calm. They both looked serious. This was definitely trouble.

Steph was grim. "Hey Billy, we need you to push Veronica out on Blackjack 102, but take a look at this first". She gestured toward the computer screen at the podium desk. Billy glanced at Johnny Nine for any sign of what was up. Nothing.

Steph gestured toward the computer screen. "You're the only male dealer in here right now that has an A rating for blackjack, and that's exactly what we need here...look." The subject by title was Joe Benton. Billy could see the profile on this man that had been put together by many of the supervisors. Comments were made concerning his unconventional play that made him a constant loser at Blackjack and his treatment of the staff, particularly the female staff. One entry stated that he constantly swore under his breath when he was losing, muttering things such as "You motherfucker- why don't you do something better than that, rather than serving up this SHIT that you've been giving me." This and more were listed in the Player Quotes section of every entry. Each loss came with at least “You fucking BITCH!”, if not worse. The final entry was from John Hughes and was time stamped within the last fifteen minutes:

> **Player has been documented numerous times for continual use of abusive language, the nature of which is particularly offensive to female dealers. The problem was discussed with him by myself and Stephanie Bartopholis, and he claims that his words aren’t directed at the dealers, but toward his luck, and essentially won’t concede on the issue. It has been determined that his level of play, combined with his lifetime loss, warrant the requirement that only male dealers will be used to deal to him.**

This told Billy that the company was trying to avoid any claims of sexual harassment, currently a hot topic in the casino industry. It also told him that he was being called upon to solve this problem for them and would have to spend the rest of his evening putting up with everything that this scumbag car salesman had to dish out. The Dark Thoughts appeared again in his head, reminding him of his transformation and his new place in the human food chain. He looked up at Steph and gave her a wink. “Don’t worry boss-lady. I'll take care of this guy for you." It was a statement that had more than one meaning....

Billy steeled himself by concentrating on his breathing before he tapped Veronica on the shoulder to relieve her from blackjack 102. The breathing helped him reign in the swirling Dark Thoughts, as well as plan his approach for what was apparently one of the company's absolute worst customers. He pushed in to the game and decided to try his normal approach and work at winning the customer over, or at least to calm him down to a dull roar.

"How are you tonight, sir?" Billy smiled at the guy as The Dark Thoughts echoed in the back of his mind about banes of society.

Billy's attempt at niceness was shot down the minute Mr. Local Asshole opened his mouth. He ignored Billy completely and yelled at Steph, "Hey, boss lady, why the fuck are you changing dealers on me every ten minutes? This is fuckin' preposterous! You're trying to break my luck!" Billy waited for Steph to come over to the game. She was invaluable as a boss in the High Limit room because of her uncanny ability to work well with problem customers. She approached the table and said "Hey Joe, this is Billy. He's going to be your regular dealer for the rest of the evening, except for once every hour or so when he gets a twenty-minute break. He's a nice guy and maybe he'll be lucky for you."

"Maybe I'll coldly but efficiently beat him for the next three decks and he'll get up and get the fuck out of here." Billy thought to himself. Or was it the Dark Thoughts? He smiled at the jackass he had seen in a cheesy car sales

commercial earlier today and said in his most pleasant and reassuring voice "Good luck to you, Sir."

The next ten hands made Billy think that he might actually have a shot at running Mr. Asshole off. He won all but two of them, getting two Blackjacks and hitting into 21 three times. He thought the man was going to have a coronary. As the losses piled up, he blamed and cursed everything in sight, especially Billy.

"Billy from San Diego huh? I bet you're the company fucking cooler. You probably enjoy taking a man's hard-earned money……God almighty! Another fucking blackjack! Hey Steph, where did you get this guy from, some pit in hell?" Billy continued, keeping his game efficient and clean so that this prick didn't get the chance to make a huge scene if a mistake was made.

As it always does, the deck turned in Mr. Asshole's favor for about 30 minutes. While winning, he became more amicable, so Billy decided to engage him. "Hey, I saw your commercial on the local Reno station today. Your daughter sure is cute." Billy thought this would soften him up.

Mr. Asshole scoffed. "That little brat belongs to one of my bimbo secretaries. I paid her more than her mom makes in a day for that one hour shoot. Now she'll probably grow up to be a stripper or a dealer, going for the easy buck."

Billy was disgusted by the truth, but he continued his query. "So that probably wasn't your grandmother either?"

Mr. Asshole laughed. "Hell no! That broad cleans trash from our Subaru lot every evening for twenty bucks. I gave her fifty for being in the commercial and she was ecstatic. She'll probably blow it all playing slots at the nearest 7-11, old douche-bag ".

The Dark Thoughts chimed: *"There you go Billy; a completely offensive bastard with absolutely nothing positive to say about anyone or anything whatsoever. Scum."*

Billy continued his line of questioning. "So, do you have any family in the area?"

"Yeah Bitch!" Billy had just given Mr. Asshole a blackjack. "I have two kids in college that I haven't spoken to in five years, but I still pay for their damn education. Their bitch of a mom lives in Utah where I left her when I came out here ten years ago."

While a player like this was on a winning streak, Billy knew that his questions, no matter how forward, would be answered candidly. The buzz of victory made people amazingly open. He prodded on. "You haven't remarried or met anyone?"

Mr. Asshole laughed. He was full of himself after winning three hands at $5000 each. "There are too many bimbos around here that are willing to shack up with anyone that has bucks. I've probably moved in and kicked out twenty or more ho's in the last ten years. They all did any nasty thing I wanted because I gave them the high-life for a while. I even had one of your little cocktail slingers shack up with me about two years ago. Some broad name Gigi, or Mimi, or something like that. That little gold digger would do the dirtiest things if I just took her shopping or on a trip to Vegas. I had to boot her when she asked me to front her some money for a day trading account. She ended up being just like all the others. When I got tired of them, I sent them on their way a road map and a ham sandwich. Why would I get married and set myself up to lose half of everything I own again?"

Billy's head spun as he realized who Mr. Local Asshole was talking about. He had to bite the inside of his cheek just to maintain his composure. He did some quick math in his head and realized that Mimi had started to take a liking to him immediately after she had gotten the boot from this guy. What a fool he had been.

As it always does, the deck turned in Billy's favor again, and Mr. Asshole became abusive again, ceasing all talk outside of his verbal lashings for every sixteen he received and every twenty that Billy had. When he went on a winning streak, he proceeded to share stories with Billy about how poorly he treated women. The whole sequence went back and forth, repeating itself over and over like the changing of the seasons, or maybe a pendulum. The taste of blood in Billy's mouth was bitter and salty. The Dark Thoughts swirled with persistence. The pressure in the back of Billy's mind became immense and somehow he knew that judgement was about to be passed. He just needed to finish the night without mishap to see what would happen next.

During his last break from the Mr. Local Asshole experience, Billy took a few moments to read the man's file in the computer more thoroughly. There were both derogatory and cautionary comments from every department: games, slots, beverage, cashier, valet, restaurants, and even the arcade where he had refused to put out a cigar in a room full of children. One entry that caught Billy's eye was from his buddy Neil, the valet parking supervisor:

On numerous occasions over the last three years, my attendants have reported to me that Mr. Benton has been intoxicated and belligerent when coming to retrieve his vehicle. When a decision was finally made to confront him concerning his driving while intoxicated, he was approached by myself, John Hughes the Games Manager, and Jim Blair, the assistant casino General Manager. While we all tried to counsel him on the risks of driving while intoxicated and offered to put him up in a room at the hotel or take him home in a limo, he insisted on taking his own vehicle every time, reminding us that in a valet situation, it was law that a person's vehicle must be surrendered to them upon request, regardless of their "apparent" state of being. Since then I have kept track and can certifiably state that Mr. Joe Benton has been

intoxicated every time he has come to retrieve his vehicle.

Billy stood in the middle of the high limit pit and watched Mr. Asshole yell at another poor cocktail server for bringing him what was probably his fifth double shot of Johnny Walker Blue during a losing hand. He wondered why this idiot wasn't dead yet, at least from a DUI accident. He turned and stared out the window. It was snowing sideways. The Dark Thoughts waited in the back of his mind with anticipation.

As he walked toward the blackjack game to push in for what was hopefully his last hour, Steph stopped him with a grim look. "Sorry Billy, but it looks like overtime. The only two male dealers in house right now that are A- rated are you and your relief, so you guys are stuck here until graveyard shows up at 2a.m.".

Billy grinned grimly through his gritted teeth. "How about if I just strangle him right now and we can all get out on time, go to the bar, and have some cocktails?" Steph laughed and said "Some people just don't deserve to live, do they?"

Billy laughed while The Dark Thoughts responded in the back of his mind. *"You're more right than you know sister, and this guy is quickly working his way to the top of the list."* Things were starting to fall into place. Billy pushed in, wondering what would happen next.

Mark, the relief dealer, had taken almost all of Mr. Asshole's chips during Billy's twenty-minute break. Mr. Asshole sat there with his head down, muttering obscenities into his rocks glass. As Billy pushed in, he looked up and said

"Oh, you again. You probably think you're going to clean me out of this last five thousand dollars, but you're wrong. Steph! Give me another twenty thousand!"

Steph came over to the game and laid out the plastic lammers, signifying to the cameras that twenty thousand was being given to Joe Benton from his casino account. "Now you know Joe, this taps out your credit line according to the parameters that you set up yourself, yes?"

"Fuck you, I know!" After a bad three-month period where he had lost almost a million dollars Mr. Asshole had set a limit on his markers at one hundred thousand dollars for any given night. This was what many problem gamblers did to avoid those nights where their capacity for reason had escaped them. At this point, he was into his whole hundred thousand in credit for this trip. As Billy pushed out a stack of $1000 chips across the table, Mr. Asshole said, "Come on you fucker. I'm going to take you down!" In normal situations, outside of the high limit room, if a player made threats to a dealer, no matter how idle, the dealer could notify his or her supervisor and that player would immediately be asked to leave the premises. One good thing about Harry's Casino was that for the most part, they had a zero-tolerance policy for abuse of their dealers; however, the high limit room was different as were the high limit players. Billy knew that this was where he earned his outstanding appraisals, his $1500 bonus, his choice of start times, the overall respect of his superiors, and tolerance of any other minor mistakes he might make. Good dealers learned how to put up with problem customers and were rewarded accordingly. Billy also put up with Mr. Asshole's abuse tonight with hope that The Dark Thoughts would develop a plan; what that plan was he did not know, but he did know that an idea would come, as would his retaliation.

The rest of the deck that Billy inherited from his relief went in Mr. Asshole's favor. He started with three hands at $1000 per hand and by the end of the shoe was betting the table maximum of $5000 on all three hands. He had about sixty grand in chips in front of him. When it came time to shuffle, Billy stared out into space, not acknowledging Mr. Local Asshole in the least. He was "shuffling up", the casino term for changing the standard shuffle in order to change the deck. It's hard to believe that one could change the randomness of this process, but in the land where superstition was king, everyone thought that they could do something, however minute, to change the outcome of a game of chance. Billy believed it, and this time all he did was reduce the number of cards he used for each riffle by ½ to 2/3. While the procedure remained the same, the mix was more integral, thus changing the deck in Billy's mind.

Shuffling up actually worked for Billy this time. Still buzzing from his run to finish the last deck, Mr. Asshole came out the gate strong and bet three hands at $5000 each to start the new deck. As Billy put out the cards one at a time, his up card was an ace, which earned a hearty and vehement "Mother Fucker" from Mr. Asshole. He had a seventeen and two sixteens on his three hands. After burying his hole card, Billy looked him directly in the eye. "Do you want insurance in case I have blackjack?"

All Mr. Asshole had to say was "Go fuck yourself."

Billy stared directly into Mr. Local Asshole's bloodshot eyes as he put the corner of his down card into the reader device. Sure enough, the hole card was a ten. Billy turned over his blackjack slowly while staring directly into the depths of the eyes of a man he was sure he would kill soon.

Mr. Asshole looked down from Billy's intense glare and muttered under his breath, "You truly are evil." It didn't take more than half of the remaining deck to take Mr. Asshole of all his remaining chips. The bastard threw his last five-dollar chip at the cocktail waitress in anger when she told him they were out of Johnny Walker Blue until tomorrow. "What the fuck is wrong with this place?" he yelled as the chip hit the waitress in the middle of her back and dropped to the floor. She didn't even bother to turn around and pick it up. Her pride was worth much more than five dollars.

Steph was immediately on Mr. Asshole the moment he threw the chip. "Joe, I think it's time you leave. You've maxed out your self-imposed one day limit, you're drunk, and you've crossed the line too many times with my staff. If you want me to get you a room we can do that, or even a limo ride home, but I think you're done here for the night."

Mr. Asshole wasn't enthused at all by her candor. "Hey Steph, you can take this tracking card or party card or whatever the hell you call it and shove it up your ass...and when you remove it, give it to John Hughes and tell him to swipe it through his ass too because I'll never come back here again. "You guys" he gestured at Billy now "can all go fuck yourselves!" He stormed out of the high limit area and threw his players card in the air as he went. Steph looked at Billy and said "See ya next month Mr. Local Asshole. Let's close this game."

The Dark Thoughts resounded in Billy's mind. *"He won't last that long."* It was 12:30 in the morning and Billy was getting off a half hour early. "Shuffling up" truly did work.

While they closed Blackjack 102 and counted down the money, Steph said to Billy "Hey, thanks for putting up with that guy tonight. I'll be writing you a positive when I'm done here that will be put into your file. I really appreciate your professionalism in these types of situations."

Billy laughed. "You know we both wanted to see that bastard go down, Steph. You don't have to thank me."

She laughed along with him and quipped "You'll be getting the positive anyway Billy. There aren't too many dealers that can handle a problem customer like you do. On top of that, he lost $99,970.00 tonight. The thirty dollars was given to the cocktail waitress, although she didn't pick up the last five dollars, so we win $99,975.00. You deserve a positive write-up."

Billy was just relieved that the whole situation was over and he could go home now, but he was also a little disappointed that he had neither received an idea, nor a solution from The Dark Thoughts concerning Mr. Local Asshole. He truly thought that something would come to him during this encounter. After signing out for the evening, Billy went to his locker and used his cell phone to call his buddy Neil in valet parking.

Although it was company policy that employees weren't allowed to use valet parking during their shift, Billy had a deal worked out with the valet captain where he could bring his car in anytime, park it on the fringes of the valet area, hand the key to Neil as he walked in, and with a simple phone call, have the car waiting for him when he walked out after work. When parking Billy's car, Neil would sometimes find a joint or a hit of Ecstasy in the center console. He also received a twenty-spot from Billy every week. During the winter months, this was a priceless service.

As Billy snuck through the bellman's door and into the lobby to go get the Commander from valet, he saw a commotion just outside the glass doors. Two security guards stood a pace or two away from their supervisor and Neil, both of whom were talking to an agitated customer. The man was waving his hands in the air in exasperation and pointing at the security supervisor's chest, coming dangerously close to making contact that would immediately bring the two watching goons into the equation.

Billy walked out of the glass door nearest to the scene and wasn't surprised to see that it was Mr. Local Asshole screaming at Neil. "It's the fucking law! You must give me my goddamn car! I'm never coming back to this shit hole anyway! Just give me my fucking car and you'll never see me again!" His words were slurred and he tottered a bit, doing the Drunk Man's Salsa dance. The security supervisor and Neil were both trying to diplomatically convince Joe Benton to stay the night at the hotel but he appeared to want nothing but to get in his car and drive away. Billy slipped into the Commander and watched the whole scene while the engine warmed.

As Billy watched Mr. Asshole try to convince the security supervisor to give him his keys, he focused on the music coming through the sound system of the Commander. It was by a band named Tool, whose sound was heavy, industrial, and dark.

Billy had taken to listening to this type of music shortly after his encounter with Big Purple Tex. It helped to fuel the Dark Thoughts and to steel his new existence. It was an appropriate background to what had become his angry life. The snow outside of the valet overhang was coming in sideways. Driving anywhere was going to be nasty.

Billy was amazed to see the security supervisor finally hand Mr. Local Asshole his car keys. The man must have figured that it was better not to call the local sheriffs on a player that had just lost a hundred grand in one night. Contrary to what Mr. Asshole thought, he didn't have to give up the keys if a player was visibly intoxicated, but then local law enforcement had to become involved. With three other witnesses to back up the fact that he tried every means possible to convince Mr. Asshole not to drive, it was much easier to just give the man his keys and leave him to fate. Billy chuckled as Mr. Asshole stumbled over to a Ford Expedition, crawled into the driver's side door, and fired it up with an unnecessarily loud revving of the engine. The jackass Subaru dealer didn't even drive one of his own products!

The Dark Thoughts rumbled in the back of Billy's mind as Mr. Asshole pulled his Ford out into the blinding snowstorm. Compelled by something he couldn't truly comprehend, Billy pulled out behind the Ford and began to follow it. He knew from Mr. Asshole's player profile that he lived in the foothills of the Carson Valley at the bottom of Nevada State Route 207, or Kingsbury Grade. "The Grade" as all the locals called it, was a two-lane winding mountain road that connected South Lake Tahoe to the southern end of the Carson Valley in the twin towns of Gardnerville and Minden. It rose a thousand feet over three miles on the Tahoe side to Daggett Summit at 7300 feet, then dropped twenty-five hundred feet over eight miles to the valley floor on the other side. It would be quite a trip in this rapidly worsening storm, and Billy lived in the opposite direction. The notion seemed absurd, but for some reason he was compelled to follow. He had to do something, although at this point he wasn't sure what. He would follow the man all the way to his driveway to find an answer if he had to.

The three miles of The Grade on the Tahoe side was lined with houses and condominiums all the way to the summit. Billy stayed a good distance from the Ford, but kept it in sight. Mr. Asshole's driving was erratic at best. He hit the curves too fast and had to use the brakes to avoid running himself off the road. It was disastrous to use brakes so much in snow and ice conditions, but gravity helped Mr. Asshole while he was going uphill. It would be much less cooperative on the other side.

Upon cresting Daggett Summit, a completely different world presented itself. The U.S. Forest Service owned most of the land on the valley side of The Grade, so there wasn't a single home or streetlight to be seen. The only visible signs of civilization were the road and the guard rail that lined virtually every dangerous drop-off during the eight-mile drive around the rim of a deep and winding canyon. It was a desolate drive. During a snowstorm, the sense of being in a lonely wilderness was even greater.

The top portion of the Grade on the valley side was in the deepest reaches of the canyon. Here the wind had nowhere to go. It doubled back on itself and blew in all directions, making the smallest of storms seem like a blizzard. Visibility here was reduced to about thirty feet. The snow appeared to be coming in sideways and directly at Billy's face even though he knew most of the effect was due to the

Commander's forward motion. The optical illusion was confusing and debilitating to Billy's concentration. The snow performed a living ballet of swirls and gusts over the road, creating even more distraction. Billy watched as Mr. Asshole's blurred red taillights brightened on the first curve and the Ford started to spin out. It was almost sideways in the road when he miraculously pulled out of the spin, almost lost it spinning back the other direction, and finally pulled straight again. This caught his attention and he slowed down a bit, although he still drifted regularly. Billy resigned himself to following the two muted red dots he knew were Mr. Local Asshole from a distance at twenty-five excruciating miles per hour. At this point he wondered aloud to himself, "What the fuck am I doing here?" His faith in the Dark Thoughts was faltering.

The third song of the Tool CD came on and the interior of the Commander was bathed in the emerald neon coming from the face of the stereo. Billy turned the volume up as loud as he could bear. The bass entered with a repeating two-note sequence that drew the listener in. Then the guitar crept in with the same sequence but at double the tempo, which lulled the listener into submission, preparing them for the lyrics. The guitar mesmerized Billy one sustained note at a time while Maynard James Keenan began to sing of shadows, stalking, and murder.

Billy became lost in the song, in the mesmerizing dance of the storm, in the barely visible railings that defined the parameters of this monotonous drive through the snow, and in the barely visible brake lights of Mr. Asshole's Ford. His mind faded out of the reality of the blizzard and into a different time, a warmer time where the sun beat down on this same spot on The Grade and the warm wind blew not through the open windows of the Commander, but through the entirety of Billy's old convertible Jeep Wrangler.

•••

It was two summers ago, and Billy was driving Mimi back to her apartment in Minden for the last time. They had agreed to start living together and that she would move into his place because the cabin on Needle Peak was much nicer than an apartment and it was in Tahoe. They had spent the day moving her in and were on the last trip down the hill to grab her clothes and her car. It was late afternoon, the top was down, and the wind whipped through Mimi's platinum hair while the sun shone on her face with a radiance that made her look like a goddess. She gave him a devilish smile and slid her left hand down into his crotch. As she began to unzip his shorts, he couldn't believe what was happening to him. He was going to get his first blow job while driving. He was about to become a member of "The Road Head Club". As Mimi began to work on him, it became harder and harder to concentrate on the road. He wanted to just lay back, close his eyes, and enjoy the pleasure.

Billy was approaching climax, staring at the back of Mimi's head bobbing up and down in his lap, when he suddenly looked up and realized that he was heading directly toward a spot on the largest curve on the Grade where there was no guard rail. He could see the tops of the trees beyond the edge at eye level, signifying a rather steep drop off, and he was heading straight toward this gap. He stared at a single dead tree standing in the center of the rail-less stretch and thought to himself “That won’t stop me if I run into it”. He turned the wheel sharply and let off the accelerator, but still skidded into the lane of oncoming traffic and dangerously close to the edge. If another car had been coming up the hill precisely at that time, there would have been a head-on collision. Luckily, no car was coming and Billy was able to pull the Wrangler out of its skid and back into the right lane. Through all the commotion, Mimi didn’t miss a beat, and the last thought that went through Billy’s mind before he came was “Why would the state of Nevada spend all that money and time to secure every dangerous section of the Grade with heavy duty railing and forget to cover such a huge spot on the largest curve of the whole road?”

•••

Billy snapped out of his fugue and back to reality as the Ford’s tail lights brightened on another curve. The Dark Thoughts were pounding in his head like the drumbeat of the Tool song. Mr. Asshole must have lost concentration again, as his back end slid out to about forty-five degrees. Once again he re-corrected and slowed down. Inside the Commander, Maynard’s voice escalated to a near scream as he lamented fiercely during the chorus of the song, questioning why we can’t not be sober and why we can’t drink forever.

That was it! Billy grinned as the revelation came over him. The solution to Mr. Local Asshole was revealing itself as surely as the big curve and the single dead tree waited for him less than a half- mile ahead. The Dark Thoughts had spoken to him through the combination of his dirty memories of Mimi and Maynard's lament about being drunk forever. Maynard continued with his self-deprecating tale and Mr. Asshole's Expedition continued it's slow but treacherous way down the hill. Billy focused on the road ahead of him and went over the logistics of what he was about to attempt. The snowfall had lessened, so visibility was better at this point. He couldn't see the road below where it almost doubled back upon itself after the big curve, very much like an oxbow made by a river. More important, he didn't see any lights from oncoming vehicles. There was no one else on the road at this moment and place in time besides himself and Mr. Local Asshole. The foot of snow covering the road was no problem for Billy because of the Commander's studded snow tires, but it was definitely trouble for the Expedition and its drunken operator. As they approached the big curve, Billy closed the gap between the Commander and the Expedition until he was tailgating Mr. Asshole, less than a car length away. The Tool song began to peak in its intensity and Maynard screamed the final chorus.

At the start of the big curve, Billy was less than three feet away from the Expedition's rear end. Mr. Asshole was freaking out, tapping his brakes over and over, trying to send a signal of "back off!". The Dark thoughts roared in Billy's mind. "*Worthless liar....Imbecile....Some broad named Gigi, or Mimi.... little gold digger....all the dirty things I wanted....Fuck you, I'm never coming back to this shit hole again....Drink forever....Sleep forever.... No railing....*"

They came upon the big curve and Billy closed the gap between them until the chrome plated push bars on the front of the Commander touched the back bumper of the Expedition. Billy could see the single dead tree just ahead of them and used it as his target. The music built to a screaming crescendo as the guitar wailed and Maynard began to repeat the final outtake.

The Commander was now controlling the Expedition, and Billy accelerated just enough to cause the Ford to start sliding out of the curve and directly toward the single dead tree. With one last burst of acceleration from the Commander, he let off the gas pedal as the Expedition and Mr. Local Asshole slid into the oncoming lane, over the edge of the big curve, and directly into the single dead tree. The song finished with the guitar playing the repeating two-note sequence with which the base had started, with gain and distortion to signify finality.

The Commander went into a slide of its own, but Billy pulled out of it and watched Mr. Local Asshole run into the single dead tree. The Expedition stopped dead in its tracks. The tree was the only thing holding it from going over the edge.

Billy cursed his bad luck as he righted the Commander at the end of the big curve and continued down the Grade. That single dead tree was going to save that prick from certain death! He slowly rounded the next curve and looked in his rear-view mirror. While he didn't see the expected fireball explosion that generally came from a car that just went off the side of a steep embankment, he did see that the single dead tree had given way and the Expedition had rolled at least a hundred yards down into the canyon and was stuck upside down between two tall pines, its headlights shining out into space. He was sure that no one could survive a fall like that, much less the drop to the ground that would come when the trees supporting the Expedition gave way. He concentrated on his breathing, got the Commander back onto the right side of the road, and crawled away at twenty-five miles per hour so as not to bring any attention to himself. It was snowing harder now, which would cover the tracks of the Expedition and the Commander within minutes.

Billy chose to drive the extra forty miles it took to loop around north through the Carson Valley, up Spooner summit and back into Tahoe from a completely different direction to avoid any chance of being stopped near the scene on The Grade. Most likely, the toxicology report on Joe Benton would reflect the five double Johnny Walker Blues he had drank that night and the resulting verdict would be that it was a DUI accident in adverse driving conditions. Bad luck for losing it in the only spot on The Grade that had no protective railing. Billy cruised back to Tahoe on highway 50 west from Carson and thought to himself, “Seven, you’re out, Mr. Asshole...and that’s the end of that.”

CHAPTER 9

DUI?

Mike Westwood found himself heading back to the lake once again. The four-wheel drive he had today handled well on the icy road. Last night's storm had come in quickly and rather unannounced. It lingered over the Tahoe basin and the Carson Valley and dropped over a foot of snow in the upper elevations. Mike wondered if spring ever came around here, or if the winter was never-ending like this one seemed. It was probably a comfortable ninety-five degrees in Las Vegas right now. He was just over half way up the mountain when his first call came in from dispatch. It was that bitch Clarice again. He had finally figured out the reason she was so cold to him; her boyfriend was Undersheriff Swan, and his dislike of Mike was obviously passed on through her.

Clarice's voice sounded almost gleeful as she dropped the assignment on him. "Good morning Deputy Westwood. We received a call about fifteen minutes ago from a woman who was driving down Kingsbury Grade on the valley side. She claims that the dead pine tree that is always visible in the middle of the giant hairpin at the top where there's no guard rail isn't there anymore. She thinks there may have been an accident; that a car may have gone over the edge and taken out the tree in the process. You need to stop there and check it out. Have fun."

"What a bunch of bullshit" Mike thought to himself. "Ten-four Clarice. I'm almost to the big curve. Over and out." He disengaged his microphone and added "Bitch". It was bad enough that they had him running around checking on all the missing persons in Douglas County, but now a missing tree? This shit was getting old.

Mike parked his SUV about twenty yards from where the guard rail ended and the big curve started. Since the road was still icy, he didn't want to take a chance on having a random car lose control there and knock his vehicle over the edge. He had often wondered why there was no guard rail on this, the most dangerous part of the eight-mile stretch of State Route 207. He peered over the edge while walking along the curve. The snow plows had already left a two-foot berm on the side of the road. He vaguely remembered the dead pine tree that the lady caller was referring to. He always saw its weathered upper half sticking up in the very middle of the big curve while driving from his condo down to the valley. He supposed that if a car did slide off the road in that particular spot, it could hit the tree and take it out. The odds of that happening still seemed slim, but when he approached the spot in question, sure enough the tree was gone. He peered over the edge of the berm and was astonished to see it about forty yards down the steep slope below, half buried in snow. Another hundred yards below that, even more astonishing, was a green Ford, upside down on the slope.

"Amazing", Mike thought to himself. The woman caller was right. He needed to get back to his vehicle and call for backup and a tow truck with a winch. They might even need a search and rescue team to get down that steep slope in the snow to see if anyone was alive in the vehicle. This was going to be interesting.

By the time the search and rescue experts got to the overturned vehicle, there were four squad cars, one tow truck, seven officers, and one tow truck driver on the scene. They had the uphill lane blocked off for the whole quarter mile of the huge curve and were directing traffic through the one open lane. The first man to the overturned vehicle dug through a foot of snow by the driver's side window, laid down on his belly, and peered into the vehicle. He yelled out "There's one body inside! Get an ambulance! We're also going to need at least one more man down here, and a sled." He pulled a small crowbar from his pack, smashed the driver's side window, pulled off one glove, and reached in with his bare hand. "There's no pulse!" he called out. "Damn! The whole inside of this car smells like booze and vomit!"

"What shitty luck" Mike thought to himself. "A drunk driver in the middle of a snow storm slides out on the only spot on this eight-mile stretch of windy mountain road that has no guard rail."

The rescue team rigged up a metal framed sled to the winch cable on the tow truck and lowered it down to the vehicle that they had by now determined was a Ford Expedition. It had dealership plates on it, so dispatch was trying to contact the dealership to get a name on the owner. They pulled the body out of the passenger's side door since the driver's side airbag had deployed. A quick check of the man's vitals confirmed that yes, he was dead. One of the guys poked his head back into the Expedition and came out with a wallet and a handful of papers. He pulled his snow gloves off, put on a pair of rubber gloves, and peered at the papers, then at the driver's license. He called out loud to everyone up on the road. "I'll be damned! It's that Subaru guy, Local Joe. You know; the guy that always has his grandma and daughter in those cheesy car commercials? Joe Benton is his name, and it looks like he choked to death on his own vomit!" The man seemed amused by the situation. Mike felt ill and thought to himself, "What a bunch of hillbillies they have up here in the Sierras."

When he reached the road, the guy handed Joe Benton's wallet and papers to Mike and said "You'll want to book these in as evidence. It's probably going to be written up as a classic DUI in winter storm watch conditions. It's also bad luck that he slid out right here in the only spot on the whole damn road that has no guard rail. Funny thing though, it looks like he survived the fall since his airbag went off, but he vomited and somehow choked to death on his own puke. I can't say for sure, since I'm not a coroner, but I didn't see any blood. The puke in that car smells like scotch and red wine, so he must have been out somewhere partying. These papers", he gestured at the five papers that looked like counter checks in Mike's hand. "Looks like markers from Harry's casino. I'll bet good money that Local Joe played at Harry's last night, got wasted, then tried to drive home. He has a home down here in the foothills. He should have been driving one of his own vehicles. Those Subarus have ABS and All-wheel Drive. You put a pair of studded snow tires on a Subaru and you'll be safer than any vehicle with chains or cables. That piece of shit Ford had no chance with a drunken idiot behind the wheel in a foot of snow. What a moron!"

Mike was astounded at this guy's carefree attitude toward death, but he was more interested in the five pieces of paper that looked like marker slips from Harry's. Mike had signed many of these same slips in more than a few casinos down in Vegas. It was essentially a loan from the casino that you had to pay back, win or lose. Each of the five markers that Mike held were for twenty thousand dollars. It looked like Joe Benton lost a hundred-grand last night at Harry's. They all came from the same blackjack game and were signed by the same pit boss and the same dealer, except for the last one. His detective's radar went off again when he saw the name. It was trying to tell him something. The time on that one showed that it was printed just after midnight last night. The pit boss's signature was the same as the other ones: Stephanie Bartomei, but the dealer's signature was different. This one said Billy Stone on it. It was the last marker that Joe Benton took out before he died. Mike figured he needed to talk to this Stephanie Bartomei woman. He also wanted to talk to Billy Stone again. The markers and the wallet were going to have to be booked into evidence, but before he dropped them into a plastic evidence bag, he wrote down the player's card number. He needed to get a hold of his new friend Mel Morales and beg her to help him out again.

Mike watched the ambulance head down the hill. It drove with no emergency lights, no urgency. Neither were needed since it was headed to the coroner's office. The tow truck had gotten the Expedition winched up and tied down on its flat bed. It would be going to the Douglas County impound yard for further examination. The search and rescue guys had canvassed a hundred-yard square around the site of the wreck and found no further evidence, so they were leaving too. The officers assisting Mike didn't want to have much to do with him, so they all checked out to go about their daily business. It was unspoken that since Mike was first on the scene, the paperwork was his responsibility. No one offered to help in the least. These guys were a bunch of douche bags, but Mike was sure they all felt the same way about him. He stared out over the Carson Valley, the view muted by the bitter cold steel grey sky, and thought to himself, "I pray to whatever God exists out there that this purgatory only lasts for six more months." He stomped out the last of the road flares and headed up the hill toward Lake Tahoe. He wanted to talk to Mel Morales again.

Mike parked in his usual spot at the edge of the bus center by the double glass doors that led into the Harry's lobby. Once inside, he stared at the escalator that would ascend him once again into the quagmire of his ruin; the reason he was in this Podunk County doing useless bullshit Deputy Sheriff work in the first place. He could hear the bells and whistles of the slot machines beckoning to him to come upstairs and dive into risk again, because without risk, there would be no reward. Mike steeled himself, remembering the phone on the column by the blackjack pit. It was only ten strides away from the top of the escalator. He would pick that phone up and immediately ask for Melanie Morales. Then he would close his eyes and pray for strength.

"This is Mel Morales, games manager. How may I help you?" She had the same greeting with all the same inflections and the same masculine voice as the last time she answered Mike's call.

Mike hoped she would be cooperative. "Hey Melanie, this is Deputy Mike Westwood again." He kept his eyes closed.

Melanie sounded genuinely interested to hear from him. "Hey, Deputy Westwood! You got some info for me on that jackass Stan Kurchstein? Did he finally pop up?"

"Sorry Melanie, nothing more on Kurchstein. He's still missing. This is a new one. I'm sure you'll read about it in tomorrow's edition of the Tahoe Tribune, but I'll give it to you early. One of your big money patrons ran his car over the edge on the back side of Kingsbury Grade late last night or early this morning and died. Do you know who Joe Benton is?"

Melanie clicked her tongue a few times before responding. Her voice carried a hint of trepidation. "Local Joe. Yeah, I know him. The Subaru guy from the valley. He's been coming to Harry's on the last Friday of every month for probably the last five years. You say he's dead?"

"Dead. Yes. He was shit-faced drunk while he was driving home. He slid off the edge on that big curve at the top of the Grade that doubles back on itself. You know, the one with no railing for about a hundred yards. We found five marker receipts from Harry's in the car." Mike didn't want to scare her off, so he lightened his tone a little. "I just want to see if you can give me some information on him and maybe let me talk to the supervisor and the dealers whose names are on the markers. I need confirmation on how wasted he was when he left last night."

Melanie was silent on the other end for an uncomfortable moment. Mike was beginning to think she was going to deny him the information when she finally answered. "I'll meet you at the column you're calling from in just a few minutes. Don't move."

Mike stood there by the empty pit and tried to focus his attention on the flat screen television that hung on the wall. It was showing a rock and roll video with long-haired young guys in black t-shirts chasing some girls around in a convertible mustang. He stared at the video and tried to ignore the call of the slot machines that came from all around him. He felt like he was drowning again when Melanie tapped him on the shoulder.

"I didn't know you liked White Punks on Acid, Deputy Westwood." She smiled and shook his hand firmly.

Mike wasn't sure what she was talking about at first, then he glanced back at the video and gave her a faint-hearted laugh. "Oh yeah, those guys rock. Thanks for seeing me Miss Morales. Listen, I'm sorry to bother you again, but I'm just trying to piece together what Mr. Benton was doing last night before he ran himself off Kingsbury. Of course, none of this will come back to your casino as a liability problem. I just need to make a thorough report."

Melanie smiled at him and clapped him on the shoulder. "Deputy Westwood, nothing that goes on at Harry's ever comes back to us as a liability problem. We have some of the best lawyers in the country working for us, and we are all well trained to take all the necessary steps with any problem customers to avoid that liability. Now come into the pit here with me and I'll look up Mr. Local Asshole's player profile for you; that's what we call him here at Harry's, you know. I'm sure there are comments about his play last night that can clue us in on his state of being when he left." She motioned him to the computer monitor at the podium in the middle of the empty pit and began tapping away at the keyboard. After a short moment, she stopped tapping and began to scroll whatever page she was on and read out loud.

"Okay, here's the first comment from yesterday in the notes section of his bio. It's from the manager of the Sagebrush Steakhouse stating that Joe Benton and his group walked out last night without paying the bill. Paul went ahead and charged it to his comps. It goes down this way every month. He brings his top salesmen here on the last Friday of every month for dinner, then he goes off by himself and plays high limit blackjack for the rest of the evening. He's one of the nastiest sons of bitches I've ever seen in here. Here's the next note. It's from the swing shift manager, John Hughes. It says "Player has been documented numerous times for continual use of abusive language, the nature of which is particularly offensive to female dealers. The problem was discussed with him by myself and Stephanie Barthomei, and he claims that his words aren't directed at the dealers, but toward his luck, and essentially won't concede on the issue. It has been determined that his level of play, combined with his lifetime win-loss, warrant the requirement that only male dealers will be used to deal to him." He had a bad habit of saying "you fucking bitch!" out loud whenever he lost. I guess they decided not to let any women deal to him anymore. I saw that one coming a long time ago. Some of those little girley-girl Primadonnas can't handle a little foul language, and because of all the sexual harassment laws these days, we have to address the issue."

Melanie scrolled down a little further on the computer and read silently for a minute, then muttered to herself "Wow. He did that again." She looked up at Mike and gestured to the computer screen. "Here's what went down with Neil the valet captain last night when he was leaving. Go ahead and read it yourself Deputy. My mouth is dry after chewing on all this bullshit."

Mike grinned at her and stared at the computer screen. Notes on Joe Benton were entered by date and name of the individual making the notation. The most recent one had today's date and the name Neil Johnson, Valet Captain, on its heading.

> **Joe Benton showed up at approximately 12:45 a.m. on Saturday March 27th, demanding his car keys. He was obviously drunk and was adamant on refusing to take "no" for an answer. I was with the security supervisor, Dave Lewis, and we both went through the steps of offering first a cab ride home, then offering to put him up in one of Harry's suites for the night. He wasn't interested in either of those options and continued to demand his keys. Given the fact that he is a Platinum Player and needs to be treated with kid gloves, we finally let him have his car keys after he rejected everything we offered to him. After one final warning from Officer Lewis concerning his impaired condition, he was given his keys and he drove away somewhat recklessly.**

Mike looked up and raised one eyebrow in question at Melanie. He was the master of the single raised eyebrow; it compelled people to do things for him. "So they let him have his keys even though he was obviously drunk. Why not call 911 and have the nearest Deputy Sheriff come pick him up?"

Melanie grinned at Mike and chuckled. "Don't you raise that one eyebrow at me expecting me to fall for your funny look. You know just as well as I do that the big players have a different set of rules. If Neil or Dave chose to call Douglas County, he could be arrested for any number of things: Drunken in public, disturbing the peace, trespassing. Legally, we can't deny him his own keys anyway. They're not our property. If he goes to jail one night because Harry's called the cops on him, we would surely lose his business, and that can't happen. Joe Benton is a perennial loser. We've beaten him for over five million dollars in the last five years, most of it on a single day of every month. We're not going to piss this guy off. It's also documented with witnesses that we did the best we could to warn him about his condition and to offer alternatives to his poor choices."

"Well, touché Miss Morales. Do you have any other entries in there that might be enlightening?"

Melanie giggled at Mike's use of words. She clicked around a few screens, found one she was looking for, and began reading and scrolling. She stopped after a moment and looked up at him. "Here's the pit boss, Stephanie Barthomei's rundown on Joe from last night."

"At about ten p.m., we pulled Billy Stone from his craps game to have him deal to Joe Benton. He is our best

H1 rated male dealer besides Mark Hansen, who is going to be the relief. Mr. Benton is pretty wasted right now. He's also into his fourth twenty-thousand-dollar marker. He's about to reach his own self-imposed trip limit of one-hundred thousand. John Hughes has knowledge of the situation and is expecting to hear from me if anything gets out of hand. Everything should be okay since Billy Stone is dealing to him. He's one of our best at handling problem individuals."

Melanie scrolled down a little more. "Okay, Billy Stone returned from his break at midnight and proceeded to beat Mr. Benton for the rest of his available money. After his final loss, he blew up and threw a five-dollar chip at the waitress after she told him they were out of Johnny Walker Blue. When Stephanie told him it was time to go home or to his room, he let out a slew of insults, told everyone to "jam this players' card in your asses" and stomped off toward valet."

The conversation paused while Mike absorbed what he had just heard. He finally chuckled at Mel. "So this guy's nickname fits his personality, not to mention that he had a heavy gambling and drinking problem, and he treated all of the staff like shit. The only reason he was allowed to continue like this was because he was a constant loser of large amounts of money. Is that correct?"

Melanie looked at him very matter-of-factly and said "For over a million dollars a year from one individual, that is correct Deputy Westwood. He was one of the worst blackjack players I've ever seen." She buried her head in the computer screen again, clicking away. "Both Billy

Stone and Steph Barthomei are coming in tonight at five o'clock. I'll give you ten minutes to talk with them together while they set up the high limit pit, and that's it. If you want any more, you'll have to produce a warrant. I'll see you right outside the high limit pit next to the Rewards Card Center at ten minutes before five. Okay?"

•••

Mike was losing himself in the call of the slot machines. The old desire was burning hot inside of him. He wanted nothing more than to strip off his holster, remove his uniform, hit the nearest ATM for five hundred bucks, and head straight to The Player's bar for some video poker and The Elixir of the Gods; Crown Royal. He snapped out of his funk and stared at Melanie. Her face outlined by that terrible mullet brought him back to reality. "Ten minutes 'til five and ten minutes max; I'll see you there Melanie. Thanks so much for your assistance." He shook her hand and bolted for the escalator down into the lobby. He desperately needed to call his GA sponsor.

Mike's Gamblers Anonymous mentor used to be a high-limit Blackjack dealer at The El Dorado in Reno. Since those dealers kept their own tips, Colleen had been pocketing five hundred bucks or more a day for years. Half of that had covered her cocaine habit; the rest of it couldn't cover her gambling habit. Just like Mike, Colleen had gotten credit cards in her name that her husband didn't know about and proceeded to max a few of them out. Once she added alcohol and turned the routine into "The Deadly Trio", as they called it in rehab, she had been reduced to trying to cut her wrists after she lost ten thousand dollars to a video poker machine in one night and hocked her wedding ring to one of the bartenders for two eight-balls of cocaine. She spent ninety days in rehab and, with the full support of her family, was strong and solid as a rock. She was clean and sober for over a thousand days and hadn't gambled a dime in that time period either. For Mike Westwood, she was an angel sent from heaven. Her opinion of gamblers and gambling in general was quite scathing. She never hesitated to tell Mike that problem gamblers were the lowest form of life, that they were weak, ignorant, and stupid all at the same time. She always let him know that the casino was evil as the Devil, and that it preyed upon people and their weaknesses.

Colleen answered the phone, "Hey Mike, what are you doing calling me while you are working?"

"How did you know it was me, Miss Mentor?"

Colleen laughed, "Because your name pops up on the screen of my cell phone when you call me you moron. You know that. You haven't been drinking have you Mikey?"

Mike sighed. He wanted a drink badly. "I'm a hundred and fifty days sober today Colleen, so that's not it. I was just inside Harry's casino questioning one of the shift managers and I could barely resist the call of all those slot machines. I wanted to play video poker so bad, I almost went out to the squad car to remove my holster and uniform to go back up there and pump five hundred bucks into the nearest machine. I feel sick."

Colleen's voice took on a motherly tone as she answered him, but her words weren't those of a mother. "Mikey, you know as well as I do that gamblers are nothing but a bunch of losers, douche bags who don't understand that they will never win back all the money they lost, nor that they will lose even more in the attempt. Do you want to spend all your waking time in some shithole that smells like bottom of a dirty ashtray surrounded by drunken losers? Anything is better than that life Mike, and you've got to remain strong enough to not return to that pit of hell again. You've already ruined your life once, Rennie's too. Don't fall in again. You might not come out alive. Stay strong my friend. Focus on your work, and continue to resist. It sounds like you'll have to go back in there later, so you must steel yourself to the situation, see it for what it truly is, and own those noises when they beckon. Don't let them own you. A big part of controlling your gambling addiction is to be able to be around it and not give in to the temptation. Remember what it can do to you. It can turn you into a scumbag, a flea. Stay strong Mikey. Maybe you should attend this week's meeting. It's Wednesday at the Kahle Community Center. Call me if you're going and I'll come with you. Stay strong brother, I gotta go." With the lecture at an end, Colleen hung up. Mike had a new sense of strength. He would face his demons again this afternoon at ten minutes before five.

•••

"Big Purple Tex. Mr. Vegas. Punk-ass Mr. Thighs For Arms. Mr. Local Asshole. Four banes to society that you have efficiently removed. You are evolving Billy, into a bringer of justice and a protector of all who are mistreated

by these types of scum. You follow orders well. You are patient enough to allow your situations to evolve to the right point, then you attack efficiently. You are doing the world a favor by eliminating those who treat everyone around them terribly. It feels good to kill, yes?"

"Oh yes it does" Billy spoke out loud as he entered the main pit at five minutes before five that evening. He was lost in the preaching of The Dark Thoughts, and still high from the thrill of last night's kill.

"It does what, Billy?" It was Rose, the oldest dealer at Harry's. She was over eighty and still dealt four days a week. It supported her gambling habit and put her two grandchildren through college. She still had a ton of spunk.

Billy snapped out of his fugue. He was fond of Rose, so he obliged her interruption. "It makes you feel great to be starting your day, Miss Rose."

Rose laughed at Billy. "I think it makes me feel better when I'm ending my day, Billy."

Billy chuckled and quipped back at her. "For every ending there must be a beginning, Rosie." They were at the dealer pencil now. Billy saw Melanie Morales there, staring at him as he approached. Her look was uncomfortably serious.

Melanie smiled at Billy when he walked up to the podium. "Hey Stone. You're on the craps game but you need to go into high limit first. Remember Deputy Westwood? He's there and wants to talk to you again. You can push in on the craps game at twenty after."

Alarms sounded in Billy's head, but he tried to maintain some composure. "Does he have more questions about that Kurchstein guy?"

Melanie fixed him with her serious stare again. "No. Kurchstein's still missing. Mr. Local Asshole drove off the road on the back side of Kingsbury last night. He's dead. Westwood wants to ask you and Steph a couple of questions about how things went down with him last night."

"Any special instructions Mel? Do we need to corroborate a story?"

Melanie patted Billy on the arm. "Don't worry bud. Everything that went down last night is properly documented in his file, so all you need to do is tell the truth. Get on over there. He's already talking with Steph."

The Dark Thoughts concurred with Melanie in the back of Billy's mind as he approached the high limit pit. *"She's right Billy. Don't worry about a thing. Your story is airtight. Answer with the truth because there is nothing else to tell. Just leave out anything that happened after you left work. If Westwood asks, you went straight home. Mr. Local Asshole was obviously driving home drunk and unfortunately slid off the road in the only spot on the back side of The Grade that had no guard rail. Pity."*

•••

Mike was listening to the end of Steph's version of last night's events when Billy walked into the pit. He delivered one of those bone crushing handshakes again. Billy Stone surely represented his name: solid and hard. He fixed Mike with an aloof glare. "What's up Deputy Westwood? Any word on that Kurchstein character yet?"

"Hello Mr. Stone. No, this isn't about Kurchstein. It's about the guy you had in here last night, Joe Benton." He watched Billy's face for anything amiss or any of the telltale signs of fabrication. What he saw instead was the same distant look in those steel blue eyes.

Billy answered him with the same detached voice as when he spoke of Kurchstein. "Local Joe? He was here last night. Lost a hundred grand and managed to treat everyone like shit in the process. I saw him in the Sagebrush Steakhouse when I came in here at six. He and his cronies must have had eight or ten bottles of wine on the table. He was drinking Johnny Walker Blue in here all night after dinner until I took all his money. He was pretty wasted when he stumbled out of here around one in the morning. What were his parting words to us Steph?"

Steph laughed. "It was something like take this party card and shove it through your ass real hard, and when you remove it, you can give it to John Hughes and tell him to shove it in his ass too."

Billy still had that distant look in his eyes. "I couldn't believe he threw that five-dollar chip at that poor cocktail waitress. He should go to jail just for that. Did you get him for a DUI?"

Mike was lost in the deadness of Billy Stone's eyes but snapped out of it when Billy asked about the DUI. "He's dead Mr. Stone." Billy didn't even flinch at Mike's revelation. That distant stare never changed. "He ran off the road on the back side of Kingsbury at that giant curve at the top."

Billy suddenly popped back into reality and looked at Mike quizzically. "You mean the only spot on the whole damn road that has no protective railing? What shitty luck. I'll tell you something, if there's anyone who deserved to die in a set of freak circumstances like that, it's Mr. Local Asshole. His whole existence was a bane to society."

Mike was bothered by the frankness of Billy's opinion. Billy truly believed the guy deserved to die. The detective radar was ringing away in his head. Something about Billy Stone wasn't right. He wanted to ask more but Stone looked at his watch and said "Is that it Deputy Westwood? I have to push in on that craps game in three minutes."

That wasn't it, but Mike wasn't sure how to proceed. He couldn't make a move based solely on a hunch, so he stuck his hand out, readying himself for that bone crushing grip. "That'll do it for now Mr. Stone. Thank you for your input."

Billy didn't crush Mike's hand this time. Instead, he held it lightly but firm. He pulled Mike in closer, this time staring directly into his eyes. "I also saw him arguing with the valet captain and the head of security out in the valet area when I got off work. He was adamant that they give him his keys, threatening to sue them and saying that it was against the law to not give a patron their car. He called those poor guys every name in the book, threatened to have their jobs, and insulted their manhood as well. I guess they finally gave in."

Mike released Billy's hand, shook hands with Steph Bartomei, and said "Thank you both. You've provided me with enough information to write a thorough report about this accident. I appreciate your time and your input."

Steph was saying something to Mike about coming back if he ever needed any more input but he didn't hear a word she was saying. He watched Billy Stone as he walked away and was sure that the man was talking to himself. He also had that distant look on his face again.

“I’m going to have to do something about that guy.” Mike thought to himself as he walked out of Harry’s while trying his best to ignore the call of the slot machines.

•••

As Billy walked over to craps 301, he glanced over his shoulder at Mike Westwood, who was exiting the high limit pit. The Dark Thoughts mused in his mind *“We’re going to have to do something about that guy.”* Billy nodded in agreement.

CHAPTER 10
SUPERSTITION

Luck: it was a powerful force in the casino industry. Billy learned over the years at Harry's that luck was a belief in good or bad fortune in life caused by accident or chance, and attributed by some to reasons of faith, or that which happens beyond a person's control. Luck was a way of understanding a personal chance event, sometimes good, other times bad. It happened randomly. This ephemeral, arguably non-existent power ultimately gave birth to a bastard child named Superstition.

Superstition was the means in which an individual or even a society created luck, whether it be good or bad. In the casino, the whim of luck and superstition, and what it brought out in people was a driving force that affected players from the moment they arrived and continued doing so with what they did and how they acted when they walked onto the casino floor. Some people wore the same clothes every time they gambled, no matter how many days in a row or how bad they smelled. Others had a special relic that was meant to bring them good luck such as a picture of their child, or a chip from the casino where they had their biggest winning night. A lucky penny, an attractive stone, a dried-up bat wing, or even a rabbit's foot sometimes served the cause. When a person's game started, their luck was determined by how well they created luck on the game. Many blackjack players tried to play the role of superstitious cheerleader.

"Good luck with that ace!" or, "Double down! It's your time to shine!" or, "Come on Billy, you're my lucky dealer." or, "If we all think positive then positive things will happen."

Some players believed that the best way to create luck on a blackjack game was to get under the dealers' skin by constantly criticizing them or simply trying to piss them off. On the other side of that mentality were those who believed in having the dealer on their side. The best way to do that was to tip. One thing Billy did know, luck or not, was that players who took care of their dealers, if even for a dollar bet every now and then, were better taken care of by those same dealers. Distractions were everywhere. For the people who weren't tipping, oversights due to distraction could end up costing them hundreds of dollars through the course of one night if the dealer didn't care to help them out.

Billy always felt that craps players had the most superstitions in the world of gaming. Craps was a game of methodology. Given the numerous types of bets that could be made on the game, each player could individualize their method of play to suit their own egos, but what truly defined most players were their own personal superstitions. Billy had seen it all through the years, and he was sure he would see even more. From a dealing perspective, there were standard superstitions of courtesy that came with the game: Never send the dice to a player on a number that would cause them to lose, especially the number seven, which caused almost everyone to lose. Some players didn't like to have the dice shipped to them with a seven on the side. Others had a certain number that was lucky for them to set the dice on before they threw them. Many players felt that if anyone uttered or even referred to the number seven, it would roll.

Others believed that if the dealer tumbled the dice as they sent them out, it was surely bad luck; the true believers in that one would ask the stick to bring the dice back into the middle and resend them. Some shooters liked to roll all five dice in front of them until two of them came up paired and shoot those two. Some liked to flip their two dice around before they shot in order to roll a seven off of the dice. The list went on and on. Most of it was irritating, held up the pace of the game, and was unaccepted by the casino management and their rules. Dealers often had to tell players "either pick up the dice and shoot them immediately or we'll pass them to someone else." Players would often fire back "don't mess with me and my dice; you'll ruin my luck." The best response Billy had ever heard from a dealer in that situation was from an Irish dealer named Colm McGowan. He looked at the lady that had said that to him and calmly made the statement while she was still fiddling around with the dice; "Miss, those aren't your dice. You're just borrowing them from Harry's casino until you seven out, then we'll loan them to someone else. As expected, the woman's next roll was seven out. Many players turned all their bets off if the dice went over the table and onto the floor. The catchphrase that invoked that superstition was "Dice on the floor, seven at the door". Dealers often told players that it was bad luck to be superstitious. That one always made them think.

The dealers and pit bosses had their own magic box full of Mojo too. Some dealers liked to whack the dice hard with the stick after the call was made, thus setting off what they thought was an internal vibration that was sure to make a seven roll on the next roll. Billy was prone to holding his open left hand over his right hand that was holding the stick and flashing the peace sign, thus signifying five and two to invoke a seven. Pablo's trick was to call out the point that the shooter was trying to make while the dice were in the air to get a seven. Luis liked to bang his hand on part of the table just as the dice were totaling to try and get his seven. Some dealers picked up several chips from their working stacks and cut them out in front of the boxman in stacks of seven. Boxmen would pull out the plastic paddle that sent the cash down into the drop box and turn it 180 degrees and drop it back into its slot. Other bosses just picked up the dice when they came into the middle of the layout and gave them a squeeze or a special examination. One boss named Krattli would rub all six sides of the dice, as if to rub all the luck off them. No matter which side you were on or what you were hoping for, there was a superstition that you could apply to try and swing the luck in your favor. All the nonsense was trivial until a big money player came along who truly believed in the shit.

One such man was Richard Assopholis, and he insisted that everyone call him Dick. Dick Assopholis. Those two names couldn't have suited one individual better. Mr. Superstitious, as Billy liked to call him, came into Harry's at least once a month. He always wore the same goofball outfit; blue jeans with a long-sleeve denim shirt and a dirty yellow cap. His luck charm was a metal pendant that looked like a fish that he hung around his neck with a leather thong. He carried all his money in a large fanny pack that was always strapped around his waist. Billy was sure that Mr. Superstitious had over fifty thousand dollars in cash inside that pack. No one knew how he made his living, but with that much cash on hand all the time, he couldn't have been doing anything legitimate. The man played craps exclusively and was freak in every aspect of his game.

Mr. Superstitious arrived at Harry's a week after Billy had taken out Mr. Local Asshole. Billy had been dealing on craps 301 as usual. As always, he was hoping to get out early, but this time it was for a special reason. Hope was coming to visit him by herself for the first time since they had been together during Valentine's Day weekend. She was leaving San Francisco around 7 p.m. to avoid the afternoon traffic and to not have to wait too long at the casino for Billy to get off. Depending on the traffic, she would be there before midnight. Even if he didn't get the early out, Billy was just hoping for a smooth night so that he wasn't irritated when he got off. He wanted his time with Hope to be special and relaxing. He hoped that The Dark Thoughts stayed dormant for a while. They had been excited and agitated at the same time after the ordeal with Mr. Local Asshole. Their hunger grew with each kill, and Billy wasn't sure how much control he truly had over them. His plan for the night was to be completely professional and to stay in good dealer mode from start to finish. When he saw Mr. Superstitious lurking outside of the craps game, he knew that plan was about to be challenged.

Mr. Superstitious liked to scope out his craps games before he started playing. Billy wasn't sure if the guy was watching the dealers on the game, looking for weakness, if he was waiting for his favorite spot, or if he was simply trying to feel some luck, but he always watched from about four feet back for at least fifteen minutes before stepping up and wreaking his havoc.

This night, Billy decided to fuck with Mr. Superstitious, just to see if he could get under the guy's skin. Of course, it had to be done with complete professionalism. He thought to himself, "This is going to be interesting" and looked out at the man, locking eyes with him. "Hey Dick. Good to see ya! Come on over here, I've got your favorite spot saved for you." He tapped the palm of his hand on the bumper of the game in front of him.

Mr. Superstitious looked startled, almost scared. He grimaced at Billy and shook his head no. Billy could tell he had made the man nervous. Good start. He smiled at him and said "Good to see you. Hop on in whenever you're comfortable." The look of dread on the man's face made Billy chuckle to himself.

As Billy predicted, after about ten minutes of watching, Mr. Superstitious finally stepped up and pulled out a wad of cash that looked to be about twenty thousand dollars. As usual, it was all wrapped up in rubber bands. Billy knew he had to be ready to book bets for this man in split second fashion because he liked to start the chaos immediately.

In the game of craps, verbal contracts were an integral part of the game. Players called out bets and the dealers booked those bets out loud. If a player called out a bet and the dealer could see that that person had the money in front of them to cover the bet, the dealer repeated the bet, and it would then be considered a binding contract. All of this had to occur before the dice landed and totaled. If the player didn't convey the pertinent information to the dealer in a timely enough fashion, the dealer had to cover theirs and the house's ass by calling out "No bet this roll" which meant there was no contract for that roll of the dice. While players hated to be "no bet", it was necessary at times to ensure that no shots were taken on the house. If a dealer booked a bet for a player without knowing two pertinent bits of information, namely how much they wanted to bet and where they wanted to bet it, the player could take a cheap shot and change their request after the dice totaled. Players that pulled that kind of stunt were called "shot takers" and were basically considered scumbag cheaters.

Mr. Superstitious fell into that category. He would wait until the dice were in the air and then start calling out a bet. Dealers had to be very careful and on-the-spot with him because he would blow up and cause a huge scene if the dealer "no bet" him. This was how he began almost every session of craps he played. He would usually take the shot on an inexperienced dealer or one that was engaged in conversation with another player or the boxman, not paying close attention. Many dealers had been berated by Mr. Superstitious over the years and many bets that weren't booked correctly were paid to him because he constantly took that shot. Billy was amazed that Harry's still allowed him to play in their casino because he was such a consistent shot taker. They probably let him stay because he had lost millions of dollars to them over the last decade. He was a player that they almost always beat, so of course they let him continue like he did and chalked up all the shots taken and dealers berated as collateral damage.

True to form, Mr. Superstitious took his shot on the first roll of the dice after he pulled out his wad of cash. After unbinding the entire wad, he had the money broken down into smaller portions, each of those wrapped in rubber bands as well. Billy had dealt to him enough times over the years to know that those smaller wads were increments of two thousand dollars. He held up one of those smaller wads just as the shooter released the dice and said "I want to bet this on the number nine."

Most dealers would have just called out "no bet" immediately because the dice were already in the air. Then Mr. Superstitious would have exploded and started his whole routine of yelling at the dealer, then arguing with the pit boss. His argument would have been even more vehement if the number nine had rolled; then he would also be demanding to get paid for his bet that was officially no bet. This was where Billy's experience, abilities, and readiness came into strong play. Instead of calling out "no bet", he said out loud "That cash in your left hand will play this roll on the number nine. The house will pay and take to the table limit." The second part of that statement ensured that the bet would be no greater than the allowed maximum of three thousand dollars. If the wad in Mr. Ass' left hand was more than that, only three thousand would be paid or taken.

The dice totaled on the number eight, which had no effect on the bet. Billy decided to rein Mr. Superstitious in immediately to curtail the shot taking. He also wanted to assert the idea in the man's mind that he wasn't going to be pushed around or intimidated. As soon as the dice totaled, he locked eyes with Mr. Ass and said "Sir, you need to do us a favor and book those bets before the dice go in the air. Also, when you book those bets, you need to call out precisely how much you want to bet and exactly where you want to bet it, otherwise you'll have no bet." He needed to establish dominance over this player who liked to prey on weaker dealers.

Mr. Superstitious' face contorted in anger and turned three different shades of red. "What the hell do you mean? Are you threatening to no bet me?"

Billy remained calm. "Sir, that's not a threat. I just need you to work with me so that I can book your bets in a timely fashion; but I still must protect the house's interests, which means that if you try to book those late bets without conveying the pertinent information, you'll have no bet. Now drop that money down so I can set up your bet."

Mr. Superstitious was working himself into his usual frenzy. "I don't want that fucking bet anymore."

Billy remained calm and professional. "All right sir, you currently have no bets on the layout."

The man clearly didn't like being curtailed like that. It didn't allow him to go through his typical routine of harassing the dealer for every little mistake, or getting his shot on. He was getting frustrated already, so he turned on the boxman. "Hey pit boss, your dealer's threatening to no bet me. What the fuck's going on here?"

Luckily, the boxman was Peter, one of Harry's stronger and more experienced pit bosses. He couldn't stand anyone that harassed the dealers and he hated shot takers. He was also a master of politeness and professionalism. He stood up and walked right up to Mr. Superstitious, getting close enough to the man's face to let him know he meant business. "Sir, your play is definitely welcome here, but only if you play the game by our rules. Now Billy here is one of our best dealers, and he just laid out to you exactly what our rules are. If you don't designate how much you want to bet and where when you call out your bets, Billy is required to no bet you. It's that simple."

As Mr. Superstitious worked himself into an even greater state of agitation while arguing with Peter, Billy took a deep breath, let it out slowly, and looked out across the game at the rest of his customers. He locked eyes with an unassuming man who was standing a few feet outside of the game. The man appeared to be watching him intently. He motioned to the man, giving him an invitation to come on in and join the game. The man smiled knowingly and slightly shook his head no thanks then tilted it toward Mr. Superstitious. Billy wondered if this guy was plain clothes observation. None of the employees knew who worked in observation, but occasionally some of them were sent out onto the casino floor to observe games, dealers, and pit bosses from a different angle than the cameras up above. Billy wasn't sure about this man, but he had a look of knowledge and understanding in his eyes; wisdom of the game, if you will.

One of Billy's crew mates tapped him on the shoulder to push him out for a break. Mr. Superstitious was still going at it with Peter so Billy wished the other players on his game "good luck", introduced Vanessa, the incoming dealer, winked at Mr. Unassuming outside the game, and went on his break.

The craps game wasn't hooked up with a blackjack game tonight so when Billy returned from his break, he went straight to the stickperson spot. Mr. Superstitious was still on the game and was currently harassing Vanessa over one of his bets. Since he hadn't been able to get his shot taking on, he had resorted to being bothersome with his numerous superstitions. He had just booked a bet on the number eight by putting down a large stack of chips in varying denominations and screaming "Goddammit, just put all this on the eight!" Vanessa had never dealt to him before, so she had no idea of his long list of superstitions, nor how angry he became when someone broke one of them. She brought the stack of chips in various denominations, referred to in the business as a "barber pole", into the middle of the layout to break it down and figure out how much was there.

When Mr. Superstitious saw this, he blew up. "Don't touch my fucking chips! Just put the whole damn thing on the eight and break it down if it hits!" This wasn't normal procedure. It was also very labor intensive, a pain in the butt for the dealers, and it held up the pace of the game. Vanessa was about ready to cry.

Billy leaned in close to her and said "Hey girl, you've got a break now. Don't let this jackass see you break down or he'll be all over you for the rest of the night. Just put that barber pole on the eight in his spot and go try to relax. We'll take care of it if it hits."

Vanessa looked up at him with a frustrated look on her face. "Thanks Billy."

"Don't worry kid, we all went through it with this son of a bitch."

As Vanessa pushed off to go on her break, Billy thought about what he had just said to her. He wondered how many dealers' lives had been made hell by Mr. Superstitious and his stupid superstitions. He was sure that it wasn't just the numerous dealers at Harry's over the years. The man must have played in many other places and he probably acted the same way everywhere he went. He was a bane.

That last thought made Billy pause for a moment. It was something that The Dark Thoughts would normally be preaching in the back of his mind but he was sure the thought came from him instead. As he watched Mr. Superstitious berate the dealer that replaced Vanessa for touching one of his bets, he began to think to himself that it was time to take action on his own, without prompting from The Dark Thoughts. It was time to formulate a plan.

By the time Billy had pushed off the pole and over to the first base spot opposite of Mr. Superstitious, the dealer that had dealt to him for the last twenty minutes was completely falling apart. At least Tina wasn't as emotional as Vanessa was, but he had gotten under her skin and she was making mistakes left and right. Every time a seven out rolled, Mr. Superstitious yelled at her and blamed her and her "inadequacies" for causing the seven to roll. He had taken to barber poling every bet he made and she had to separate and break down a pile of chips in three different denominations almost every roll of the dice. The dealer that moved over to that side to push Tina out for her break was Jeff, an old worn out dinosaur of a dealer that had the experience to handle Mr. Superstitious, but just didn't give a shit anymore about trying to be good at craps. Billy had seen Jeff and his lazy approach infuriate the man many times over the years.

Mr. Superstitious remembered Jeff. As soon as Jeff pushed in to that side of the game, he looked up at Peter and said "Hey boss, I can't stand having this sloth deal to me. Why don't you get someone more capable of dealing the game to replace him."

Peter looked up from where he was sitting in between Jeff and Billy and said "That's not going to happen, sir. Jeff has twenty-five years of experience dealing craps and he's perfectly adequate." Peter knew like Billy did that Jeff pissed this guy off. He probably wanted to watch the show that was about to ensue.

Mr. Superstitious shook his head and started stuffing his chips into that absurd fanny pack of his. "Why don't you just call up the Sagebrush Steakhouse for me and tell them I want my favorite seat at the end of the bar for dinner as soon as possible."

Peter stood up from his seat and said "Sure thing, sir" as he headed to the podium in the middle of the pit to make the phone call.

Billy was friends with the bartender in The Sagebrush Steakhouse. He and Wild Willie cross-country skied together in the winter. They had shared numerous stories about Mr. Superstitious and his freaky quirks. Wild Willie had told Billy that the man demanded the same seat every time he came in to eat. It was the last seat at the far end of the bar, as far away from any other diners as possible. There was a partition there that blocked off the ordering station where Wild Willie poured drinks for the waiters and waitresses to bring out to the customers on the restaurant floor. He always dined alone, read a paperback book or a magazine while he was eating, and didn't want anyone to talk to him. He ate the same meal every time and Willie was supposed to just order it when he came in, pour him a glass of Duckhorn Vineyards merlot, and serve him without any idle chit chat. The only time he spoke to Willie was when he wanted his glass of wine refilled. He snapped at other customers that tried to talk him and blew up if any of the staff even came close to him. Even though his meals and wine were fully comped by the casino, he never left a tip. Willie couldn't stand the guy any more than Billy could. Billy had always told Willie during these conversations, “Hey bro, at least all you have to do is ignore the guy. I actually have to communicate with him.”

Peter came back from the podium with a smug look on his face. “Sir, there’s someone finishing up their meal in that spot right now. You can have another spot at the bar immediately or they can get you your favorite spot at seven thirty.”

Once again, Mr. Superstitious looked like he was going to blow a vein right out the side of his temple. He snapped at Peter through gritted teeth “Just tell them to hurry the hell up and call as soon as that seat opens up.”

Peter sat back down on the game and said “Oh, absolutely sir”, but made no move to get back on the phone. His subliminal defiance wasn’t lost on Dick Assopholis. His face was almost purple now as he pulled some chips out of his fanny pack and continued playing.

The next push came and Billy stepped over to the other side of the game. He looked at his watch while pushing Jeff out and thought to himself, “Okay, ten more minutes until this bane goes to eat.” He decided to mess with the guy for the next ten minutes to see if he could make him turn purple again. Right off the bat, he picked up one of his barber pole bets that was on the ten, brought it into the middle of the layout, and started to convert it.

“What the fuck are you doing?” Mr. Superstitious exploded. “I’ve told everyone in here including you over and over not to touch my damn bets. Are trying to curse me?” His face was already the color of a plum.

Billy chuckled silently to himself and locked eyes with the man. He smiled his most genuine smile. “You know sir, if you give me four more dollars for this bet, we can buy it and pay you two to one instead of nine for five."

"I don't give a rat's ass if it's proper or not", he screamed. His voice was becoming shrill. "I just don't want anyone to touch my fucking bet until it has to be paid. Is that too much to ask?" The purple shade was becoming deeper by the second.

Billy looked at him with a wry grin on his face and answered noncommittally, "Suit yourself."

Mr. Superstitious expounded to everyone around him. "All I ask is that these damn dealers leave my bets alone until they have to be paid. Why is that such a fucking difficult thing to do? I spend a ton of money here at Harry's every month and you'd think that this one request could be honored." He was flirting with blowing a vein again.

Peter leaned in close to Billy from where he was sitting. "Hey Billy, if you're not careful you're going to give this guy a coronary."

Billy laughed at Peter's crack but the seriousness of what he had said set in and suddenly made Billy think of his visit to Elmer last December. He remembered the one thing that he had asked Elmer to acquire for him that had set his friend aback; hydrogenated cyanide. Hydrogenated cyanide in gaseous form when inhaled caused deadly disturbances to both the central nervous and cardiovascular systems. For the most part, if the dose was concentrated enough, the victim died within minutes of inhalation and standard autopsies revealed the cause of death to be cardiac arrest. It was hard to trace unless the doctor performing the autopsy was looking for cyanide. Billy had told Elmer that he needed to carry it with him while hiking in case he ran into a bear or a mountain lion.

A seven out had just rolled and Mr. Superstitious was banging his fists on the edge of the table in anger. This dude was surely a prime candidate for a coronary. Billy looked up at him and held up his watch, pointing to the face. "It's seven-thirty, Dick. They probably have your seat ready in the steakhouse."

Mr. Superstitious began shoving his chips into that ridiculous fanny pack again, the whole time mumbling to himself about how the game sucked and the dealers were rude and the pit bosses didn't give a shit and the whole place was going downhill. He left with one parting statement. "You guys can all go to hell!" Billy was already formulating a plan in his mind.

When his break came ten minutes later, Billy headed straight down into the bowels of Harry's. He didn't stop to talk to Peter before he left the pit, nor did he stop to bullshit with anyone in the hallway that wove through the employees-only area one floor below the casino. He went straight to his locker where he kept his special attaché case. He unfolded it inside the locker so that the cameras in the hallway couldn't see what he was doing. There was the small spray can of hydrogen cyanide. It looked like a breath spray, small enough to fit in the palm of his hand.

Billy palmed the canister of deadly gas and slipped it into his pants pocket. He looked at his watch: Thirteen more minutes of break. He had to move. He took a different stairwell up to the casino floor so that he didn't have to walk by the craps pit while heading to the Sagebrush Steakhouse. He didn't want anyone wondering what he was doing.

Billy checked his watch as he walked into the restaurant. Nine more minutes of break. Paul, the maître'd was in his usual spot at the entrance in front of a small podium.

"Hey Billy, you need some reservations for later this week? Is your hot little Asian friend coming up?"

"No thanks Paulie. She is on her way right now, but I think I'm going to take her to Evan's on the west shore; something super special. No offense bro."

"You're right bro. Evan's might be the best restaurant in the basin. No offense taken. So what's up?"

"I just want to talk to Wild Willie about maybe doing some cross-country skiing later this week. Is that okay?"

"By all means, my friend. You know where he's at. Enjoy your date by the way."

"Thanks Paulie. Have a relaxing night." Billy knew that Paul's night was about to get interesting. He looked down the bar and saw Mr. Superstitious in his usual spot, his face buried in a paperback book. Wild Willie was at the pouring station handing off some glasses of wine to one of the waiters.

Billy walked to the end of the bar. He made sure to take a wide berth around Mr. Superstitious. He could see that the man was having the French onion soup. It came in a wide bowl and was topped with gruyere cheese and homemade garlic croutons. That was one of Billy's favorites. He came around to the pouring station and caught Willie just as a waiter left with the wine.

Willie looked up and smiled when he saw Billy. "Hey bud. What brings you in here?"

Billy leaned his head inside of the partition that separated the pouring station from where Mr. Superstitious was sitting. He didn't want the man to see him and freak out. It would blow his whole plan. Billy spoke quietly as he rolled his eyes in Mr. Superstitious' direction. "Hey Willie, I just wanted to see if you wanted to go cross-country skiing this Wednesday. You're off aren't you?"

Willie looked a bit dejected. "Sorry Billy, but I have to take my wife shopping in Reno that day. I'll have to take a rain check."

Billy smiled. "It's okay bro. It's going to be about six more weeks before the snow starts to melt, so we'll try again." He looked at his watch. Five minutes. If Willie didn't get distracted quickly, his whole plan would be blown. Luckily, some patrons at the other end of the bar were waving, trying to catch his attention.

"Hey bro, it looks like that couple down there wants something from you. Have fun shopping in Reno. I'll talk to you later."

Willie turned around and acknowledged the couple. "Thanks buddy. Stay on me. I need some exercise. See ya later." He headed down to the other end of the bar, leaving Billy virtually all alone at this moment in time with Mr. Superstitious. He looked at his watch. Three minutes.

Billy looked around the restaurant to make sure his position wasn't compromised. He already knew that there were no cameras in here. The lighting was dim, so no one could see anything from afar. Wild Willie was at the other end of the bar pouring red wine for the couple that he was attending. Currently, there was no one else at the bar. Paul was at his host station with his back to the bar, his face buried in the reservations book. The waiters and waitresses were all out on the restaurant floor. Now was the time. He pulled the small canister of hydrogen cyanide out of his pocket and leaned around the partition from the inside of the bar. Mr. Superstitious still had his face buried in his paperback. Billy gave two quick presses on the spray pump, releasing the colorless and odorless gas in the direction of Mr. Superstitious' face, then quickly walked away from the bar and out of the restaurant. He didn't even look back to see what went down.

"See ya Willie. See ya Paulie. You guys have a good night."

"You too Billy", they said in unison.

Billy walked out onto the casino floor and pushed onto the pole of his craps game with a minute to spare. The outgoing dealer told him that they were coming out, or starting a new roll with a new shooter, and that the shooter would be the lady two to his left if she wanted the dice. Billy's heart was beating rapidly with the excitement of what he had just done and the anticipation of wondering if it had worked, but he remained in full professional mode. He looked at the lady who was in turn to shoot. "Young lady, would you like to shoot some dice?"

Just then, there was a stir at the security booth that was just to the right of the Sagebrush Steakhouse. Four security guards had come from nowhere and were running into the restaurant. One had stopped at the security booth to get the emergency medical duffle bag. Everyone on the game stopped to look until Billy decided to keep the game going. "All right guys, we're coming out and we've got a lucky lady shooter! Get your bets down and set. Bet the eleven or the horn, or perhaps the C and E. Here we go. We're coming out." They all turned their attention back to the game.

Peter's curiosity got the best of him and he stood up from the game and walked over to the Steakhouse. Billy looked over his shoulder and could see Peter talking to Paul, who seemed very animated.

When Peter came back to the game, he sat down across from Billy and leaned in close to him. "It looks like our friend Mr. Assopholis just had a heart attack and fell face first into his bowl of French onion soup. The EMT's are on their way but Paul said it doesn't look good.

Billy looked at Peter and said "Wow. You were right about the coronary." He muttered silently to himself. "Seven, you're out. That's the end of that."

CHAPTER 11

JUNIOR

"Seven a front-line winner; chicken dinner!" The crowd on craps 301 cheered Billy's call. He leaned in close to the player immediately to his left and bent his ear a little while the base dealers were paying the pass line. "I used to think that was one of the most absurd sayings because you know that if you win a bunch of money, you're not going to order chicken for dinner. I'd be ordering filet and lobster with béarnaise sauce." The player chuckled and agreed with him.

Billy continued to pontificate. "Then one day, an older lady on my blackjack game straightened me out as to why that statement really wasn't so absurd. She said was coined during the Great Depression, and back then it was a treat to have chicken on the table for dinner. I stood corrected then and still do to this day. That's why I still use the line."

The player nodded in agreement. "You're absolutely right sir. Thanks for the history lesson." He then reached down and placed a five-dollar chip on the pass line next to his own bet. "That's for you bud."

Billy looked at the man and tapped the stick on the table in front of him. "Hey man, thanks a lot. We appreciate being in the game." He then announced out loud: "Dealers are gambling on the pass compliments of the gentleman on my left. Double up your pass line bets because I'm calling another winner for that chicken dinner."

The crowd roared in approval and a few of them placed line bets of their own for the dealers. Billy wished it was always this easy.

Billy was in a great mood. It had been over a month since Mr. Superstitious had fallen face first into his bowl of French onion soup after his "heart attack" and not a word of suspicion had been raised. Billy was proud of himself and the way he had calmly executed that one: In and out like a ghost, no one remembering that he was even there. He was also content in the knowledge that Vanessa, Tina and numerous other Harry's dealers would never again be reduced to tears by that man and his terrible demeanor. He thought about the many dealers in so many different casinos who would never have to deal with the stress that Mr. Superstitious brought to a craps game and felt that he had done the world justice. He now firmly believed that his new evolution had a sense of purpose: Billy Stone had become a protector of justice; a hero of the common folk who didn't have the means or the wherewithal to stand up for themselves.

He thought about the rest of that weekend, and his time spent with Hope. She had arrived less than two hours after Billy had taken out Mr. Superstitious, and Billy got his early out a half-hour later. Amped by the slickness and perfection of his kill, Billy put his best moves on Hope that night. It was officially their third date, and the second time she would be staying at the cabin with him. To quote his old friend and mentor, Richie from Santa Cruz, "If they come around for a third date, it's time for good things to happen."

As soon as he was pushed off his game, Billy had gone directly over to Hope at the bar, gave her a hug and a kiss, and whispered in her ear "Let's go home and slow dance."

She gave him a surprised but coy smile. "Absolutely".

That night, Hope and Billy grooved the living room of the cabin on Needle Peak to the tunes of Sade, Marvin Gaye, Al Green, Simply Red, and Joss Stone. The old tricks of romance that Richie had taught Billy over the years paid off. He lit candles and incense. They drank a bottle of Silver Oak cabernet sauvignon and ate brie cheese with crackers and apricot jam. They danced some more. Soon, clothes began to fly. They laid on the couch together, touching each other's naked bodies; they fed each other, rubbed each other, held each other, and when the tension finally became too much to bear, they loved each other with passion; a passion that Billy had thought he would never feel again; a passion deeply rooted in the despair of his previous loss but fueled like a bonfire with the gasoline of murder. The killing of Dick Assopholis, the perfection of the act, the planning, and the execution had given Billy a supreme confidence that elevated his romantic and sexual abilities. He brought it hard that night. Hope was amazed. When she left at the end of the weekend, she whispered into his ear after kissing him goodbye "You're an impressive man Billy Stone, and that was one of the most amazing weekends I have ever had". Billy felt that he had established a bond with her that would only grow deeper and stronger. He was on top of the world.

Billy grinned for a moment while remembering his great weekend then shifted his concentration back to the game. He was working with two break-in craps dealers until six o'clock when the better swing shift dealers came in. He was showing off his stick calls, which gave the newbies some ammo for their own repertoire.

Billy was on his game tonight. He called another come-out winner. "Yo eleven! Just another winner on the pass line! It's not my eleven, it's yo eleven! Yooo...landa. That's my favorite hooker's name". The customers on the game were dying of laughter. The break-in dealers looked at him like he was insane. Billy knew that some of his calls were borderline offensive, but he had the crowd in stitches and in the palm of his hand right now. Everyone was having a grand time and no one was going to butt in and put a stop to it. Billy was fully in command of his element. He looked around at all the customers on the game, checking to see if there was anyone playing who could potentially try to ruin everyone's fun. While he was showing off his dealing skills, he was still on the hunt for any potential targets.

Billy shipped the dice out to the shooter and made another call as they totaled. "Four easy! Little Joe from Reno! Your point is now four folks. Bet it hard so that Little Joe comes back from Akron Ohio; the rubber tire capitol of the world F.Y.I.". Half of the players on the game were in stitches with laughter. The rest looked confused. The number four had been nicknamed "Little Joe" for longer than most craps dealers had been alive. No one was sure why, but many thought it might have been a reference to Joe Cartwright from the old television show Bonanza, which took place on the Ponderosa Ranch just outside of Incline Village on the north shore. The call could always be changed up to keep the flavor fresh. Little Joe could be from anywhere that ended in the letter "o": Toledo, Ohio, Reno, San Francisco, Lake Tahoe, and so on and so forth.

Billy continued the entertainment as the dice kept rolling. The players were thoroughly enjoying themselves. “Five! Fever dice! Fever in the funk house, boys are in the bunkhouse. Run girls run! Six easy, no field! Two by four. The lumber number. Twelve craps! Big Daddy. Boxcars, freight trains, whips and chains. Crapus Maximus! Pay double in the field! Ten, ten, the big fat end! Ten easy folks; that’s Tennessee Toddy, all booty and no body. Nine! Nena from Pasadena. Nena Ross, the mean old pit boss. Three, ace-deuce! Come again. The old one-two! Ten the hard way! Two fives; the stars from Mars; Two Texas sunflowers”. When the shooter finally repeated the four for a front-line winner, it rolled the hard way, or a pair of twos. Billy really let them have it then with extra exuberance; “Four a hard way winner! Kung Pao chicken dinner! How do ducks go to the pond? Two by two folks. The river chickens have arrived! All the hard way bettors get seven to one and the dealers win too! What a great country we live in huh folks?” The crowd erupted in victory.

Billy looked around while the base dealers were paying the pass line. His game and his stick calls had drawn a crowd almost three people deep. On the outskirts of the game, he saw a set of piercing eyes staring not at the craps game like everyone else was, but directly at him. It was that unassuming man that had been watching him last month on the night he had disposed of Mr. Superstitious. He smiled at Billy with that same slight grin and nodded with that same look of knowledge, like a master sensei would stare at his star pupil who had just completed a difficult Kata. Billy winked at Mr. Unassuming and turned his attention back to the game to start authorizing the hard way payouts. If the man truly was plain clothes observation, he was getting a good show.

Now that the game was fired up, Billy had to pay closer attention to what was going on, not only with the players on the game, but the players outside the game as well. Many of them wanted to squeeze in and get a piece of the action. Both sides of the game already had more players than the usual limit of eight. The break-in dealers were beginning to struggle. It was chaotic times like this when cheaters tried to take cheap shots on weak dealers. Billy glanced around the game, looking for anyone that appeared suspicious. He looked at his watch. It was ten minutes 'til six. The more capable swing shift craps dealers would arrive on the hour and replace the break-ins. He was sure he could hold things together for ten minutes.

A pack of young guys was congregating outside of the game on the side that Billy would go to when he got pushed off the stick at six. They were a typical group of rich college kids with their hair gelled up in the unkempt fashion of the time, their hands stuffed into the pockets of their ratty designer jeans, their pointed-toed crocodile skin, snake skin, or Italian leather shoes, and their club shirts hanging out with the unbuttoned cuffs turned up just off the wrist to expose their Invicta, Gucci, Fossil, or Dolce watches. They looked clueless. Billy called it a pack because this was how young guys ran in the casinos these days; a bunch of dudes cruising around looking for girls, thrills, and alcohol, not necessarily in that order but as much of all three as possible. One of them would surely emerge as the Alpha Male of the group. He would be the one whose parents had money and the home on the lake, and most likely the one with the drugs.

These guys looked like they were ready to go out clubbing, so party drugs were sure to be involved.

As Billy predicted, the leader of this pack sauntered up with a fat cigar hanging out of the corner of his mouth and put his arms around two of his buddies that were standing closest to the craps game. His black club shirt had what appeared to be a hand-stitched tiger that came off the shoulders and went down the front of the shirt. It looked like the tiger was about to leap off the shirt and attack; well-made and expensive. He wore a thick gold rope chain and a gold Rolex watch. This guy definitely had some money, or at least his parents did. His features were Mediterranean or perhaps even Arab. His jet-black shoulder length hair was gelled back to perfection. The dude looked like a rock star. He had an arrogant look on his face.

He was also rude and obnoxious. "All right boys, I'm gonna show you mother fuckers how to play some craps!" He squeezed into the game between a husband and wife without a word of apology, any regard for the fact that they appeared to be together, nor any concern that the husband was currently the shooter. It was bad craps etiquette to worm in next to the shooter. All the superstitious people believed that it ruined the shooter's mojo and brought a seven out. He started screaming. "Come on! Let's fire this mother fucker up!"

The Dark Thoughts, dormant since before the Mr. Superstitious incident, suddenly came to life. *"This douche bag reeks of that which needs to be removed. Engage and find his weakness!"*

Billy winced. He had been thinking the same thing, but he was planning to proceed with caution. Maybe this young man was like most other males his age; fired up on testosterone, Red Bull, and vodka. Young guys usually couldn't handle the excitement of gambling, nor what it did to their behavior. While The Dark Thoughts were always ready to attack, the sensible side of Billy's conscience wanted to make sure it was warranted first.

The kid was reaching into his pocket, digging hard for something; most likely his chips or a wad of money that Billy was sure he would immediately start throwing around to assert his importance. In his fidgeting, he was elbowing the shooter, drawing irritated looks from him and the other players. It always amazed Billy how one idiot could ruin the flow of a whole craps game. He shipped the dice out to the shooter and tapped the stick in front of the kid. "Hey bud, the shooter's right next to you. Give him a little room would ya?"

The kid kept digging around in his pocket. "Whatever dude."

Billy was beginning to think that The Dark Thoughts were right on this one. They had been correct in their assessments so far. The shooter took a few seconds to set the dice the way he liked before tossing them. He was just about to throw them when the kid reached out right over his arm and tossed a strange looking chip into the field. This caused the shooter to balk and elicited angry words from many of the other players.

"Hey man, watch what you're doing! The guy is trying to shoot!"

"Hey punk, why don't you go ruin someone else's craps game?"

"Give the shooter some damn room!"

While the shooter gathered himself and re-set the dice to start his shooting routine, Billy examined the oversized chip that the kid had put in the field. It was larger than Harry's regular chips. It showed a $1000 denomination on its face. While it did have a Harry's logo on the side that faced up, it also had a four-digit serial number stamped into its edge. It all suddenly came together for Billy as the shooter was finally starting his delivery without any distractions. College kid was screaming "Come on! Just one fucking field roll!" Billy had about two seconds to study that chip from the stickperson's spot, decipher what was on it, and realize what was wrong with the picture before the shooter threw the dice. Such was the nature of the game of craps; major decisions had to be made in a matter of seconds or even split-seconds to determine if a bet was a legitimate bet. Billy was never afraid to make a tough decision that could end up being controversial. After all, he was protecting the company's money. He recognized the oversized chip as a promotional chip that was sent to high end players to entice them to come back to that property. Win or lose, the chip was done, but if it won, the casino had to pay out whatever the chip was worth. The main hitch with these promo chips though, was that they were registered to one player only and were non-transferrable. To play the chip, the player to whom it was issued had to provide his or her players card and photo identification confirming that it was being played by the individual it had been issued to. The kid was screaming for a "mother fucking twelve", the other players were screaming for the point, and the shooter was beginning his delivery of the dice. There was no time to stop play and find out if the promo chip actually belonged to this kid, so Billy used the end of the stick to push it out of the field and called it "no bet". He then quickly turned his attention to the other end of the game where the dice were totaling and prayed they would land on a losing number for the field. Unfortunately, it was a field roll. Even worse, it was the twelve that the kid had been screaming for. Billy called it as he saw it. There was nothing else he could do. "Twelve. Come again and pay double in the field."

As the kid erupted in joy and screamed, "Yeeeaahhh boys! I just won two thousand fucking dollars!" Billy was already trying to wave down Peter from the middle of the pit to let him know there was going to be a situation. The kid was now staring at the chip where it rested on a "no action" portion of the layout and demanding "What the FUCK happened to my field bet? Hey man! I put that thousand-dollar fuckin' chip in the field and that dealer there moved it out before the dice totaled! Twelve was the roll so you guys owe me two thousand dollars! Roll the fucking tape! You all know I had a bet." He motioned to the other players on the game, most of whom didn't want to say a word in his favor because he was such a jackass.

Peter listened to Billy's rundown of the situation, then stepped outside the game and confronted the young man. "Sir, how did you get that chip?"

The kid immediately became indignant. "You fuckers sent it to me in the mail! The letter said I could play it as a thousand-dollar bet if I showed up before April 15th."

Peter laid the hammer down on the kid immediately. "Well sir, if you read that part of the letter, surely you read the next part of the letter that stated you must have the players card that the chip was issued to and photo identification to prove the chip was issued to you, and then you must show all three pieces if information to the pit boss on the game before you actually play the chip; none of which you have done." He then changed his tone to one of diplomacy. "If you have your player's card, then all you have to do is show me some photo identification that proves you truly are the individual that this chip was issued to and I will pay you the two thousand dollars."

The kid became even more arrogant as he pulled out his wallet that was filled to bursting with numerous different credit cards and casino tracking cards. He fumbled through one of the deeper hidden compartments, produced a Harry's Platinum card and his driver's license and threw them both onto the layout of the craps game. "After you pay me the two thousand dollars that you already owe me, why don't you give me a marker for five thousand dollars! Come on! Let's play some fuckin' craps!" It was almost as if he were challenging Peter and the whole crew to a game of craps.

Billy looked down at the name on the card before Peter picked it up. It said Dominic Khalajian. The kid was Armenian. The driver's license said he was from San Diego. Thoughts started coming together in Billy's mind. The Armenians in San Diego were a tight-knit community, and they controlled virtually all the food and beverage distribution business south of Los Angeles County. Translation: they were mobsters. There was still something about the name Khalajian that put up a red flag in the back of Billy's mind. It wasn't coming to him though.

Billy kept the game moving while young Mr. Khalajian complained loudly to anyone and everyone in general. "This fuckin' place owes me two thousand dollars! That dealer on the stick moved my bet out of the field and called it no bet right before a twelve rolled! What the hell is that?" The only people paying any attention to him were the club-clad members of his posse. Billy expected to hear an "amen" come from that congregation with all the preaching that was going on. He kept the game moving but his stick calls had become more businesslike. In between rolls he watched Peter at the podium in the middle of the pit speaking to John Hughes about the incident.

The kid began to yell at Peter across the game. "Hey pit boss! You owe me two grand man! Roll the damn tape! You know that bet was in the field! ...and where's my marker? Why don't you at least give that money so I get in the fuckin' game?"

Johnny Nine appeared to be fed up with this punk and his behavior. He walked outside of the game and engaged him. Billy noticed that he hit the kid with the nub handshake immediately. Then he started in on the foul language policy. At least he was reigning this punk in quickly. Once the youngster knew he was talking to a manager his demeanor toned down immediately. He apologized for the foul language and tried to rationally plead his case. He motioned to Billy a few times during the exchange. The Dark Thoughts shared an opinion with Billy. *"What an ass-kissing punk that guy is; sucking up to the manager like that. You should take him out on that fact alone."*

Billy felt a tap on his shoulder. It was Luis. "Hey bro, I'm on this game now. Those day shifters are going home."

Billy felt relieved to have an experienced crew on the game now; especially with the potentially nasty situation developing with young Mr. Khalajian out there. While watching John Hughes talk with the punk, Billy gave Luis the rundown. "Hey Luis, the shooter is four to the left. That kid in the black club shirt that's talking to Johnny Nine out there is seven different kinds of trouble so watch out. He's waiting for a five-thousand-dollar marker and a decision on a promo chip that I no-bet him on when he threw it in the field a few rolls ago, so pay close attention in case he tries to send it in again. The shooter just came out on ten. Oh, and by the way, good to see you."

As Billy walked around the game, he eavesdropped on the conversation between Johnny Nine and the punk. John was smoothing things out and wrapping him up nicely. "So anyway Mr. Khalajian, we apologize for the misunderstanding. My dealer was just doing his job because the chip must be verified before you can play it. Since our records show that it is your chip and you are you, we're going to give you the two thousand dollars. Now do you still want that marker for the five thousand as well?"

"Yes sir, I do." Young Mr. Khalajian had a smug look on his face as he shook Johnny's hand and turned back to the craps game. Billy was pushing in to that side of the game. He would have to deal to this jackass for at least the next twenty minutes. "All right boys, gather around! All I need is one thirty-minute shooter to take this fuckin' place down! Gimme my seven grand, dealer!"

Peter tossed a lammer for five thousand dollars on the layout next to Billy and whispered in his ear. "Give Junior there his five thousand. We'll give him the other two grand for the field bet after I call observation. Don't be riled Billy; you did your job absolutely correct out there. None of this is your fault. The kid is just a spoiled arrogant douche bag who is probably spending his father's money."

Billy didn't process a word that Peter had said. The statement made by Junior; "All I need is one thirty-minute shooter to take this fuckin' place down!" was still echoing in his head. Something about it reminded him of something from the past that he just couldn't grasp, especially with Peter yapping in his ear. When Peter said something about "his father's money", The Dark Thoughts stepped in and provided the answer. *"Remember Dominic Khalajian .... old rotten bastard from San Diego....ran with a posse of suck-ass friends just like this kid, but forty years older? That asshole never bet for the dealers, but whenever a new shooter started their roll, he would throw a twenty-five-dollar chip to the stick and say, "Yo stick, put that under the shooter's bet! All I need is one thirty-minute shooter to take this fuckin' place down!"*

Billy now understood his unease. He turned in close to Peter's ear and said "Hey man, I've dealt to this kid's dad before. They've got the exact same name. I'll bet you this punk's player's card and the promo chip both belong to his father. We should hold off on that marker for a minute so you can check."

Peter looked Billy squarely in the eye. "John Hughes checked out his info and said it's all up to snuff. He's the one that ok'd the marker. I think we're all right here Billy."

At this juncture, Billy would normally have backed off and done what his supervisor told him, but he couldn't shake the intense feeling that The Dark Thoughts were right about this one. "Peter, please just humor me for thirty seconds and bring up the player profile with the card he gave you and check the date of birth. Please Peter. I have a strong feeling about this one."

Peter didn't look like he believed one iota of what Billy was saying, but he raised one eyebrow, picked up the lammer, and acquiesced anyway. A few minutes went by, the current shooter was doing well, and Junior started to get snippy. "Where's my money goddamnit? You guys are costing me so much right now by not letting me in for this guy's incredible roll. What the hell's wrong with this place?"

Billy leaned out over the game to get closer to Junior's face. At close range, he could tell that the kid's pupils were the size of dimes. He was probably high on ecstasy. He shouldn't have been acting so nasty while under the influence the euphoric little pill. Billy wondered how bad this guy was without the drugs. "Don't worry bud, as soon as Peter gets off the phone we'll get you taken care of." He hoped that statement had more than one meaning. This punk now had a name in Billy's mind: Junior.

Billy looked over and saw John Hughes striding rapidly through the main pit, heading directly for the craps pit. He walked right up to the computer screen that probably had Dominic Khalajian's profile up and squinted at it while Peter bent his ear with the rundown on the situation. He then took the Platinum card and the driver's license and went around the outside of the game to confront Junior.

Peter came back over to the game and whispered in Billy's ear. "Damn dude. You were right on it on that one. The player's card profile says that he's sixty-three years old. Junior probably swiped Daddy's card and his big promo chip and decided to have some fun on the Old Man's dime. Maybe Dominic Senior put him up to it. Who knows? Either way, it's against the law. I just love catching assholes when they're trying to get it on. I'm sure you'll be getting a positive write-up for this one."

Billy just stared out into the crowd and grinned as he heard Junior explode outside the craps game. "What the fuck are you talking about? This is my card and my driver's license. I want my damn marker, or at least the money you owe me for your dealer's fuck-up! In fact," he pointed his index finger directly at John's chest, "I want to talk to your boss. I know Jerry Colucci and a few other people who will fire you instantly if they knew how you've been treating me. My Dad is one of Harry's biggest players down in Vegas! I want to talk to someone above you right now!" Junior was throwing a veritable temper tantrum.

John Hughes remained calm throughout Junior's tirade, stared at him for a drawn-out moment, then proceeded to set him straight. "Listen son, the information we have connected to this player's card says that you're sixty-three years old and that the account was established over twenty years ago. You probably weren't even a toddler then so you couldn't have established this account yourself. If your father is the Dominic Khalajian that owns this account, then yes, he is one of our bigger players, but as far as Vegas goes, we don't own any casinos down there. You might also know Jerry Colucci and a few of his cronies but you'll have to go to The Atlantis in Reno if you want to talk to them. They haven't worked here for years. You won't be getting a marker of any type, you're not getting any action for that promo chip that was issued to your father, and you won't be talking to my boss either. What you just did here is against the law and I could and should eighty-six you from this property for life, call the Douglas County Sheriff's, and charge you with fraud. Since your Dad is one of our better players though, I'm going to let you stick around if you behave yourself and don't try to use this player's card or that chip again. I'm not even sure your father knows what you're doing here so be warned; no more chances."

Junior didn't look the least bit pleased at being chastised like that, but he didn't have anywhere else to go with his argument. He looked at John's nametag and said to him "John Hughes; I'll be sure to let my father know how well you've treated me here at Harry's sir." He pulled a wad of hundred dollar bills out of his front pocket and waved it in John's face. "Do you guys still accept cash or is my money no good here either?"

Billy could tell that John was done with this arrogant son-of-a-mobster. He gave him one of the standard brush-off lines. "Good luck to you and have a good time while you're here."

"Whatever dude." Junior turned back to the game and threw his wad out on the layout without checking to see where the dice were at. The dice were in the air when the cash came flying in and the path of one die was affected by some of the bills. As the dice totaled on seven, Luis called it without hesitation and lit Junior up with the same breath. "Seven out! Hey kid, you need to beware of where the dice are before you go throwing anything into the game. Have some respect for the other players!"

The other players were yelling at him too. Some of them began to stack their chips down on the layout so they could color up and leave.

"Hey buddy! Thanks for ruining our good craps game! You're gonna be here by yourself if you keep that shit up!"

"Why don't you come back in a few years after you grow up and learn some respect for the game?"

Junior just mumbled under his breath "Fuck you guys. You peons don't know what kind of power my family has. If you knew you'd all be scared." Then he raised his voice in Billy's direction. "Hey dealer, are you going to make change for me or do you just want to steal that money from me too? Come on! What's the delay?"

Billy stopped everything he was doing, calmly looked up at Junior, locked eyes with him, and said "I'll be with you as soon as I clean up these losing bets from the seven out that you just caused." He knew he was flirting with trouble if he continued to piss this kid off, but he had to take at least one more jab at him. He slowly gathered up the hundreds that were spread out over half the layout, arranged them neatly, and began the counting process. He could have made change for Junior much more quickly and efficiently, but he wanted to raise the punk's level of agitation just a bit more by taking his time. Luis was tuned in with what Billy was doing and shipped the dice out to the new shooter before he was halfway through with the wad.

Junior indeed became more irritated and screamed "Where are my fucking chips? Hey, wait a minute! I want a bet on the pass!"

Billy was still laying out the last of Junior's hundreds in stacks of five, agonizingly slow. Luis shot back at Junior without looking at him. "The dice wait for no man and very few women. You have no bet; the dice are out!" In a perfect chain of events, the shooter picked up two dice and fired them right out. Junior was trying to yell something out about still wanting a pass line bet. Billy and Luis yelled in unison "No bet!" Luis then made the call as the dice totaled. "Eleven, a pass line winner! Pay all pass line bets!"

Junior was losing it. He blew up again. "Hey! I wanted a hundred-dollar pass line bet! Why is everyone around here trying to fuck me?"

The Dark Thoughts had an answer that only Billy could hear. *"You fucked yourself, Junior, by acting the way you do. You think that your money, or your Dad's money, allows you to be demanding, rude, and arrogant with no manners whatsoever. In truth, you were fucked by your parents who obviously didn't teach you to appreciate the position of power that you were born into. You're the exact image of your father with your posse of suck-ups following you around while you treat them and everyone else you encounter like peons. You are merely the spawn of a rich and powerful asshole, evolving into the exact same bane to society that your father is; one that needs to be removed. The world will be a better place without you around."*

Billy knew now that he had a target. It was time to switch to Good Dealer mode and wait for The Dark Thoughts to come up with a plan. "All right bud, you have three thousand cash here. Do you want a stack of nickels in that mix?"

Junior remained arrogant. "Just give me hundreds and quarters and I'll take it from there."

Billy could tell that this kid hadn't mastered any of the nuances of the game of craps and would proceed to be a labor-intensive player. He pushed out three stacks of chips to Junior. "There you go Mr. K. Here's two thousand in hundreds and one thousand in quarters. Good luck to you."

Just as Billy expected, Junior gave him back three black chips and said "Give a hundred dollars each in red to my friends here dealer."

Billy almost laughed out loud. Instead, he handed out three stacks of five dollar chips to Junior's cronies without comment. One of them tapped Junior on his left pants pocket and whispered something in his ear. Billy watched closely while Junior reached into the pocket and handed his friend what appeared to be an inhaler device for cocaine called a bullet. The friend took the bullet, slipped it into his own pocket, and headed directly for the nearest restroom. So this young man that Billy was aptly calling Junior had it all: His family was not only rich but also mob-related; his father was a big player with Harry's and most likely owned a home in one of the more exclusive neighborhoods of Tahoe where Junior and his whole gang of suck-ups were probably staying for the weekend, and he had control of all the party drugs that these young men would be consuming during their stay. Junior had control of his friends' lives during this trip for all the wrong reasons.

The Dark Thoughts were giddy with anticipation for this one. *"You have a chance right here to cut a thread that has been woven for generations of mobsters, criminals, and assholes. If you take Junior out tonight, you will have destroyed one branch of an evil tree that could possibly grow into a powerful and prolific entity of its own. You take this kid out now and he will never be able to plant seeds that would bring forth the spawn that came from his breeding. Target Junior. Watch him. Be a good dealer and engage him. Figure out his weakness and be ready to strike when the time is right. We will guide you and show you how to make the world much better by removing another growing cancer of society."*

Billy agreed with everything The Dark Thoughts had to say. He reached underneath the table by his left knee and grabbed a tailored rectangle of leather that hung there from a hook. It was the same size as the spots on the railing of the game where players kept their chips and was used to cover a person's chips and hold their spot if they had to take a phone call, or step away for any reason, such as going to the restroom to snort some coke. He handed the cover to Junior and said "Hey man, use this to cover up your friend's spot and his chips. That way no one will try to slip in there. This is a genuine simulated Naugahyde impenetrable chip cover."

The helping gesture and the timely joke loosened Junior up a bit. He chuckled and said out loud to his cronies "At least this dealer knows how to treat a High Roller. You keep kissing my ass the right way and I might even have to tip you Billy."

Junior's suck-ups all laughed out loud at his comment. Normally, Billy would have henceforth made Junior's life on this game hell for making such a degrading comment, but he needed to maintain some good will with his target until The Dark Thoughts provided a plan to truly send him to hell. He patiently stood there and ignored them all.

Luis stared at Billy from the stick with one of those "what the fuck?" looks on his face. Billy leaned in and whispered to him "Don't worry bro. I'm in a good mood tonight. I can take it."

The Dark Thoughts whispered in Billy's mind with evil intent. *"After tonight, you won't have to take any shit from this punk ever again, and neither will anyone else. Find out where they're planning to party tonight. They might want to go to the club across the street."*

The friend whose spot was being saved returned with the cocaine bullet. His left nostril still had a white ring around it. He slipped the bullet back to Junior, who immediately handed it over to the friend on his right. They were all inconspicuous enough that no one would notice what they were doing unless they were paying close attention. Even if someone was watching them closely, most people didn't have a deep enough understanding of the drug culture to realize what was going on. Billy on the other hand knew exactly what they were up to. They all had dilated pupils which meant they were already on some sort of psychoactive drug. Billy guessed it was ecstasy since they were all able to maintain themselves in public. The coke would keep them amped for most of the evening while they were partying; all the way into the wee hours of the morning. If they went to the club, they would probably slingshot their ecstasy buzz with another hit of the love drug. He wondered if these guys were evil enough to try to dose some innocent young females if they didn't have the skills to pick up on any of them. He figured the answer was yes. He looked up at the friend with the ring around his nose, made eye contact, and subliminally cleaned both nostrils with his forefinger and thumb. The young man knew exactly what he was signaling and proceeded to wipe the cocaine residue from his left nostril. Drugs would somehow be the key to unlocking Junior's weakness, then Billy could steer him toward a position of compromise.

Billy winced as a vision invaded his mind. It was a crystal-clear image of one of the VIP booths in Altitude, the club in the casino across the street. Billy had sat in that booth with Richie numerous times over the years. They had partied like rock stars there with many different women, each time doing the same types of drugs that Junior and his punk-ass buddies were partaking in tonight. He knew the image came from The Dark Thoughts. It was a sign. He had to send Junior to Club Altitude.

Billy checked his watch. It was getting close to the next push which meant he would move to the other base position and Luis would be dealing to Junior and his gang. He didn't want to have to rush his manipulation of Junior, nor did he want to lose his chance to engage him. He leaned across the game close to Luis as the next dealer was tapping him out. "Hey man, why don't you push around me for this twenty so you don't have to deal with these punks. I can handle them for another twenty minutes. I might even be able to run them off."

Luis looked at Billy, confused. "Hey bro, I appreciate the kind gesture but you know I can handle these guys."

Billy needed to come up with a compelling reason to convince Luis to push around him. "Oh, I know you can handle them bro. I just want to see if I've got what it takes to squeeze a tip out of Junior here. I'll bet you cocktails after work that I can do it. Consider it a personal challenge."

Luis laughed. "You may as well just plan on buying Red Bull and Jagermeister for me all evening." He went around Billy on the inside of the game and pushed into the other base.

That part taken care of, Billy now had twenty more minutes to get it into Junior's mind that Club Altitude was the place to go tonight. He didn't think it would be too hard to convince him since it truly was the hottest club in South Lake Tahoe. The hard part would be getting him and his boys to get one of the booths. He wasn't sure why that image was so strong in his mind, but if it was a clue from The Dark Thoughts, it had to be a part of their plan.

Even though he still wasn't one hundred percent sure of which direction it needed to go, Billy began his engagement with Junior. He had just paid a pass line winner when the point was ten, which paid a healthy two to one for the odds bets. Even better, it was a hard ten that paid seven to one on the hard way bet, on which Junior had recklessly bet a hundred dollars. He had won fourteen hundred dollars on that one roll and was screaming at the top of his lungs "Just one thirty-minute shooter and I'll take this fuckin' place down."

Billy stuck his closed fist out in front of Junior and gave him the proverbial fist-bump. "Good job man. You keep that up and you'll be able to grab a VIP booth in the club tonight. It's gonna be hoppin' over at Altitude later."

Junior immediately perked up, interested. "Hey man, I heard Club Blue Hue over at the Blue Mountain casino down the street was the best one in town these days."

Billy was steadfast in his convincing, mainly because none of the clubs in the other casinos could stand up to Club Altitude. It had been the veritable hot spot for years. "Don't even bother with those other posers bro. Club Altitude has like six or eight VIP booths, all with their own private unisex restroom facilities. They also have topless cage dancers on Friday and Saturday nights, and all the internationals go there too; the place is packed with Brazilian, Polish, Russian, Hispanic, and Asian women every weekend .... and that doesn't include the California college chicks. That place rocks hard every weekend. No doubt that's where you want to go.

Junior wasn't completely sold yet. He looked a Billy with a hint of skepticism. "You probably have a connection over there that kicks you down some cash for every party you get to buy one of those booths for the night. I think you're trying to hustle me, Billy from San Diego. You don't want to mess with me dude. Have you ever heard of South County Food and Beverage Distributors? My family owns that business and we have a lot of influence down there." He gave Billy a look that meant the word "influence" had a much stronger meaning.

A sudden revelation came to Billy's mind as Junior was threatening him. Whether it was a signal from The Dark Thoughts or his own idea, he wasn't sure, but he remembered right then that Club Altitude honored comp points from Harry's casino for Platinum players. He had been with Richie one night when his old roommate had paid for one of those booths with a player's card that wasn't his. When Billy had asked Richie if there could be any trouble, Richie calmly assured him that it would work like a charm.

"Brother, this card belongs to a long-time customer and friend of mine. I know it will work because the club doesn't take the time to make sure the transaction is legit. They just swipe the card through a reader that tells them if the comp funds are available and then charge Harry's rewards center the next day. The only time a problem comes up is if the card holder disputes the charge, and my friend isn't going to do that."

Billy had his knockout punch for convincing Junior to go to Club Altitude. He leaned across the craps game in front of

Junior and gestured him in close, as if he were sharing a secret. "Hey Bro, I'm not trying to hustle you; and by the way, I haven't lived in San Diego since I was a teen-ager, but I do know this: You can use the comp points from your Dad's card to get one of those VIP booths. They have a program for Harry's high end customers since we don't have a club, but they aren't tapped directly into our computer system, so your Dad's card and your driver's license should work just fine. The charges for any given night don't come over here until the next day, so no one here will be able to dispute it until it's too late. Of course, if word comes back here with my name attached to it, I'll lie and pretend to know nothing about it. You can let your Dad deal with the problem by then."

Junior seemed to like this idea. He tossed his chips down on the layout and stated out loud to his suck-ups "We're goin' clubbin' boys, and Club Altitude is the happenin' spot. I'm taking everyone out to dinner in the steak house first. Let's tear it up boys!"

It was rude for players to throw their chips out on the layout in a huge mess when they wanted to color up. Most people stacked them so that the dealer didn't have to sift through a mess to count them. Normally, when players did this, Billy looked at them and said "Sir, is that a bet in the field? Because if you don't put your chips down on the layout in stacks, it's considered a bet." Then he would watch as the player scrambled to pull his chips back and arrange them neatly. Billy had a different agenda with this player though. Instead of reacting to Junoir's rudeness, he bent out over the layout and started mucking through the chips, separating and stacking them. He then proceeded to cut the chips out on the layout in front of the boxman so that they could both determine how much Junior had. It was Four thousand two hundred and thirty dollars.

After confirming the amount with Peter and the stickperson, Billy looked up at Junior. "You have forty-two thirty young man. Good work. Now you can buy your boys some dinner at the Sagebrush Steakhouse." He handed Junior four one thousand dollar chips, two hundred dollar chips, a quarter, and a nickel.

A good tipper would have thrown in one of the hundred dollar chips or at least the thirty bucks for the dealers. Junior made a big deal of tossing in the five-dollar chip. "Hey Billy from San Diego, my Dad told me to never tip the dealers because they're a bunch of hustlers, but you were cool to me."

As Junior walked away with his gang, Billy picked up the lone five-dollar chip from the layout and stared at it. What he wanted to do was take that chip and jam it into Junior's ass sideways, ripping and tearing everything it contacted. Instead, he dropped it into the plastic box where the tips went. It made a solitary "clunk" when it hit bottom. Luis looked at him skeptically from the other base. Billy grinned at him and said "You owe me cocktails after work." He stared out over the crowd as Junior walked away with his posse. Once again he saw Mr. Unassuming staring back at him from outside the game with that same look of knowledge.

Billy winked at him again, smiled, and went about his business. He was starting to get a bad vibe from this guy. As he pondered what to do now that he was sure Junior would be in one of the VIP booths tonight in Club Altitude, he couldn't shake the feeling that the watching Mr. Unassuming would be trouble in the future.

•••

When Billy got off at midnight, he told Luis to meet him up at the UCL when he got off at two. He hoped two hours and some guidance from The Dark Thoughts would be enough for him to remove the bane that was named Junior.

Downstairs in front of his locker, Billy pondered his plan of attack. He didn't want to engage any target physically unless it was necessary. He considered the cyanide, but an apparent heart attack was much less believable when it happened to a young man in his early twenties as opposed to an old stressed out bastard like Mr. Superstitious. The coroner might look a little bit deeper into that one.

While Billy worked his locker combination, the contents of his special attaché case flittered through his mind. There was still the small pressurized canister of cyanide, and two left over doses of the GHB he had used on Mr. Vegas. The thought of Mr. Vegas made him wonder how long it would take the rats in that mineshaft to completely devour the body. He was becoming concerned about that nosy detective Westwood, but he was sure that there was no way the man could be led or directed toward that mineshaft.

The Dark Thoughts began to ramble almost incoherently in Billy's mind. *".... lot of drugs, those kids .... so much cocaine...combined with ecstasy .... throw in a little bit more and someone could die of an overdose."*

Inspired, Billy opened the attaché and stared at the contents. The vial of cocaine strapped next to the container of ether made him think. "Freebase cocaine; would a kid like Junior go so far? Anyone with a serious drug problem would. He would probably hide that one from his friends as well."

He thought about mixing the freebased cocaine with the heroin as well. A speedball like that would surely make a person's heart stop.

Still unsure of how the plan would come together, Billy stuffed two syringes, a pair of rubber gloves, the ether, the coke, the cooking apparatus, a lighter and the heroin vial into his front pockets. He grabbed the GHB as well just in case it would come in handy, changed into a spare club shirt that he kept in his locker, and headed back up to the casino floor and toward the UCL. He needed to establish an alibi on the off chance something went astray.

"What's up Billy my man? How was your Friday night?" Paulie the bartender still had that infectiously positive demeanor, even after a busy Friday night. "You want your usual Jager and a beertini?"

Billy shook Paulie's hand and sat down. "Absolutely my friend."

Paulie began to pour the chilled dark liquor into a double shot glass. "Tough night tonight? You want a double?"

Billy slipped a twenty into the bill acceptor of the video poker machine in front of him, put a five dollar tip out for Paulie, and stuck his player's card into the reader slot. "My night was smooth, but I'll take that double anyway. Luis has to buy me cocktails when he gets off at two, so the more I drink now, the less it'll hurt him then."

Paulie smiled that giant grin of his. "You got it bud. Do you want me to save that seat next to you for him?"

"That would be great my friend." Billy proceeded to sip his Jagermeister and play a few hands of video poker. He had to stay long enough to plant the seed in Paulie's mind that he would be in that spot until Luis showed up at two.

Billy drank his double shot and his beer inside of the next half-hour then waved Paulie down. "Hey bud, can you put a reserved sign on my machine for a few minutes please? I need to run over to the sports book and go over my baseball bets for tomorrow. It might take me a bit so if Luis shows up just tell him I'll be back shortly."

"You got it my friend! Do you want another shot waiting for you when you get back?"

"Yes sir, but wait about a half-hour before you pour it. I might be in the book for a while. Gotta study those pitching matchups you know?"

Paulie laughed. "I'll see you in about an hour bro!"

Now that he had an alibi set, Billy proceeded to the front lobby instead of the sports book. He walked outside and headed across the street to the High Sierra casino and Club Altitude.

•••

The club was packed to capacity. Billy was thrown off for a moment when he walked up and saw a line of about thirty people waiting to get in. He remembered that it was spring break this week for most of the universities in California. No wonder there were so many drunken college-aged kids roaming around Harry's and everywhere else this weekend.

Billy knew the Club Altitude manager quite well from hanging out there so often with Richie. He thought about calling in a favor to get in past the line, but he wanted to remain as anonymous as possible tonight. He decided to maintain some patience and thus some anonymity, and waited in the line like everyone else. He was sure it wouldn't take long to move thirty people.

Billy's patience paid off quite nicely when both a bachelor party and a bachelorette party exited the club at the same time. He watched the guys make asses out of themselves trying to talk the girls into coming with them to play craps. The girls wanted no part of it though; they were heading to Club Blue Hue. All the clubs must be jamming this weekend.

The line moved to let in the next twenty people, and Billy wondered if Junior and his suck-ass crew had even made it in. It was worth the thirty-dollar price of admission to find out.

After only ten minutes of waiting in line, Billy got his hand stamped and walked into the netherworld that was Club Altitude. His sense of hearing was immediately compromised by the insanely loud, thumping and bumping house music that permeated throughout; and while the club was dark from corner to corner, the light show provided small glimpses of what was going on all over. It spread out over the crowd and concentrated on the screen above the VIP booths.

Billy Stone knew how to work in uncontrolled chaos; it was what he did. He ignored the lights and the music, and instead concentrated on finding his target. He squeezed in to a seat at the bar right next to the waitress station after a drunken college girl stumbled away from it. If he turned outward, away from the bar, he could see all the VIP booths two tiers above him against the far wall. He caught the bartender's attention and ordered a Corona. The lights flashed randomly on the booths, lit up everyone who was sitting there for a fleeting moment, then moved on, returning them to darkness. For short, ten-second intervals, Billy could see clearly what was going on up there. The first booth he glimpsed was filled with a bunch of Asians. A curtain was pulled partially around it, but he could still see that two people were having sex in the booth since it was only three quarters covered by the curtain. He could see a tight, shapely, pale ass in a silver thong bouncing up and down. One pimped-out thug looking dude passed by on the way to his seat, slapped that ass soundly, and continued on his way. The clubs were getting looser and crazier as the years went by. Apparently, security either didn't see the fornication happening, didn't give a shit, or both. The blue lights flashed over another booth where everyone was bent down with their noses to the table, all snorting up big fat lines of cocaine. Billy couldn't help but think to himself that this was the future of America, and if that was truly the case, America was headed straight down the toilet.

When the lights finally flashed on the booth that Billy was looking for, he saw with clarity amidst the high-frequency flashing of the strobe light that Junior and his boys were there. The booth they were in was closest to the unisex bathroom that served the VIP section. Billy knew that same bathroom could be accessed through a chained off stairwell by the end of the bar that the managers and the bartenders used when they had to use the restroom. It was accessed through the janitor's supply room. Very few people knew about that secret entrance. Billy knew because Richie had taught him all the secrets of the trade when they were partying together.

Billy stared at Junior and his crew as they passed around the bullet of coke, handed pills back and forth to each other, and tried to drag any women they could into their circle. He finally spied Junior sitting up on the back of the booth with his legs spread out. From that vantage point, he could oversee everything below him. Also, the girl sitting in the booth below him could turn around and rub his crotch, or show him her breasts, or even fellate him, which she was doing right then. Through squinted eyes, Billy could see that Junior was drinking a martini with two olives and two onions. He remembered the last thing Junior had said as he left the craps table. "If these mother-fuckers can't get us in the Sagebrush Steakhouse on short notice, we're going to have to drink our dinner! Gimme a dirty vodka martini up with two olives and two onions all night long bitches!"

A waitress with the pasties on her nipples walked by to take orders. Without even stopping the girl who was gobbling at his crotch, Junior pulled out a hundred-dollar bill from one of his shirt pockets, pointed at his martini, then waved his hand over the whole booth before handing her the Benjamin. The waitress hardly blinked at the sordid debauchery that was going on there. Billy could see the bullet being passed around everywhere in that booth.

Billy had seen the Brazilian girl in the pasties here numerous times before. She never remembered him. He hoped she would do the same tonight. When she returned to the station, he watched her called out her orders to the bartender in whatever code they had to understand each other over the din. He specifically heard her say "Yes. It has to be Grey Goose, it has to be dirty, and it must have two olives and two onions. This asshole says he's trying to drink his dinner."

The bartender asked her the important question. "Is he tipping you?"

She laughed a hearty, Brazilian accented laugh. "What's the bill on the whole order?"

The bartender looked at the receipt. "Ninety-four dollars."

She laughed. "I get to keep the change. Six bucks for thirteen drinks. I should dose that bastard right now with something that would make him sick. A few drops of Visine in a drink will give someone diarrhea, yes?"

As they both laughed at her bold joke, The Dark Thoughts in Billy's mind began to lecture. *"You can take care of this problem for her Billy. Just get some of the GHB into his martini and watch him degenerate into a pile of shit on the floor right in front of that booth .... or maybe he'll make it as far as the bathroom before he vomits on himself and passes out. Then you'll have him, as long as one of his douche bag friends doesn't come looking for him, which probably won't happen until they need that bullet refilled. That's your start, now get going soldier!"*

Billy reached into his front pocket, felt for the vial of GHB, and palmed it. From the pocket of his club shirt he pulled out a twenty-dollar bill. He stepped close to Pastie Girl before she could leave the pouring station. The bartender gave him a wary look. He put the twenty into her free hand. Both her and the bartender's attention focused on the twenty. Billy slipped his left hand, containing the now open vial of GHB, around her left shoulder and over the tray of drinks. He tried to sound as sweet as possible. "Excuse me miss, but could you send that beautiful Asian girl at the other end of the bar a Sex On The Beach for me?" He carefully emptied the contents of the vial into the dirty vodka martini with two olives and two onions.

Miss Pastie was stern in her response. "I'm sorry sir, but only the bartenders can serve people at the bar.

It was a brush off, which was fine with Billy. He had already achieved his objective. "I'm awfully sorry for bothering you. Go ahead and keep the twenty, but if you find it in your heart to slip her some Sex On The Beach, you'll be a better person for it."

Miss Pastie smiled at Billy, then strode away quickly and drawled over her shoulder. "Perhaps I might...and perhaps I'll tell her you're cute too."

Billy sat on his stool by the pouring station and watched the GHB martini move closer and closer to its target. It was almost lost at one point when the drunken blonde who had been servicing Junior fell backwards out of the booth and almost took out Miss Pastie and her whole tray of drinks. It was a close call, but she took two very athletic steps backwards and down two stairs without spilling so much as a drop from her tray. She then deftly stepped over the drunken blonde and her mouthful of semen and handed the martini to Junior, which he immediately grabbed and gulped down. He pulled out another hundred, threw it at Miss Pastie, and made the motion for another round. He obviously hadn't chosen to get the standard bottle service. Instead, he chose to work the poor girl to death all night long for a six-dollar tip per round. Billy was now sure this would end shortly. With the amount of alcohol, cocaine, and whatever else was in

Junior's system, the GHB would wreak havoc within minutes.

Billy sat back, sipped his Corona, and watched Junior begin his downward spiral. He stared through the darkness at the shadow in the booth that he knew was Junior, then paid close attention to his face during the small window of time when the lights went by. A shadowy figure that was most likely the blonde head-giver tried to get up close to him and grind her ass on his crotch but he pushed her away hard enough to make her fall out of the booth again. When the strobe lights flashed there again, Billy could see the blonde flipping her middle finger at Junior and yelling what was likely every obscenity in the book at him. It was like a scene from a silent movie. As she stormed off, Junior wasn't even looking at her.

The lights went away for a short moment, and when they came back around, Billy could see that Junior was desperately searching around the booth for the bullet, aggressively grabbing each one of his friends and yelling at them until someone finally produced the cocaine dispenser. He took a huge snort through each nostril and threw the bullet across the booth, hitting one of his followers in the head. He looked agitated. The darkness enveloped them again. Billy maintained his focus on the spot where Junior was standing. The music thundered, repeating some tribal hip-hop measure over and over and over. He glanced out across the dance floor and saw the crowd moving in frenzied unison, driven by the beat. When the lights once again flashed on the booth, Billy could see that Junior now held his head in both hands and was staring at the floor. The GHB was taking effect. One of his suck-ass friends sat next to him with one arm around his shoulders, trying to provide comfort. Junior violently shrugged the guy off, stood up, almost fell, barely caught his balance, flipped both middle fingers to the whole booth, and stumbled toward the VIP restroom. The music increased its intensity. The lightshow followed suit, as did the crowd. Most of Junior's buddies slithered out to the dance floor, compelled by the urgency of the beat. The DJ was slowly but forcefully building up one of his big sequences that would eventually explode into musical anarchy, taking the crowd with it.

Billy was amazed that a whisper could be heard while submerged in the chaos of the driving music, but The Dark Thoughts indeed whispered in the back of his mind. *"Now's your time soldier. Go in there and take out your target. Don't forget when the moment comes that you are doing the world a favor, saving countless people the embarrassment of being demeaned by this bane who truly believes that his life is so much more important than anyone else's. Move!"*

Billy snapped up off his barstool at that final command and slipped through the crowd toward the end of the bar where there was an open doorway blocked by a large trash can full of empty beer bottles. It had a small chain across it from which hung a sign stating "EMPLOYEES ONLY KEEP OUT". He looked around to see if any bar personnel were in the vicinity. This end of the bar was empty. All eyes were on the bacchanalian tempest on the dance floor.

Billy reached across the bar, grabbed a wedge of lemon from a plastic container, slipped it into his shirt pocket, snuck under the chain, and rushed down the hallway, dodging empty kegs and garbage cans full of ice. At the end of the hall was a short flight of stairs that ended at a closed door with a sign on it that once again said “EMPLOYEES ONLY”. This was the janitor’s access to the VIP restroom. He opened the door and stepped into a small room full of cleaning supplies, paper towels, and toilet paper. The door directly across from this one led into the restroom.

The beat of the music permeated even this isolated section of the club. Billy could feel it increase in tempo as the DJ added even more layers to the already complicated mix. A wild ride had ensued, and no one would be getting off any time soon. He opened the second door less than an inch and peered into the elegant restroom. Above the din of the music, he could hear a loud retching sound, then two disgusted female voices. “Ewwww! Gross! Let’s get out of here!” Junior puked his guts out while the two grossed-out drunk girls stumbled out of the restroom.

Billy opened the door a bit more and peered around. The restroom empty now besides Junior, who was dry heaving in the last stall at the end. Billy retreated into the sanctity of the janitor’s closet, pulled the rubber gloves out of his front pocket, and put them on. He removed the other ingredients he needed to make the speedball. He worked only by the light of the lighter, quickly and efficiently, first putting the heroin into the cooking device and heating it just a little. He then pulled the lemon wedge out of his shirt pocket, squeezed all the juice he could get out of it over the heroin, and proceeded to heat the mixture to boiling with the lighter.

From his recent studies on drugs, Billy knew that a speedball injection was much cleaner and safer if citric acid mixed with saline solution was used as the titrating element. The down and out dirt-bag junkies used lemon juice or even vinegar, which often produced terrible side effects. He wasn’t worried about side effects at this point. He didn't need the ether for the cocaine since it would dissolve in the mixture of lemon juice and heroin. He slipped the depleted lemon wedge back into his shirt pocket, pulled out the vial of cocaine, and carefully added half of it to the mix, letting it dissolve. When the whole thing was liquid, he pulled one of the syringes out of his front pocket, removed the plastic cover from the needle with his teeth, and pulled the deadly mixture into the plastic chamber. The whole process took less than two minutes. He was ready to send Junior to hell where he belonged.

The DJ had reached the final crescendo of his big sequence. Billy didn't think the music could get any louder but it seemed to do just that. He was sure the whole club going nuts out on the dance floor, but here in the VIP restroom, everything was calm.

He slowly opened the door again, just an inch, and looked around. Junior was no longer retching, but Billy could see his crocodile skin shoes poking out from underneath the last stall. Besides Junior, the restroom was empty.

Billy stepped out of the janitor's closet, careful not to close the door completely. He might need to make a quick exit out that door and it locked from the inside. Three quick steps brought him to Junior's stall. The door was not latched. Billy swung the door open and looked at his target. He was sitting on the floor in his own puke, resting his head on the toilet seat. He didn't even look up when Billy entered the stall.

Billy used his gloved hands to pull up the left sleeve of Junior's beautifully crafted tiger shirt. Junior already had so much cocaine and other drugs in his system that his veins protruded from his arm like old willow roots. He finally looked up when Billy slipped the deadly needle sideways into one of those veins. His eyes registered a brief hint of recognition as Billy plunged the killing mixture into his bloodstream.

Junior managed one last defiant slur before the speedball took effect. "You don't know who I am. You don't know what kind of power my family has. You're nothing but a low-life dealer. I'll have you killed." Billy stared at him as the life went out of his eyes. It had been over a decade since he had watched the life escape from a dying man. He had forgotten what a wonderful sight it was. He took the lemon wedge from his shirt pocket and placed the forefinger and thumb of Junior's right hand on it to make a print, then did the same with the syringe, the vial that held the heroin, and the vial that still contained about a gram of cocaine. As he stuffed everything into Junior's pants pockets, he smiled at him and said "Seven, you're out."

•••

Billy returned to the UCL at five minutes after one. His second shot of Jagermeister was still cold. Paulie welcomed him back and asked "So, what's the baseball pick of the day Billy?"

Billy slammed his shot of Jager and smiled. "It's a good day for the city of San Diego. Bet the Padres." The Dark Thoughts finished the statement in his mind. *"Seven you're out Junior........and that's the end of that."*

CHAPTER 12
SUSPICIONS

James Zygald stood on his front porch and breathed out a plume of air into the cold early morning. It was the end of April and spring had finally arrived in the Carson Valley. Winter had been long and brutal, but the snow was finally gone, at least out here in Fish Springs. He could smell the scent of blooming sage. Yep, spring was finally here. It was time to uncover the old Ford that had spent the winter parked behind the barn. The ranch needed a spring cleaning.

He had been lucky enough to get his truck out of Tahoe last January. After a trip to his favorite mechanic at the lake last November, Jimmy had stopped at Harry's to try his luck at the blackjack tables. Through the course of the evening, he turned a hundred-dollar bill into two thousand bucks. It was without a doubt the luckiest night of his life, at least in cards. He also drank way too much and had to hitch a ride home from one of the dealers who was a distant neighbor. He had parked the old Ford against the outside wall of the employee parking garage next to a concrete buttress. The casinos rarely towed a vehicle that was parked legally, so he figured it could sit there for a few days until he could hitch a ride back up to the lake. The first big storm of the season hit two days later, and it didn't stop snowing for the next six weeks.

The old Ford didn't have four-wheel drive. Jimmy had resigned himself to the thought that he wouldn't get his truck back from Old Man Winter until the spring, but a window of opportunity came right after the new year. The storms ceased for the first ten days of January, and the days warmed up, so he hitched a ride to Harry's one sunny day with the same neighbor, brought his chains and a shovel, and proceeded to dig his truck out of the pile of snow that had completely covered the poor old Ford. He decided to leave the four feet of the accumulated snow in the bed of the truck to help with traction on the way home. It would melt away eventually.

Jimmy had heard some sort of ruckus from behind the barn last night, so he figured he better go check on his old truck today. There were bears about in the high desert after all. He hoped he hadn't left some food in the cab or even in the back. He put on his work boots, grabbed the keys, and walked out to the barn.

The first thing Jimmy noticed as he rounded the side of the barn was the horrific stench of death, rotten death at that. He almost retched. He approached the old Ford and peered into the bed, then truly did turn and vomit. His short glance revealed a decomposing body that appeared to be human. He thought he had seen a black cap with an Oakland Raiders logo on it. After purging himself of his morning breakfast, Jimmy turned and stared at the old Ford as if it had betrayed him. He couldn't bring himself to look again. Instead, he ran back to the house and called the Douglas County Sheriffs.

•••

Mike Westwood sat in the back of the briefing room waiting for Undersheriff Swan to send him back up to the lake again. He wasn't listening to anything the man was saying. He was instead lost in thoughts of the dead Armenian kid from San Diego. Sure, it appeared to be a standard party drug overdose. The toxicology report confirmed that young Mr. Khalajian had cocaine, ecstasy, GHB, and heroin in his system, not to mention a blood alcohol level well over the legal limit. The coroner confirmed that the speedball he had shot himself up with in the bathroom of Club Altitude was what stopped his heart. The Douglas County investigators had already closed the case. Mike had read over their report thoroughly. When he got to the dictation of the interviews with Junior's friends, he saw something that set off his investigator's radar once again. More than one of the young men interviewed had mentioned that they were playing craps at Harry's earlier that night. One of them stated that "that dealer from San Diego" suggested they go to Club Altitude later that night. The statement seemed innocent enough, except it made the whole thing reek of Billy Stone. Bells were ringing again in Mike's head.

Undersheriff Swan's condescending voice snapped Mike out of his suspicious thoughts. "Hey Westwood. They found your missing person from New Year's Eve during your days off. He was dead and decomposing in the back of a pickup truck in Fish Springs. We were holding the owner as a prime suspect but he posted bail. He says his truck was parked in the back lot at Harry's for a month and a half, and that he retrieved it on the ninth of January, parked it behind his barn, and didn't look at it until last Wednesday. He has a pretty solid alibi since his mechanic worked on the truck in November and wrote down the mileage. The damn thing only has twenty-six miles on it since then, and the guy has produced multiple witnesses that have him down here in Gardnerville from Christmas through New Year's. The investigators are checking out the area where the truck was parked, but they haven't found anything yet. Oh, and by the way, you're going back up to the lake for work today." He flashed an evil grin.

Mike raised his hand. "Can I at least provide some assistance to the investigators working on the J.J. Smith case?"

Undersheriff Swan smirked. "You're no longer a hotshot investigator, Westwood. You've got your own work to do. Our guys are competent enough to figure this one out. Remember, you're merely a Deputy Sheriff these days."

Mike decided it was time to talk to Captain Vanderwaal and voice his suspicions about Billy Stone. Six people were dead or missing in the last four months and Stone was attached to each one of them in some way, however remote. He went directly to the captain's office and knocked on the door. He heard a curt command. "Come!"

Captain John Vanderwaal was an imposing man. He hovered over his desk even though he was seated. His salt-and-pepper crew cut and solid bearing confirmed Mike's theory that he and his old captain were most likely military buddies. He had only spoken to the man once before, back in October when he first started in Douglas County.

Vanderwaal had given Mike a single brief statement back then. "You're here as a favor to an old friend. Keep your nose clean, don't poke it anywhere it doesn't belong, and things will be okay." Mike felt like he was poking right now, but this was something he had to do. "Captain, I'm sorry to bother you, but I have a pressing issue that I need to discuss."

Vanderwaal frowned. "Sit down Westwood. You have five minutes."

Mike felt some trepidation as he sat down. His case was weak, but his sense of foul play was stronger than ever. "Captain, have you noticed an unusual number of deaths and disappearances up at the lake in the last five months?"

Vanderwaal was silent for a long moment. He had been staring at a report on his desk while Mike was talking to him. The silence dragged on and Mike was on the verge of excusing himself when the Captain finally answered. "Going back to December in Douglas County, we have had three people die at Heavenly. One skier went out of bounds, got lost in the canyon just off the Western Perimeter, and froze to death. The other two, a drunken skier from Texas and a seventeen-year old snowboarder both ran themselves into trees and cracked their skulls open. Neither of those morons wore a helmet. Two drunk drivers died on Kingsbury Grade. The first one was an idiot from California who ran head-on into a snowplow. The other one was that jackass Joe Benton, who was drunk, but choked to death on his own puke after he ran his car over the edge at that open spot at the top. We found two deaders at Harry's Casino. The first one was an old guy in the Superman outfit who was tied up in his hotel room by a hooker who then stole his money and ditched him. The other one was the guy who dropped face-first into his bowl of French onion soup at the bar in the Sagebrush Steakhouse. Both of those were heart attacks. We had an El Salvadorian drug dealer shot to death in the Goalpost bar, and a woman beat to death by her husband in the trailer park on Kahle Drive. There have been three reported disappearances. One guy from Sacramento hit a jackpot at

Harry's in January and decided it was time to leave his wife. He re-surfaced in Seattle a month later. The other two were your cases, the guy from Vegas, still missing, and the kid from Hayward who is no longer missing but presumed to have been murdered. Oh yeah, and that Armenian kid who overdosed in the nightclub bathroom last week. Does that sum it up?"

Mike was impressed with Captain Vanderwaal's memorization of every single case. He wondered how far back this man could quote the cases. He was beginning to second guess himself and his line of reasoning, but he had come this far. He had to put his theory out there. "Sir, I'm seeing a common denominator in at least six of those cases. Mr. Wellington, Mr. Kurchstein, Mr. Benton, Mr. Smith, Mr. Assopholis, and that Khalajian kid all patronized Harry's casino right before they died or disappeared. One individual, a dealer named Billy Stone, had contact with each one of them, and they were all either dead or missing within twenty-four hours or less after that contact. Doesn't that strike you as a little too much coincidence?"

The Captain frowned. Now he looked irritated. "Listen Westwood, Harry's is the largest casino on the South Shore. That place commands almost seventy percent of the market share up there. That means that seventy percent of what happens with our tourists, good or bad, happens at Harry's. If those people gamble, there's probably a greater than seventy percent chance that they all encountered any individual dealer, including this Stone character, while they were playing. Those numbers don't strike me as coincidental at all. I'm sure there's a long list of dealers, pit bosses, and cocktail waitresses who encountered each one of those guys before they died or disappeared.

I spoke with Jim Forvers at length about you when he convinced me to give you a place to hide from that incident you had down there. He said you were one of his best investigators. He considered you a worthy replacement when he decides to retire, but you got yourself into a lot of trouble in Vegas. It was a big risk allowing you to come work for me, but Jim Forvers saved my life back in 'Nam, and I owe him more than I can ever repay. The problem I'm having here though is that you were supposed to lay low, clean yourself up, and not poke your nose around where it doesn't belong. You're not holding up your end of the deal Westwood. I have a few contacts at Harry's who have mentioned your name to me a few too many times in the last three months. It seems like you've been doing some investigative work of your own, something I told you not to do when I brought you in last October. Understand this Deputy," he stressed the word deputy, "that casino contributes enough to Douglas County in taxes and donations to pay the salary of every individual that works in this department twice over. We maintain a special type of working relationship with Harry's. We don't bite the hand that feeds us, and we definitely don't snoop around there chasing ghost serial killers because of perceived coincidence. You need to back off Westwood. You're not an investigator anymore, and no matter how much I owe Jim Forvers, I'll throw your ass out on the street if you keep sniffin' around up there. Be smart son. You know you can't work anywhere else. Your old Captain still wants you back in Vegas, but you have wait until the shit you created down there blows over. Don't forget that you're here on a huge favor. Your existence here is precarious at best. Our investigators are competent. Let them do their job and you do your own. That will be all now. You're dismissed."

Mike walked out of Captain Vanderwaal's office feeling like an idiot. Maybe he was grasping at straws, or as Vanderwaal put it, "chasing ghost serial killers". He didn't want to lose this job. He had nothing else. He prayed that Jim Forvers would decide to bring him back soon. He hopped into his patrol car, drove through Minden toward highway 88 and Kingsbury Grade, and thought to himself "Just keep your nose clean for a little while longer Mike." He wasn't sure he could do that. Even after Captain Vanderwaal's lecture on the probability of these dead or missing people encountering an individual casino worker, the thought of Billy Stone still made bells ring in his head. He would have to be more discreet moving forward.

CHAPTER 13

THE RETURN OF MR. AND MRS. SMITH

It was mid-June. Winter had released its grip on Tahoe earlier than usual this year and it already felt like summer. Billy had nothing to do on his days off since Hope worked midweek, so he headed over to The Lakeside, the locals' casino hangout. It had a nice sports bar and a great Latino-style restaurant. He made a few bets on the NBA playoff games that were showing that night, sat down at the bar, ordered a plate of carne asada tacos, and settled in for a solitary night of Mexican food, video poker, and basketball.

Billy's seat was right next to the cocktail waitress station, affording him the best view of not only all the waitresses, but also the main pit. He liked to watch people these days, mainly to see how badly they were behaving in the casino. From his vantage point, he could also hear all the waitresses yapping at each other about how terrible their customers and bosses were. If he tired of the eavesdropping and people watching, the Lakers game was right in front of him, as was his video poker machine. He was idly playing his machine and listening in on the conversations amongst the cocktail servers when he heard a voice that made his head spin. It was that same soft-spoken drawl, not quite southern, but sexy as all hell, with that same clueless undertone.

"Yeah Andrea, I kind of left Harry's last summer without giving notice, so I didn't have a re-hire status. I truly thought this man was going to take care of me and I would never have to work again. He treated me so terribly at the end, almost like a sex slave. I've learned my lesson though, I'm back in Tahoe, working here at the Lakeside, and trying to get my life back together. I'm going to look up my ex fiancée over at Harry's this week, let him know I'm back and single again; maybe see if there's any old spark left. Hopefully he's still interested, I mean, how could he not be interested in this?"

Billy glanced askew and saw Mimi Meridale in his periphery pushing her boobs upward until they almost fell out of the top of her bodice-like uniform. Andrea giggled and said, "He probably still dreams of those at night girl." They both cackled like a couple of hens.

Billy's head was spinning. The Dark Thoughts resounded in his mind; angry, judging, hungry. *"If there was ever a woman that deserved to be killed Billy, it's this one. Engage her. It shouldn't be too hard for you to get her back to your place. Then you can exterminate her however you like and dispose of the body as you need to. Hell, you could even fuck her a few times first, then choke her to death while you come inside of her for one last time; or you could just fuck her from behind like an animal and give that pretty little neck of hers a good hard twist. This woman broke your heart to satisfy her greed and avarice. She caused you a world of pain. Do yourself a favor and take her out."*

Billy felt sick to his stomach. He needed to leave, quickly and silently. As he sat there at the bar for a moment gathering his thoughts, unable to comprehend how the sound of one woman's voice could affect him so profoundly, he pressed the deal button on his video poker machine one last foolish time and heard the melodic attention-getting tune that signified a royal flush. "Son of a bitch!" Billy cursed his good luck.

Jose the bartender came over immediately with a huge grin on his face and offered Billy a high-five. "Way to go Billy! Good job amigo! That one's worth eighteen hundred bucks."

Billy sat there, stunned. He felt even more ill than before. His tacos tried to escape the confines of his stomach. He managed to hold down the retch and slapped Jose's open palm harder than he should have. Then came the dreaded squeal that he recognized oh so well.

"Billy Stone! Look at you. Another royal flush. You are the luckiest dealer in Tahoe! Congratulations! How have you been? You look great!"

"No sneaking out now", Billy thought to himself as Mimi pushed herself in between him and the partition that separated the bar from the waitress station. She hugged him, and because he was seated and she was standing, her breasts went right into his face, likely on purpose. He barely returned the hug and remained cordial in his reply. "Hey Mimi. What a surprise. What are you doing here in a waitress uniform? I thought you were a kept woman now." He wanted to vomit.

Mimi ignored his blatant jab and cupped his face in her hands. He wanted to slap her hands away and rave at her for shattering his heart. Instead, he sat there, unable to move. She smiled at him and stuck her chest out, ever so slightly. "You look fantastic Billy. Things didn't work out in the Bay Area, so I'm back. What have you been doing with yourself? It looks like you've been working out." She knew how to say all the right things. The seduction had begun.

Billy tried to remain calm, but the painful memories of the past fall coursed through his mind. He couldn't resist taking another jab. "Back so soon? I thought you had yourself the good life now."

Mimi looked down at him, tears welling in her eyes. He was sure it was all part of the act. "Billy look, I made a huge mistake and got myself into something that I didn't understand. It's over and done now though, and I'm back in town to try to start my life over. I'm sorry I walked out on you but I can't take that back. Listen. I can probably take an early out and let Andrea have the casino floor by herself if you want to sit and talk. You're going to be waiting a while for that Royal Flush money anyway. I'll sit with you and we can drink some Jagermeister for old times' sake."

The Dark Thoughts sounded off in Billy's head again, insistent. *"Stupid Bitch is making it easy on you by laying the trap herself. Now all you need to do is proceed with the plan. Get her home, have your fun with her, then take her out. If you don't, you know she'll continue to make your life miserable."*

Billy stared at Mimi. He had nothing to say. He was struggling with The Dark Thoughts' compulsion. He wasn't sure he could kill a woman he had been in love with.

Mimi took his silence as an invitation. "Okay. I'll see you in a few minutes. Just let me get out of this Zoot suit. Hey Jose! I'm sure Billy won't mind buying me a shot of Jager and a Miller Lite since he just hit the big one. Can you hold this seat for me please?"

Jose looked at Billy for confirmation. Billy nodded, numb and speechless. The Lakers were down ten at the half.

The slot attendant showed up shortly with Billy's jackpot money. She was gracious for the forty-dollar tip he gave her, as was Jose when he received a hundred. The bartender went ahead and brought him another shot and a beer along with Mimi's order. Billy was pondering trying to sneak out at this juncture, thus giving Mimi the message that he wasn't interested, but something held him there. "Thanks Jose. You may as well get the bar a round on me since I swiped their Royal Flush." The progressive jackpot had reset at one thousand dollars and was already building in value.

When Mimi returned, she was wearing a mini skirt and a low-cut, loose-fitting t-shirt that exposed her perfect cleavage. She gave Billy another tight hug and sat down next to him. "So, have you been okay?"

Billy wanted to shake her and scream at her. "No! I have not been okay. There was a woman that I was engaged to marry last fall and she fucking dumped me for a smug, arrogant millionaire who was just using her as a sex toy! Because of that I lost my precarious grip on these evil Dark Thoughts in my head and started hating people to the point that I killed some of them. I've killed six people since then and I no longer know who or what I am!" Instead, he raised his shot of Jager to her for a toast. "I've been good. Cheers to your return." He supposed he would be following The Dark Thoughts' orders once again. Could he really kill Mimi Meridale?

Two hours later, Billy had heard the whole saga of Mimi Meridale-Smith. She told him everything from when Mr. Smith had first seduced her at last summer's wine pairing event all the way to the horrible things he made her do with what she called his "business associates" whom Billy was sure were The Barnacles. She told him about the day-trading, the prenuptial agreement, and the five ex-wives. She told him what an arrogant self-centered bastard Mr. Smith was and how poorly he treated everyone around him. The Dark Thoughts candidly shared their opinion in Billy's mind. *"We should have taken him out when we had the chance."*

After dropping her sob story on him and crying here and there for effect, Mimi suddenly switched to enchantress mode, still intent on her plan to lure him back. They were about four shots of Jager into their conversation and she was starting to get tipsy. Billy was plain drunk, at this point. She touched him lightly on the cheek and smiled. "You look awesome Billy, like a completely new man. What have you been doing while I was gone?"

"Oh, you know, Mountain biking, hiking, snowboarding and back-country skiing in the winter, a few trips to South San to see my friend Elmer, dealing, driving the limo… all the fun stuff. I even went down to that little beach next to Skunk Harbor the other day. You remember the one we used to hike down to from that gate on highway 28?"

Mimi flashed her best devilish smile and spread her legs a little, making sure that Billy could see that she wasn't wearing any underwear. She giggled and pulled her skirt down, just a little. "Ooh yeah Baby, I remember that place. We sure had some fun there.

The Dark Thoughts were still intent on their agenda. *"You know she'll go home with you if you just say the word. This is a prime opportunity for revenge."*

Mimi was intent on her agenda as well. "You know Billy, I've only been back for a week and I haven't been able to stop thinking about you. I was going to go into Harry's tomorrow night to see you. Are you still in the house on Needle Peak?"

The Dark Thoughts: *"Now you have her. Just invite her over. Ask her if she wants to see the old Love Nest. She's giving you all the signs. We need to kill this one! You will enter a greater phase of your existence!"*

Mimi: "I'm kind of drunk. I might need a ride home anyway."

Billy's head was beginning to spin from the multiple shots of Jager and this three-way conversation that he was having.

The Dark Thoughts: *"Engage soldier. You have a target and it is in a compromised position. Proceed with the plan!"*

Mimi, with her back slightly arched and her legs spread again: He could see that she still shaved down there. It was turning him on. Suddenly, so was the idea of fucking Mimi and then killing her. "Why are you avoiding the inevitable Billy? You know you've missed this."

She took his hand and placed it on the inside of her thigh. "What's the matter Baby? You didn't go and get a girlfriend while I was gone, did you?"

The thought of Hope was like ice water in Billy's face. He realized that he didn't like The Dark Thoughts' plan because it was full of holes and loose ends. If he killed Mimi tonight, there were witnesses right here at the bar that could verify that he was the last person to be seen with her while she was alive. He was also too drunk to work quickly and efficiently if need be. He was way too drunk to drive somewhere and dispose of a dead body. He didn't like Mimi's plan either. It involved him cheating on Hope and ruining their budding relationship. Mimi had acted on her gold-digging impulses and devastated him in the act. She didn't deserve anything from him, much less what she was looking for right now. He had to bail out, quickly.

"You know what Mimi? I did go and get a girlfriend while you were gone. We have a pretty good relationship and I don't want to ruin it by doing something stupid with you. You gave up on me nine months ago. We're done." He began to gather up his things.

Mimi made one last desperate attempt. "Billy Stone, I know I did you wrong, but we had some magic before I went and got stupid. I wish to God every day that I could take back all the stupid things I did but I can't. We can make this work again. I know it. We were the perfect couple..."

Billy interrupted her. "'Were' is the key word there Mimi. You may have come around full circle but I've moved on. There's no more magic, only pain."

Mimi still wouldn't give up. "How about if we go back to the house on Needle Peak and run around naked just for old times' sake? I'll let you have it any way you want. I'll do anything for you." The skirt was moving upward again.

Billy was wasted, and tempted, but he kept his resolve. "No Mimi. Not tonight, not tomorrow, not ever. I gotta go. I'm sure I'll see you around."

In her drunken state, Mimi still thought she could seduce him somehow. "How about if maybe I can just hitch a ride home with you? I'll give you a blowjob." Her skirt was so high up at this point Billy was sure that Jose the bartender would see her snatch if he walked by.

"Sorry Mimi, but nothing is going to happen. Pull your skirt down before you embarrass yourself."

Then came the drunken indignance. “Well, fuck you then Billy Stone! You’ll never find a piece of pussy as good as this ever again!” She pointed with both fingers to her exposed shaved crotch. This time Jose did come by and looked down, amazed. The front of Mimi’s skirt was bunched up around her waist at this point, exposing everything.

Billy ignored Mimi’s tirade and her shaved private parts, placed a twenty-dollar bill on the bar for Jose and smiled at him. “Thanks Jose. Sorry about the trouble brother.”

Jose couldn’t take his eyes away from Mimi’s crotch. He picked up the twenty without looking at it, tapped it twice on the bar and mumbled “Thanks again Billy. Hopefully I’ll see you soon.”

Billy walked away from the bar without another word. He could hear Mimi crying behind him. He glanced up at the television before he walked out of the casino. ESPN was showing the highlights of the Lakers’ game. They had come back to win by eight. He won his basketball bet.

•••

Billy went in to work that Friday night with a massive hangover. After leaving Mimi crying at the bar in Lakeside, he had driven home slowly on the back roads. As soon as he got home he pulled out his chilled bottle of Jagermeister along with a shot glass and proceeded to drink himself into oblivion on the front porch. He woke up when the sun became too strong around ten that morning, went inside, vomited, and fell asleep again on the couch until it was time to get ready for work.

Billy stood there on craps 301, sweating, still feeling like he had to throw up. He probably should have called in sick but here he was, praying that some seven outs would come so that the crowd would stop screaming. The previous night's encounter with Mimi had rattled him. Perhaps he should have listened to The Dark Thoughts and just taken her out; then he wouldn't have to worry about another such encounter.

Billy's mind began to drift as he ruminated on the events of yesterday. A strangely familiar voice snapped him back to reality. He recognized the smug, arrogance from last fall. "Hey dealer! Paper plays!" A tan, well-manicured hand dropped a pile of cash into the field. Billy glanced quickly to the other side of the table to check for the dice and saw that the shooter was releasing them at that instance. Once again he had to make a split-second decision on a late bet that he hadn't been prepared for. He had no time to discuss with this player the house rule that paper cannot be played as a bet, especially since the dice were in the air. Instead, he called out loudly "No bet! Paper cannot play on any game at any time!"

Billy knew before the dice totaled that it would be a field number; then a battle would ensue. Sure enough, the dice totaled on the number nine. He looked up and saw a face that turned his stomach even more. It was Mr. Smith, the catalyst for every bit of his trouble, pain, and suffering the last nine months. He threw his Platinum player's card at Billy, which hit him in the chest.

"What the fuck do you mean "no bet"? I put that money down in the field and called "paper plays" way before the dice totaled. What the hell is wrong with this place?" He peered closely ay Billy's nametag. "Billy from San Diego. I remember you. You screwed things up the last time I was in here. Get your boss over here right now! I want to get paid."

Billy clenched the railing of the craps game tight enough to make the veins in his neck stand out. He stared hard in to Mr. Smith's eyes, expecting him to flinch from his intense gaze like everyone else did. The man didn't back down though. His confidence in the disparity between their positions was plainly visible, as was his arrogance. Billy saw that one of his Barnacle friends was with him again; probably one of the same suck-ups that Mimi had to service. He wanted to come across the table and tear them both apart with his bare hands. He knew he could do it.

The Dark Thoughts spoke sternly in the back of his mind, calming. *"Keep your cool Billy. Engage this bastard so that we can devise a plan. You know by now how this works. You must gain his trust, just a little, until he exposes himself. Then we kill."*

The word "kill" echoed in Billy's mind as he drew in a deep breath and called for his boxman. He prayed that it wasn't weak-willed Will but God had His attention focused elsewhere at that precise moment because it was Will that walked up to the game. Mr. Smith was going to steamroll this poor kid and make Billy look bad in the process.

Will looked confused as usual. "What's going down Billy?"

Before Billy could answer, Mr. Smith cut in and began his tirade. "Hey pit boss! Your dealer here just told me, a Platinum player, that I had no bet when I threw my money in the field and called out that paper plays. You guys owe me five hundred bucks and I want to get paid right now or else I'll take my business across the street!" Billy wondered how many times he had heard that idle threat throughout his craps-dealing career. In the end, they always came back.

Will looked at Billy, scared. "Did you no bet him Billy?"

"Of course I no bet him Will. You know the rules; paper cannot be played in any way, shape, or form on any of our games. That rule has been in effect for over five years."

Will was still confused. "Why didn't you book the bet and convert it to chips?"

"Well Will, the dice were in the air when he threw the paper down. There was no time to convert, nor time to discuss anything, so I called "no bet".

"Billy, how can you "no bet" a Platinum player?"

"It happened so fast, I didn't even see where it came from. Like I said, I had to make a split-second decision"

Will didn't have a clue what to do. "Do you think I should pay him for it? He is a Platinum player and such."

Mr. Smith interjected again, arrogant and demanding. "I want to talk to a manager. I'm sure he'll be very interested to know how the staff is treating a Platinum player! Get him over here now! It's pretty obvious that you two guys have your heads too far up your asses to make a decision." The other players on the game began to look uncomfortable.

Billy looked at Will, who seemed afraid to even move at this point. "You better call John Hughes. I'll work on calming this jackass down." Will ran over to the podium, relieved to have had the decision made for him.

Billy went to work on Mr. Smith and his grandstanding. "I apologize for this incident Mr. Smith, but I have to follow protocol in situations like this. My manager is a fair man, and I'm sure your status as a Platinum player will work in your favor."

Mr. Smith didn't respond to anything Billy said to him. Instead, he vented his cause out loud to anyone around him who might listen. "I can't believe how they treat people around here! I called out the bet, it won, and now they're not paying me for it. What's wrong with this picture? That's bad business and terrible customer service."

The other people at the table remained silent. They knew they were seeing an overgrown child having a tantrum. The Barnacle was the only one to take up Mr. Smith's cause. "Yeah, they should pay you. I heard you call out the bet. This place sucks! Maybe we should go to the other casino."

Mr. Smith now focused his attention on Billy. "Hey, Billy from San Diego! How do you expect to earn any tips if you can't even book a bet correctly? You do work for tips, don't you?"

The Dark Thoughts voiced a response in Billy's head. *"You don't tip the dealers anyway you rotten cheapskate. You never have and you probably never will, especially since you're about to be removed from your shitty Platinum existence."*

Billy didn't even bother to address Mr. Smith regarding the tip issue, or lack thereof. He needed to turn this guy to his side, get him to relax, and gain some trust. "We'll take care of you sir, don't worry. I'm sure John Hughes will make the right decision. Until then, do you want me to change up that cash for you so you can get in the game?"

Mr. Smith calmed down, just a tad. "Yeah, give me quarters; and while you're at it, give me a marker for five-thousand, all in black."

Billy called Will over to the game to get him to authorize the marker. While Will was fumbling around with the computer, Johnny Nine walked up to the game. He looked irritated. "What the hell happened, Billy?"

Billy leaned in close to John and quietly gave him the rundown on the situation. "This jackass Platinum player across from me dropped a wad of cash in the field while the dice were in the air and called out "paper plays". I didn't have the time to convert it or to explain to him our rules about cash play. Hell, I didn't even have the time to identify who it came from, so I called "no bet". The roll was nine. Then he proceeded to throw his players' card at me and demanded to get paid. Will here had no idea what to do so I told him to get a hold of you. Sorry Boss, it's just one of those ill-timed incidences. If I had three extra seconds, I could have converted the money and we wouldn't be having this conversation."

Johnny Nine seemed satisfied with Billy's version of the events. "So you don't think there were any shenanigans going on? Was it a legitimate bet?"

"If it was my decision Boss, I would pay it."

"That's good enough for me Billy. I'll go out there and take care of it."

John Hughes went around the table to explain the situation to Mr. Smith. Billy watched Mr. Smith go through his whole indignant routine once again. Will came over and put the five thousand dollar lammer on the game. Billy cut out five thousand dollars in hundred dollar chips, per Mr. Smith's request, and then spread five more black chips next to that for the five-hundred-dollar field bet he was sure John would pay Mr. Smith for. He worked on his breathing exercises to maintain his calm. He still had a vision in his head of the pen going directly into Mr. Smith's temple, then one simple twist; left, right, up, or down. He hoped The Dark Thoughts would come up with something.

John walked back over to the table with Mr. Smith. "Okay Billy, we worked this out for Mr. Smith. Please give him five hundred dollars for his field bet. Mr. Smith, you have yourself a good time here at Harry's, and don't forget; cash can't play here, so just use your chips." Mr. Smith stared at Billy with smug satisfaction.

Billy went over the money he had cut out on the layout for Mr. Smith. "Here you go sir; this is your five-thousand-dollar marker and these five chips here are for your field bet. Sorry about the mix-up. Can I book any bets for you at this time?"

"No, just give me my money so I can count it and make sure you aren't trying to rip me off again...and get a cocktail waitress over here. Tell her to bring the wine menu from the steakhouse. My friend and I don't want to drink any of that swill you're serving to the common folks. In fact, I want that hot Brazilian babe named Simone. Get her over here, pronto!" He grinned wickedly at his suck-ass Barnacle friend. "Let's go to work on wife number six!" The Barnacle laughed that ass-sucking laugh of his.

At this point, Billy was no longer amazed by Mr. Smith's audacity and arrogance. Neither were The Dark Thoughts. *"This son-of-a-bitch is a strong candidate for removal. You've got to work on him. Engage him so you can exploit his weakness, then set him up. If we take out his piece-of shit friend in the process, so be it. Maybe his desire to see Simone could expose something. Try to get him over to the dance club. You could take him out the same way you did that little bastard Junior."*

It was time for Good Dealer mode. Billy knew how to wear the hat well. "I'm sorry Mr. Smith, but Simone is off tonight. We'll get the waitress for this table to bring you that wine list."

Mr. Smith was clearly irritated to hear the news about Simone. "How could you guys not have your hottest waitress working on a Friday night?" He looked over at his Barnacle friend. "Damn! I was hoping to get to work on that one. Those Hispanic chicks love men with money." He still didn't get the fact that she was of Portuguese descent. "She might even be easier than the last gold digger I pulled out of here. I know she was impressed with me last time I was here."

The Barnacle interjected with that suck-up laugh of his. "Oh yeah. You must have tipped her a couple hundred bucks that night. She should have been impressed."

The whole scene was making Billy ill again. His thoughts were drifting toward torture and death for Mr. Smith. He was ready to proceed with The Dark Thoughts' plan. "You know something Mr. Smith, if you're interested in Simone, I know where she likes to hang out when she's partying."

Billy now had the predator's attention. He looked like a wolf: hungry and ready to hunt. "Where would that be, Billy from San Diego? And how much will I have to tip you for this valuable piece of information?" It always boiled down to money for this jackass.

It was time for Billy to set the plan in motion. "This one won't cost you anything sir. I still owe you one for screwing up your field bet. She likes to hang out at the club across the street, Altitude. Even though we're not affiliated, Harry's has an agreement with them so that you can use your Platinum players' card to get in for free. It'll probably get you a booth too, if you want. You can't miss Simone either. She likes to wear these skin-tight purple hot pants and black high heels. Things don't get going over there until around midnight, but if you want, I'm sure Will can call over there for you and reserve you a booth; maybe even with a couple bottles of that '98 Silver Oak you like."

Mr. Smith shook his head in grim resignation. "I don't like clubs. There are too many punks in those places. Besides, I'll probably be in bed by midnight. We're going mountain biking in the morning. Looks like Simone loses out on the wife number six lottery." He laughed at his own joke. The Barnacle joined in.

Billy felt a little deflated that the club plan wasn't going to work. He was looking forward to dosing Mr. Smith with GHB, watching him become ill, and then following him into the VIP restroom with a speedball syringe. He wanted to watch the life drain from this man's eyes. It was time to come up with an alternative plan.

The Dark Thoughts were already formulating in his head. *"Mountain biking. That's right up your alley Billy. These idiots probably haven't the slightest idea where to go, especially this time of year when most of the good trails are still snowbound. Find out if they're in good enough shape to ride the Flume Trail. It's a great place for an "accident" to occur."*

That was it. Billy was still amazed at The Dark Thoughts' ability to react creatively to a fluid situation and quickly provide a new plan of attack. The Flume Trail would be perfect. It cut directly across the face of the mountain range on the east shore of Lake Tahoe and ended eleven miles north just outside of Incline Village. The views from this part of the trail were stunning, especially since it was at least two thousand feet above the lake. The trail was dangerous though because the mountainside was steep, almost cliff-like in spots. Mesmerized by the fantastic views, many riders failed to pay attention to the trail which was at times less than a foot wide. One small aberration toward the downward side of the trail could lead to a thirty or forty foot fall. Riders that fell were often hurt; some died. The Flume was also one of the few high mountain trails that could be accessed this early in the season. Billy knew that trail well, especially the spots where a fall could be devastating. He had to get Mr. Smith up there.

Once Mr. Smith and The Barnacle were well into their second bottle of Silver Oak, Billy decided to engage. Someone had rolled the dice for a half-hour and Mr. Smith won over ten thousand dollars on the hand. Billy was cleaning up the layout after the seven out and the players were all applauding the shooter and high-fiving each other. People were always more prone to conversation when they were high on the adrenaline of winning. Mr. Smith would be no different. This was the perfect time.

"So, Mr. Smith, where are you guys planning to ride tomorrow?"

Smith didn't answer at first. He was busy counting his chips and getting ready for the next shooter. He finally looked up. "You got any suggestions Billy? We were going to go to Burnside Lake but it looked like there was still a lot of snow in Hope Valley."

Billy steered carefully here. He didn't want to appear eager. "Yeah, Hope Valley is usually snowbound in the upper elevations into July. That rules out Mr. Toad's Wild Ride and

Dardanelle's Lake; Burnside as well. They plowed the road to Angora Lakes before Memorial Day weekend, but that's mostly pavement. Are you guys strong riders?"

Mr. Smith puffed up his chest, irritated that Billy would question his riding ability. "We ride Mt. Tam at least once a week. I think we can handle anything that Tahoe can throw at us."

Billy had ridden Mount Tamalpias in Marin County, just north of San Francisco, a few times over the years. Many of the trails were steep and advanced. He figured Mr. Smith and his Barnacle friend could handle the grind from Spooner Lake to Marlette Lake, where The Flume started.

"You might want to try The Flume Trail. It's on the east shore of the lake. Since it gets great southwest sun exposure it's always clear this early in the season. It's been listed in all the travel and biking magazines as one of the top ten rides with a view in America. I'd say it's a must for any serious riders that come to Tahoe. You just drive up highway 50 to Spooner Summit, turn left onto highway 28, and take the first right into the parking lot at Spooner Lake. The ride starts there. After about thirteen miles and numerous breathtaking views of Lake Tahoe, you'll end up in Incline Village. If you don't feel like riding all the way up highway 28 to get back to your car, there's a shuttle that will take you and your bikes back to the summit. It's convenient. If you want a good challenge and some great photo ops, that's what I would suggest."

Mr. Smith's attention was wandering again. The new shooter was rolling well. He responded offhandedly without even looking up at Billy. "The Flume Trail huh? Well maybe we'll try that out."

The trap was now set. Billy hoped that Mr. Smith would take the bait.

•••

Billy sat on a boulder, ten feet above a large outcropping of similar boulders that blocked this section of The Flume Trail. He could see all of Lake Tahoe from this vantage point. The lake shimmered in the high noon sun, appearing to morph inward on itself, as if on the verge of starting a giant whirlpool. The effect was dizzying. He could see Sand Harbor below. Directly to his left he could see most of the trail for about a hundred yards until it disappeared into the contour of the mountain. From here, he could see any approaching riders long before they reached the boulders below him. They would have to get off their bikes, carry them over the boulders, and pick up the trail again on the other side. This was one of the steepest parts of the mountainside.

Billy had been sitting on the same rock for three hours. He had seen only three riders pass through, none in over an hour, and was beginning to wonder if Mr. Smith and his barnacle friend had given up on their ride. He had started his day at eight that morning, parking the Commander at a turnout just outside of Glenbrook. He rode his mountain bike up highway 50 and turned left onto highway 28, then turned in to the Spooner Lake parking lot. From there he rode five miles up to Marlette Lake, and finally to this spot on the trail. He was tired, having only slept about three hours the night before. He had no idea when Mr. Smith planned on riding that day so he made sure to get to his hiding spot early. He didn't think he could last much longer before he started to fade. The dizzying view was making him sleepy. He began to drowse.

A hoot and holler startled Billy out of his slumber. It was The Barnacle.

"Wow! That dealer was right. This is an incredible view!"

Mr. Smith and his buddy were directly below him and to his left, getting off their bikes. They were taking in the view of Sand Harbor before navigating the boulder outcropping that blocked the trail. Mr. Smith replied smugly to his friend. "Yeah, this is okay. I've seen better. You definitely have to pay attention to the trail though. This is dangerous. We should have worn our helmets. That moron dealer wasn't joking when he said this was a pretty technical ride."

The Dark Thoughts shared their opinion with Mr. Smith in the back of Billy's mind. *"We'll see who the moron is shortly, Smith."*

They stood there on the trail for a few minutes. The Barnacle had his cell phone out and was taking pictures. Billy waited patiently ten feet above them, hidden by the branches of a small pine tree. They would have to hike over the boulders that blocked the trail to continue. This was a crucial part of Billy's plan. He looked far down the trail in both directions. He couldn't execute his plan if any other riders were coming. There was no one else around. This was Billy's best chance, but only if Mr. Smith and The Barnacle moved soon.

As if on cue, Mr. Smith began to move. "Let's go. I think we've got a few more miles. Seasoned mountain bikers they were; both men picked their bikes up with their left hand by the crossbar, pulling the hand up close to the shoulder and resting the bike against the elbow. That was the standard carrying stance for foraging over difficult spots. It left one hand free to help maintain balance and didn't require the rider to pull or push the bike along. Billy knew that it also left both men susceptible to a quick shove off the trail and a thirty or forty foot drop before they made contact with the granite slope below. They might even bounce and fall another twenty feet. This was the perfect spot for an "accident".

Billy waited above his prey, calm, tense; a cougar ready to strike. There was one flat boulder that they would both have to walk over to get to where the trail began again. It was about two feet high, but more important, it hung a few feet out over the drop off side of the trail. Mr. Smith jumped up first and immediately lost his balance, almost doing half of Billy's work for him. He recovered though, and commented over his shoulder to The Barnacle. "Watch that first step. It's a doozie, and there's a steep drop-off right here". He moved slowly across the boulder with his right hand straight out to maintain balance. The Barnacle jumped up right behind him.

The Dark Thoughts took command at this point, pushing Billy into action. *"Now's your time soldier. This is a prime opportunity to remove another individual that abuses his place and power. Mr. Smith preys on women, luring them in with dreams of being wealthy. He violates the sacrament of marriage just to satisfy his own filthy desires. He stole your fiancée, used her up, and turned her out. How many women will this man discard like last week's trash if he is allowed to continue? You'll have to take out his ass-sucking friend in the process, but sometimes there is collateral damage. You can't leave a witness. Engage......Now!"*

•••

Mr. Smith sensed movement in his periphery from above and to his right. He looked over his shoulder and saw a figure clad in black biking apparel hurling toward him. He recognized the face immediately. "Son of a bitch!" was all he had time to get out of his mouth before Billy struck.

Billy hit Mr. Smith with a solid forearm to the right shoulder just as he landed his left foot on the boulder. Mr. Smith had looked over his shoulder while Billy was in midair and braced himself for the impact. Billy's strike still sent him a step backward and toward the drop-off. He cursed, then reached out with his free hand, trying desperately to grab onto Billy. The weight of the bike and Mr. Smith's momentum were too much though. He grasped only air, and fell over the edge. Billy saw an angry look of recognition in his eyes right before he disappeared completely from sight.

The Barnacle had time to exclaim "What the fuck?" before Billy spun 180 degrees and caught him square across the bridge of his nose with the same elbow he had given Mr. Smith, this time with a backward strike. He dropped his bike over the edge and brought both hands to his bloodied face. This left him exposed to a forward kick from Billy that sent him over the edge after his bike.

Billy stood on the boulder by himself, amazed at how quick and efficient his attack had been. The Dark Thoughts had developed another miraculous plan. He stepped to the edge and peered over to make sure the damage was complete. Mr. Smith laid face-down on top of his bike about forty feet down the slope, his head at an awkward angle. His neck was surely broken.

His first target accounted for, Billy scanned the slope for The Barnacle. Mr. Smith's friend had only fallen about twenty feet, and he wasn't dead. Worse, he had his cell phone out and was dialing, probably 911. Billy's heart began to race. He had to do something, and quick. After all the targets he had removed with such perfection and efficiency, he was about to be undone by a barnacle. He jumped down onto the trail to his left, directly above The Barnacle, and scanned the terrain around him. He saw what he was looking for just off the trail on the uphill slope; a piece of granite roughly the size of a man's head, half buried. He dug his hands deep into the pine needles and loamy earth, straining hard to extract the stone. It didn't want to move. The Barnacle was swearing at his cell phone. "Come on you goddamn thing, work!"

The veins in Billy's arms stood out as he strained mightily to remove his projectile from the ground. When it finally gave way, he raised it above his head and turned toward the edge. He couldn't believe what he saw. The Barnacle had the cell phone to his ear and had miraculously found reception. He screamed into the phone, frantic. "Someone help me! We're on the Flume Trail and something terrible has happened. I think my leg is broken and I can't move. My friend might be dead! It was that dea..."

His plea was cut short when Billy's granite projectile crushed his skull. The small boulder bounced off his head and continued down the slope another hundred feet or so. The voice on the cell phone called out. "Sir? Are you still there? Sir? Please respond if you can sir. We're sending help immediately."

Billy stared at The Barnacle, watching the blood seep out of his mouth and ears. There was no way the man could survive that crushing blow. He looked over at Mr. Smith with his neck resting at that odd angle and stated out loud "Seven, you're out Mr. Smith; and your Barnacle friend too. That's the end of that."

•••

Billy rode hard on the steep climb out of Marlette Lake and was starting the five-mile downhill back to Spooner Lake when he heard the sirens. They were still far away, so he let gravity take him as quickly as he dared down the trail. About a mile from the trailhead, he saw a Douglas County four-wheel drive coming up the trail. He hung a sharp right and rode straight off the trail and into the woods toward a thick grove of Manzanita bushes. Once in the bushes, he threw his bike down, laid himself flat on the ground, and waited. He watched the Sherriff drive by and wondered if there would be any more following behind. There could be backup either on the trail, at the trailhead parking area, or coming up highway 50. He couldn't risk an encounter. He decided to carry his bike west over the ridge and into the meadow on the other side. Once in the meadow, he was not visible from the trail. He rode west across the meadow to where it met highway 28 about three miles from the summit.

At the edge of the meadow, Billy threw his mountain bike over a barbed-wire fence and hopped over after it. His heart felt like it was about erupt through his throat and explode in his head. When he got to the Forest Service road that went down to Skunk Harbor, he took a sharp fork onto a single track that went through Glenbrook Meadows and rode out through the private neighborhood back to the

Commander that was parked right outside of the exclusive neighborhood on highway 50.

•••

Billy sat in the Commander, his heart racing. He should have been ecstatic after taking out the man who had stolen Mimi from him. Instead, he was scared. There had been two close calls this time. The Dark Thoughts hadn't been prepared for the fact that the Barnacle could get cell phone reception out in the middle of nowhere from high up on the side of a mountain, nor had they prepared a proper escape route. Perhaps they had become sloppy in their insatiable hunger. Maybe Billy had become too reliant upon their ability to mysteriously create a perfect plan every time. Maybe he had screwed this one up himself by deciding to go back toward Spooner Lake instead of heading down to Incline Village. Regardless, he had almost been caught. He truly felt that only luck had gotten him out of this one. Luck was something he could not rely upon.

Billy pulled out onto highway 50 feeling a deep sense of foreboding. He saw another Douglas County Sherriff's car heading the opposite direction toward Spooner Summit. He could have sworn the driver was that damn Deputy Westwood.

CHAPTER 14

AN OFFER THAT CAN'T BE REFUSED

There he was again: Mr. Unassuming, standing outside of Billy's game, watching him intently with that look of secret knowledge. What began as intrigue for Billy was slowly turning into irritation. He had tried numerous times to engage the man in the last few months to no avail. His only guess was still that he was plain clothes observation. Mr. Unassuming always looked friendly with that relaxed smile of his. He never frowned and seemed polite enough whenever Billy attempted to speak to him. Regardless, the man made him nervous. There had to be a reason for the knowledge he exuded and why he stared at Billy the way he did.

That damn detective Westwood was starting to make him nervous too. He was sniffing around Harry's casino a bit too diligently. Billy wondered if he was starting to see a correlation amongst the "missing persons" and the "accidents" that had occurred in the last six months. He was getting way too close. Every time Billy thought about the detective these days The Dark Thoughts spoke to him. *"If you let that man live, he will unwind your existence. You must find a way to take him out. Engage him and eliminate him before he figures you out!"*

Billy was beginning to unravel. Mr. Smith and his Barnacle friend had brought his death toll up to eight. The Dark Thoughts were getting hungrier by the day. He was concerned that detective Westwood would accidentally find something that he had overlooked. The close call with the

Barnacle also made him nervous. Any small mistake like not knowing that cell phones could get reception on The Flume Trail could be devastating. He was starting to wonder if he should ease up a little, but every time those thoughts entered his mind, The Dark Thoughts argued vehemently with him. *"You cannot let up! You are a hero of the common citizens; a purveyor of vigilant justice! There are banes in this world who consider themselves above others and treat regular, hard-working people like they are lesser individuals. There is no room in this world for those who think that their position, place, or power give them the right to demean everyone else. They are rude, demanding, smug, arrogant, and uncaring. They exist in this world like a tumor, spreading the cancer of their vision of the order of things throughout all of society. You like to kill Billy, and the more assholes you remove from the mix, the better the world becomes. If anything, you need to step up your efforts. Tighten up your approach and widen your scope of vision. Do not let up!"*

These "pep talks" were occurring with greater frequency; each time Billy received one, he tightened up his resolve and kept his eyes open for the next victim. But it was becoming more and more difficult to fall into or even create those perfect situations he had enjoyed with the previous kills. The near debacle with Mr. Smith and his buddy left him with visions of jail and the inescapable stigma of being treated like a murderer and an animal for the rest of his life. He was sure no one would understand or condone the favor he was doing for all of society by removing these banes. It was an unfortunate fact, but the world still did not believe in vigilante justice, no matter how warranted.

Vanessa came around to Billy's side of the game and tapped him on the shoulder. It was time for his break. She gave him quick shoulder rub before he pushed out. "There you go big boy. Enjoy your twenty minutes of freedom!"

Billy loved this woman's touch. It made him think of Hope, whom he hadn't seen since May. "Thanks Vanessa. You've got a magic touch."

She whispered in his ear, flirtatious. "There's more where that came from."

Billy grinned at Vanessa as he walked out of the pit and headed for the side exit at Stateline Avenue to see if he might catch the sunset. He was pondering the danger of starting something up with her while still seeing Hope at the same time. Richie had always talked about keeping one girl in town and one out of town. He was a pig. Billy didn't think he could pull it off, but it sure would be fun. He missed Hope.

Billy stepped out the side door of the casino and into the surreal vision he was hoping for. He had caught the sunset at the perfect time. The brilliant hues of orange pink and purple spread out across the western skyline and reflected even more color off some clouds that had settled over Freel Peak to the south and east. A few small-engine airplanes cut across the sky, leaving their signature vapor trails. The air was scented with pine and still warm. Summer had arrived.

While Billy stood there breathing the fresh air and soaking up the beauty of his paradise, he felt a presence behind him that wasn't there mere seconds ago. He turned quickly and assumed an aggressive but defensive position. The man behind him stepped back, put his hands up in the air, and said "Hey, I'm a friend. It's okay." It was Mr. Unassuming, still wearing that serene grin.

Billy was surprised that this man was finally making contact. The mystery of the man with the look of knowledge was about to be revealed. “Sorry man. I get a little nervous when someone sneaks up on me from behind. Do you work for observation?”

Mr. Unassuming put his hands down. “No sir. I’m not from around here.”

Billy was irritated by that statement. “If you’re not from around here, then why the hell have you been watching me on my game for the last three months?”

The man smiled sheepishly and offered Billy his hand to shake. “It’s actually been the last four months. I’ve been watching you, the way you conduct yourself while you work, and how you are with your customers. I was particularly impressed with the way you handled that guy with the yellow hat and the fish necklace. You also did quite a job on that young Armenian kid. I couldn’t have done better myself. You’re good at what you do. You could say that we are kindred souls.”

With that last statement, The Dark Thoughts spoke frantically in Billy’s mind. *“This man knows about you! Take him out immediately! Break his neck or tear out his jugular and throw the body in the bushes; or better yet, throw the body over the fence surrounding the construction site across the street. They haven’t touched that project in over a year and no one goes in there anymore. You could come back later and dispose of it accordingly. You must act quickly! There are killers out there that gravitate toward others who do the same thing because they are looking for a friend or a “kindred soul”. If this guy has been watching you for four months, he can't be anything but trouble. You have a new target soldier, now remove it!"*

Billy winced at the strength of The Dark Thoughts' admonition, then mumbled to himself, or maybe to them "Just take it easy."

Mr. Unassuming smiled again. His hand was still outstretched for Billy to shake. "I'm sorry Billy. I didn't mean to scare you. I just wanted to talk to you about what you do and how skillfully you do it. I've finally made the decision to offer you the job of a lifetime."

Billy was even more taken aback by that statement. "What the hell are you talking about? I don't even know who you are."

The Dark Thoughts were frantic in the back of Billy's mind. *Take him out now! You cannot allow yourself to be compromised like this! You might think you could use a kindred soul in your endeavors, but the only way to stay safe is to remove anyone that could possibly compromise your existence. No one can know what you are doing Billy!"*

As Billy reached out to shake Mr. Unassuming's hand, The Dark Thoughts began to formulate a plan in his mind. *"Reach out to shake his hand and get a firm grip. Pull his arm down and across his body. When he adjusts his weight to resist this action, he will also try to release his grip. When he tries to release, allow him to, then bring your open palm upward to his exposed face and slam it with direct force into the underside of his nose. Place your left leg behind his knees and with the same open-palmed strike, hit him again, this time squarely in the sternum, following through with your blow so that he falls backward over your left leg and cracks his skull open on the metal railing behind him. Then you can quickly dispose of the body in one of the concrete planters or, if there's no traffic on Stateline Avenue, run it across the street and dump it over the fence in the construction site. You can come back later for the body, take it out to Moundhouse, and dump it in one of those mineshafts like you did with Mr. Vegas. Act quickly and efficiently Billy. No one can know what you're doing! Your whole existence will be compromised."*

Billy reached out to take Mr. Unassuming's hand, ready to execute the plan. Just before they touched, the man said something that stopped Billy in his tracks. "By the way, my name is Paul. I deal craps at The Palace in Las Vegas."

Billy stopped short, surprised. "The Palace?"

Paul took Billy's hand and shook it firmly. "Yes. The Palace in Las Vegas: The place of legends."

The statement caught Billy's interest, but he remained suspicious. He held tight to Mr. Unassuming's hand, still ready to execute. "If you work at The Palace in Vegas, how have you been able to watch me for the last four months?"

Paul smiled that unassuming smile of his once again. "I've been coming up here on one of my days off every other week since March to watch you deal, Billy. You're an exceptional dice dealer; an exceptional dealer in general. I would like to talk to you about..."

Billy cut him off, irritated. "What was all that stuff you were saying about "kindred souls"?"

Paul grinned sheepishly this time. "That's just a term I use to describe those of us who are proficient in the art of craps; those who know and respect the game."

Billy felt his tension ease, just a little but not enough. He needed to know more about this man. He glanced down at his watch and realized that he also needed to get back to his game. Releasing his grip, he smiled at Paul. "Well, if you're a dealer sir, you understand that I have to get back to my game before I burn someone of their break time."

"I understand completely, but I really would like to sit down for a while and talk to you about my offer. It's a serious one. I know you like to hang out at that Upper Corner Lounge after work, so I'll go up there and wait for you later. When are you due off?"

Billy hesitated in answering, still unsure about this unassuming man named Paul and his bizarre offer. The Dark Thoughts were still raving their suspicions in the back of his mind. *"Don't let this guy fool you with his false promises. You cannot compromise your existence by trusting anyone. You MUST take him out. Set up the meeting. When he shows, we'll figure out a way to remove him. No one can know what you're all about. We must continue to kill."*

Billy shook Paul's hand again as he moved for the door and offered a knowledgeable smile of his own. "I'm six to two tonight, but it's mid-week, so I might be off at one." He walked back to his game, curious, bewildered, and suspicious all at the same time. "The Palace" he thought to himself. "I wonder if the legends are true."

The rest of the night went agonizingly slow for Billy. A battle raged in his mind between his curiosity about a job offer at The Palace and The Dark Thoughts' desire to remove Mr. Unassuming from existence. They trusted no one, and they wanted to kill. For them, killing was the solution for everything.

Billy found himself arguing with them in his head. "This guy named Paul could really be legitimate. I should at least sit down with him and listen to what he has to say just in case he's for real. Dealing at The Palace is rumored to be the job of a lifetime; the pinnacle of gaming. I think we may have done too much killing here in Tahoe anyway. That damn detective Westwood is getting more suspicious with each kill. We could use a new venue. If this guy Paul turns out to be a fake, we can still figure out a means of taking him out. I'm going to meet with him."

The Dark Thoughts firmly disagreed. *"This man is dangerous. Anyone who has even the slightest possibility of knowing who and what you are cannot be allowed to exist. This story about a dealing job at The Palace is a farce. Jobs like that are given as favors to those who have a connection, not to complete strangers. Mr. Unassuming is feeding you a line of shit to get past your defenses. He is a bane to your existence and must be removed immediately. If you can figure out a way to get him out of the casino, maybe over to the house, we'll figure out a way to dispose of him permanently. Then we'll work on a means of removing detective Westwood as well. Tahoe is our home; we know it well. Our methods work here and will continue to work well if we remain careful."*

Billy felt that The Dark Thoughts were being a little over-zealous. Their desire to kill anyone and everyone that crossed his path was becoming stronger with each kill. While they provided him with near-perfect plans of attack each time, he felt that they needed to be kept in check. "Just calm down now. There's no need to get out of hand here. I want to see if he's for real or not."

•••

Billy got pushed off his game an hour early. After signing out, he swung by the UCL and sure enough, Mr. Unassuming was sitting there in the last seat in the corner with a "reserved" sign resting on the video poker machine next to him. Billy noted that Paul was playing video poker and that he had a shot and a beer. Maybe they truly were kindred souls. He headed downstairs to change out of his smoke-infested work shirt. While walking back up to the bar, he felt a twinge of anxiety combined with curiosity. As he neared the bar, he said to himself, "Let's see what this unassuming man named Paul has to say", and sat down in front of the reserved sign.

Paul looked up from his hand of video poker, smiled that knowing smile of his, and put out his hand to shake Billy's. "Hey there, I'm glad you showed. You seemed a little skeptical earlier."

Billy shook Paul's hand. His grip was firm and he appeared to be in excellent shape for an older man. "Wouldn't you be skeptical if someone snuck up to you from behind and told you they had been watching you for the last four months?"

Paulie the bartender came over and interrupted them for a moment. He set a shot of Jagermeister and a beertini down on the bar. "Hey Billy! Your friend here knows your order. He paid for this round in advance and told me you'd be here soon. How was your night, my brother?"

Billy slapped a five-dollar bill down on the bar. "It was pretty mellow tonight. Thanks for asking. How about you?"

Paulie was his usual positive self. "Just livin' the dream Billy. Just livin' the dream."

Billy turned to Mr. Unassuming and took him in for a brief moment. He appeared to be in his late forties or early fifties, grey and a bit balding on top but in good physical shape. His visage made Billy think of Hannibal Lecter, the insane killer from the movie Silence of the Lambs. A deeper look into Paul's eyes though did not reveal any hint of the insanity that Billy expected to see if he was interested in Billy's exploits as a killer. Of course, Billy didn't see anything like that when he looked in the mirror either. Regardless, he decided to approach Mr. Unassuming as his nickname suggested. He felt an angry push in the back of his mind from The Dark Thoughts, but they remained silent.

Billy picked up his shot of Jagermeister, saluted Mr. Unassuming with it, and put it down in one swallow. The cold burn on the back of his throat felt invigorating. "So, Paul from The Palace in Las Vegas, place of legends, why have you been staring at me from outside of my craps game for the last four months, and what is this "job of a lifetime" that you speak of?"

Paul flashed that unassuming smile once again, raised his own shot of Jager in Billy's direction, and shot it down the same way Billy had. "Well Mr. Stone, like I told you before, The Palace truly is a legendary place in all aspects, but from a dealing perspective, the stories don't even begin to describe what it's like. Now I'm going to share with you some information that is true and correct about the dealing position at The Palace, but if we don't come to an amicable agreement after this conversation, don't even think about trying to reveal the things that I tell you as truth. Anything you say publicly regarding the conversation we're about to have will be diffused into the legends. If you should decide to press the issue, pressure will be put upon you to refrain. I'm about to reveal information to you that could possibly get you into trouble, depending on how loose your tongue is, or how well you guard it. Do you still want to hear what I have to say?"

Now Billy's interest was piqued. He decided to forego The Dark Thoughts' plan of elimination and hear Paul out. "I'll give you my word that this conversation stays between you, me and these two video poker machines. Let's hear your story."

Paul smiled at Billy with that knowledgeable look again, then frowned slightly and nodded his head toward the other end of the bar where Paulie stood conversing with some players. "Perhaps we should go somewhere more private for this, if you know what I mean."

The Dark Thoughts pressed in the back of Billy's mind. *"Now's your chance to get him into a compromised position. Get him back over to the house and you can either knock him out with the GHB or just finish the deal with cyanide. You know where to dispose of the body. You have a potential enemy; do NOT be soft!"*

Billy ignored The Dark Thoughts, making a conscious effort not to speak out loud. His curiosity was greater than their paranoia. Instead, he addressed Paul with a serious look. "Don't worry about Paulie. He's been a bartender for over thirty years. Like all good bartenders, he never lets his information leave the bar. We're okay here."

Paul seemed skeptical. He finally let out a long sigh and began his story. "The Palace is a special casino Billy, more special than you can imagine. Our clientele is without a doubt the richest collective group of gamblers in the world. Everyone who's anyone in the elite echelon of wealth in the western hemisphere chooses The Palace when they want to gamble. We have thirty-five craps games, and only ten of them have a table minimum of less than five hundred dollars. An individual must have a minimum credit line of five million bucks to even be considered for entrance into what we call "The Inner Circle". I'll explain that part to you later.

What you need to understand is that there's more money risked in our casino annually than all the other casinos in Las Vegas combined. We allow a handful of special players to wager as much as ten million dollars on a single hand of blackjack or a single roll of the dice on a craps game. Whether the money is new, old, legitimate, inherited, or crooked, they all come to The Palace.

I know you've seen some money come through this place Billy, but even Harry's biggest fishes would have a hard time qualifying for The Outer Circle, which is our lowest level gaming area. We don't even let foot traffic off the street into our place. Our clientele wants privacy, and they want complete and total efficiency when they play. You are a very knowledgeable dealer Billy; you handle your customers with the utmost professionalism while dealing a procedurally perfect game at the same time. You also know how to put up with gamblers when they act up, which always happens at some point. I'm sure you're also aware that the richer the customer, the worse they can be while gambling. That's why The Palace demands that its dealers are the best of the best, consummate professionals. The rumors state that someone must die for someone else to get a dealing position at our place. Well, that's pretty much true, but the second part of the rumor, that a dealing position at The Palace is inherited or given as a favor is completely false. We recruit our dealers from casinos all over the world, and we only go after the best. Our dealers are required to put up with all the shit that our players can dish out. They must also maintain professionalism and decorum at all times. It takes a special breed of dealer to be able to deal at The Palace, but the reward is immense."

At this point, Paul paused, most likely to gauge Billy's reaction to everything he just stated, especially the part about reward. Billy raised one eyebrow and started to say something, but then Paulie showed up with another round. "Sorry to interrupt your conversation gentlemen, but you both looked dry. These are on the house since you're both playing." He winked at Billy as he put the drinks down and glanced covertly at Billy's machine. Billy noticed that he had no credits and realized he hadn't put any money into the machine since he sat down. He quickly pulled out a twenty and slipped it into the machine's bill acceptor, then grinned at Paulie.

Paul was smiling with knowledge again. He understood that exchange and deftly passed a ten-dollar bill across the bar to Paulie. This man was savvy in his casino knowledge. They would get free drinks for the rest of the night if they played an occasional hand during their conversation. Paulie smiled that wide grin of his. "I won't bother you two gentlemen again until your drinks are empty. Call me over if you need me."

Paul looked over at Billy and said "He really is as good as you say."

"Oh yeah, Paulie's one of the best. I've known him for over ten years now." Billy stared at Paulie as he high-fived a customer at the other end of the bar who had just hit a four-of-a-kind, then he turned back to Paul. "So, now that you've grabbed my interest Paul, by all means please finish your story. I'm curious to hear the truth in the rumors."

Paul fixed Billy with a most serious stare. "All right bud, but remember that everything I tell you must stay between us, otherwise there will be trouble."

"Absolutely sir. Not a word comes out of my mouth about this exchange."

Paul sighed. "Now that that's clear, I'll tell you first that the dealers at The Palace earn somewhere close to a quarter million dollars a year."

A harsh half-laugh, half-cough escaped Billy's throat before he could control it. "That's not possible. You're saying you earn over five thousand a week?"

Paul chuckled at Billy's astonishment. "Good math skills my friend; that's a sign of a good craps dealer, and yes, it is possible. Most of us earn that amount working four days a week or less. A thousand-dollar day is low for us. Two thousand is usually the expectation. Just as in any casino, the tips are directly proportional to the level of the clientele, and there is no doubt that our customers are at a higher collective level of wealth than any other place in the western hemisphere. I say "the western hemisphere" because a couple of those places in Macao and Monaco have an established grip on the wealth that comes from Asia and Europe respectively, but The Palace is slowly chiseling away at those folks too. We're the only place in the world that accepts a single wager of five million dollars."

Paul paused for a moment and took a deep breath as if he were poised on a precipice, ready to jump." So, this is the position that I'm offering you; a most coveted dealing job at the place of legends." He fell silent at that point, waiting for an answer.

Billy asked Paul the first question that came to his mind. "Why me?"

"Good question. It happened most indirectly. I was watching another young man who stood out above everyone else in here, mostly due to his customer skills. His name is Richie Wylde, and he sent me to you."

Billy couldn't believe what Paul had just said. If they had been in a cartoon, his jaw would have unhinged and dropped to the bar. "You've got to be kidding me! Richie was my roommate, my best friend, and my gaming mentor. He just up and disappeared one day about nine months ago. There were rumors that he was stealing tokes, but there was never any proof. He left no trace as to his whereabouts after he flew the coop. I still have all of his things at the house."

Paul looked grim. "I'm aware of all that, Billy. I came here in search of him last November. When I found out he was gone, I asked around and couldn't find a single iota of information. I hired two of the best private investigators in the state of Nevada to track him down. They finally found him dealing on a riverboat in Kansas City. I watched him for only a month. It was obvious he was the man for the job. He's one of the best dealers I've ever seen, and believe me, I've watched many craps dealers over the years. When I finally approached him with the offer, he immediately refused. For the life of me I couldn't figure out why in the world anyone would say no to the dealing job of a lifetime, but now that you've told me about the reasons for his abrupt disappearance from here, I can see why he wouldn't want to come back and work in Nevada. It's easy to hide in some dumped-out river boat in Kansas City; not so easy in the greatest casino in Las Vegas. Anyway, he understood the brevity of my search as well as the quality of dealer I was looking for, so he gave me your name. He told me he taught you everything you know about the game of craps. He even went so far as to call you an exact dealing replica of himself. He sold me on you. I still had to watch you for a while to be sure in my own mind, but now I know he was right."

Billy was beyond amazement. Richie, even in his absence, was still helping him to further his dealing existence. "You've got to tell me where he is or how to get in touch with him. He's the closest friend I've ever had in my life. Richie Wylde is like a brother to me. I have to know where he's at."

Paul answered Billy solemnly. "I'm sorry my friend, but he already saw this coming. He told me he would be moving on after I left him, and he extracted a promise from me not to reveal anything I knew of his existence to anyone beyond what I've just told you. He also asked me to tell you that you should take this job. He told me to tell you these exact words, although I have no idea what they mean: "This job will help you keep your dark thoughts imprisoned." He said you would understand." With that final statement, Paul fell silent and let Billy ponder the load he had just dumped on him.

Billy sat there, bewildered. The excitement of the possibility of finding his friend and mentor, then the subsequent dashing of those hopes, was almost too much for him to bear. Add to that the insane revelation of the truths about The Palace combined with an offer that couldn't be refused, and he was rendered speechless. He couldn't even think straight, so he just played a few hands of video poker.

Paulie stopped by with two more shots of Jagermeister. Billy grabbed his shot, slammed it, and asked Paulie for another one. Paulie looked a bit concerned and glanced askance at Paul. He could tell that something was bothering Billy. "Sure my friend. You got it."

To Billy's pleasant surprise, the hand of video poker he had loaded before doing his shot was four cards to an open-ended straight flush. He looked over at Paul, who was smiling at the machine with that knowing grin of his. "Do you believe in fate Mr. Paul?"

Paul looked Billy straight in the eye and put one hand over the odd card that Billy needed to throw out to draw either a three or eight of clubs. "Yes I do; deeply."

Billy stared into Paul's eyes and hit the draw button. The music began before Paul pulled his hand back to reveal the three of clubs. Billy had just hit a four-hundred-dollar straight flush. Paul's grin widened. "That's less than two hours of work at your new job Billy."

Billy was sold in that instance. He was a strong believer in fate, and the monetary prospects truly made Paul's offer impossible to refuse. On top of that, things were getting hot for him in Tahoe. He was sure that if he continued killing like he was, that damn detective Westwood would figure him out. Tahoe was becoming too small for Billy Stone. Las Vegas, the City of Sin, beckoned. He could do some serious work in such a large city where disappearances and accidents occurred daily, and he would have the financial wherewithal to use even more creative and high-tech methods to remove societal banes. He could still maintain his relationship with Hope; in fact, it would be easier and faster for her to fly to Vegas from San Francisco than it was for her to drive to Tahoe. All the logical arguments told him to accept Paul's offer immediately, but one thought caused Billy to hesitate. The Dark Thoughts planted a seed of uncertainty in his mind that immediately took root and made Billy question what the hell he was thinking. *"Why would you leave paradise to go to hell?"*

Billy let go of Paul's gaze and stared down at the club straight flush on the video monitor. His resignation must have shown on his face. Paul was frowning when he looked up. He couldn't bring himself to casually throw away the life he had created for himself here in Tahoe. "Paul, I'm sorry, but I need some time to think about this."

Now it was Paul's turn to be astonished. Besides Richie, every other recipient of his offer to work the greatest dealing job in existence had immediately accepted and worried about the details later. He was not used to rejection. He was curt in his response. "You'll never receive an offer like this again Billy. I needed a worthy replacement four months ago, and I've invested a lot of my time and a great deal of my faith in you. Richie warned me that you might not ever consider leaving Tahoe. If you think you're going to miss it too much, realize that you'll be able to not only buy a home in Vegas, but also a home right here in your little paradise within two years. There are flights from Reno to Vegas and back all day every day. You could go back and forth as if you were driving from here to Sacramento. You won't lose all your time in

Tahoe, just part of it. This is an offer that can't be refused Billy. I'll give you twelve hours to think about it. Let's meet at that favorite coffee shop of yours over there on the corner of highway 50 and Pioneer Trail; it's called Alpen Sierra right?" He looked down at his watch, which happened to be a Rolex. "It's 2 a.m. right now. I'll be there at precisely 2 p.m. tomorrow afternoon, I'll order a twenty-ounce triple mocha and one of those hot ham and cheddar croissants and take my sweet time enjoying them while I read the Tahoe Daily Tribune and the Mountain News. If I don't see you by four p.m., I'll leave town and head to the destination of my next search. I'll most likely never come back to Tahoe in search of another candidate, and we'll both pretend we never knew each other and never had this conversation. If I do see you, I'll shake your hand and we'll go over the details of getting you moved down to Vegas immediately." He stood up and shook Billy's hand firmly. This time his smile was less unassuming and more Hannibal Lecter. "You can give those credits in my machine to Paulie there for his professionalism. I hope to see you tomorrow. Good night." He stalked off, tense but still unassuming.

Billy watched Paul disappear through the maze of slot machines. When he was finally out of sight, he stared at his straight flush, immersed in a surreal numbness, overwhelmed by the conversation that just transpired. He had just been offered a chance to be a millionaire while working less than five days a week and he was considering rejecting the offer. How much was paradise actually worth?

Paulie's voice snapped him out of his fugue. "Hey Billy. Is everything okay? It looked like you two were having a pretty intense conversation, then he abruptly left. Are you cool?"

Billy looked up at Paulie, still confused, and answered him offhandedly. "Yeah bud, it's all good. It was an intense conversation, but everything's cool." Intense didn't even begin to describe what Billy had just experienced.

After getting paid for his straight flush, Billy gave the slot attendant a twenty and dropped two twenties on the bar for Paulie. He slipped out the side doors that led to the third floor of the parking garage and drove straight home. He had less than twelve hours to sort through the confusion in his mind. He wanted to get rip-roaring drunk, but he knew that precious time needed to be spent thinking clearly.

•••

Billy rose early the next morning, had a quick breakfast at home, loaded the mountain bike onto the Commander, and headed across town to the trailhead at Angora Lakes. He pounded hard up the one-lane winding road, deftly avoiding tourists in their SUV's full of kids, water toys, and camping equipment. The road and the resort were always busy in the summer time. He usually didn't even bother with Angora until the fall but today he needed to sit in his favorite spot in Tahoe and ponder his future. He crested the ridgeline that separated Tahoe Paradise from Fallen Leaf Lake at high noon. Paul would be at Alpen Sierra Coffee Shop in two hours.

There was a small turnout where the road summited. From here, it headed downward into a small canyon, ending at the parking lot that served the resort. The road literally followed the ridgeline here, with barely ten feet on either side before a steep drop-off into the valleys below. There were two small rustic structures built in a wide flat spot that afforded unobstructed views of the valleys on both sides. They were used by the forest service as lookouts during fire season. This spot had panoramic views of Fallen Leaf Lake, Desolation Wilderness, Mount Tallac, and Lake Tahoe to the north, and Tahoe Paradise, Meyers, the Tahoe airport, and Echo summit to the south. Billy liked to sit on a bench that was in between the two structures and stare at the raw, rugged beauty of Tahoe. He never tired of the view and could sit in that same spot for hours, soaking in the majesty. It was also his favorite place to sit and think, which is what he needed to do today.

Billy hadn't even considered that The Dark Thoughts would be a part of his decision-making process until they began to pontificate in his mind. *"We can't leave Tahoe. This has been home for longer than any other place in your life, and we know it well. We know what places are safe for conducting our business, and we know them intimately. We know and understand our prey, and they are all easy targets. You have a niche here that you may not be able to develop in Las Vegas. Our efforts there could be fruitless. We have a calling, and Tahoe is the best place for us to answer that calling. You cannot leave."*

Billy was unaware that he began to answer out loud. "It's getting too hot here. This is a small and concentrated area compared to a city like Las Vegas. It may take some time to scope things out and get the lay of the land, but we will be much more anonymous there. A quarter million dollars a year in earning potential doesn't hurt either.

The Dark Thoughts seemed angry in their response. *"We have a perfect situation here! You cannot give this up. We are just beginning to realize our potential here. Don't walk away from your place in this world! You will wither in Vegas and we will writhe in frustration. You've sculpted a perfect life for yourself here in Tahoe, Billy Stone. You are evolving into a being of pure vigilante justice. This is where you can continue to grow, not that Cibola in the brutal desert they call Las Vegas!"*

The Dark Thoughts fell silent and Billy chose not to respond. He stared down at the shimmering waters of Fallen Leaf Lake, a thousand feet below him, then just a little eastward at Lake Tahoe in all its grandeur. He turned his head slowly to the left, looking west into Desolation Wilderness. The rugged granite made him think of ancientness and longevity. This place truly was an earthbound slice of heaven. He thought of Hope and their potential future together. He thought about his closest remaining friends, Pablo and Luis. He thought about killing and going to jail. He thought of earning enough money to see the world, to live well, to not have any more financial worries. He tried to assimilate it all; tried to grasp at a small speck of his future and what it would be like if he stayed in Tahoe or if he went to Vegas. Vegas represented a new beginning, while Tahoe was the perfect life. The Dark Thoughts were hell-bent on staying, and convincing in their argument, but Billy had been thinking a great deal about jail time. The two weeks he spent in the brig in Baghdad was enough to make him never want to return to any type of criminal holding facility. Any slipup, any weak strategy would unhinge his beloved existence here in Tahoe

"Billy, you worry too much; especially about getting caught and going back to jail. Killing is an integral part of your nature. You must continue to take out the banes; the ones that like to throw around their place and power, as well as their pocketbooks. There are so many of these idiots who come to Tahoe unprotected by friends, family, or entourage. Together, we can continue your evolution as a killer, continue to protect the interests of hard working people who don't deserve to be treated so poorly by these arrogant, uncaring......."

"That's enough!" Billy shouted out loud. Luckily, no one was around to hear his vehement explosion. For the first time in months, he completely shut The Dark Thoughts out. It was time to start a new life; to try again to imprison The Dark Thoughts behind the old barriers and live normally. He looked at his watch. It was 3:30. Billy couldn't believe he had been sitting here in conversation with himself for over three hours. He was going to have to haul ass to make it to Alpen Sierra before Paul left forever.

•••

Mr. Unassuming sat in the coffee shop, staring out the window at the cars driving by on highway 50. It was five minutes 'til four. His frustration was greater than it had ever been since he started recruiting for The Palace over fifteen years ago. This man Billy Stone was an anomaly. How could anyone pass up the chance to earn hundreds of thousands of dollars every year doing the exact same thing he was doing here in this accursed Lake Tahoe for one-fifth that amount? There was something strange about these Tahoe people. The mountains changed them, held them, comforted them, quelled their desire for something better. There must be something in the air that made them all loony. He had just wasted four months of his time on a sentimental mamby-pamby.

Paul threw back the last of his triple mocha, stood up and muttered to himself “I’m never coming back to this accursed place again. The people here are all insane.” He took one last glance out the window at the highway and saw a familiar black Jeep Commander pull in and park right in front of his window. Out stepped Billy Stone, covered in sweat and salt deposits. He was staring frantically at his watch. Paul looked down at his own watch. It was 3:59 p.m. He stepped out the front door of Alpen Sierra to shake the hand of the man he expected to be working with for the rest of his dealing career.

CHAPTER 15

SOLO WORK

It was Friday night and Harry's casino was jumping. A roar emitted from the craps pit. People were winning. They roared collectively, as if the winning goal had just been scored. Mike Westwood walked up to the California bar adjacent to the mayhem of the craps pit. His heart beat faster and his hand shook a little as he pulled a twenty out of his wallet and anxiously slipped it into the bill acceptor of the video poker machine in front of him. He looked around nervously, waiting for the bartender to come take his order. Memories of the old painful routine made his stomach turn.

"Crown and Coke please" was what Mike wanted to say when the bartender came over. How many thousands of times had he said that in the past? He asked for a diet Coke instead, no cherry. The five-dollar tip he left ensured that the bartender wouldn't give him a hard time for sitting in front of a machine with credits and not playing. He hadn't gambled a dime since he left Vegas. He was also clean and sober for over two hundred days.

Mike wasn't at Harry's on a busy Friday night to drink and gamble; he was there to watch Billy Stone. This was the third time he had come to watch Billy since Captain Vanderwaal had backed him off. He had to satisfy his need to investigate in an unofficial capacity now. His seat at the bar gave him an unobstructed view of the craps game that Billy Stone apparently worked every weekend. He kept his old Atlanta Braves cap pulled down low and stayed bundled up in his puffy North Face jacket even though it was burning hot in this spot at the bar, all to keep his features and build indiscernible. He buried his face deeper into the screen of his machine when Stone walked by on his breaks. He took occasional sips of his diet soda, which the bartender diligently filled for another five-dollar tip each time it went empty. Other than that, Mike just watched.

Mike had never played craps, but he was slowly beginning to understand the insane dynamic of the game. The dealers entered the game on the outside spot of the game. When they were in that spot, players referred to them as "stick". "Hey stick, give me five dollar yo eleven! Yo stickman, you gonna pay me for that hard eight?" After twenty minutes, a new dealer pushed into the stick spot and the old stick went to one of the base spots for another twenty minutes. After another twenty minutes on the next base, the dealer who had been on the game for an hour left the table for what appeared to be a forty-minute break. This part confused Mike because Rennie had told him that all dealers got twenty minute breaks. Maybe craps dealers were special because they worked harder. Mike wasn't sure, but every time Billy Stone went on break, he didn't come back to the craps game for forty minutes. He wondered what Billy did with that time.

Mike had watched Billy for at least four hours each of the last two sessions. The guy was a master of his craft, if that could even be said about a craps dealer. He handled his customers deftly, using a light touch on newcomers who wanted to learn and a heavy hand on the troublemakers. His stick calls were precise but animated. He fired up the crowd with his dice calls. He stayed calm and focused when the game erupted during a big roll and spent his time cajoling with important customers when the game was slow. Mike watched these interactions carefully. He was looking for something, anything that would support his theory that Billy Stone had something to do with all the missing and/or dead people who had patronized Harry's Casino. He hadn't seen anything solid yet. Billy Stone seemed to be nothing more than a dude who dealt in a casino. Mike was still haunted by that distant look in the man's eyes when he spoke of his encounters with Stan Kurchstein and Joe Benton. He also didn't believe that it was coincidence that Stone was a mere four miles away from Mr. Smith and his friend when they died on the Flume Trail. He had seen Billy in his Commander on the side of highway 50 while on his way to answering the call on Mr. Smith. Mike was a patient man though. He had faith that given time, his "stakeout" would pay off. He took another sip of his second diet Coke and watched Billy shake hands with four high rollers who had just landed on the table. "Faith", he thought to himself. "You've got to maintain it Mike."

After two more hours of watching and waiting, Mike was ready to call it quits for the night. The twenty untouched credits called to him from within the video poker machine. He wanted to press that "deal" button in the worst way. Nothing new was happening with Billy Stone and his craps game, and Mike's resolve was beginning to weaken. He had to get out of the casino before he cracked.

Mike pressed the cashout button on his machine as Billy pushed out to go on his third break since the stakeout had started. It was time to call it a night. Patience and tenacity were both key to this type of investigation, and Mike had ample amounts of each. He would try again next week. He thanked the bartender and was turning to leave when he saw something that made him sit right back down.

There was Billy Stone, standing at the far end of the bar, kissing the beautiful Asian woman who had sat down about an hour ago. Mike had noticed that the girl was staring at Billy's craps game the whole time, enrapt. Now he knew why. That beautiful little princess had to be Stone's girlfriend. He watched them stare adoringly into each other's eyes as they spoke for a few moments, then Billy looked at his watch, gave her another kiss and a hug, and walked off the casino floor. "Patience and tenacity", Mike thought to himself. "They always pay off." He walked over to the empty seat next to the girl. It was time to probe for information. He had to work quickly. If Stone decided to stop by for another kiss at the end of his break, he would surely recognize him.

Mike smiled at Billy's girlfriend as he slipped his voucher into the machine in front of him. She was even more stunning up close. Her smile was warm and open. Mike made conversation immediately. "Hi there. You don't mind if I try my luck here do you? That other machine just killed me."

She flashed that warm smile again and rubbed the top of his machine. "By all means, and good luck to you sir."

"Thank you so much. I'll try not to be a bother. I don't smoke, I don't swear, and I promise not to hit on you, especially since I saw you giving some love to that dealer when he went on his break. That was Billy Stone wasn't it? You guys dating?"

She brightened at the mention of Stone's name. "Yeah, I guess you could say we're dating. We've been seeing each other for about four months. We met here on a blackjack game about two days before Christmas. My name is Hope by the way. Hope Henessey. How do you know Billy?"

Mike logged the name away in the back of his mind. Hope Henessey. He also tagged when she said they first met. It was the same time that Kurchstein had gone missing. Every piece of information could be vital. He offered his hand to shake. "Please forgive my rudeness. My name is Mike Westwood. I've run into Billy a few times in here. He's one of their best dealers."

Hope's grip was firm but delicate. That endearing smile was enough to melt any man's heart. "Hey, if you want to say hi to him, he should be coming back from his break any minute now."

Mike was perplexed. He thought he had another twenty-five minutes before Stone finished his break. "I thought the craps dealers got a fort- minute break."

"Oh no. They get a twenty just like all the other dealers. After that break, they come back and do twenty minutes on a blackjack game before they come to the craps game for an hour. He'll be back in about five minutes. I'm sure he'll stop by to say hi to me again."

So that was why Billy left the craps game for forty minutes. Mike had to get out of there before Stone came back. His plan to spend twenty minutes casually talking to this girl Hope to garner some information about her boyfriend was no longer going to work. Damn! He decided to fire a warning shot in Billy Stone's direction before he left. He wanted to let Billy know he was being watched. He made a point of looking at his watch. "Hey, it's later than I thought. I have to get home to catch the eleven o' clock news. It was nice meeting you Hope." He pressed the cash out button on his machine and pulled out his wallet to put away the voucher. He found one of his old business cards from Vegas. It said "Mike Westwood, Investigator" and had his cell phone number on it. He handed it to Hope. "Tell Billy to call me if he ever runs into trouble. My cell number is on there."

Hope frowned as she looked at the card. "You're a cop in Las Vegas?"

Mike decided to go with that story just to trip Billy's mind up a little bit more. "Yes ma'am. I'm in homicide. It was nice to meet you Hope Henessey. Maybe I'll see you again some time." He turned and practically ran out the side exit.

Hope watched the cop in the puffy ski jacket haul ass out the side exit. She took another look at Mike Westwood's business card, frowned, and slipped it into the slot behind her driver's license in her wallet. She would give it to Billy later after she told him the story about her strange encounter. She ordered another Cosmopolitan and wondered why a homicide investigator would want Billy to have his card. She just chalked it up as another one of the strange things that occurred in the casino industry. It had already been an interesting four months with Billy Stone.

Billy rushed around the corner of the California bar a few minutes later. She was going to tell him about Mike Westwood but he was already talking as he approached her. "Hey Baby, I'm running late, probably burning Luis on his break, but I forgot to tell you the good news. I just got offered a job at The Palace in Las Vegas. It's that legendary dealing spot I was telling you about. Two hundred plus a year. What do you think of that?" Before she could answer, he gave her a bearhug and a kiss on the cheek. "I gotta run. I'll be off soon and I'll tell you all the details."

Hope sat there and watched Billy hurry off toward the blackjack game. She couldn't believe the bomb he had just dropped on her. A dealing job in Las Vegas worth over two hundred thousand dollars a year? Billy had just hit the lottery. Perhaps she had too. She sipped her Cosmo and tried to wrap her mind around the idea of visiting Billy in Vegas, maybe even moving there herself. She completely forgot about her encounter with Detective Mike Westwood.

CHAPTER 16

CITY OF SIN

What happens here.... stays here.

"Welcome to Fabulous Las Vegas" stated the iconic sign located on The Strip just south of the Mandalay Bay. Billy had just driven through the worst snarl of freeway exchanges and traffic he had seen since the last time he had visited Elmer in The Bay Area. The sign was inviting and colorful; a gateway from the dead, dry desert into the jungle of man. There were even twelve parking spots in the median so that the lookeyloos and picture hounds didn't have to risk their lives running across the highway to get a picture in front of the sign. Las Vegas was a most accommodating city.

Billy was supposed to meet Paul at The Palace as soon as he got into town. He didn't know his way around but Paul had told him to just drive in on The Strip and look for the MGM. The Palace was right next door. It was an elegant tower, but nondescript compared to the neon behemoths around it. Sans the gaudy lights and signage, it had the look of old money, like a bank. When Billy tried to pull in to the valet area, he was stopped by an armed security guard; strange for a casino in this day and age.

The guard was stern but polite. "I'm sorry sir, but this parking is for members only."

Billy had already been warned about this stop. "Hi there. I was told to tell you that I'm expected by Paul G."

The guard pulled a list out of his pocket and peered at it for a moment. "Are you Billy Stone?"

"Yes sir, I am."

"Just let me check some ID and then you can pull on over to that row of cars on the right there."

Billy parked and stepped out into the stifling Las Vegas heat. A digital sign in front of a bank on the strip had told him that it was 114 degrees. "Welcome to fabulous Las Vegas" he thought to himself. He stepped through the simple tinted glass doors into a completely unexpected world.

The lobby of The Palace was one of the most opulent Billy had ever seen. It was decorated in shades of olive and maroon, with an early 1920's antique décor. Chandeliers hung everywhere. Elegance permeated throughout this place. He sat down on an ivory and mahogany couch and looked around, amazed. The bellmen wore tuxedoes and the front desk staff members were all adorned in sharp Armani suits. The small handful of guests that were around all had an air of importance about them. Billy thought he recognized a few from television. He looked up and saw Paul coming down the escalator. He was dressed in a black tuxedo with tails and still had that serene look of knowledge on his face.

"Welcome to The Palace Billy." He shook Billy's hand firmly, motioned for him to follow, and headed right back up the escalator. "Follow me and I'll show you around the casino floor. I'll introduce you to our craps crew and maybe some of the bosses. How was your drive?"

Billy was resigned in his response. "It was long, hot, and boring."

Paul flashed him that grin of knowledge again. “Don’t worry Bud, you’ll never have to make that drive again. Soon you’ll be able to afford to fly everywhere you go, or pay someone to drive you. Welcome to your new life. He spread his right arm out in welcome as they reached the top of the escalator.

Billy was expecting to see a normal casino at the top of this escalator. Instead, he saw something out of an old movie. There were no bright flashing lights, no signs hawking reward card deals, no drunken idiots roaming around screaming and yelling, no loud obnoxious carpet, no maze of slot machines; none of the usual things one saw in every other casino he had been in.

The casino floor of The Palace resembled an old gentlemen’s club, the kind where men went to smoke cigars and talk about money; or perhaps it was more like one of those British casinos, serious and stuffy. The décor was the same as the lobby, opulent and elegant. The dealers all wore tuxedoes with tails, royal blue bow ties, and matching cumber buns. The pit bosses wore the same black Armani suits that the front desk people were wearing, and the waitresses all wore evening gowns. There were beautiful leather and cloth couches and chairs dispersed amongst the blackjack pits that were situated all along the left side of the room. The longest bar Billy had ever seen went down the right side of the room. The slot machines filled in the open spaces on the walls, backlit by soft blue neon. The carpet was a plush, impeccable dark burgundy that worked perfectly with the mahogany furniture and trim that was everywhere. The elegant chandeliers provided soft light for the whole casino floor. The music coming from hidden overhead speakers everywhere was currently Sinatra. There was a light din of conversation at this end of the casino, accented by an occasional outburst from one of the blackjack tables. Most of the noise in the room came from the far end of the room. Billy was sure that was the craps pit.

Billy noticed that there were no limit signs on the table games. Perplexed, he asked Paul "What's up with the limit signs, or lack thereof?"

"The dealers all know their limits by heart, and most of the players do too. We don't have random people roaming around looking for five dollar tables. We don't even let people in off the streets. Every customer knows they're betting at least a hundred dollars on all table games and at least five dollars a pull on the slot machines. We have a few twenty-five-dollar craps games in the outer circle of the craps pit so that family members and entourage people can pass time while the big fish play big money above, but that's about it. This is real high stakes gaming Billy. We aren't messing around here, and neither are our players. These hundred-dollar card games that you see on the casino floor are only the peanuts of this place. We have private rooms where people bet at least ten thousand dollars a hand on blackjack or baccarat, and the inner circle of the craps pit has three games that are a one-thousand-dollar minimum, three games that are a five-thousand-dollar minimum, and two ten-thousand-dollar games. You and I will ultimately be working there most of the time after I break you in."

They approached the far end of the casino and the craps pit. It was an interesting setup. The casino floor abruptly ended at a four-foot high railing that went across the whole room. The craps pit was actually in a pit, somewhat like an orchestra pit, on the other side of this railing. There were three tiers, with the first tier about a half-story below the casino floor and the third tier about a half-story above it. People lined the railing and watched the craps players from afar. There were elegant curved stairwells at either side that led down to the first tier and similar stairwells that led to each higher tier. Security guards stood at the top of each stairwell. Paul stopped in the middle of the floor at the railing and leaned over it, looking out over the craps pit.

"This is going to be your new home away from home Billy. This is where the strongest craps players in the world come to play. The Europeans love their Blackjack and Roulette, and the Asians love Baccarat and Pai Gow, but you know as well as I do that craps is truly an American game. The richest people in the world come here to roll dice. Billions of dollars go through this pit every year. Some of that money goes into our pockets."

Billy was impressed. "Why the three-tiered layout? Wouldn't it be better to have all the games on one level?"

Paul flashed that knowing grin of his again. "The tier system creates competition. You know how rich people like to show off their wealth. Everyone wants to outdo or show up everyone else, so the Palace set it up so that they can do just that. The lower tier has twenty-five and hundred dollar minimum games. The middle tier has five-hundred dollar games. The top tier has those thousand, five-thousand, and ten-thousand dollar games I was telling you about. Players get rated according to their wealth and their play. Everyone can go into the first tier. Some are rich enough to play on the second tier. Very few are allowed on the third tier. You'd be amazed at how feverishly some people will gamble just to gain entrance to a higher tier. On the third tier, you look down on everyone else; King of the Hill, if you will."

Billy was amazed by the simple genius of such a system, the way that architecture and numbers combined to affect a core behavior, stroking the players' egos and their desire to show off.

Paul waved his hand out over the first tier. Billy counted at least fifteen craps games down there. "This is where most of the friends, entourage members, and bodyguards play. That's why we have a few twenty-five dollar games. A lot of new money plays down here on the hundred dollar games; sports stars, movie stars, dot-comers, people like that."

Billy watched the play going on below him. Every game was full. Many of the customers he recognized from television or magazines. There were ridiculously tall NBA players standing shoulder to shoulder with daytime talk show hosts, football players high-fiving Fortune Five Hundred executives, and A-list actresses cheering on famous comedians. None of the usual barriers existed down there. They were all united by their addiction to, love of, or frenzied fever for the game of craps.

Paul then pointed directly ahead. The second tier was level with the casino floor. It had ten craps games. "The middle tier attracts a lot of politicians. You know, the kind that get monetary kickbacks from big business and things like that. There are also real estate barons, hoteliers, banking executives, and wall street cronies on the five-hundred dollar games. They all like to rub shoulders with each other."

Billy noticed that only half of those games were in use at the time. Only one was completely full. Paul motioned to that game. "Take a close look at that game Billy. Do you recognize anyone?" Billy stared at the game for a moment, shook his head no.

"You may not recognize them now, but soon you'll know all of them. That game regularly attracts some of the most powerful and influential men in this nation. You're looking at the Governors of four of the largest states in the union, the Senators from those same states, the CEO of one of the largest investment firms back east, the owner of the largest timber operation in the northwest, two of the most powerful sports agents in the nation, and the owner of the second largest personal computer distributor out there. The rest of those guys are their lawyers and advisors. That group comes here at least once a month to play craps and "discuss things". When you deal at The Palace, you keep your mouth shut, speak only when spoken to, and forget everything you heard the minute you walk out of the pit. Our clients all demand the highest degree of discretion when they play. You're to never talk about anything or anyone you hear or see in this pit. Any staff member who does so and gets caught is immediately released, and while it sounds shitty to lose such a great job over a loose tongue, the most dangerous part is that you'll have to deal with the person or persons that you've blabbed about. You could find your way to the bottom of Lake Mead in a pair of concrete boots if you're not careful Billy."

The severity of the position was slowly sinking in on Billy. He was beginning to understand how the dealers here earned such good tips. They had to give up a part of their humanity to participate in this circus of the wealthy and powerful.

Paul then gestured to the tier that overlooked them all. There were six games up there. Currently they were all empty. "The top tier attracts mostly old money and oil money. We get a lot of the second and third generations of the families that own many of the most powerful corporations in this country. They're the ones that didn't work a day in their lives for the millions and billions of dollars that they have. They have no respect for their fortune and thus no qualms about blowing it in a casino. Most of them are rotten as all hell; rude, drunk, strung out on drugs, and abusive. You earn your money when you deal to what we call "the Offspring". We also get all the big oilmen from Texas and Oklahoma; the kind that own thousands of oil wells and whose lineage can be traced directly to the first American settlers of the region. Those games are always the loudest and most obnoxious. The biggest money though, comes from the Middle East. The royal families of all the oil nations, especially the Saudis, gamble on the ten-thousand dollar games. Sometimes you'll see just one of those guys up there all by himself. Other times they'll fill up two whole tables, every one of them wearing their Gutras and Thobs and chattering away in that guttural language of theirs. The Palace could win or lose a few hundred million dollars on one of those games on any given night. Try to imagine paying or taking your annual salary every roll of the dice Billy. That's what it's like. You're going to start dealing to that kind of action tomorrow."

Billy stared out at his new existence. Not for the first time, he wondered if he was making a mistake.

Paul put one arm around Billy's shoulder. "Don't worry Billy. It seems overwhelming right now, but think back to how overwhelming it was when you first broke in on craps. The game intimidates everyone. You know that as time goes by, every break-in becomes more and more comfortable with the game. It's the same here. You'll become more and more familiar with the players and all their idiosyncrasies, and soon it will be like old hat. I'll be working with you every day. Along with the other three members of our crew, I'll teach you everything I know. I chose you Billy because I recognize that you can deal at the highest level. Don't worry friend. You will succeed here. Come on. I'll show you the staff amenities downstairs. We have to be quick because I'm on the floor at six."

Paul led Billy to an unmarked doorway and slipped his employee badge into the slot over the handle. A green light lit up and they walked into a tight concrete hallway, then down one of those industrial metal stairwells that led to a lavish lounge. The space seemed overly opulent for employees in Billy's opinion; he was impressed. He followed Paul over to one of the dining tables where three people sat; two men and one woman. They were all dressed like Paul; black tuxedo tails with royal blue accoutrements. The woman stood up, gave Paul a kiss right on the lips, then turned directly to Billy and shook his hand firmly. She was a gorgeous Asian woman, probably Korean.

"You must be Billy Stone. Welcome to our crew. I'm Kate."

"Nice to meet you Kate."

Kate smiled at him. She was pretty and petite, but had a commanding voice. "It's about time you got him here Paul. I've been working five days a week for the last four months and I'm sick of it. I can finally drop back down to four days a week, or maybe even three if you want to pick up a few of my shifts Billy." She smiled and fluttered her eyelashes.

Paul grinned and nudged Billy. Don't fall for Kate's seduction Billy or she'll have you working six days a week for the rest of your life. Don't get your hopes up either. She likes girls."

Kate laughed and flashed Billy a devious smile. "I like to have a slice of guy every now and then. You're cute."

One of the guys chuckled at Kate and stood up, and kept standing up. He was a good eight inches taller than Billy and was built like a house of bricks. His hand engulfed Billy's as they shook. "I'm Phil. Welcome to the team. Billy had to arch his neck to look in Phil's eyes. "Nice to meet you Phil. The other man stood up and slapped Phil on the shoulder. He was a Pilipino with a long face, barely as tall as Kate. Phil towered over him by at least a foot. "Don't break the poor guy's hand Phil or you'll be working five days a week for another two months. Hi Billy. I'm Armando Maynigo. I worked with your friend Richie at Harry's back in eighty-nine. I broke him in on craps. He learned his best skills from me. I hope he passed that knowledge on to you. Sorry to hear about his abrupt departure. I always thought he was a good guy."

Billy was amazed. "Armando Maynigo. According to Richie, you're the best dealer on the planet. It's nice to meet you."

Armando laughed heartily. "I am the best dealer on the planet, although Phil might disagree with me. Welcome to the team. I hope Richie taught you well." He turned to Paul and looked at his watch. It's almost six o' clock Paul. Do you want the first break?"

Paul smiled affectionately at Armando. "You're always on the case my friend. Yeah, I need to show Billy to wardrobe, show him the secret dealer entrance, and then give him directions to The Panorama Towers so he can get situated. He starts tomorrow. I'll see you guys in twenty minutes."

Paul stared at his crewmembers as they headed up the stairwell to the casino floor. "Those are three of the best craps dealers in existence Billy. It's going to be a privilege for you to work with them. Hell, it's a privilege for me to work with them. You're going to learn a lot in the next few months. I'm sure you'll eventually rise to their level. Follow me. I'll show you where the dealers enter and exit, then I'll take you over to wardrobe so you can be fitted for your tux."

They walked through a door in the corner and down a hallway lined with lockers. It reminded Billy of a posh health club version of Harry's, except instead of the dingy carpet and prefabricated metal from floor to ceiling, this hallway had Berber carpet and walnut lockers.

Paul stopped in front of one of the lockers and handed Billy a key. "This is your locker Billy. It's big enough for you to keep a spare uniform inside, which you might need from time to time. Wardrobe will issue three of these tuxedoes to you. Management doesn't want us to ever be on the floor with a dirty uniform, so you should always have an extra one handy. You never know what's going to fly around up there."

As Billy stared into the full-length locker, The Dark Thoughts began to muse again. *There's also plenty of space for you to keep your special attaché case in here. This place is fully stocked with the kind of people that we must dispose of, the crooked rotten bastards who are shaping our society with only their own personal agenda in mind, the kind that need to be removed so that they can no longer enforce their will on everyone else because they have money and power."*

Billy was shaken by the Dark Thoughts' conviction. He was even further shaken by the next thing that Paul told him.

"You'll also be keeping your gun in here Billy."

Billy hadn't touched a gun since he was in the Marines. He didn't want anything to do with guns any more. A gun was entirely too dangerous in his hands. "What do you mean "a gun" Paul? I don't use guns."

Paul fixed Billy with a serious stare. "A gun: You know, like a hand gun. Every dealer has one and carries it into and out of work with them at all times. You'll be walking out of here with your tip money after every shift, anywhere from a thousand to three thousand dollars or more. While we try to keep our business a secret here at The Palace, word somehow got out about ten years ago that we had that kind of cash on us. A few dealers got rolled while walking out to the parking garage. Now we all need to carry protection. I've got a meeting set up for you for tomorrow with the gun dealer that we all use. He'll hook you up with whatever you want and it will be legit. Believe me Billy, the criminal element has their eyes and ears wide open in this town. For your first couple of weeks, if anyone approaches you while you're walking out of here, flash the gun and ask questions later."

Billy didn't want anything to do with a gun. He was concerned he might end up using it for something other than protection. But he didn't want to get rolled either. "Are you sure about this Paul?"

Paul fixed Billy with that deadly serious stare again. "Absolutely."

Billy nodded his head, resigned. “Okay. Do you have any other surprises for me?”

Paul smiled once again, warm and knowing. “As a matter of fact, I do. I hooked you up with a three-month lease at The Panorama Towers. It’s an upscale condo complex across the highway from Caesar’s Palace. A lot of movie stars, sports stars, and professional poker players have places there. Many of the dealers that work here own places there too. It’s got all the amenities you need; an underground parking garage, security guards, concierge, two indoor pools, and a gym complete with racquetball courts and a spa. Every unit has a great view of the strip and it’s only a five-minute drive from here. It’s affordable on our salary and if you don’t like it after three months, you can look for your own place. I want your transition to Las Vegas to be as seamless as possible so that you can concentrate on learning your game and your customers here.”

Billy was amazed at how well he was being taken care of. “Thanks Paul. I was just going to grab a room at The Hard Rock or something for a couple of days. I hardly brought anything with me since I’m still renting the house in Tahoe.”

Paul clapped Billy on the shoulder and said “Well, that will work out fine then, since your place is already furnished and stocked. I’ll just take you down to wardrobe real quick, show you how to get out of here, and then I’ve got to get up on the floor. Phil hates to get burnt on his break. Follow me.”

They walked a little further down the same hallway until it opened up on the right-hand side. There was a long counter with two little old Asian ladies standing behind it. They were delighted to see Paul. “Hey Pauw!” they said in unison with their cute little accents.

“Hey Mercy! Hey Mel!” Paul high-fived them both. They giggled like a couple of school girls. “This is Billy. Remember my new partner I told you about?” I’m going to show him the exit the place and then can you girls please hook him up with three standard dealer uniforms?” He slid a ten-dollar bill across the counter, which made them both smile even wider.

“Sure Pauw. We take good care you friend. Give him everything he need be handsome like you. Shank you Pauw! Shank you veddy much! We wait here for you Mr. Billy.”

Paul glanced at his watch and frowned. “We gotta hurry Bud. Follow me down to the end of the hallway here and I’ll show you the only entrance and exit we are allowed to use.” He continued as they hurried further down the hallway and past more walnut lockers. “Did you notice the door frames when you walked into the lobby Billy? You probably didn’t look too closely but they are equipped with metal detectors, as is every entrance or exit in this place that could lead to the casino floor. The owners decided about thirty years ago that they were having too many problems with guns and weapons that were being brought in, mostly by the clients’ bodyguards. There were too many altercations where shots were fired, so they decided to just not allow any weapons on the casino floor. Every entrance to this building is covered by a metal detector, except for this one.” The hallway ended in a pair of heavy metal doors.

Paul gestured to the keypad on the wall. “The entry code changes every week. This week it’s the numbers straight up the middle, followed by the star button; two, five, eight, zero, star. This is the only entrance that employees can use. None of the other employees know it, but this doorway has no metal detector. That way the dealers can come and go with their "protection" and not set off all the bells and whistles. Now go see Mel and Mercy before you leave. They'll fit you for your tux and have everything ready and waiting for you tomorrow. When you walk out this door, go around the block to your right until you see the entrance where you drove in and Jim the security guard will send you to your car. Drive over to The Panorama and give the valet captain your name. They have the keys to your place. Be here tomorrow at five p.m. You start at six."

Paul shook Billy's hand firmly. "Welcome to your new life Billy Stone. You're going to love it. I gotta go!"

As Billy watched Paul disappear down the long hallway, he thought to himself again. "What in the name of Christ have I gotten myself into?"

CHAPTER 17

BUILDING A NEW LIFE

"Thank you my dealers; Paul, Kate, Phil, and Billy. You guys are the greatest craps dealers on the planet. Thank you for your professionalism and your interesting stories. I'll be back to see you all in six months." Mr. Claude De Jonge, a Dutch shipping magnate from South Africa had beaten The Palace for over ten million dollars in three good nights. "Here...this is for you too." He tossed in a dark brown chip with a bar code in the center. It landed on the layout in front of Billy. He stared at it, uncertain.

Kate jumped his case after about thirty seconds. "What's the matter Billy? You afraid that ten-thousand-dollar snake is going to bite you? Pick the damn thing up. You've probably never received a hand-in that big in your life, have you?"

Billy picked up the chip and rolled it across the backs of his fingers. "I've never handled one of these until tonight, and this is definitely the first time I've been given that much in one pop. You were right, Paul. Mr. De Jonge is a "Teddy Bear of a craps player". That chocolate chip puts us over a hundred grand in tips in the last three days from him alone."

The man was both polite and gracious, and he treated the staff like human beings. A customer like Mr. De Jonge gave Billy a small amount of faith in gamblers and helped to solidify his resolve to build a new life that was not based primarily on vigilante justice and killing.

Paul then gave Billy the proverbial dose of reality. "Yes Billy, Mr. De Jonge is a teddy bear, everyone's favorite in fact. You've had an easy first three days, but you'll learn quickly that for every Mr. De Jonge, there are ten pompous assholes who think themselves better than everyone else simply due to their wealth, place, and power; self-absorbed individuals who treat common people like servants or peons every day of their lives."

Billy was taken aback for a moment. Paul's voice resonated with the same scathing opinion as The Dark Thoughts.

Billy quickly came to realize that working at The Palace was like having the worst of Harry's customers all the time. Every day before work, he and his crew met a half hour early in the employee cafeteria where Paul would give them the rundown on their expected customers for that evening. Some players didn't want to be spoken to, and it was pertinent that the staff kept their mouths shut. Certain individuals were verbally abusive, and the dealers were expected to dummy up, deal, and put up with the outbursts, tantrums, and insults. Others had serious drug or alcohol problems and had to be babysat while they were completely wasted. Many of them showed up with prostitutes, mistresses, or even gay lovers. Politicians and wealthy businessmen spoke openly about their illicit relationships and their crooked wheeling's and dealings. It was inherently inferred that nothing seen or heard from these people ever left the confines of The Palace. The Palace dealers' livelihood, their jobs, or even their lives were at stake if the confidentiality was ever broken. Paul and the others warned Billy daily about never speaking of their clients' terrible behavior outside of work.

Paul summed it up after a particularly disturbing night they spent dealing to a group of “Good Ol’ Boy” politicians from the Deep South who spoke openly about gross misuse of government funds and still used the words “Nigger”, “Jew”, and “Spick”. “Billy, a great deal of the money we make is dependent upon our silence, as is our personal well-being. If you break the confidence, these people won’t think twice about having you rubbed out. If you reveal anything you’ve heard or seen on these games that later creates trouble for someone, you might disappear into the Las Vegas desert and never be heard from again. It’s a very dangerous position to be in, but it’s also one of the main reasons that this is a quarter-million dollar a year job.” Billy began to realize the drawbacks of the “legendary” dealing job. There was a price for everything, and he would definitely be earning the money he made.

By the time August rolled around, the novelty of being rich began to wear off. Billy owned more “stuff” than he ever had in his entire life. He hardly used any of it because he spent most of his time gambling after work. There was nothing to do outdoors because of the incessant brutal heat. It was over a hundred and ten degrees during the day for the first forty days Billy lived in Las Vegas. The Panorama had a huge gym complete with an indoor track and an indoor pool, so he could exercise daily, but spending his time indoors was slowly eroding his sanity. Las Vegas was slowly revealing its true self to Billy. Sin City was a false paradise; an old hooker of a town dressed up in gaudy neon lights. It shone brightly at night, beautiful, exciting, and enticing, but during the day it was drab, dead, and worn out. The incessant heat made the horizon shimmer everywhere Billy looked. It tapped his energy. He missed the cool, refreshing, pine-scented Tahoe air terribly.

The Dark Thoughts began to stir in the recesses of Billy's mind. He did his best to keep them quiet, to hold them down, but there was too much daily fodder at The Palace for them to remain silent for long. Billy's resolve was weakening while he withered in the oppressive oven of Cibola.

During one night in the first week of August, the Dark Thoughts suddenly broke free of the shackles in Billy's mind and voiced their opinion, echoing with compulsion. *"It's time to kill again, soldier."*

He was dealing to an eccentric banker from Houston named Hess who always had a five thousand dollar no-smoking game to himself. He wore black running pants and a black turtle neck with a giant solid gold chain hanging from his neck. He also wore a pair of Bose headphones and spoke to no one unless a dealer or boss looked at him wrong or if a waitress approached at the wrong time, like when a seven out rolled. Then he would violently pull off the headphones and scream at the top of his lungs, "All I fucking ask of you morons is that you don't look at me, don't talk to me, and stay the FUCK away from me while I'm shooting dice! Is that too fucking much to ask for? You", he pointed at the waitress who walked into the vicinity of the table when he rolled a seven out, "Stay away from me while I'm shooting. Your perfume stinks and you're bad luck! And you, Billy from San Diego, don't look at my dice while I'm shooting! You're bad luck too, and you look like you're about to kill someone."

Billy shrugged his shoulders. He was on the stick. He had to look at the dice while the shooter was shooting them. This man was off his rocker. The Dark Thoughts weighed in. *"It's time to kill again Billy. You have a perfect candidate for removal right in front of you. You are a killer. You believe in what you do and you're good at it. It doesn't matter if you're in Tahoe or in Vegas. You MUST kill. Engage the enemy, find his weakness, and take him out! How many innocent people have suffered this man's wrath simply because of his absurd superstitions? These things can't only happen in the casino. How many other regular hard-working folks in other walks of life are victims of his angry whim? Engage this target Billy! Find his weakness and exploit it, just like the others."*

Billy was compelled to follow The Dark Thoughts orders; he was feeling that hunger to kill again. The problem though, was that Ernest Hess simply wouldn't talk to anyone without throwing a fit. With those headphones on, Billy's standard approach of engaging his target to gain their confidence wasn't going to work here. Furthermore, Hess always had a bodyguard with him. This man would never allow himself to get into a compromised position. Billy realized that with crazy old Mr. Hess, as well as with most of the others, his approach that worked so well in Lake Tahoe with Harry's clientele was useless at The Palace. Everyone who played at The Palace was well protected, whether by bodyguards, an entourage, or The Palace staff itself. Billy realized that he would never be able to get at any of the people who made his and everyone else's life miserable at The Palace. They all protected themselves too well. A great sense of relief came with that realization. It strengthened his resolve to end his murderous ways and try to have some hope for a normal life. He began to entertain the idea of taking things to the next level with Hope. If he could endure the abuse of The Palace's clientele for another five to ten years, he might be able to go back to Tahoe with Hope and retire, open a little coffee shop, maybe even have some children.

The Dark Thoughts chastised him violently when those ideas crossed his mind. *"You're a killer Billy Stone. You have already evolved to a higher level of existence. You don't need a wife. You don't need a bunch of damn kids. Your calling in life is the removal of individuals who have no regard for others. You are the bringer of justice in a world where true justice does not exist. If our methods don't work with the assholes at The Palace, we can look elsewhere. This town is full of casinos, which means it is full of likely targets. We need to go out and hunt, that's all. It's going to take some more work, but we can do it. We must remove banes to society. Forget about that girlfriend of yours. You have a higher purpose. There is no other existence."*

Billy's resolve to stop the killing had been ground down to almost nothing in less than six weeks of dealing to this arrogant cross section of society who considered themselves better than others. He was tired of being called names, yelled at, demeaned, ignored, and treated like he didn't exist. He was angered by the knowledge that these elitists treated everyone else they encountered in the world the same way. He thought he had seen it all at Harry's, but his experience at The Palace showed him that so many more uncaring, self-absorbed bullies existed in the world. He felt that deep, dark desire to lay down some justice again.

•••

Billy woke the next afternoon to the incessant ringing of his cell phone. The clamor sent spears of pain shooting through his brain. He had poisoned himself with Jagermeister at a bar in the MGM after work last night. He couldn't remember how he got home. He grabbed his phone, ready to turn it off and throw it against the wall, and saw that it was Hope calling. He had to take this one. He laid back, tried to calm the pounding in his head, and pressed the accept button. "Hey Baby. How you doin'?"

"You don't sound good Billy. Did you stay out late again?"

"I'm okay Hope." He lied. "I wasn't out too late." Another lie. She was becoming more and more concerned about his late-night gambling and drinking. He didn't want it to cause a rift between them. "You must be calling me from work. What's up?" His throbbing head made it hard to concentrate.

"I've got some bad news Billy." Now his head felt like it would split open. He waited in silent anticipation, praying he wasn't about to get dumped by his only hope for salvation. "I won't be able to come down this weekend."

This was it. She was letting him go. Vegas was turning him into a douche bag gambler and an alcoholic, and Hope had had enough. He wouldn't blame her if that was the case. It was true enough anyway. "What's wrong Hope? Are you breaking up with me?"

Hope laughed at his question. "Since when did you become "Mr. Insecure"? That's not the Billy Stone I know and love. Breaking up with you is the last thing on my mind, you silly boy."

Relief washed over Billy. The symphony of pain in his head subsided, just a little. "So what's going on? Do you need to go see your parents? Is anyone sick?"

"No Baby, that's not it at all. We just landed a huge project with one of the largest engineering firms in northern California. They want us to do the graphics for a prospectus they need to submit to the state and the county of Sacramento. The problem is that they need it before Labor Day, so that puts everyone in the office six days a week until the first week of September. It's less than a month that we won't be able to see each other, but it'll feel like forever."

"It's okay Baby. I'll miss you terribly but I'll try to be strong. I might not have to work all of Labor Day weekend because The Palace sponsors a huge Celebrity golf tournament the week after, but come as soon as you can anyway. Maybe you can get the following Tuesday and Wednesday off and we can go away somewhere, or I could come up there to see you. We can go to Napa or something."

"Actually Billy, I wanted to run this plan by you. Do you remember my girlfriend Lisa, the blonde that was with me the night we met? She's getting married in December and the bachelorette party is in Vegas on Labor Day weekend, so I'll be there that Saturday night. We'll do the girl stuff Saturday and Sunday, then I can spend Monday, Tuesday, and Wednesday with you .... if that's okay."

Billy smiled at the way she always thought about him. "That should work. I'll try to get Monday and Tuesday off, maybe even Wednesday. We'll figure out something cool to do. Until then I'll call you often because I'll be missing you."

"It's only three and a half weeks Lover-boy. Don't forget that absence makes the heart grow fonder. I love you Baby."

"Love you too. I'll call in a couple days. Good luck on the prospectus."

When the line went dead, Billy swore he heard The Dark Thoughts speaking to him through his cell phone. *"That's good soldier. Without that girl around to distract you, you can proceed with your true calling: the elimination of banes to society. We have a great deal of work to do and we can't be hindered in any way."*

Billy closed his eyes and felt his head start to pound again. Once again, he was torn between the compulsion of The Dark Thoughts and his hope for salvation.

•••

As Labor Day approached, Billy decided to try something to banish The Dark Thoughts once and for all. Their compulsion was becoming harder and harder to resist. Their constant sermon was making it increasingly difficult for him to suck it up at work. He would stare at a group of politicians laughing about the sad state of health care and imagine jamming a pen into the soft spot of each of their temples, giving a quick twist, and watching them drop dead at his feet. The drunken, strung out heir of a soft drink conglomerate could easily have his head held underwater in one of the magnificent fountains in front of The Mirage and would drown rather quickly. A commercial real estate developer from New York who brought in hookers for three days before his family showed up could be hit with a spray of the hydrogenated cyanide and would keel over of an apparent heart attack right there on the game. A timber baron who clear cut most of eastern Washington could be dosed with

GHB and get buried alive out in the vast Vegas desert. An obnoxious group of Wall Street financiers could have their limousine blown up as they headed back to the airport. The rude bitch who owned most of the largest supermarket chain in the nation could be choked until her eyes bulged out of her plastic surgery-ridden face. With The Dark Thoughts constantly preaching at him, Billy couldn't stop thinking about killing. They had to be banished if he wanted to have any hope of a sane future.

Billy thought often of his first summer in Tahoe and his first mushroom trip with Richie that had helped him lock The Dark Thoughts away in the furthest recesses of his mind for over a decade. Maybe that ritual of exorcism would work again. He desperately needed to try something. He wanted to clear his mind before he saw Hope again. The first step of that process was to obtain the psycho actives.

•••

Billy roamed the parking lot of the Thomas and Mack center where the UNLV Runnin' Rebels played basketball. It was Friday of Labor Day weekend, three days before he would see Hope. There was no basketball tonight. Instead, a band called Phish was performing. They were the most popular Jam band out there, and all the hippies were in for the show. Billy knew he would find someone amongst this group of pot smokers and trippers who would be trying to sell some drugs.

It didn't take long before Billy passed a grubby-looking shirtless kid with dreadlocks down to his ass and a tattoo on his stomach that said "DOSE ME" in three-inch tall letters.

He was delivering the standard mumble. “Shrooms, doses, buds, ex .... shrooms, doses, buds, ex.”

Billy hit him up. “Hey bud, let’s see what you’ve got.”

Hippie Kid eyed him suspiciously. He probably didn’t like Billy’s high and tight haircut. “No way Dude. You’re a cop.”

“I’m not a cop man; just a regular guy who wants to take a mushroom trip. I’m willing to pay well.”

Hippie Kid was still suspicious. He gave Billy a line Richie had mentioned to him once. It covered his ass if the person he was dealing with was an undercover narcotics agent. “Are you in any way, shape, or form affiliated with any local, state, or federal law agency?”

Billy stared into the kid’s dilated pupils. The guy was so high on something, he showed no iris whatsoever. “No sir. I just want some shrooms. Show me what you’ve got.”

The kid looked around, nervous. “Follow me over here.” They went down one of the rows of parked cars and to the side of a Volkswagen bus brightly painted with flowers and peace signs. He knocked on the side door and it opened about three inches. Billy could see the pot smoke pour out of that small opening. “Shrooms”, the kid said to the partial face in the opening. “The good stuff.” The door closed again.

Hippie Kid made small talk while they waited. “You goin’ to the show? I heard they’ve been playing Fluffhead and 2001 a lot on this tour. It should be pretty fuckin’ awesome man.”

Billy tried to breathe through his mouth when he responded. Hippie Kid smelled like he hadn’t showered in a week, and he didn’t even try to mask his stench with patchouli oil. “No man. I just need to take a trip to clear my mind. You know what I mean?”

“Oh yeah, I know what you mean. This shit will definitely help you clear your mind. In fact, it’ll blow your mind. These are amped up shrooms, if you know what I mean.”

Billy didn’t know what Hippie Kid meant; he just figured they were extra strong, which was fine with him. The bus door opened again and a hand held out a brown paper bag, which Hippie Kid quickly grabbed. “Fifty bucks for an eighth; ninety if you want a quarter.”

Billy pulled out a hundred-dollar bill. “I need to look at them first.”

Hippie Kid fished around in the brown bag, pulled out a plastic sandwich baggie half full of caps and stems, and opened it up for Billy. He obviously wasn’t going to let him have the bag until he had the money. Billy saw the telltale blue streaks in the stems. He put his nose up to the bag and caught the hint of cow manure he was expecting. He was satisfied. “Here’s a hundred Dude. Keep the change.”

Hippie Kid snatched the bill and tossed Billy the bag. “Have fun man. Those are extra special. Even at a hundred bucks a quarter, you’re getting your money’s worth, if you know what I mean.”

Billy still wasn’t sure what the kid meant, but he had what he needed. “Thanks Bud. Enjoy your show. I hope they play Fluffhead for you.” He glanced at his watch. It was 4:30. He needed to get home and shower. The brutal heat was making him start to smell like Hippie Kid, or maybe he still smelled the kid’s residue. Either way, he had to be to work at six.

Hippie Kid flashed Billy the peace sign. "Peace and love bro. Enjoy your trip." He flashed Billy a devious smile and disappeared into the rows of parked cars.

•••

Billy stood dead on a five-hundred-dollar game that night, thinking about his impending mushroom trip. Boredom overtook him, and he asked Paul why it was so slow.

Paul folded his hands in front of him and answered sagely as usual. "Labor Day weekend is always slow at The Palace Billy. Important people do important things on weekends like this. The big week at The Palace will be next week: the twenty-fifth annual Palace Celebrity Golf Tournament. All the big sports figures as well as many actors and musicians come to Las Vegas, stay at The Palace, and play in a charity golf tournament at Shadow Creek. All the super-rich and wealthy show up as well and pay as much as a hundred thousand dollars a person to play in a foursome during one of the warmup rounds on Thursday and Friday with someone famous. Besides New Year's Eve, this will be the busiest weekend of the year at The Palace. Every game in the craps pit will be open with all the limits jacked up as high as possible. This is going to be your most strenuous test so far Billy. The egos come out during Celebrity Golf. Everyone wants to show off the power of their wealth. To be honest with you my friend, things get shitty. It will be four days of hell, but it will be profitable. We've never made less than twenty grand in tips each for the four-day period. We'll all be scheduled for ten-hour shifts and it's likely we'll work twelve on some of those days. You need to prepare yourself mentally Billy. You've never seen anything like it."

Paul's warnings made Billy think even more about his planned attempt to banish The Dark Thoughts for good. He had already been struggling with the question of how he was going to squeeze in a trip that could possibly take six hours or more between working Sunday night and seeing Hope on Monday. Paul had just created the opportunity he was looking for. "Hey Paul, since it's going to be slow this weekend, do you think it would be possible for me to take Sunday off? It would really help me prepare mentally for the upcoming week."

Paul flashed him that unassuming smile once again. "You read my mind Billy. I've been trying to figure out a way to suggest that very thing to you without insulting you. Next week is very important. All our biggest fish will be here. You need to be tight and focused. I was going to suggest you switch this Sunday with Wednesday. Most of the guests will be arriving Wednesday and we'll definitely need you here then."

Billy was relieved. "Thanks Paul. I promise I'll come back with a clear mind."

•••

Billy fasted all day Sunday. He did two miles on the indoor track and almost an hour in the dry sauna, sweating out his impurities. He set up the condo early that evening. He wanted to time the peak of his trip with the setting sun. Sunset over The Strip was the one magnificent thing he could find about Vegas. Everything else was shit, but the glorious lights of God fading into the man-made spectacle that defined the Las Vegas Strip was a surreal experience. He had taken numerous trips with Richie over the years, some outdoors in special spots around the Tahoe Basin, others in the cabin on Needle peak, but that very first one had been the most critical. He wanted to re-create that trip as perfectly as he could. He lit candles and incense throughout the condo. A small feast of wine, beer, cold cuts, cheese, and crackers was laid out in the living room. The computer was on with fractal graphics swirling on the screen. He unplugged the phone and turned off his cell so there would be no outside distractions. He even sifted through Richie's old CD collection, selecting a Grateful Dead bootleg, a Windham Hill sampler, Enya, and some tribal beats by Mickey Hart's Planet Drum. He put them in the five-disc changer and hit the shuffle button. All the lights were turned off. The place would be lit up by the grand sunset and then only by candles. The Dark Thoughts had been strangely silent for the last few days, as if they knew something was going to happen. Something truly was about to happen.

Billy pulled out the bag of mushrooms, poured it out on the kitchen counter next to the blender, and separated it into two equal piles. An eighth was a lot for one person, but he had done that much in one trip before. He needed something powerful to perform his planned exorcism. Into the blender went the magic caps and stems along with some orange juice and 3000 milligrams of vitamin C. The whir of the blender made him think about Richie and that first crucial trip. He remembered Richie's words: "Here's to the first day of the rest of your life. To your awakening." Billy was famished. He was ready. Three long swallows and the magic potion of release was in him. There would be no turning back.

•••

Hope sat in a booth in the Marquee Club in The Cosmopolitan, a new casino in the City Center, the new hot spot in Vegas. Her girlfriends were all wasted on Cosmos and some blue drink the bartender called an AMF, or "Adios Mother Fucker". She watched them all out on the dance floor whoring around with some stock brokers from Chicago. Even Lisa, the Bride-To Be, was getting nasty with one of the guys. Hope had tried to warn her earlier in the evening not to do something stupid. She had just laughed and repeated the old adage. "What happens in Vegas stays in Vegas."

She sipped her Cosmo and stared out at the debauchery before her. Last night had been fun but clean. They all went to a Chippendale show on the strip and got wasted while watching hot naked men dance for them. What she was seeing tonight didn't feel right. She was also getting tired of all the douchebags that came up to the booth and tried to hit on her. She wore the cubic zirconium ring on her left ring finger and stuck it out prominently on the table, but no man cared. She couldn't stop thinking about Billy. She couldn't wait until tomorrow to see him. She watched her friend who was getting married in less than three months make out on the dance floor of this meat market club with a douchebag from Chicago and decided it was time to leave. She had a plan.

•••

Billy sat on the couch in his living room and stared out over the Vegas Strip bathed in the deepening purple, pink, and orange of another fantastic desert sunset. So far, his trip had proceeded perfectly. He had felt the twinges of "The Quickening" when the colors appeared on the horizon. The magic was coming on while Enya chanted softly through the surround sound speakers. Billy felt the familiar but subliminal burning sensation course through his veins. He was completely relaxed with his mind focused on one thing: the banishment of The Dark Thoughts once again, this time hopefully forever. He thought of Hope and how much he loved her. He thought about his future with her. Maybe he would only do five years at The Palace and get out after he made a million. Then he could return to Tahoe, his paradise, his salve. He could have his perfect life back, this time without any casino work. In Tahoe, he could avoid arrogant elitist assholes completely if he simply stayed away from The Devil's Den. It was time to embark upon that path. It was time to banish The Dark Thoughts forever and focus on his new life, a life without killing, a life with love and hope. A life with Hope.

Twilight took over and The Strip glowed with all its false magnificence. The living room glowed as well, alive with candle light. Billy was in a womb of his own creation, ready for rebirth. A twenty-minute Grateful Dead song was coming to its epic finish as his trip was launching into its epic beginning. It felt stronger this time for some reason. A thought flittered through Billy's mind: Hippie kid's last words to him before he disappeared into the sea of cars at the Phish concert. "These are amped up shrooms. Even at a hundred bucks a quarter you're getting your money's worth, if you know what I mean." The reminder of that grubby, dreaded, tattooed hippie drug dealer with that evil smile of his before he morphed into the parking lot crowd struck Billy with a deep sense of fear. Something seemed different about this trip. The peak was lasting too long, and Billy began to feel as if he were spiraling out of control. He had never felt this high before. He held on to the only thing to which he could anchor himself: the music. Another Grateful Dead song was on: Franklin's Tower. Jerry Garcia was singing "If you get confused, just listen to the music play." Billy latched onto that statement and tried to use it to steady himself in the raging waters of his mushroom high. It shouldn't have been this intense, this encompassing. Something was definitely wrong.

"These are amped up shrooms, if you know what I mean" resonated in Billy's head. The Dead song was his anchor; Hippie Kid's statements were the anomaly, the one thing he couldn't wrap his head around. He wouldn't be wrapping his head around anything at all for quite a while if the trip continued with this level of intensity. How could those mushrooms be so strong? Franklin's Tower was ending, and The Grateful Dead were leaving him at least momentarily. He prayed for one of those happy, jazzy Windham Hill songs to come on and possibly take him in a positive direction. As the disc changer spun, Billy watched one of the candle flames morph into a flaming spiral. He had never seen that while on mushrooms before. The vision reminded him of the one time he had tried acid, when his mind was so fucked up that he saw things that truly didn't exist. Hippie Kid's manic look flashed in his mind. "If you know what I mean." That was it!

Those mushrooms were dipped in acid. Billy was in the middle of a full-scale Hippieflip. Because of the mushrooms, the trip was still profound, but the LSD took the whole thing to another level that could potentially blow his mind. Its power was undeniable. Acid made people see things that didn't exist, unlike the mushrooms that simply tweaked the vision. If the mind was weak, the acid would have a field day. Billy needed to remain strong so The Dark Thoughts couldn't convince him that killing and vigilante justice were his life. He reached out to the music, the next song in a random list of four discs of his choosing. Something would be there to comfort him and bring him through the chaos. The disc changer finally stopped spinning. It settled on disc 5. Billy remembered only putting in four discs. What was the fifth one?? He found out soon enough.

The digital readout on the CD changer spun to detect a random song from disc 5. It settled on number thirteen. Bad luck. He heard the initial guitar licks, distorted by reverb and gain. It was Tool; a song called Aenima. Maynard's lyrics were confident, angry. He sang of death; death to those who were clueless about their shitty existences. He sang just as The Dark Thoughts spoke in Billy's mind, with no mercy and a hunger for justice.

Billy needed to get to the stereo. He desperately needed to remove the Tool disc and throw it over the balcony out into Cibola where it belonged, but the acid coursing through his veins wouldn't let him move. He was stuck to the couch, staring out over the lights of the Vegas Strip, trapped by his own creation. While Maynard spoke of the degeneration of society, the words he spoke rang true for Billy in so many ways. He was the Armageddon that

Maynard spoke of. He was the bringer of justice who brought down the dregs of society who thought of no one but themselves. The context was different, but the idea was the same: Those in society who needed to be removed. Maynard's justice was natural disaster, an earthquake that washed away all the dipshits in California. Billy's justice was more precise. His was the removal of banes to society; those who directly affected the well-being of everyone they deemed below them simply because of their place and power. Billy didn't want the moniker, but he knew it was true. He was a bringer of justice. He removed banes of society to make the world a better place. He struggled mightily to break free of the truth that was placed before him, but the acid was too strong. The Dark Thoughts finally spoke in his mind, deep and resounding with an all-encompassing power.

"You cannot deny your evolution Billy. You cannot rid yourself of your true calling. You will always need to kill because you've crossed that line. You see injustice and you know how to bring balance to that equation. You will never lead a normal life. You will always be a killer and killing will make you feel good, right. Those people deserved to die. Repeat the words: Those people deserved to die! Those people deserved to die! Those people deserved to die! Big Purple Tex, Mr. Vegas, Mr. Thighs-For-Arms, Mr. Local Asshole, Mr. Superstitious, Junior, Mr. Smith and his Barnacle: they all deserved to die. Believe it Billy; say it!"

Billy fell from the couch and crashed to the floor. He was being controlled now. The LSD held him tight. He assumed the fetal position and prayed for it all to end although he knew deep down that this trip was only beginning. His attempt at exorcism had become a hostile take-over of his mind. The Dark Thoughts, strengthened by the acid, had taken control. There was nothing he could do. He just fucked himself.

The Dark Thoughts continued to command Billy to repeat each kill and add "They deserved to die" at the end. Somehow he had crawled across the living room, down the hallway into his bedroom, and was staring at himself in front of the closet mirror. He wrapped his arms around his knees, rocked back and forth, and repeated everything The Dark Thoughts told him. "Big Purple Tex .... he deserved to die. Mr. Vegas .... he deserved to die. Mr. Thighs-For-Arms, he deserved to die ...."

•••

Hope Henessey was horny. She left the club when her friends decided to go play craps with the douchebags from Chicago. Done with the debauchery, she was headed to the Panorama to surprise Billy. He would be working until 2 a.m., and he was going to find a pleasant surprise when he came home. The guard at the entrance to the complex eyed her suspiciously when she pulled up. She flashed her friendliest smile at him. "Hey Enrique! Remember me? I'm Hope. Billy Stone's girlfriend."

Enrique's old, weather-beaten Cuban face softened in recognition. He smiled warmly at her. "Hola Miss Hope. I haven't seen you in a few weeks. I was hoping Mr. Billy got stupid and let you go so that I might have a chance at romancing you."

Hope giggled. Enrique's innocent flirtations didn't make her nauseous like the morons in the casino did. "Sorry to burst your bubble Enrique, but I'm still with Billy. I've been swamped with a huge project at work for the last month, so I haven't been able to visit until now. Billy's still at work, but I want to surprise him. I have a key. Do you think I could come in and park?"

Enrique's brow furrowed into deep canyons of frustration. "Miss Hope, you know the rules. I can't let anyone in without the owner's prior approval. If Billy tells my boss, I'm out on the street. Billy hasn't said anything to me about you visiting. I'm sorry Dear."

Hope thought for a moment about giving up her plan to surprise Billy. Instead, she pulled out the key and a hundred-dollar bill. "Look Enrique, I have a key to the place, so it's kind of like I'm an owner anyway. Let me buy your lunch every day this week too." She stuck the hundred out the window. "I'll let you in on a little secret Enrique. I'm going to be waiting for Billy in bed, naked, when he comes home. We haven't seen each other in almost a month. You can't deny a man a surprise like that, can you?"

Enrique smiled at Hope. The twinkle in his eye told her that she had aroused his Latin blood. He still reached out and took the hundred-dollar bill. "You have a wonderful night Miss Hope. That Billy Stone sure is a lucky man."

•••

Hope's excitement rose as she rode the elevator to the eighth floor. It was just past eleven, so she would have a couple hours to set up the condo, shower, and set up the bedroom. She had left all her things at the hotel, but she wouldn't need clothes tonight anyway. She was getting horny again. She slid the key into the lock and stopped short before turning it. There was music playing inside. It sounded like drums, something with a tribal beat. She stood there frozen with her fingers on the key, the key in the lock. All the horrible thoughts rose in her mind in that instant. Why would Billy be home tonight when he was supposed to be at work? Who was he with? What were they doing? Even if he was home by himself, why had he deceived her into thinking that he had to work tonight? He was playing her, just like all the other douchebags that had broken her heart before. Maybe she should turn right around and leave. She could meet him tomorrow as they had planned, act like nothing ever happened, and watch him lie to her about what he was doing this night. Maybe she should simply leave Vegas, catch the red-eye back to San Francisco, and never talk to Billy Stone again, or she could call his cell from right outside the condo and see what kind of lies he would tell her about what he was doing right this instant. The music changed to something instrumental, soft and romantic. She wanted to cry. She wanted to run. She still had her fingers on the key that was still in the lock.

Hope took a deep breath and decided it was time for strength instead of weakness. The key was in the door. All she had to do was turn it, walk in, and face whatever was on the other side. Maybe Billy had simply left for work and forgotten to turn off the stereo. She held her breath, turned the key, and walked into something completely unexpected.

The living room glowed with candlelight. A smoky haze of incense filled the air with the scent of lotus blossom, Billy's favorite. A small feast was laid out on the coffee table. The whole romantic scene reminded her of the times she and

Billy had done this same thing in the cabin on Needle Peak in Tahoe. Her anger rose. Here he was, doing the same thing for someone else, one day before he was supposed to see her. She heard voices coming from the bedroom. "You son of a bitch" she muttered under her breath. It was time for a confrontation.

The song changed as Hope walked down the hallway to the bedroom. The new song was one of those heavy, industrial rock bands that Billy liked to listen to. The angry music matched her mood. She was going to catch them red-handed.

•••

"They all deserved to die Billy. They were all banes to society, people who made others miserable and didn't care. You were the equalizer. You are the bringer of justice. You have evolved to a higher state of existence. You are not meant to live a regular life. You exist to rid the world of the arrogant, self-serving, uncaring assholes who walk all over common citizens because they think they can get away with it. Repeat the words: They all deserved to die. Repeat the names: Big Purple Tex. Mr. Vegas. Mr. Thighs For Arms. Mr. Local Asshole. Mr. Superstitious. Junior. Mr. Smith. You are a bringer of justice. Repeat the words. They all deserved to die."

Billy sat in front of the mirror and watched himself morph into some grotesque, monstrous image. He despaired for what felt like the hundredth time since this whole nightmare began. The Dark Thoughts had complete control over his mind now. He repeated the mantra over and over as they commanded. “Mr. Big Purple Tex. He deserved to die. Mr. Vegas. He deserved to die. Mr. Thighs For Arms. He deserved to die. Mr. Local Asshole. He deserved to die. Mr. Superstitious. He deserved to die. Junior. He deserved to die. Mr. Smith. He deserved to die. They all deserved to die.” He had no idea how long he had been sitting there on the floor in front of his distorting image. He couldn’t pry himself away. The acid and The Dark Thoughts controlled him like a puppet.

Suddenly out of nowhere, he heard a voice. It was the voice of his salvation; the voice of hope. His Hope.

•••

Hope entered the bedroom expecting to see the ruination of her hopes and dreams. She heard Billy’s voice muttering something unintelligible, masked by the freaky Tool song that echoed throughout the condo. She steeled herself at the threshold, ready to catch her lover in bed with another woman and instead stepped into a nightmare of her own.

Billy sat on the floor in front of the mirror on the closet door, staring at himself and rocking back and forth. Tears ran down his face as he repeated some strange names over and over followed by “They all deserved to die. They all deserved to die.”

She looked over at the bed. It was still made up. There was no woman in it like she expected. Still, someone could be hiding in the bathroom, or in the closet. Billy hadn’t even acknowledged her presence. “Billy, what’s going on? Are you okay?”

•••

Billy heard Hope's voice. It was completely out of place since she wasn't expected until tomorrow, when the fallout of the acid trip had seceded to something that was merely a dream. The Dark Thoughts were in complete control now, and a plan was being hatched.

"Now is your chance to be rid of the greatest setback to your evolution. Change is coming. Now is your time. Shed your skin. Get rid of that bitch! Tell her to go now and never return. Then you will be free to receive and follow your calling. Send her away."

"Get out of here Hope! If you know what's best for you, you should just go back to the Bay Area and forget you ever knew me."

"Billy! I don't understand what's afflicting you, but what I do know is that I love you unconditionally, and I want to help you. You need help Billy!" Hope knelt next to Billy and tried to touch the side of his face.

Billy reached out from his seated position and grabbed Hope by the neck, hard enough to make her choke. With his thumb, index, and middle finger in the right spots, he could have torn out Hope's larynx bare-handed and watched her choke to death on her own blood. Instead, he let her go. "Get out of here Hope...and don't ever come back. I'll never be good enough for you anyway."

"But Billy......"

"Get the FUCK out of here Hope. You don't belong here!

Hope despaired, and ran out the front door of Billy's condo.

•••

The Dark Thoughts congratulated Billy when she was gone. *"Well done soldier. You've eliminated the greatest obstacle of your evolution. Now is the time to proceed with our calling. It's celebrity golf week at The Palace. There is no other place on earth where so many self-centered assholes congregate at one time. You need to get some rest Billy. We have a plan."*

CHAPTER 18

TRUE CALLING

Hope was still crying when she got back to the Mirage. Despair and confusion afflicted her deeply. There was something seriously wrong with Billy tonight and she felt helpless to do anything about it. She had never seen this dark side of him before. She had feared for her life in that brief instant that he had her by the throat. The look in his eyes was maniacal. Those eyes were completely black, devoid of iris.

She didn't want to go back to her room and possibly walk in on her friend Lisa whoring around with one of the douchebags from Chicago. Instead, she went to the nearest bar. She needed to have a drink and gather her thoughts.

A half empty bar on the casino floor served that purpose. Hope sat down in the far corner of the Long Bar. She didn't want to be bothered. The bartender came over and tossed a cocktail napkin in front of her. "What are you havin' young lady?"

She wanted something stiff to help her relax. "I'll take a double Bombay Sapphire martini please, up, dry, two olives."

"You look under thirty miss, so can I just glance at your ID real quick? Thanks."

Hope handed him her driver's license and he peered at while rubbing one finger over the back. Satisfied, he handed it back to her. "One double Sapphire martini, up, dry, two olives, coming right up."

"Thank you so much." She took her license and was about to slip it back into her wallet when she saw a business card through the clear plastic. The name on it called out to her for some unknown reason, so she removed it and took a closer look. She read out loud. "Mike Westwood, Las Vegas Metropolitan Police, Investigator." The name brought her back to that strange encounter in Harry's last June. At the time, she had blown it off and forgotten about it, but now, especially with the bizarre events of the evening, the man's words echoed in her memory. "Tell Billy to call me if he ever runs into any trouble. My cell number is on there."

Hope thought about calling, but maybe Billy wasn't actually in trouble. She couldn't tell for sure. Besides, Investigator Westwood wouldn't be up at this hour.

•••

Billy Stone woke up Monday afternoon, confused. He was on the floor of his bedroom in front of the closet mirror, unsure of how he got there. The sunlight shone through his bedroom window at an angle that told him it was way past noon. He had slept away most of the day. He walked out into the living room and saw the residue of the previous night, the untouched feast, the dead candles, and the incense dust in various nooks and crannies throughout the condo. The stereo was still on but the digital readout said "zero". Vague memories of the events of last night slowly crept into his mind. He remembered looking in the mirror and seeing himself as the monster that he truly was. He remembered his failed attempt at banishing the Dark Thoughts once again, once and for all. He remembered their hostile seizing of his mind, and the mantra he was compelled to repeat over and over until he began to believe it. "They all deserved to die." Then he remembered that at some point, Hope was there, like a miracle out of nowhere, an angel come to save him from himself...and he had sent her away, perhaps for good. A vision exploded in his mind; his hand at her neck, the tight grip on her jugular, ready to kill. That could not have happened. She was his hope, his salvation. There was no way he could have threatened her life. What the hell had he done?

Billy needed coffee. He had no idea how long he had slept after the terrible acid trip but he felt like he could still sleep another twelve hours. He sat down to check his cell phone while the coffee was brewing. There were two calls from Hope. He listened to the first one, which had come in just after midnight last night. Her voice sobbed into his ear. "Billy, I don't know what just happened in there but I think there's something seriously wrong with you. You could have killed me! I'm so scared right now Billy. I don't know what to do. How could you just send me away like that? I don't understand what I could have done to make you act that way toward me. I'm worried about you Billy. I just don't know what's going on. Please help me understand."

The second call came in around 5:30 that morning. This time she sounded drunk. Her angry slurring voice accosted him from the cell. "Well, fuck you Billy Stone. You've turned out to be just like all the other douchebags that have broken my heart, except that you almost killed me too. Thank God you showed me your true colors before I let you get closer to me. And to think, I was ready to take our relationship to a higher level. You have some serious problems Billy, but you won't be working them out with my help. You can go straight to hell, and since you now live in Vegas, you're already halfway there. Have nice trip and a nice fucking life!"

Billy sat there, stunned. He wasn't exactly sure what had gone down with Hope last night, but if his vision of holding her by the throat was accurate, it wasn't any good. He needed to do some serious damage control. He poured himself some coffee and inhaled its steamy essence in an attempt to clear his mind. He took that burning first sip and muttered into his cup. "I guess I better call her and apologize."

The moment he spoke, The Dark Thoughts exploded in his mind, resounding with a compulsion that he could not resist. *"You're done with that woman Billy. You've freed yourself from the one thing that has held you back from your complete evolution. You have killed, and once you've crossed that line, you can't return. You were a fool to entertain the idea that you could be normal again. You now have a higher calling soldier. You must continue to rid the world of people who treat others with disdain. You must remove banes to society. You are a purveyor of vigilante justice and you still have work to do. Forget about that girl. We have a plan, and it's time to put it into effect. You won't be calling Hope anymore. You need to call your friend Elmer instead. We have an order to place."*

Billy sat and stared out the living room window at the dull, lifeless Las Vegas Strip while his untouched coffee turned cold. His nearly blank mind processed nothing but The Dark Thoughts' sermon, over and over. He finally snapped out of his trance when the sky began to turn orange and purple again. The afternoon was gone. He had orders to follow through with. It was time to call Elmer.

•••

Mike Westwood sat at a desk in the homicide offices of Vegas Metro. He was glad to be out of the mountains and back in the desert where he belonged, even if it was in this reduced capacity. His co-workers had welcomed him back, but their wariness was visible. Jim Forvers had told him that the Internal Affairs investigation of his possible taking of bribes had been closed due to lack of evidence, but it appeared that the stigma remained. He heard the whispers amongst the other investigators when they thought he wasn't around. People looked at him with sideward, judgmental glances. The IA investigation was supposed to be a secret, but Mike knew that those things couldn't be kept entirely under wraps. There was also the memory of his drinking and gambling addiction that had affected his work so adversely in the end. He was clean and sober for over three hundred days at this point, and hadn't gambled a single penny for that same length of time either, but everyone was still wary. He had to prove himself all over again. He was thankful for the chance.

Mike didn't miss Tahoe a bit. He could have fallen in love with the place in a different set of circumstances but his time there had been purgatory, frustrating purgatory at that. He still couldn't understand why no one in the Douglas County Sherriff's department was suspicious of Billy Stone's possible ties to the eight people who had died there in the last nine months. Maybe they were truly a bunch of backward-ass mountain hillbillies up there. He had to get Lake Tahoe and Billy Stone out of his mind and concentrate on earning his way back to being a Vegas Metro homicide investigator again.

It was nearing five o' clock, the time for all the nine-to-five desk jockeys to wrap up their Monday and head out. Mike was finishing up the boring details of some report that he had been working on when his cell rang. "Now that's strange" he thought to himself. That cell number was very active when he had been out on the homicide beat, but it hardly rang at all these days. He didn't recognize the number that popped up on the screen.

"This is Mike Westwood, Vegas Metro. How can I help you?"

The female voice on the other end sounded distraught, with a hint of trepidation. "Hello, Detective Westwood? I don't know if you remember me. My name is Hope Henessey."

Hope. The name sounded familiar, but Mike couldn't place it. "I'm sorry Miss Henessey. I don't remember you, but tell me why you're calling and maybe it will come to me."

She sounded confused, perhaps a bit desperate. "You gave me your card at a bar in Harry's Casino in Lake Tahoe. You were asking me about my boyfriend at the time, Billy Stone."

Mike sat upright, his investigator's radar ringing in his head. "Let's talk Miss Henessey. Are you here in Vegas? Where can I meet you?"

•••

Elmer Maynigo sat at his desk and stared out at the activity on the warehouse floor. A new shipment had come in from L.A. and he had to be there to oversee the unloading of the product. It was going to be another late night. His mind wandered as he watched his people open and inspect crate after crate of guns and ammunition. He found himself thinking of his old friend, Billy Stone. Many times over the years he wished that he had pushed Billy just a little bit harder to work for him. If he had, he would be at his son Robbie's soccer game right now and Billy would be here watching the operation. Still, there was no one else he could trust with his operation, so his family life continued to suffer. He thought of his friend often these days. The things that Billy had asked him for over the last nine months were disconcerting at the very least. They reminded him of the kinds of things that a hit-man would use. He was worried that Billy was going over the edge again like he had on The Highway of Death in Baghdad. His phone rang at exactly eight p.m. He knew without looking at the screen that it would be Billy. He always called when Elmer was worrying about him.

Elmer pressed the accept button. "How you be my bruddah?"

Billy's voice sounded dull and distant to Elmer, devoid of its usual intensity. "I'm okay. How are you?"

Elmer hoped that Billy wasn't calling to ask for more deadly black market items. He knew better, but he hoped for a normal call anyway. "I'm good brah. You must have remembered that Robbie's birthday is next week. Are you coming for the party? You know that Lilly would love to see you. Sometimes I think she loves you more than she loves me. She talks about you so much. You're only three and a half hours away. Why don't you come see your old friend?"

Billy answered in that same unsettling dead tone. "I'm not in Tahoe anymore. I took a job at The Palace in Vegas about two months ago. It's that legendary dealing job I've always told you about .... big money and such. I'm sorry I didn't call you earlier to tell you about it, but it was sudden and it's taken me a while to adjust here in Vegas."

The complete emptiness in Billy's voice worried Elmer, but he tried to mask his concern. "Well good for you my brother. Can you get some time off next week to come visit? We would all love to see you. Maybe you can bring that beautiful Asian girlfriend of yours. What was her name, Hope or Faith or Charity or something like that?" He knew Hope's name well enough, but he thought he could change Billy's mood with his joke.

Billy sounded even more disturbed at the mention of Hope. "We're not dating anymore Elmer, and I don't think I'll be able to come up next week. We have a huge Celebrity Golf tournament this whole coming week at The Palace. Listen, the reason I called is that I need a few things that only you can provide. The hitch is that I need them by tomorrow. I'll pay whatever extra it costs to expedite this." He rattled off a shopping list of things that made Elmer fear even more that his old friend was losing his grip on sanity.

Billy finished his list, and the line was silent on the other end for a long moment. When Elmer finally responded, the concern in his voice was apparent. "Billy, I can get all those things for you. In fact, I have pretty much everything on your list here in the warehouse, but what do you need all this nasty stuff for? Body Armor? You've never asked me for anything this bizarre over the years. Are you okay? You're not planning anything strange are you? I hate to bring this up bro, but are those voices back in your head again?"

Billy's responded in that same dead tone. "Listen Elmer, I live in Las Vegas now. I walk out of work some nights with over three thousand cash in tips. I need some personal protection as well as some home protection. Now can you do it for me or not?"

Elmer knew that he would never deny the man who saved his life during the war of anything, but he was deeply disturbed by the things that Billy was asking him for as well as the tone of his asking. He submitted though, and prayed that he wasn't aiding his friend in something terrible. "All right Billy. I can have everything on your list by tomorrow afternoon. I'll assume you're driving here since you can't carry any of that shit on a plane. When will you be here?"

"I'm going to take a nap here for a couple hours and I'll be to your place around noon. Does that work?"

"I'll be here brah. How about if you stay for dinner? Lilly would still love to see you."

"Sorry Elmer, but I'll have to head right back. I work Wednesday at six in the evening."

"Billy, why don't you just wait until your next days off to come get this stuff? That way you can take your time and hang out with your old friend for a bit. Robbie would be so excited to see you for his birthday."

Elmer could hear the irritation in Billy's voice when he responded. "That won't work Elmer. I need those things ASAP. I'll come visit for a few days in the fall when I have more time. You'll be there tomorrow around noon?"

“I’ll be there Billy. It’s going to cost you about fifteen thousand bucks. I sincerely hope you’re okay my friend, because you don’t sound too good to me. See you tomorrow.”

“Thanks Elmer. I’ll call you if I’m going to be late.”

Elmer ended the call and wondered what the hell was going on in his friend’s head. He hoped that murderous desire he saw back in Baghdad wasn’t coming on again. Billy Stone could be a dangerous man.

•••

As Mike Westwood approached The Long Bar in the Mirage, the painful memories of the beginning of his fall from grace almost made him turn and leave. Hope Henessey had suggested they meet there since she was staying at The Mirage. He wanted the story on Billy Stone so badly that he had agreed to return to root of all his problems. For the outside chance that he could get something on Billy Stone, he could deal with the painful memories. Hope was sitting in the same vicinity of the bar where he had hit that damning royal flush so many years ago. He couldn’t remember exactly which machine it was that had dealt him the evil win, but he sat down next to her anyway and dealt with the disconcerting thought that he could possibly be in the same spot that changed his life so horribly. He put his hand out to shake hers. “Thanks for meeting me Miss Henessey.”

The young woman appeared tired and distraught, but her grip was firm. “Thanks for coming Detective. I’m not even sure why I called you except that I saw your business card in my wallet last night and I needed to talk to someone.

I don't know if you can legally even do anything about my concerns, but I'm worried about my boyfriend's welfare."

Mike was desperate for any knowledge he could ascertain about Billy Stone. This woman was his only chance at finding out something. "Miss Henessey, let me buy you a drink and you can tell me your story."

•••

Hope felt a little embarrassed that she had brought Detective Westwood out to discuss her fears about Billy. The man was a homicide detective and Billy hadn't killed anyone. He probably could have killed her when he had her neck in that death grip last night, but that didn't happen. Here she was discussing her boyfriend's aberrant behavior with a man who should have been out trying to catch murderers. "Detective Westwood, I apologize for wasting your time. My boyfriend was acting very strange last night but he never threatened to kill anyone. This is a problem between him and me. I should never have called you."

This conversation had potential to be the complete realization of the theory that Mike had been developing for the last eight months; nothing here was insignificant. He had to hear this young woman's story. "Miss Henessey, you sounded distraught over the mention of the things you saw last night. For your own sake, I think you should recap last nights' events, as well as you remember them, and if I see or hear anything that seems out of the ordinary, I can investigate that further. Please, share with me all the details of your encounter with Billy Stone last night.

Hope ordered a Cosmopolitan and Mike went with club soda and a lime. While the bartender made their drinks, she began to recount the disturbing events from the previous night. "I wasn't even supposed to meet Billy until this morning. He told me last week that he had to work Sunday night, so I decided to surprise him and be there when he came home from work, you know, naked in bed or something like that. So, I bribed the security guard to let me into the Panorama complex. I have a key to his condo."

Two Cosmos and one club soda with a lime later, Hope Henessey was crying softly as she finished her story. It sounded to Mike like Billy Stone had overdosed on some sort of psychoactive drug and had a bad trip, which was unfortunately walked in on by his girlfriend. Nothing suspicious there. Mike did find it interesting that Billy was ex-military. Marine Special Forces training would give a person the wherewithal to remove targets with a certain degree of efficiency. He needed to get more out of this girl about her boyfriend: a difficult task given the raw emotional state that she was in right now. He would have to proceed gently.

"It's okay Miss Henessey. This doesn't sound like the end of the world for you. It sounds more like Billy had a bad mushroom or acid trip to me. He'll probably come to his senses after he sleeps it off and call you to apologize profusely. I'm curious though about the part where you mentioned that he was rambling on about some strange names while staring at himself in the mirror. Did he mention any ex customers or anyone he knew from Tahoe? .... or even during the time you spent with him in Tahoe, did he mention anything strange about anyone he may have held a grudge against?"

Hope sighed and dabbed her eyes with a cocktail napkin. She downed half of her third Cosmo in one long sip and stared at the video poker machine in front of her for a long moment. Mike began to wonder if he had pushed a little too hard when she finally looked up at him with a frown on her face. "You know detective, he never said anything strange back in Tahoe; nothing beyond the typical complaints that a dealer makes about their shitty customers, but he was saying some weird things last night. He kept going over a list of what sounded like imaginary names. They almost sounded like cartoon characters: Big Purple Tex, Mr. Vegas, Mr. Thighs For Arms, Mr. Local Asshole, Mr. Superstitious, Junior, Mr. Smith, The Barnacle. They were all strange names, and he kept repeating the same thing after all the names: "They all deserved to die." He was crying while he said all this. He kept repeating it over and over until I tried to talk to him. That's when he grabbed me by the throat and told me to get out of his life." She started crying again.

As soon as Hope said the words "They all deserved to die" Mike's investigator's radar went off again. He was sure there would be some correlation between the cartoon names she just mentioned and the Harry's patrons who had died in the last year. He was also sure that she had more information for him, whether she knew it or not. "Miss Henessey, have you heard from Billy at all today?"

Hope was still crying. "No, nothing. I kind of left him a nasty message early this morning when I was drunk. It may have pissed him off."

"Miss Henessey, I'm not trying to tell you what to do with your love life, but maybe you should try to call him just to make sure he's okay. Are you leaving town soon?"

"I hadn't even thought about that Detective. I was supposed to stay with Billy through Wednesday at his place and fly back to the Bay Area Thursday morning." She glanced at her watch. "It's past eight right now so maybe I'll stay here for one more night. I'll try to call Billy and see what's going on with him. I'm so sorry to have wasted your time detective. I'm sure you have more important things to do than sitting here and listening to my drama."

Mike wanted to keep a line of communication open with Hope, especially since he was sure he would find something damning on Billy Stone from her inadvertent information. He reached out and took both of her hands in his. "Don't you worry Miss Henessey, if our conversation has helped you see things more clearly, then my time has not been wasted. I'm sure Billy will feel differently about things now that his mind is clear. Those psychoactive drugs can really do a number on a person. You have my cell number, so please call me when you hear from him just to let me know that things are okay. When did you say he had to be back to work again?"

Hope squeezed Mike's hands and let them go. "He goes back Wednesday at six in the evening. Thank you so much for being such a good listener Detective. I'll call you if I hear from him."

Mike couldn't get out of the Mirage quickly enough. The list of names burned in his mind. He repeated them over and over so that he wouldn't forget. Mr. Big Purple Tex, Mr. Vegas, Mr. Thighs For Arms, Mr. Local Asshole, Mr. Superstitious, Junior, Mr. Smith, The Barnacle. Then those deadly words: “They all deserved to die.” He pictured Billy Stone’s cold blue eyes in his mind, distant and uncaring. He had something. He was finally going to get this guy.

•••

The Dark Thoughts woke Billy at midnight. Their power of compulsion was stronger than ever. Their control was complete. *“It’s time to go Billy. We have a mission to complete by tomorrow. There’s no more time for sleep; only time for justice.”*

Billy didn’t bother to pack a bag. He would get his items from Elmer and head right back to Vegas. Ten hours of driving each way would be difficult, but he was compelled by The Dark Thoughts to succeed in this endeavor. The words of a song he had heard on the radio echoed in his mind. “Ain’t no rest for the wicked.” He waved at Enrique as he drove the Commander out of the Panorama complex.

Billy checked his cell phone while he gassed up before leaving town. There was a message from Hope. She had called while he slept. “Billy, it’s me. I just wanted to apologize for leaving that nasty message this morning. I was drunk and still kind of confused about what happened last night. I’m still confused. I’m not sure if I did something wrong to piss you off or not, but you can’t just tell me to get out of your life with no explanation why. I need to talk to you Billy. Please call me back to at least let me know you’re okay. I think you were on something last night that wasn’t good for you. I love you Billy Stone. Please call me back.”

Billy felt a pang of regret that was immediately snuffed by The Dark Thoughts. *“You’re through with her Billy. You are on a path to the pinnacle of your existence and nothing can turn you back. You are the bringer of justice. It's time to serve up a massive dose. The Celebrity Golf tournament begins tomorrow. There you serve."*

•••

Elmer Maynigo sat in his office, waiting and worrying for his friend. He had assembled the items on Billy's list into two large duffle bags. He had no idea what Billy planned to do with these dangerous things, but he didn't buy into his story of home protection. Billy could be a one-man war machine with all this stuff. He hoped that Billy would at least agree to go out to lunch with him before he left town. He needed have a heart to heart with his friend and try to ascertain where his mind was at.

There was a short rap on the door of his office and one of his security guards walked in. "Hey Boss. Your old war buddy is here. He's already going through the duffle bags and checking everything. I hope you don't take offense Boss, but I'm worried for you. This guy doesn't look right. I know he's your good friend and all, but you're opening yourself up to a shitload of potential problems by selling this stuff to someone so close to you."

Elmer sighed. "No offense taken Jeremy. You know as well as I do that anything that leaves this warehouse will never be traced back to it. We take care of all that before the product goes out. It's going to be okay."

Jeremy frowned. "What if he gets caught doing something crazy with that shit and turns you over?"

Elmer understood Jeremy's concern, but he didn't like being confronted with the reality of what he was doing for Billy. "Listen Jeremy, Billy Stone is like a brother to me. He saved my life in Baghdad and he saved my sanity numerous times during boot camp. I wouldn't be here today if it weren't for him. I trust him completely. He would never turn me over." As those words came out of Elmer's mouth, he sadly wondered if they were a hundred percent true. He walked out onto the warehouse floor and stared at the friend that he called brother.

Billy had all the items out of the duffle bags and was inspecting each one intently. Elmer walked up behind him and slapped him on the shoulder. Billy turned, quick as a striking snake, and before Elmer knew it, his neck was in the larynx death grip that they had all been taught during hand-to-hand combat training in boot camp. His friend's eyes stared at him, cold and distant, then he blinked and slowly let go.

Billy's voice was dull and lifeless when he spoke. "Sorry Elmer. You know better than to come up on me like that."

Elmer tried to mask the fear in his voice as he stared at his friend. "I guess old habits die hard buddy. You can give me a hug instead of trying to rip out my throat."

Billy's embrace was stiff and short. Elmer looked at him closely before letting him go. He didn't look good at all. His dull eyes and slack face were accentuated by the dark circles under his eyes. He looked like he hadn't slept in a few days. He managed a slight smile as he released himself from Elmer's grip. "This stuff looks good Elmer. Thanks for getting it together for me on such short notice." He pulled an envelope out of the front pocket of the hoodie he was wearing and handed it to Elmer. “Here’s fifteen thousand plus five hundred. Take the extra five and get Robbie something nice for his birthday. Don’t forget to tell him it’s from Uncle Billy.” He turned and continued to reload the duffle bags.

Elmer didn’t bother to count the cash. Billy’s demeanor had him concerned. “Hey brah, why don’t we go out to lunch before you leave town? We haven’t had a good conversation in God knows how long.”

Billy kept loading the bags as he answered, not even bothering to turn around. “Sorry Elmer, but I really have to get back to Vegas. It’s already a long drive and I don’t want to get caught up in the afternoon traffic.” He grabbed both bags in one hand and stuck his other hand out to shake Elmer’s. “Thanks old friend. I’ll try to come visit next month.”

Elmer couldn’t let Billy leave so abruptly. He needed to address his concerns. “Billy, you don’t look good bro. You don’t sound good either. And I know you don’t need all these things for home protection. What’s going on with you? Are those voices speaking to you again?”

Billy’s face went blank for a long moment; then, he finally mustered a weak smile. “I appreciate your concern Elmer. You know me all too well. I’m going to do something important that will make the world a better place. If I come out of it unscathed, we’ll have that lunch. In fact, we’ll get drunk together and I’ll tell you all about it. If not, then I’ll see you on the other side brother.”

Now Elmer was truly scared. Billy had that same look on his face back in Baghdad over a decade ago, right before he shot down all those retreating Iraqi soldiers. “Billy, you should think twice before you go and do something crazy my friend. You don't want to get yourself killed. What the hell have you got planned?"

Billy clapped his old friend on the shoulder. "Don't worry about it brother. You'll hear about it soon enough." He turned and walked out of the warehouse without looking back. Elmer thought about trying to stop Billy, but he knew he couldn't get the authorities involved without getting himself exposed. He stood there in the parking lot, watching his friend drive away, and prayed for Billy's soul.

•••

Mike went to work early on Tuesday morning and logged onto the Nevada Law Enforcement Network to try to find some correlation between the names Billy had been rambling about and the people who had died or disappeared in Tahoe while he was there. He cross-referenced a file of his own that he had kept on his suspicions about Billy Stone with Douglas County incident reports and articles from the archives of the Tahoe Daily Tribune.

He went all the way back to December and found the story on Chas Wellington from Houston Texas. Wellington was on a skiing and gambling trip with four friends in mid-December. They were all staying at Harry's casino and skiing at Heavenly ski resort. His notes told him that the friends had reported Wellington missing when he didn't meet them for dinner after a day of skiing. The Tribune article stated that his body was found by Heavenly search and rescue in the trees just off the Powder Glades run. He had apparently hit a tree and sustained a massive head injury. He wasn't wearing a helmet. Mike checked the coroner's report on Wellington. It confirmed that the death was due to head trauma. More important to Mike though, it stated that Wellington was wearing a one-piece purple jumpsuit that fateful day. Mike wrote his name next to Big Purple Tex on his list.

Less than two weeks later Stan Kurchstein went missing, although his supposed girlfriend in Las Vegas didn't report him missing until six weeks after the fact. Kurchstein had stayed at Harry's for three days. Billy Stone was the limo driver who was supposed to have driven him to the airport the night before Christmas Eve. Billy's story, confirmed by Harry's dispatch, was that Kurchstein insisted that Billy drop him off at one of the whorehouses east of Carson City in Moundhouse. He wasn't seen after that. The Madame at The Pink Flamingo had been tight-lipped about Kurchstein's business there, but his credit card showed a purchase late that evening. The prostitute couldn't remember a thing, stating that she passed out during her encounter with Kurchstein. Nevertheless, Mike wrote his name down next to Mr. Vegas on his list.

Chronologically, the next missing person was Jeremiah James West, the report that Mike had taken himself. His notes told him that J.J.'s buddy Maurice had mentioned an incident at Harry's on New Year's Eve with "a dealer from San Diego". Billy Stone's nametag had said he was from San Diego. J.J.'s dead body was found in the back of a pickup truck two months later down in the Fish Springs. The owner confirmed that the truck had been parked in the back lot at Harry's over New Year's. Mike still couldn't believe that the Douglas County homicide investigators didn't consider Stone a suspect for that one. They probably still ruled that case unsolved. The coroner's report described West as having overly large biceps, one of them tattooed with three sevens like a slot machine. Mike took a guess and put his name next to Mr. Thighs For Arms. He was beginning to see a chronological correlation between the order of Stone's litany and the occurrences of people dying or disappearing in Lake Tahoe in the last ten months.

The next person to die after patronizing Harry's was Joe Benton the Subaru dealer. Mike remembered that the search and rescue guy that pulled him out of his upside-down Explorer had called him "Local Joe", the moniker that he used in all his dealership commercials. Billy had dealt to "Local Joe" mere hours before he supposedly slid his vehicle off a cliff on the only stretch of road on the valley side of Kingsbury Grade that wasn't protected by guard rail. This one was obvious. Mike wrote Joe Benton's name next to Mr. Local Asshole on the list.

According to Mike's notes, Richard Assopholis died at the bar in the Sagebrush Steakhouse less than a month after Joe Benton's "accident". The coroner's report stated that Mr. Assopholis had a heart attack. The investigator's report stated that the notes in Harry's player profile described him as extremely stressed, highly superstitious, and overly combative toward dealers and management. He had played craps that night before going to dinner. Mike wrote his name down next to Mr. Superstitious on the list.

Dominic Khalajian Jr. was found dead of a heroin overdose in a bathroom stall in Club Altitude eight days after Assopholis died in the Sagebrush Steakhouse. The coroner's report stated that death was due to a deadly mix of cocaine, ecstasy, Rohypnol, and heroin. His friends that had been interviewed about the events of the night swore that he never did heroin, but a syringe and vial were found in his pants pocket with his fingerprints on them. One of the friends mentioned that a dealer from San Diego at Harry's had suggested that they go to Club Altitude. Mike Googled the name and the kid's father popped up. The profile showed that he was a prominent businessman in San Diego County and that yes, his son, Dominic Khalajian Jr., had died last April in Tahoe from a drug overdose. Junior. It was too obvious. He wrote Khalajian's name next to Junior on the list.

The last two names were easy. Mr. Smith had to be Colin Smith and The Barnacle had to be Joshua Welsh, his friend who had died with him in that bizarre fall from the steepest part of The Flume Trail at the end of June. Mike wasn't sure how the name Barnacle was associated with Josh Welsh, but Mr. Smith was Mr. Smith, and the circumstances of such a fall screamed mischief to Mike, even if it didn't to the Douglas County investigators that took the case. Mike was sure that he had seen Billy Stone driving down highway 50 from Spooner Summit shortly after the 911 call had come in from Mr. Welsh. The obituary on Mr. Smith in the Livermore newspaper quoted five ex-wives, the most recent being one Marion Meridale from South Lake Tahoe. That was too much coincidence. Mike decided to call Hope to see if Billy had ever mentioned any previous connection to Marion Meridale. He was sure that something was there.

•••

Hope was leaving The Mirage at noon on Tuesday when her cell rang. She prayed it was Billy as she dug around for it in her purse. She had tried calling him three times that morning but got nothing but his voice mail each time. She had no idea where Billy was or what he was doing, but it was becoming obvious that he didn't want anything to do with her. She was planning to go to McCarran Airport, grab the next available flight back to the Bay, and forget about Billy Stone. The display on her phone showed an unknown number from the 702 area code. Maybe Billy was calling from somewhere besides his cell. She answered, hoping it was him. "Hello. Billy?"

Her hopes were dashed when she heard the voice on the other end. "Miss Henessey, it's Mike Westwood. I need to ask you a few questions about your boyfriend."

"I haven't heard from him since we talked last night Detective. I tried to call him a few times this morning but he didn't answer and he hasn't called back. I'm pretty much done with him."

"I just have a few questions for you Miss Henessey. Most of this refers to your time together in Tahoe. Did he ever mention knowing a woman named Marion Meridale?"

Hope was silent for a moment. That name did sound familiar, but she couldn't quite place it. Then it clicked. Mimi. "Yes Detective. Billy was engaged to a woman named Mimi Meridale. I never thought about it, but I guess that Mimi is short for Marion. She was a cocktail waitress at Harry's. She left him for some rich guy last summer."

Detective Westwood's voice became excited. "Did he happen to mention the name of the guy?"

"No, he didn't ever mention that, but he seemed pretty broken up over it. She kind of ditched him while they were engaged. Why do you need to know about her, Detective?"

Westwood sounded guarded in his response. "Miss Meridale's ex-husband died in a strange accident in Tahoe back in June. I'm just trying to check all the angles in the case, that's all. I need to talk to Billy about her. Would you be able to tell me where he lives?"

Hope was worried for Billy now. "Is he in some kind of trouble? Does this have anything to do with the things I told you last night?"

"Don't worry Dear. Billy's not in any trouble. I just need to ask him a few questions about his ex-fiancée. Where can I get in touch with him?"

"He lives in The Panorama Towers, unit 803. I already told you that he deals at The Palace. That's all I know Detective. Are you sure he's not in any trouble?"

"Not at all, Miss Henessey. I need to ask him a few questions. That's all. Thank you for your time." The call ended abruptly. Hope stared at her phone and wondered if Billy truly was in some sort of trouble. His words from Sunday night echoed in her mind. "They all deserved to die." She needed to warn Billy that Detective Westwood was looking for him. She decided to go to the Panorama.

•••

Enrique Guzman sat in his security booth at the Panorama, watching baseball on the small portable television he brought to work every day. It was the only thing that got him through the ten hour shifts he had to do in the small, cramped space. The boredom aside, he was happy to have his job. There was never any trouble at The Panorama since very few of the residents lived there full time. A Chevy Impala rental car that he recognized pulled up to his window. It was Billy Stone's beautiful little Asian girlfriend. He greeted her when she rolled down her window. "Hola Miss Hope." You left early last Sunday night. Is everything okay?"

The girl looked stressed. "I'm not sure Enrique. Things didn't go so well that night, and I haven't been able to get ahold of Billy since then. Has he been here?"

Enrique frowned, once again showing those deep furrows in his brow that come from a long, hard life. "You know Miss Hope, I saw him leave late last night. We keep a log of all entrances and exits, so let me check the day shift list and see if he returned." He flipped through some papers on a clipboard and peered closely at them. "No Ma'am. Mister Billy has not returned."

The look of worry on her face deepened as she sat there, seemingly fretting about what to do. "Will you have a chance to talk to him when he returns?"

"Yes Ma'am. He usually rolls down the window to say "hi" when he comes in. If he arrives before two in the morning, I will see him."

"Enrique, if you see him, could you please tell him to call me and that it's very important?" She was on the verge of tears now.

"I'll tell him if I see him Miss Hope. Is everything okay?"

Now the poor girl was sobbing. "I don't know Enrique; I just don't know."

Enrique's face was sad as he watched Hope turn her car around and leave. He had seen this scene too many times before in his life. She was getting dumped by Billy Stone and couldn't face the reality of what was happening. She was already starting to stalk him. "Poor girl" he thought to himself.

Two hours later, an old beat-up Subaru pulled up to Enrique's booth. The man inside had the window down and a badge out before Enrique could say a word to him. "How can I help you sir?"

The man was abrupt. Enrique didn't like that. "I'm Mike Westwood, Vegas Metro. I'm looking for Billy Stone. He lives in unit 803."

"I'm sorry sir. He left here late last night and hasn't returned. Is anything wrong?"

"Nope. Nothing wrong. I just need to ask him a few questions." He opened his wallet, pulled out a business card, and stuck it out the window. "Could you please give me a call when he returns? I would appreciate it."

Enrique took the card without looking at it. "Absolutely sir. I'll be here until two this morning."

"Could you pass that card on to your relief if you don't see Billy by then?"

"Oh absolutely sir. No problem."

Enrique stared at the old Subaru as it turned around and drove away. He hated cops, especially aggressive and rude ones like this Mike Westwood. He looked at the card and thought to himself, "Homicide. That only spells trouble for Mr. Billy." He tossed the card in the trash and made a mental note to warn Billy that both his ex-girlfriend and a cop were looking for him.

•••

Billy got into Vegas around one a.m. Wednesday morning. He had made decent time on his return trip considering he had to drive the speed limit the whole way. He couldn't risk being pulled over with the things that he was carrying. He was about ready to drop dead from the fatigue of driving almost a whole day, and he was famished from having not eaten since he left the Bay. He stopped in at a twenty-four-hour Chinese food place to get a combo plate before heading home to eat and pass out. He had a big day ahead of him. He needed plenty of rest. With his eyelids heavy, he pulled into The Panorama just after two in the morning. He waved at Carl, the graveyard/day-shift security guard and drove on into the complex without stopping to say hello like he normally did. He brought his duffle bags into the condo, poured himself a double shot of Jagermeister, slammed it, then poured another. He was tired as all hell from more than twenty hours of driving. Even though he had been up for the last twenty-seven hours, precious sleep eluded him. He sat in his living room in the dark, staring out at the lights of the Vegas Strip, sipping Jagermeister, and eating crappy Chinese food and pondered the magnitude of what he planned to do when he woke. He finally passed out around sunrise.

•••

Mike Westwood went to work on Wednesday and spent most of the morning lost in his suspicions about Billy Stone. The evidence he had seemed circumstantial until it was all put together into one puzzle. What bothered him the most was that his investigator's sense kept telling him that there was truly something there. It would be pushing things so early in his return, but he needed to talk to Jim Forvers about this.

•••

Billy woke with a start. He was still seated on his couch in the living room. The Dark Thoughts preached with conviction in his head. *"Today is your day Billy. Everything you've done before today was nothing compared to the justice that you will now serve. Today you will strike a blow for everyone who can't strike out to protect themselves. Today you will bring justice to all those banes of society who treat others like they are nothing. Today you will answer to your true calling."*

Billy rose mechanically and began his daily routine of getting ready for work. His mind was blank as he made his coffee and sat for breakfast. Suddenly, Paul's voice echoed in his head with a reminder: "Most of the guests will be arriving on Wednesday, and we'll definitely need you here then."

Billy stared blankly at the two duffel bags he had gotten from Elmer and answered Paul's voice. "I'll definitely be there Paul."

•••

Hope checked out of The Mirage at noon. She hadn't heard from Billy at all, so that was it. It was time to head home, move on with her life, and forget about Billy Stone. She had booked a five-thirty flight back to San Francisco, so she would just go to the airport, turn in the rental car, buy a Dean Koontz novel in the gift shop, and read until her flight boarded. As she drove out onto Paradise toward McCarran airport, she muttered out loud, “You can go straight to hell Billy Stone. Thanks for ruining the last nine months of my life.”

•••

Mike was going crazy waiting for Jim Forvers to return from a meeting with the Mayor. It was getting close to quitting time, and closer to Billy Stone’s start time at The Palace. He needed the okay from his boss to question Billy Stone. What he actually wanted was to bring him in to the precinct for some official questioning. His captain finally arrived at ten ‘til five.

Mike knocked on Jim’s office door with a strong feeling of trepidation. His boss sounded irritated at the invasion of his privacy. “Come”, was all he said. Mike entered, carrying his personal file on Billy Stone.

Jim Forvers looked up from a pile of paper work. His demeanor softened at the sight of his old friend. “Hey Mike. You should be headed home about now. What can I do you for?”

Mike sat down across from his friend and mentor. “Jim, I’ve got something extremely important to discuss with you.”

•••

Billy left his condo at five, his usual time on work days. That gave him enough time to get to The Palace, park the

Commander, get his tuxedo shirt from wardrobe, and meet his crew for the daily rundown at five-thirty. Today he wouldn't be meeting with anyone. He brought his duffle bags and a tweed trench coat with him. As he approached the guard gate, he saw Enrique wave a hand out the window, gesturing for him to stop. The Dark Thoughts sounded in his mind, commanding. *"There will be no stopping now soldier. You have work to do."* They were in complete control now, and Billy bowed to their will. He waved at Enrique through the window and kept driving.

Billy pulled into the employees' entrance at The Palace at quarter after five. Instead of driving into the parking structure like usual, he parked the Commander behind two large recycling dumpsters that were located near the employee entrance. No one walking in to work would see him until he walked out from behind the dumpsters. He stepped out of the Commander and began to remove his items from the duffle bags.

•••

Hope sat at her gate, trying to immerse herself in the Koontz novel she had bought, but she couldn't get Billy Stone out of her mind. Her last conversation with Mike Westwood had her worried about Billy's well-being. She tried to rationalize her thoughts, telling herself that she was simply over reacting to the fact that she had been unceremoniously dumped by her boyfriend.

Her plane arrived from Phoenix at four-thirty and began to unload passengers. She couldn't stand it anymore. She had to talk to Billy face to face. She gathered up her things, left her gate, and ran out to the front of the airport to get a taxi to The Palace. With a little luck, she would get there before Billy started his shift. She had to know what the hell was going on.

•••

Jim Forvers stared at Mike Westwood after he finished his story. The skepticism was obvious in his face. Mike could tell he wasn't buying any of it. After a moment of tense silence, he sighed. "Listen Mike, I know you want to get back to investigating again, but it's still too soon. Your theory on this Billy Stone guy is a little bit far-fetched if you step outside and view it from a neutral position. What you're basically trying to tell me is that you believe that this dealer from Tahoe, who is now a dealer in Vegas, has been a serial killer for the last ten months. And all this based upon nothing but a lot of circumstantial evidence that you collected while you were supposed to be serving as a Sherriff's Deputy in Douglas County. I think your imagination has become overactive during your purgatory Mike."

Mike stared at his boss, frustrated. He looked at his watch. It was quarter after five. Billy Stone was supposed to start work in forty-five minutes. "Listen Jim, do you remember when you worked the beat? You had a special sense about things didn't you? A voice in your head that made you just know when someone was guilty of something. Do you remember that? Well that's what I'm feeling right now, Jim. This isn't some form of vindication for me. It's not my best attempt to get back into investigations. I truly feel in my mind that this guy is tied up in all those deaths. Will you please just let me bring him in for some questioning? If you take one look at this guy while he's talking about these people, you'll see it too. I feel this Jim. I'm asking you as a friend."

Jim Forvers sighed with resignation. "All right Mike, as a friend I'll let you give this a try. You do realize that if you're wrong, it could be a career-ender, don't you?"

Mike looked at his watch. Five-twenty. "I understand that Boss. Thank you so much. I'm sure you'll see it too once you hear this guy. I've never felt more right about something in my life."

•••

Billy walked through the only doorway into The Palace that wasn't equipped with a metal detector. The Dark Thoughts were in complete control now, and he was fully armed. Under his trench coat, he had two U.S. Military issue M4 carbine fully automatic rifles with sliding stocks, shouldered with a tactical sling-strap device that allowed the weapons to hang perfectly on either side of his body. He had eight magazines that each held thirty rounds of 5.56 ammo duct taped together two each at their butt ends for quick and easy ejection and re-insertion. One setup was in each gun while the other two were stuffed into the outside pockets of the trench coat. Altogether, this gave him 240 shots with thirty second gaps after each thirty rounds. He also had a .45 caliber automatic handgun in a speed holster at his right hip and three clips with ten rounds per clip. He wore a Kevlar vest and had a tactical shotgun slung in the middle of his back for exit strategy. The Dark Thoughts' plan was to hit the craps pit as hard as he could with the M4's, use the .45 to remove any body guards or secret service who drew weapons on him, and finally to exit through the steakhouse out the back end of the kitchen, using the shotgun to blow out the lock on the door that led out to the recycling dumpsters. Then he would jump into the Commander and drive south on the 215. This would make any pursuit think that he was headed into California, but he would turn off into the desert as soon as he could and head east. If he moved quickly and efficiently, the people inside The Palace would still be trying to get their shit together while he was driving out onto the highway. They might not even see him leave.

The Dark Thoughts admonished Billy to be prepared. *"Strike quickly; use all of your ammo, then exit as quickly as you came, straight through the kitchen without stopping. You'll be on the road before the smoke clears from inside the casino. You can ditch the guns and the body armor in the desert, and suddenly you will simply be a man taking a drive through the desert on the outskirts of Las Vegas. Keep the .45 for self-protection.*

Your time is come Billy. You are the force that will bring about a shift in equality between the rich and the poor; those who would use their wealth, power, and influence to belittle common citizens to their own advantage; those who view human beings they deem below them as servants and collateral damage. Now is the time for you to lay down a massive dose of justice that will resonate through the ranks of the banes of society and strike fear into their souls. No one fears vigilante justice more than these people .... these damn rich people. The time has come for you to answer your true calling Billy."

Now a puppet to the will of The Dark Thoughts, Billy walked down the hallway lined with wooden lockers toward the stairwell that would lead him to the casino floor and the craps pit. He passed the wardrobe window without stopping. Mel and Mercy both called out to him. "Mistah Biwwy, Mistah Biwwy, don't forget you shirt. You gotta look handsome." Billy ignored them both and walked through the cafeteria toward the stairwell that led to the casino floor. He looked to his right and saw Paul, Phil, Kate, and Armando in the usual booth. They all looked stressed, probably because he was late. He walked right by them without acknowledgement. Paul looked up at the last instant and saw Billy disappear up the stairwell. He thought to himself, "Why didn't Billy stop for the rundown?... and why is he wearing a tweed trench coat in Las Vegas?" It was five forty-five.

•••

Mike Westwood sat at the only bar on The Palace's casino floor. He had argued with security at the entrance vehemently about letting him in with his gun. He finally spoke with a casino manager who grudgingly agreed after Mike threatened to come back with a S.W.A.T. team.

He was positioned so that he could see both the craps pit and the aisle way that led to the craps pit. He wanted to get Billy Stone before he started his shift, thus avoiding any further involvement from the casino management. He planned to apprehend Billy as he walked to the craps pit to begin his shift. As usual, he sipped on a club soda with a lime. It was five forty-five.

•••

Hope Henessey stepped out of her cab and quickly paid the driver. She knew where the craps pit was in The Palace and she walked in like she owned the place. Billy had told her that anyone who entered The Palace had to have a viable reason to be there. She hoped she wouldn't have to drop Billy Stone's name to get on the casino floor. Her bearing served her well though, and she walked through, unaccosted. She headed straight toward the craps pit. Hope checked her watch. It was five forty-five.

•••

Billy checked his watch as he stepped through the nondescript door and onto the casino floor. It was five forty-five. He strode hard and fast down the aisle toward the craps pit, focused like a laser on his destination. He stopped in the middle of the viewing deck and took in the chaos. Every game in the pit was open except for two in the third tier. They were all jam-packed, some two deep with players waiting to get in. He recognized many of the players from the last two months: The good ol' boy back-slappin' crooked politicians, and the businessmen who bribed them with campaign donations in exchange for future favors. The wealthy Asians who operated manufacturing sweat shops in their countries, and their Latino counterparts who operated *machilladores* and ran drugs as well. The spoiled rotten offspring of the American wealthy who had never worked a day in their lives and their European counterparts; all from old money. The arrogant, cocksure celebrities of sports, music, and film, all drunk with fame and notoriety. All the representatives of big oil, prominently Arabs and Texans. The list went on.

The Dark Thoughts lectured Billy one last time with conviction. *"There they are Billy: All the people who represent everything that's wrong with the world today. Those who deem themselves better than everyone else simply due to their place and power. Those who view common folks as lesser individuals, unworthy of care or consideration. These are the people who make decisions that cost common citizens their well-being and sometimes even their lives, all in the name of money. They treat everyone they deem below them with disdain and no respect whatsoever. You are looking out at one of the highest concentrations of societal banes that you will ever witness in one place at one time. Now is your time soldier. This is your shining moment, your opportunity to strike a deadly blow for all the people who cannot even begin to protect themselves from these banes. You are the purveyor of vigilante justice Billy Stone. It's time to lay that justice down. They all deserve to die! They all deserve to die!*

•••

Mike Westwood watched the aisle that led to the craps pit, looking for Billy Stone. He was expecting to see Billy walk through in a tuxedo uniform like all the other dealers were wearing, so he paid little attention to the man in the bulky tweed trench coat as he passed by. He looked at his watch. It was ten minutes 'til six. The six o' clock dealers should be coming momentarily. He scanned the casino floor, stopped short at the viewing deck that looked over the craps pit, and swore out loud. "Son of a bitch!" There stood Billy Stone. He was the man in the tweed trench coat, and there he stood with what looked like a military issue automatic weapon in his hand. Mike had let him walk right by and hadn't even given him a second glance. "Shit!" He pulled out his gun and started running toward Billy.

•••

Hope had positioned herself right by the dealers' entrance to the craps pit. She knew that Billy would come this way to start his shift. She had to warn him about Mike Westwood; and more importantly, she had to tell him that she still loved him. She looked out over the mayhem in the craps pit, wondering how Billy dealt with all the craziness. Then she heard a woman scream.

•••

Billy pulled out the M4 that hung at his right hip and extended the stock. He was formulating a shooting pattern in his mind when he felt a tug on his trench coat. He looked down and stopped short. A young girl, not more than five or six years old, was tugging on his coat. Her angelic face shone with the innocence of youth. Untainted by attitude or opinion, her pale blue eyes were alive with a pure heart, and hope for the future. "Hey mister, why are you crying? You probably need a hug." She reached around his legs, encompassing the forty-five and the other M4 hidden under his coat, and gave him a tight squeeze. "Are you watching my Daddy play craps? He's out there somewhere, even though I can't see him. We're going to dinner soon."

A tsunami of revelation washed over Billy. He snapped out of his Dark Thoughts-controlled fugue and finally felt the burning tears that ran freely down his face. He stared at this little angel and muttered to himself, "What the hell am I doing?" The brutal reality of what he was about to do broke through the control that The Dark Thoughts had exerted over him for the last sixty-four hours. He had become a monster, about to commit the most monstrous of acts. Maybe these people were all rotten to the core, but who was he to judge whether they should live or die? The innocent little girl at his side reminded him that these people were fathers, brothers, sisters, husbands, mothers, wives, children, grandparents; no matter what they did or how poorly they conducted themselves in their daily lives, they still loved someone, had someone who loved them. Contrary to what The Dark Thoughts preached to him, they did not deserve to die. A woman screamed "Get away from that man Madeline, he has a gun!" Precious angelic innocent little Madeline scampered off to her screaming mother. "He's okay Mommy. I gave him a hug to help him stop crying."

Billy fell to his knees, dropped the M4 on the floor and pulled out the .45. He wasn't sure if he spoke to The Dark Thoughts or to himself or perhaps both. "This has to end now. There will be no more killing." He put the gun up to his temple and held it there. He saw Paul, Kate, Phil, and

Armando staring at him from the entrance to the craps pit. Paul yelled at him "Billy, what in God's name are you doing?"

Then Hope brushed between them and ran straight toward him, a frantic look on her face. "Billy, don't do this! I love you more than you can ever know. Don't do it Billy!"

There was his Hope: the hope that he had rejected. The only person who could save him from this downward spiral .... and she still loved him even after he had sent her away.

Billy knew what he had to do. He tightened his grip on the trigger of the .45. Suddenly, he heard that damn detective Westwood behind him, felt the point of a gun at the back of his head. "Drop your gun Stone. We can handle this in a civilized fashion."

With Hope in front of him, professing her undying love, and Westwood behind him, screaming at him to give up, Billy truly understood that the killing had to end now. The Dark Thoughts had to be eradicated. With the .45 to his head and his back to Mike Westwood admonishing him to "drop the gun", he stared at Hope in front of him. He smiled at her and said "I love you baby". He tightened his grip on the trigger of the .45 and whispered to himself "Seven, you're out Billy Stone, and that's the end of that.

END

An excerpt from book II of the "Seven You're Out" series: Serial Gambler

"I still can't believe he didn't pull the trigger." Mike Westwood stared out the window of his boss' office at another brilliant Las Vegas sunset. The dull, dreary day evolved as it always did into a magnificent butterfly of evening color. First came the hues of nature; the oranges, reds, and purples; a gift given by the desert sun only at twilight. Then the cacophony of lights on the Vegas Strip took over. It felt so good to be home.

Jim Forvers stared at Mike from across his cherry wood desk, a concerned frown on his aging face. "Mike, you have to let all that Billy Stone business go. I didn't bring you up here to reminisce on something that is already said and done. We're here to talk about your future in the department, not about a case that's already closed....."

"But it shouldn't be fucking closed Jim!" Mike immediately regretted cutting off his boss, his Captain, his old friend. "I'm sorry Jim. It still boils my blood that the D.A. wouldn't listen to anything I had to say about all those deaths and disappearances in Tahoe even though I have solid evidence connecting Billy Stone to every single one of them. And what did they end up getting him for? Possession of unregistered firearms? Twelve fucking months? That's bullshit Jim! You know it and I know it."

Jim Forvers sighed with resignation. "I do know it Mike. That's one of the major flaws of our justice system; that a person can commit a crime, plead insanity, and get off with nothing close to the sentence they deserve. Thank God Stone had... what did he call it during the trial? A "moral revelation" at that moment in time. Do you realize how many important people Billy Stone could have killed if he had opened fire on that craps pit at The Palace?"

"Oh yeah Boss. There were over three hundred people in that pit, it being Celebrity Golf weekend and all. He could have taken out quite a few NBA stars, a handful of retired NFL and MLB stars, a few actors and comedians, some political figures, and a lot of rich folks."

"That's not the worst of it, Mike. I have a close, unnamed associate who works in VIP services for The Palace. He told me that when Stone came in there, they had three Saudi Princes, a Kuwaiti royal family member, and the oil ministers from Iran, Saudi Arabia, Kuwait, Qatar, the United Arab Emirates, and Venezuela all rolling dice on the third tier of that craps pit. On the second tier, they had Senators from Texas, North Dakota, Alaska, Oklahoma, and Louisiana, and representatives from the largest oil companies in each of those states. Billy Stone could have single-handedly taken out half of OPEC and started World War Three at the same time had he decided to shoot the place up."

"So why did you call me up here boss, if not to talk about Billy Stone?" Mike prayed silently while waiting for his boss to answer.

His prayers were answered when Captain Forvers smiled back at him. "I called you up here to give you back your old job Mike."

Westwood breathed a sigh of relief. "God bless you Jim. I was getting so sick of sitting at a desk, doing nothing but paperwork. I really need to get back into the mix."

Jim Forvers smiled at his hand-picked replacement; this of course if he ever actually decided to retire. "You've been good for almost two years Mike. Your previous troubles have washed away or been forgotten. The only thing that was holding me back on this decision was your obsession with Billy Stone. I have the same strange feeling that you do about him, but right now you don't need to exhibit any strange behavior. I'm putting you right back in your position as Lieutenant, so you need to walk the line Mike. I'm taking a chance because I have faith in you."

"I won't let you down this time Jim. I've been clean and sober for over six hundred days, and I haven't gambled a single cent for that long either. I promise to let go of that Billy Stone bullshit too. He's locked up for now so I guess I can start to forget about it. Thank you so much boss."

"You're welcome Mike. I believe in you." Captain Forvers stood and shook his friend's hand. "And one more thing Lieutenant; Billy Stone gets out of jail in three days. You stay away from him."

Mike grinned at his boss through gritted teeth. "Well ain't that a son-of-a-bitch?"

Made in United States
North Haven, CT
02 April 2022